Envision Wonder

Founder | CEO | Creative Director | Lovietta Simpkins
Editor in Chief | Leevette Simpkins
Literary & Creative Agent | Travis Walker
Author | Kassana Wilson

This is a work of fiction. Not a portrayal or representation of any persons living or deceased. Not a portrayal of any organization or event. This novel is a product of the author's imagination and a work of fiction.

Envision & Wonder
First Edition Month & Year: April 2020
Publisher: Envision & Wonder
ISBN: 978-0-9961561-6-5

BURIED
SKELETONS

Kassana Wilson

Table of Contents

Table of Contents Continued

CHAPTER 1 -KIA

I was standing on a doorstep of a home that I was no longer familiar with. I raised my right hand to knock on the tan door in front of me but something held me back. So I turned around breathing in the late night air and took a deep breath. I took my belongings out of the plastic bag I was carrying in my left hand. This was the only few dollars I had left to my name. I pray that this money in my hand is enough to get me a hotel for the night.

I pulled out my shoe strings that were inside the bag and a folded up paper. I opened up the paper and it was a drawing from my daughter five years ago. She drew the sun and three stick figures at the park. The figures were me, my daughter and her father. I kissed the paper and folded it back up. I threw the plastic bag down on the empty sidewalk then knocked on the front door.

"Well, look who decided to show up on my fucking doorstep." Aunt Tasha said swinging the door open and looked at me up and down.

I put the drawing and money in my back pocket. I tried to move around my aunt and walk inside the house but she stood in front of me.

"What the fuck are you doing Kia," Aunt Tasha asked while pushing me back a little.

I balled up my face and pointed inside the house.

"I'm coming to pick up my daughter Aunt Tasha. Where is Nyla at?" I asked.

Aunt Tasha just chuckled. She had a silk bonnet on her head, dressed in a pink robe with slippers on her feet. She reached in her right robe pocket pulling out a cigarette and a lighter.

"Nah uh...Step the fuck back Kia! You know better than that *little girl*." Aunt Tasha said standing in the doorway. She lit the cigarette up and dropped the lighter back inside her pocket.

"Little girl," I asked confused.

"Where the fuck was all this mouth when I was taking care of your daughter for the last five years?" Aunt Tasha asked me while blowing smoke in my face.

"Where the fuck is my daughter at?" I asked getting aggravated as I started coughing on the smoke a little.

"Nyla!" I shouted trying to get my daughter's attention.
Aunt Tasha shook her head no and she closed her front door a little to confront me.

"Lower your muthafuckin' tone while you're in my presence Kia." Aunt Tasha said exhaling again.

"Let me ask you a question. Didn't you just get released from prison for a robbery and an assault charge? Speak up...I don't have all day. Of course you did! That's why you're on my doorstep now asking for your daughter back," Aunt Tasha said ashing her cigarette.

Aunt Tasha is my mother's blood sister. My mother passed away when I was seven. I don't remember much about her but I do remember my mother mentioning that my Aunt Tasha wasn't completely stable.

"You know I just got out of prison." I said to my Aunt Tasha then bent down to put the shoe strings back in my boots.

"I can call the police right now Kia and tell them that you're trying to rob me...Oh, let me be more dramatic and fall down. So the cops would think that you assaulted me too. They wouldn't hesitate to take your black ass back to prison and do you know why that is? Because now you're just a fucking convict in the eyes of the law...With a fucking list of felonies that can't be expunged." Aunt Tasha said laughing.

Y'all see what the fuck I mean? Something was wrong with this bitch...

"All I want is my daughter Aunt Tasha." I pleaded standing up on my feet.

Aunt Tasha looked around her neighborhood and puffed on her cigarette again.

"You know what's funny Kia...I've been taking care of your fucking child while you were behind bars. Since you been in my presence tonight, did you once say thank you to me?!" Aunt Tasha yelled out.

I took a step back and just stared at her.

"Say thank you for what? You're family...We are blood! That's what you're supposed to do." I said.

"I'm not obligated to do a muthafuckin' thing sweet cheeks." Aunt Tasha said winking at me. "That's your daughter. That's your fucking responsibility...Not mine Kia. You need to show me more respect...You need to be thanking me for not giving Nyla up and putting her ass in the system. I swear y'all Graves kids are something else yo." Aunt Tasha said while referring to me and my siblings last name; speaking as if she didn't share the same name as us.

"Excuse me?" I asked dumbfounded.

"You heard what the fuck I said Kia...Let me make it more clear for you. Your mother kids are appalling. Your sister runs in and out my fucking house stealing shit and doesn't think I realize it. She touches whatever she can get her hands on just to feed that nasty ass drug habit of hers. You know I had to put locks on my fucking cabinets? She steals my cereal and even my ramen noodles just to sell it on the street and get a profit back. She saves up all the change she can just to get some heroin and she does it about six times a day.

You know Nyla walked in the bathroom yesterday and saw your sister sleeping with a fucking needle hanging out her arm. Your brother Mir walks around my house breaking shit because he's blind as a bat and can't see worth a damn. I don't have money for them fucking fancy programs let alone for someone to come out to the house to teach him how to get around. Last but not least you Kia...You just getting out of prison. All three of your mother kids are..." Aunt Tasha said.

Once she mentioned my mother I stepped to her ass...Let my mom rest in peace. She had nothing to do with the way our lives turned out. We chose to go down this path everyone except my brother Mir, he couldn't help that he lost his vision and got blind before I went to prison. My mother did the best she could raising us when she was alive but Aunt Tasha was that bitch that would pick at you until you explode on her ass.

"Leave my mother out of this Aunt Tasha." I said.

She looked at me and started laughing with the cigarette still in her hand.

"What are you going to do about it Kia? Fight me? Go ahead...Show me some new fighting moves you learned in prison. No! Show me how y'all make shanks in there. Don't be stingy show me Kia." Aunt Tasha said while getting tough sticking her chest out at me.

Lord knows I didn't know where I was going to go. I lost my section 8 housing due to me being incarcerated and I didn't have shit to my name but a few bucks. I just wanted my daughter...I just wanted my daughter back with me!

"You're trying to provoke me." I said under my breath as I rubbed my bottom lip.

"Excuse me? What the fuck did you say?" Aunt Tasha asked me then flicked her cigarette and got closer to me.

"Aunt Tasha...I just want my child." I said looking up at the house to see what lights were on.

I knew Nyla was in one of these rooms. I needed to see my baby. I spoke to her throughout my five years of being incarcerated, but I never wanted her to see me locked up like a fucking animal. Nah, I refuse for her to see me like that!

"You can have your daughter when you do me a favor." Aunt Tasha said.

"What is it?" I asked nervously.

"Show me you can provide for Nyla," Aunt Tasha said smirking.

Did this bitch hear me say I was incarcerated for five whole fucking years?! I don't have a job or a pot to piss in.

"I just got home from—" Before I could finish, Aunt Tasha cut me off.

"Stop making excuses...Come back here with food and medication because Nyla has been feeling a little under the weather lately. If you can come back and show me that you can fend for your own child, I will give Nyla to you with open arms." Aunt Tasha said smirking.

"I don't have any money to—" I said getting emotional.

Aunt Tasha raised her finger up at me and shook her head.

"Do what you do best Kia...Go steal to feed your fucking child, you fucking thief. Wait right here for a second." Aunt Tasha said.

Then she walked in the house closing the door behind her.

I looked up at the sky and just took a deep breath. Was I going to risk my freedom again to get my daughter back? I sure was...I was incomplete without Nyla and my aunt knew that shit.

"Take him...My house is getting too fucking crowded." Aunt Tasha said opening up the door as she pushed Mir outside.

"What am I suppose to do with Mir? He can't even see Aunt Tasha." I said.

I watched Mir hold on to the silver rail to walk down the stairs. I got out his way and once his feet hit the concrete I held on to him. I looked at Mir and he had on these black shades to cover his eyes.

"Use your brother to your advantage. The corner store is right there." Aunt Tasha said pointing down the street.

"*Your mother would be so proud.*" Aunt Tasha spoke again but this time she was trying to be fucking funny. She reached inside her pocket to pull out another cigarette.

"Make sure Nyla bags are packed and she's dressed by the time I get back." I said as Aunt Tasha entered back in her home. She turned around and looked at me.

"If you make it back..." Aunt Tasha said under her breath then she slammed the front door shut.

I squeezed on to Mir's arm and shook my head.

"Mir...Come on baby," I said.

"Kia is that you?" Mir asked finally opening up his mouth.

"Yes...It's me baby bro." I said while turning in the direction of the corner store.

I looked down as we walked and noticed Mir had a hard time adjusting...He was hesitating to move.

"Nigga you can't see? Watch where the fuck you're going yo." I heard someone say.

I looked up and Mir bumped into a guy walking down the street.

"He didn't mean it...I'm sorry." I said apologizing for my brother.

"It's cool Kia...I'm used to people treating me like that." Mir said as he stopped in his tracks. He held on to me tightly, exhaling like he was uncomfortable and I felt bad for my brother.

"Aunt Tasha always saying fucked up shit about you in front of Nyla yo...I think she wants Nyla to look at you differently." Mir said as he followed my lead to the store.

"What do you know about look— I caught myself before I could finish speaking.

—I apologize Mir...I'm just frustrated and I didn't mean to take it out on you. How is Nyla? Does she ask about me?"

Mir pushed his dark glasses back on his face and held his right hand out.

"Put your hand down...I got you bro." I said trying to reassure him.

"I just don't want to fall Kia." Mir said confiding in me.

"I GOT YOU." I said raising my voice a little more this time so he could understand me.

"Nyla asks about you all the time." Mir said finally answering my questions.

"I know my daughter is so disappointed in me." I said shaking my head at my damn self.

"If you were my mother I wouldn't be upset Kia because the system failed you. You were trying to get by the best way you knew how. You and your baby dad were just trying to make some money, keep a roof over y'all head, and feed Nyla. Things in life happen sis...Just don't make the same mistake twice." Mir said.

Hearing them words come from him eased my pain a little more.

"I haven't seen or heard from you in five years Mir...You have definitely changed." I said giving him a compliment.

Mir was only two years younger than me but he was intelligent than a muthafucka.

"I watch a lot of Dr. Phil now." Mir said chuckling.

I shared a laugh with him.

"Mir can I ask you a question...Does Aunt Tasha take good care of Nyla?" I asked with concern.

"To be honest Kia—"

I noticed we were right at the corner store so I cut him off while he spoke.

"We are here but I need you to listen to me loud and clear do you understand Mir?" I asked.

Mir shook his head yes.

"I know that you're blind but I need to use your disability to help me out in this situation. I know it's fucked up to ask but I need you brother. You're going to walk in before me...The candy is to your right side, exactly six steps ahead. Ask questions and knock things over to distract the clerk from me. Let the clerk know that you're blind and you need assistance. I'm going to grab food and medicine for Nyla.

Before I walk out I'm going to cough and that's your cue to walk out after me, understand? Walk straight out and I will meet you at the corner. I need your word Mir...I can't go back to prison my nigga." I said while releasing my grip on his arm and moving it down to his hands.

"*I got you sis.*" Mir said squeezing my hands.

I nodded my head and walked into the store heading straight to the back aisle. I grabbed some juices, two sandwiches, chips and fever medicine. I looked around to make sure I was in the clear and stuffed everything into my jacket. I heard some commotion going on in the front of the store but I didn't look to see exactly what was going on.

"What are you doing?! What are you doing my friend?" I heard the clerk ask in his Indian accent.

A few items fell in the front of the store and I could hear in the clerk's voice he was becoming more annoyed.

"Put it back...You break it, you buy it!" The Indian accent was rolling off his fucking tongue.

"I'm sorry sir...I'm blind." Mir said to the clerk and I was smiling in the back of the store.

"Good boy Mir." I said to myself. Then headed to the front door to leave out, I was two steps from smelling the night air again.

I coughed and so did the clerk.
"What the fuck?" I said to myself.

I made it outside and walked quickly to the corner. I turned around looking for Mir but he was nowhere to be found. Once I made it safely I held my head and leaned against the wall, closing my eyes for a moment.

"You think that I don't know what goes on in my store?! I'm calling the cops! You're stealing from me!" The Indian clerk said to me.

I looked down and he had a white telephone in his hand which looked like a house phone. I held on to my jacket making sure none of the things that I stole from his store would fall down on the ground. I looked back down the street and Mir wasn't visible at all. The clerk tried to grab on me but I pushed him off of me.

"You looking for that blind boy? You niggas always want something for free in this country." The Indian clerk said.

"Did you just call me a nigga?!" I asked still holding on to my jacket. Then I heard a voice speak from behind me.

"I got it Papi...Go back into the store." This nigga said.

I turned and he pulled out a bankroll from his right pocket.

"I'm calling the cops... I want her black ass in jail. She stealing from my store! I lose money like that." The Indian clerk said with anger in his voice.

"Nah, here take this Papi...Keep the change." He handed the Indian clerk a hundred dollars and put the rest of his money back into his pocket.

"You lucky girl." The clerk said turning around heading back to his store.

"Watch your mouth next time, calling me a nigga." I said to the clerk as he walked away.

"Oh! Fuck you!" The clerk said in his accent. He put up his middle finger while carrying the white cordless phone in his hand.

I watched around still looking for my brother and I still couldn't find him.

"You didn't have to do that...I don't have much money but here is a few dollars." I said pulling out the thirty-four dollars I had to my name.

"I don't want your money beautiful." This man said to me denying my offer.

I looked at him and he was Spanish, his hair was pulled back in a pony tail. He was dressed in an all-black polo sweat suit with timbs on his feet. He was wearing a gold ring on his wedding finger and a gold chain. I bit the inside of my mouth after observing him...I was skeptical and unapproachable.

"What do you want from me?" I asked with attitude.

"Relax Mami...I just want to know your name." He said putting his hands up like I offended him.

"My name is Kia." I said embarrassed that I had all of this shit hidden under my shirt...

I looked like I was five months pregnant from this shoplifting spree. I looked around again praying I would see Mir but it didn't happen.

"Why are you looking over there? Are you looking for someone?" This Spanish nigga asked me when he noticed I was looking in every direction but at him.

"Nah...I'm good. I have to go...Thank you for paying for my items." I said and I turned around.

"Let me give you a ride." He offered.

"I'm literally walking down the street." I said pointing down in the opposite direction.

"I don't bite Kia...To make you more comfortable allow me to introduce myself beautiful, my name is Angel." He said smiling.

I shook my head no and continued to walk.

"Please, I would *enjoy* the company." Angel said.

I stopped in my tracks and turned back around. Angel pointed to the parking lot so we could get in his car. He opened the passenger door up to his range rover and I jumped inside.

"Thank you." I said.

I opened up my jacket and allowed every item to fall out of my jacket. I picked up the plastic bag Angel had on the floor of his car and put everything inside.

"Mir, where the fuck did you go bro?" I asked under my breath.

Angel got in the car and looked at me.

"You're looking for someone, aren't you?" Angel asked as he readjusted his driver's seat.

"Nah...I'm just watching my surroundings." I said lying.

"Is someone after you?" Angel asked laughing.

"No one but the devil..." I said and I always believed in that.

"Can I ask you a question?" Angel said.

I just looked at him without answering yes or no.
"Why are you stealing from a corner store Kia," Angel asked me.

"What I do isn't your fucking concern nigga!" I yelled reaching for the passenger door so I could get out.

"I was just—" Angel said.

I knew I was wrong so I let go of the door and took a breath before speaking, trying to apologize.

"I apologize...To make a long story short, I have a child that I'm trying to feed and provide for. I guess a mother has to do what she has to do, right?" I said.

Then he nodded his head up and down. Angel reached under his seat and pulled out a handgun. Lord knows if the cops approached this vehicle right now I would be heading right back to prison.

"Wondering why I have a gun? It's just for protection...I'm not going to hurt you." Angel tried to reassure me as he opened his glove compartment and placed the gun inside.

But in the corner of the glove compartment there was a picture of a woman.

"I see you staring at that picture right there...It's okay you can pick it up," Angel said to me.

I pick up the picture and the beauty this woman had in this photo was like no other.

"This woman is beautiful." I said shocked still looking at the picture.

"That's my wife...she was murdered." Angel said while looking down at the picture.

My mouth dropped from him bringing up his past.

"I'm sorry to hear that Angel...I don't mean to pry but do you know who murdered her?" I asked.

He pointed back inside the glove compartment.

"Pick up the picture right there...He did it." Angel said clearing his throat.

I put the picture of his wife back inside the glove compartment and pulled out the other picture that was underneath it.

"What the fuck?!" I said out loud and Angel just looked at me suspicious.

"You know him?" Angel asked me taking the picture out of my hand.

I couldn't believe it was a picture of my brother Mir.

"Nah...I don't know him at all. How do you know that he was the one who murdered your wife? I think this nigga is blind...He's been blind most of his life that's all I know." I said playing dumb.

"That nigga Mir ain't blind Kia...He never was beloved." Angel said to me.

—KASSANA WILSON

CHAPTER 2 KIA

"Your total for the night is $49.99 and that includes taxes and fees." The motel clerk said to me.

I looked at his appearance as he stood up behind the desk. Dressed in an all-black button up shirt, his fade was low and he had a scar under his left eye. I couldn't see what he was wearing from the waist down. His dark skin gave me an uncomfortable feeling. I was uncertain of why this was. His eyes were cold with no emotions shown. I guess that's how white muthafuckas feel when they walk on the same street as a nigga. I looked down at the name tag pinned to his shirt "Jason," was his name. My only child had her arms wrapped around my thick thighs depending on me to give her shelter for the night. I looked down at Nyla and forced a smile.

"Nyla...Go over there and look out the window. When I'm done talking to this nice man, I will come over there and ask you a question. Make sure you stay where I can keep an eye on you," I said pointing over to the window of the motel office.

Nyla let me go and looked at me without a smile of tranquility on her face. I didn't blame her though. I abandoned her for five years, what the fuck was my daughter suppose to be happy about yo?!

"What question mommy?" Nyla asked me. Her colorful book bag was on her back with everything she owned inside.

I bent down to her level to speak to her. I heard the tapping of a pen against the desk and I knew it was the motel clerk rushing me.

"Uh...Tell me how many cars pass by on the street. Can you handle that job?" I asked rubbing Nyla on her cheek.

"I'm the girl for the job." Nyla said still not granting me with a smile.

She turned and skipped over to the window as I took a deep breath, rising up to my feet and approached the motel clerk again.

"Are you paying with debit or credit ma'am?" Jason asked as he continued to tap his pen on the desk.

I reached down in my back pocket and presented the embarrassing brokenness I had left of me.

"Sir... This is the last of the money that I have to my name. I know it's not much but this is all I have to offer you." I said in a low tone then looked back at my daughter as she studied faithfully the vehicles that drove by.

"No you don't...I know you have more to offer me." Jason said licking his cracked lips. He leaned forward on his desk and I took a step back.

"Excuse me?" I asked balling up my fist.

He scanned my body up and down smiling, revealing his secret that he doesn't visit the dentist often.

"You have an hour glass shape pretty thing and your mouth looks like you can work wonders." Jason said as he dropped the pen on the desk.

I shook my head and walked over to my daughter.

"Nyla...Let's go baby."

As soon as I reached for my child's right hand I heard the deep chuckling behind me.

"What the fuck is so funny?" I asked with more attitude than I was born with. I turned around and stared this muthafucka down.

"Where are you going to go? It's storming outside and you have a child with you. If you travel in this weather I guarantee the two of you will be sick by the morning time. You don't have enough bread for a room so I damn sure know you don't have health insurance. Think about your daughter pretty thing," Jason said winking at me.

I looked down at my daughter who wasn't paying me any mind. Her eyes were glued to the rainy scenery outside.

"I am thinking about my daughter muthafucka! That's my first priority nigga," I said raising my voice a little.

Nyla stopped what she was doing and looked at me with worry in her eyes but she didn't say a word. I moved away from her and walked back up to the desk.

"You're a feisty little bitch, aren't you," Jason asked still chuckling like he hasn't laughed in years. "If you were thinking about your daughter, then you would take me up on my offer." Jason said shrugging his shoulders.

"Which is what?" I asked confused.

Jason rubbed on his bottom lip and looked at me in my eyes.

"Suck my dick until I cum in your mouth… I want you to swallow all of me." Jason said with no filter.

I looked back at my child who was still concentrating on the outside world. I dropped my head in shame as I became emotional.

"Nyla…Nyla." I said under my breath.

"Your child needs a roof over her head tonight, doesn't she?" Jason asked being funny.

I wiped my tears before I lifted my head up to speak.

"Will you allow me to bathe my daughter and put her in the bed first? Once she falls asleep I will come back in here and do whatever you want me to do." I said with more shame in my body than a sinner.

Jason turned around and grabbed something off the wall. He put an object down on the desk but covered it before I could see it clearly.

"Room 6," Jason said removing his hand.

It was a silver room key. I quickly reached for it and turned trying to rush out.

"I will be waiting baby and ayo...If you don't bring your ass back in here within an hour, I will contact the police and tell them that you're trespassing with a minor. You understand?" Jason said.

I didn't answer him I grabbed Nyla's hand and left out of the motel office. The rain was soothing to me...Like music to my ears.

"Nyla come on baby..." I said.

She squeezed my hand as we walked out. I followed the numbers on the room doors so we could enter our motel for the night. Luckily this motel was covered with outside shelter or else me and my little one would have been wet from the rain.

"Seven cars mommy...The number you're looking for is seven. That's how many cars drove by out the window. I would say eight but there was a nigga on the four-wheeler and I don't consider that a vehicle. It would have been more people driving but it's raining hard." Nyla said while looking down at her fingers.

I looked at her in shock as she spoke.

"Nyla...Don't talk like that where did you hear the word nigga from?"

She giggled, "Aunt Tasha and Mir say it all the time in the house. So does the kids in my school and you just said it too mommy." Nyla said calling me out.

I gently dropped her hand and put the key in the door. Once the door opened, I slammed it shut and locked it. I didn't even know my child was listening to me speak I feel like I was fucking up already. I leaned my head back on the door and cried silently.

"Wait, why are you crying mommy," Nyla asked.

I wiped my face before I turned around to approach her. Nyla looked at me like she was broken...I remember being her age and feeling the same exact way. Nyla was five years old when I went to prison and now my little princess is ten. More beautiful and brilliant than when I last laid eyes on her. Being in my child's presence is a gift...She didn't know how precious she is to me. Being her mother is a tough job but it's an honor as well.

"Mommy is just a little frustrated and tired baby but don't you worry about me. I'm just trying to be the best mother to you now that I'm back in your life. Will you allow me to do that Nyla?"

Nyla pulled out the wooden chair that was underneath the table in the room and placed her bookbag on the back of the chair. I held the room key in my hand for a second and dropped it in my pocket.

"I love you mommy...I always have," Nyla said.

This time my daughter showed me a smile...That didn't seem forced. I walked up to her and gave my beauty soft kisses on her forehead.

"Can I ask you a question Nyla?"

She nodded her head up and down.

So I asked her inquiringly,"Uh...I don't really know how to ask you this but it's about your Uncle Mir. Did you ever see Mir do things around the house without help...Like him having his vision?"

Nyla's face became uncomfortable and she started to stumble. I walked up to her helping to keep her balance.

"What's wrong Nyla?"

Nyla looked at her bookbag and pulled away from me not as aggressively as I thought she would.

"Uh, uh...There are things you don't want to see and I don't want to get in trou—" Nyla spoke so low it was becoming hard to understand her words.

Before I could ask what she said she opened up her back pack and pulled out a black ripped up book.

"What's that Nyla," I asked.

Nyla held the book like it was her best friend. When I reached for it she took a step back away from me like I was going to hurt her.

"My book mommy...I write and draw everything that I see in this book. I've been doing it since you and daddy been locked up." Nyla said while squeezing the book tighter.

I heard the sound of a phone going off and I looked at the back pack. Nyla looked at me like she was frightened but she didn't say a word. I gently grabbed the book out of her hands and placed it on the table.

"Nyla, go in the bathroom and run the bath water I will check on you in a minute," I said.

Then Nyla looked back at her bag but she didn't argue with me. She walked into the bathroom and closed the door behind her. I dug in her bag until I found the phone ringing. I picked it up and held it to my ear.

"You have a collect call from...Reem...If you would like to accept the charges press 1 or to decline press 0," The operator said through the phone.

I pressed 1 and held the phone back up to my ear. I heard the water in the tub running and I knew Nyla was doing what I asked her to do.

"Reem?" I said confused.

"Kia...Damn it feels so good to hear your voice baby. Did you get Nyla back?" Reem said unbothered.

I was confused...Why the fuck did my ten year old have a phone and who set up this operation for her?!

"Nyla is with me now but you know my Aunt Tasha didn't make it easy to get our daughter back..." Wanting answers, I continued, "where did Nyla get a phone from Reem and how are you making calls to this phone?"

"What the fuck did your Aunt Tasha make you do yo?" Reem said disregarding the questions I asked him.

"Reem how the fuck is Nyla receiving jail calls from this phone?" I asked again, even louder this time.

"Can I speak to my daughter Kia?" Reem said ignoring me again.

I looked up at the painting that was above the motel bed. I looked in the corner of the room seeing movement and I see a few roaches go in and out the hole in the our room.

"Reem she's in the tub right now...How did your parole hearing go? Are you getting released early or not Reem? Because I really need you right now...Me and your daughter need you," I said getting a little upset.

Me and Reem were unstoppable before we went to prison. Any amount of money you named, *WE HAD IT!* We were a couple that got money together and did what we had to do to make sure our child ate. Reem? Yeah, that muthafucka was my partner in crime. We took a lot from muthafuckas, we started off robbing small apartments then we elevated and started robbing mansions. I always kept my section 8 housing no matter how much bread I was making. I didn't want a sneaky muthafucka to expect anything. Our last robbery *we got caught up* and I still blame myself for this shit.

We'd been staking out this mansion for roughly a month or so. I decided that we were ready and Reem was down. So that night we grabbed over fourteen million worth in jewelry and other items but one thing we didn't know, was that the owner was still home. It was my job to make sure every room was secured but I just became greedy during the robbery. The owner...That white muthafucka was hiding out in the closet and alerted the police on me and Reem.

All that money was gone in a blink of an eye. Me and Reem both got arrested and he was looking to do ten years flat behind bars. Reem told the DA that this was all his idea and he forced me to do it otherwise he was going to harm our daughter, which was a lie. Reem, the father of my child was looking out for me...He wanted me to go home and be a mother to our daughter but I couldn't allow that shit. So I told the DA that I was involved just as much as he was and I asked that we split the ten years. We had more than a quarter million saved up and I knew that money could help us in this situation hiring a lawyer. I asked my Aunt Tasha to use that money to hire me and my baby dad some legal aid and she told me the money was *GONE.*

Nothing was left but a fucking silver quarter yo! This was first offenses for both of us so we got off a little easy. I love Nyla too death y'all but I wasn't allowing my baby dad to do all the dirty work...I COULDN'T! Unfortunately, Reem got into some shit in prison and he picked up more charges.

Now I was out here in these streets...Raising my daughter ALONE. *I lost everything that night...*

"I'm doing the best I can Kia...I have some niggas out there that I trust that can look after you and Nyla," Reem said.

I totally forgot that I was thinking about the past.

"Niggas that you trust Reem?! Where were these muthafuckas when our daughter needed formula and diapers years ago?! Where the fuck were they at when you got locked up my nigga?! Me and your child are out here struggling—"

Reem interrupted me while I spoke.

"Kia, baby I am trying behind bars. What the fuck else do you want me to say yo?!"

"You know what...Fuck it. I have something to ask you," I said changing the subject.

I reach for Nyla's notebook on the table but I hesitated to open it.

"I'm listening Kia," Reem said.

"You've been around Mir before you went to prison..." I said then paused.

"That's not a question Kia that's a statement but yes I have...Mir is my nigga you know that," Reem said clarifying their relationship.

"Did you ever question if he was really blind?" I asked while turning around and scratching my head.

"What yo? You're bugging" Reem said laughing. "What made you ask some shit like that?" Reem said seriously.

I heard the water in the bathroom turn off.

"You have one minute remaining," The operator said.

I felt fucking crazy for even asking questions about Mir. Who knew my brother better than me?

"I apologize Reem...I have to go" I said taking the phone away from my ear.

"Wait, Kia—" Reem tried to speak but I ended the call and put the phone on the table. I walked over to the bathroom and knocked on the door before I opened it.

"Nyla...Are you okay baby?" I asked opening up the door.

She was sitting in the tub with her back turned to me.

"I'm better now that I'm with you...Mommy did you talk to dad yet?" Nyla asked turning around to face me.
Her curls were wet as they dripped down her back and shoulders.

"Speaking of your dad...Who gave you a phone Nyla?" I asked.

She turned back around and didn't answer my question.

"That's fine you don't have to talk about it if you don't want to. Aunt Tasha told me that you have been under the weather lately...But you seem perfectly fine and healthy to me." I said from a distance.

Nyla dropped her head and played with the tub water.

"I lied to Aunt Tasha...Sometimes I fake being sick because at night he comes into—" Nyla began to speak but someone was knocking at the door of my motel room.

"Who is it? I will be right back Nyla," I said.

Nyla started shaking her head like she was upset with me.

Even so I excused myself from the bathroom and walked over to the door.

"I told you I would be back in your office once I put my child to sleep—Angel?" I said confused as I opened up the door.

"Don't look *too* surprised Kia," Angel said smirking then invited himself into my motel room.

"What are you doing here?" I asked confused closing the motel rooms' door then walked back over to the table.

"I was kind of worried about you so I decided to come check on you," Angel said checking out the room as he sat down on the queen size bed.

"How did you know I was at this motel? I didn't tell you that." I said while thinking about the things I told him earlier tonight which...wasn't much.

"I figured this was the closet place for you and your daughter to lay y'all head for the night," Angel said.

Then he got up off the bed and walked over to me. I slowly moved back and caught myself; nearly stumbling over the chair.

"Why are you backing away from me Kia?" Angel said with a straight face.

"You said daughter," I said softly looking at Angel.

"What about what I said?" Angel asked shrugging his shoulders.

"Angel whenever I mentioned my seed I always said my child...I never clarified whether I had a son or a daughter. So how the fuck do you know that I have a daughter?"

Angel smirked at me. He has been in my motel room more than a few minutes and I also noticed that he wasn't wet from the rain.

CHAPTER 3 MIR

"Why the fuck do I always have to come home to fucking dishes in my sink?! If y'all eat in my kitchen then clean y'all shit the fuck up!" Aunt Tasha yelled coming in through the back door.

She was dressed in tight pink scrubs...Knowing at her age that she needs to wear loose fitting clothes. Her name tag above her right titty dangling back and forth from too much excitement. She slammed the door and threw her purse on the kitchen counter. I was sitting at the table with my back towards the wall. Sitting in this angle I could see everything coming at me. My dark shades covering my eyes from the truth...Though I had a feeling it would all be revealed soon.

"Who are you talking to Aunt Tasha?" I asked watching her throw a temper tantrum like a little ass girl.

My Aunt always came home and bitched about something. She would yell at everyone just because the sky was blue and I knew exactly why her attitude increased every day.

"Obviously not you...Right, Mir? I mean how the hell are you going to wash dishes my nigga?! You can't even see." Aunt Tasha said while opening up the refrigerator to grab a bottle of water. "Is your sister here?" Aunt Tasha asked twisting the top off the water then she took a few sips.

"What sister?" I asked confused.

Aunt Tasha was making unacceptable faces...Faces that she didn't know I could see but me being blind was just a front. Only me and one other person knew my secret.

"What other sister do you have besides Kia nigga? I'm talking about Jada..." Aunt Tasha said getting smart swallowing her water then she placed the top back on the bottle.

"Nah, I haven't seen Jada in two days" I said telling the truth.

Honestly I was starting to get worried about Jada...Her ass never stayed away for this long before.

"She's probably running around this fucking city getting higher than a muthafucka," Aunt Tasha said laughing.

"Watch your mouth Aunt Tasha," I said standing up to my feet. I reached out in front of me pretending to be blind.

"What are you going to do Mir? Hit me...Goodluck, you have to see me to catch me and nigga, this is my muthafuckin' house...Which means I can say what the fuck I want to say in this bitch! What's wrong Mir? I hit a nerve...Didn't I sugar? Why don't you do something about it then nigga?" Aunt Tasha said going off on a rant as she put the bottle of water down on the kitchen counter.

"That's what the fuck I thought...I don't know who y'all think y'all are, Jada walks in and out my house whenever she wants too. If I start putting the fucking lock on my front and back door then where the hell is she going to go? You run around here defending your no good ass sisters when you know they will never amount to shit. Nyla doesn't even have a chance in this world and the funny part about that is, that little girl knows it.

"She sits up in that room all day coloring and writing God knows what in that damn notebook but that girl...That girl is too smart for her own good. Kia can try to be a good mother but without that nigga Reem...She will crumble. It's only a matter of time before she brings Nyla back to me. Kia can't stand on her own two feet without Reem," Aunt Tasha said laughing again.

She rubbed her right hand through her short dreadlocks and walked over to her purse. The strands of gray hair were screaming her real age...Funny how Kia went to prison and Aunt Tasha's stress started to take a toll on her and it shows through her hair.

"This house..." I said feeling for the table so I could walk around it.

Aunt Tasha eyed me coming her way and she stopped fumbling in her purse and looked at me.

"What about my house Mir?" Aunt Tasha asked looking at me up and down.

I stopped in my tracks and decided to give her space until she started being disrespectful again.

"Whatever Kia and Reem were doing before on the street *you* NEVER complained about it and do *you* know why Aunt Tasha? Because my fucking sister and her baby dad made sure *you* were stable! Whatever you asked for they gave to you with no hesitation.

"Let's not forget you were living in the projects with no heat or hot water. Kia bought you a house and never asked for anything in return until she got arrested. The only thing she asked you Aunt Tasha is to take care of Nyla and you still throw shit in her face. Tell me sugar...What's really the issue?" I said tapping on the steel chair under the table.

Aunt Tasha looked at me with a straight face but both of them fucking eyeballs watered up.

"I know you hear me talking to you," I said letting go of the chair.

I walked over to her reaching my hand out...You know? playing dumb than a muthafucka.

"I don't have to stand here and listen to this shit!" Aunt Tasha yelled.

She grabbed her belongings and tried to storm out the kitchen into the living room. I stepped in front of her and extended my arm out. She looked at me in shock and I knew questions were starting to fill up in her head but I couldn't take this shit anymore.

"Nah, you're going to listen to what I have to say...You and me both know what the real issue is. You got too fucking comfortable with the money and the lifestyle Kia provided you with. Now that she got caught your true colors are showing. The fact that you have to work fifty or sixty hours in the hospital; overworking yourself just to pay the bills. You never loved my sister…Kia was just convenient for you and that's what you loved," I said.

Everything I said was straight facts and Aunt Tasha allowed tears to roll down her face but she expressed herself silently. She was one to never let herself look weak in front of ANYONE, but I just broke her ass down.

"Get out my face…GET YOUR BLIND ASS OUT OF MY FACE MUTHAFUCKA!" Aunt Tasha yelled, pushing me.

I stopped myself before I fell over the chair behind me. Aunt Tasha looked at my little performance I did and she scratched her head.

"How dare you? How fucking dare you speak to me like that Mir—" Aunt Tasha said while holding on to her purse and wiping her face.

"Muthafuckas never want to hear the truth," I said smirking.

"You talk about me not being there for your sister? You almost got her ass arrested tonight…Why wasn't you watching her back Mir? I mean not literally, right? Since your ass can't see." Aunt Tasha said stepping to me as she smirked.

Her bipolar ass was nothing to mess with but I'll tell you one thing she had the right nigga today that was going to put her ass exactly where she belonged…In her place.

"You left her and disappeared...But my question is where did you run off to Mir and how did you get away so fast?" Aunt Tasha asked, getting suspicious.

"FUCK YOU!" I yelled while pushing my dark shades further back on my face.

"See...Muthafuckas never want to hear the truth," Aunt Tasha said using my own lingo on me.

She was about to speak again but her phone started ringing. She reached down in her right scrub pocket and pulled her phone out placing it to her right ear.

"Hello? Yes this is Tasha...Well I could use the money. I'm on my way back to the hospital now," Aunt Tasha said hanging up her phone.

Then she dropped it back in her pocket and looked me up and down but didn't mumble a word...I knew she was thinking of some shit to say though. She turned to grab her bottle of water and walked forward like she was exiting out the kitchen.

"Let me tell you something nigga...If you ever come at me like that again I will kick your blind ass out my fucking house," Aunt Tasha said speaking with nothing but rage in her voice.

"This isn't your house, remember Aunt Tasha? This crib isn't in your name," I said reaching behind me to feel the chair.

Once I knew I was safe I sat down in the steel chair. Aunt Tasha looked at me like she was distraught; then left my presence. A few seconds later I heard the front door close. Yes, Kia purchased the house for my Aunt Tasha but the mortgage and everything was in Jada's name. Aunt Tasha walks around this crib thinking someone owes her. Fuck out of here! Kia did a good deed because she has a good heart, plus Aunt Tasha looked out for us when our mother passed away. So Kia gave her something in return but she was smart enough to put it in Jada's name. I thought about the shit I said to my Aunt Tasha and I put this on my mother's grave, I wouldn't apologize for anything that I said. I was deep in my thoughts when my phone vibrated. I pulled my phone out my back pocket and held it to my ear.

"Yo?" I said on the phone but it was quiet.

"You have a collect call from...Reem...If you would like to accept the charges press 1 or to decline press 0," The operator said.

I started smiling because I haven't heard from this nigga all week. I pressed 1 then held the phone back up to my ear.

"What's good my nigga?" I said.

Reem started chuckling.

This muthafucka always laughed when he was nervous about something.

"Ain't shit my nigga. I'm just waiting to hear something back from the parole board next week. To be honest I didn't really call you for this," Reem confessed.

The gut feeling in my stomach knew it was more to the story...It always was.

"Well Wassup my nigga?" I asked tapping my right hand on the table in front of me.

"I have to hurry up before the CO's come in and do a headcount in here," Reem said.

I shrugged my shoulders because I didn't give a fuck about no correctional officers, prison guards whatever the fuck y'all call them.

"Talk Reem," I said getting up from the chair then walked over to the cabinet.

"I spoke to Kia earlier tonight," Reem said.

Again, why the fuck was this so important for me to know?

"I seen her—I mean we spoke Reem...What the fuck is this about my nigga?" I asked getting impatient then opened up the cabinet and grabbed the bottle of Hennessy.

"I don't know how to say this but she brung up your disability Mir."

Instantly my hands became sweaty.

"My disability?" I asked confused. I tilted my head to the side to hold my phone so I could pop open the bottle of liquor. "My sister knows that I'm blind," I said lying.

"That's the funny part about it...I don't think *Kia believes* that you're blind," Reem said chuckling.

"What the fuck? Are you sure?" I asked confused then I leaned back my head to take a huge gulp of the liquor. I put the top back on the Hennessy and placed it on the shelf.

"Nigga...Chill you don't have anything to worry about, *everyone* knows your condition. Kia has been locked up for a long time I'm pretty sure she seen a lot of shit that spooked her. Maybe she's just questioning everything in her life right now,"

Reem was trying to give me reassurance but I needed more than that at the moment.

"Nah yo, what made her ask you some shit like that?" I asked, trying to get information out of him.

Even though Kia is his baby mom and his loyalty lies with her, Reem was my muthafuckin' nigga...I knew he wouldn't steer me wrong.

"My nigga it ain't that deep...It's not like you're walking around the hood *pretending to be blind*, right? Because if that's the case then that's fucked up Mir," Reem said.

But that was the case, he just didn't know that.
"You know me better than anyone Reem...Why would I fuck around with some shit like this?" I asked trying to play stupid.

"That's why I laughed when Kia mentioned it to me because it don't make sense. CO's just came in to do a headcount...I got to go, one love my nigga and you keep your head up!" Reem yelled through the phone.

"You're the muthafucka that's locked up" I said laughing. "You keep your head up in there Reem," I said and I took the phone away from my ear as I ended the call.

As soon as I put my phone back in my pocket there was banging at the back door and it made me jump. I turned around and JoJo was smiling through the window looking at me.

"Damn nigga you scared me," I said walking up to the window.

"Open up the door nigga...You ain't really blind," JoJo said tapping on the window.

I opened up the back door and JoJo walked in dressed in his cop uniform. I closed the door behind me and rubbed my lips.

"What you want nigga?" I asked looking as JoJo as he walked to the refrigerator and pulled out some left over spaghetti from last night.

"Where your sister at? And take them glasses off Mir," JoJo said to me. He sprinkled water in the plastic container of spaghetti and put it in the microwave.

"Which one? You know Kia just came home earlier tonight." I said while walking over to the table and sitting down.

"Not her I'm talking about your other sister Jada," JoJo said pushing numbers on the microwave then he turned around to face me.

"I don't know nigga...She's not here, why?" I asked concerned and thinking something happened to my sister Jada.

JoJo looked at me with doubt on his face, it was tension in the room. The only noise was the timer going down on the microwave.

"Man, why the fuck do you look *so nervous* JoJo?" I asked sitting up in the chair.

"This shit is hard to say," JoJo said looking down at his hands.

The lack of communication was scaring me.

"Well, I will let you think about what you're going to say. Just be honest with me my nigga. In the meantime, I have to tell you some shit," I said shaking my head.

"I'm listening Mir," JoJo said. He grabbed a metal fork out of the dish rack and pulled the spaghetti that didn't belong to him out of the microwave.

"My Aunt Tasha made Kia steal some shit from Papi's store tonight in order for my sister to get Nyla back," I said.

JoJo sat across from me leaning back in the chair letting his food cool off.

"Why didn't you just give Kia money for the shit she needed? Before she got locked up she made sure everybody ate," JoJo said.
He had a point but that was too risky for me. JoJo loosened up the two buttons on his cop uniform shirt and got comfortable.

"If I would have gave Kia the money that would of raised more suspicion my nigga; like how the fuck does a blind nigga have all this bread?"

JoJo rubbed on his chin hair with his right hand.

"Disability check, social security check, nigga I don't know," JoJo said while shrugging his shoulders.

"Hard to get that shit JoJo when I'm not really blind muthafucka. Plus I have a feeling that she thinks something is up with me."

JoJo picked up his fork holding spaghetti.

"Anyway, I do what Kia asked me to do, ya know? Make a mess in the store to get the attention off of her, when all of a sudden I see this nigga pull into the parking lot. What bothers me about *his presence* is I been hearing in the street that this nigga is asking questions about me. So I dip my nigga! I get as far away from the scene as I could...I even disappeared from Kia leaving her all alone but she's safe and she has her daughter back," I said.

JoJo tossed the food in his mouth and swallowed a chunk without thinking twice about it.

"Nigga maybe it's some drug territory shit...Maybe we just making more money on the streets than this nigga and he wants a word with you Mir," JoJo said.

Yes, JoJo is a cop but he was a crooked cop...One that sold drugs for his side hustle. He would pull over black niggas in the hood because they were the ones holding so much weight in the trunk of their car. He would always let them go but he would take the drugs and the money.

"Nah, JoJo...His face, the look in his eyes reminds me of the devil. To be honest my nigga, I think it's personal. Anyway, what the fuck do you want to talk to me about?" I asked jumping out my seat.

JoJo blew on his food because it was too hot then he dropped the fork. He reached in his pocket and pulled out two sheets of paper.

"What's that?" I asked walking back and forth in the kitchen.

"Remember that woman you murdered Mir?" JoJo asked me while whispering like it was someone else in the crib with us.

"That was my *first love*...How could I forget?" I said. Then stopped in my tracks thinking about Bella.

"This girl comes in today holding a flyer...At the top of the paper the reward money is $50,000 and she says that she seen everything that happened that night," JoJo said.

My heart started pounding. I felt like he could hear how surreal my anxiety was getting.

"This random bitch tells you and other officers that she seen me murder Bella?" I ask confused holding my right hand on my chest.

"I'm the only one that knows this information and she didn't name you *yet* Mir. So right now you're in the clear but you have to get rid of her before tomorrow morning. That's when this witness is suppose to be coming down to the station and telling what she saw that night." JoJo said pushing the container of spaghetti away and focusing on me.

"We made sure no one else was there when this shit happened JoJo so how the fuck is there a witness—" I asked running my hands down my face.

"That's not all my nigga...Did you know Bella was married?" JoJo said.

I stopped and looked straight at him. JoJo grabbed one of the papers he'd pulled from his pocket and slid it over to me.

"What the fuck? That can't be true...I was the only nigga she was fucking." I said then looked down at the paper. It was a wedding ring on her ring finger that I didn't notice until now.

JoJo grabbed the second sheet of paper and gave it to me.

"Mir...Bella was married when you murdered her my nigga. This is her husband," he said.

When I saw the paper my eyes blew the fuck up!

"THAT'S THE NIGGA THAT PULLED INTO THE PARKING LOT JOJO! I TOLD YOU THIS SHIT WAS PERSONAL YO!" I yelled running over to him as I tapped him lightly on his shoulder with my fist.

"We can deal with him later...Right now you need to get rid of that witness." JoJo said while reaching for the container of spaghetti again.

I walked away from JoJo and sat down in the chair.

"Well who the fuck is the witness?" I asked dumbfounded because I was.

"Damn yo...It's Jada that's the witness that came into the precinct asking for the reward money in Bella's case," JoJo confessed.

"MY SISTER YO?!" I said yelling then slamming both of my fist down on the table.

JoJo reached down in his pocket then placed a few packets on the table.

"What the fuck is that?" I asked confused looking at the substance through each bag.

"A bad dose of heroin mixed with rat poisoning," JoJo said looking me in my eyes when he spoke.

"I can't do that to my sister yo," I said shaking my head.

"You're the one that got Jada strung out on drugs in the first fucking place...Does Kia know that?" JoJo said revealing yet another secret of mine while he started smirking.

—KASSANA WILSON

CHAPTER 4 REEM

"Yo!" I yelled through the phone.

I was becoming frustrated talking to Kia. I looked up and saw a post above the phone that read, *"These telephones shall be subject to recording and listening."*

I was a careful muthafucka I always watched what came out my mouth. I felt like since Kia been back in the world and got released from being in the cage she didn't respect me. I was just a prisoner with a plastic band around my right wrist with numbers that I remembered the first three days I got in this muthafucka.

"Ayo Kia...I know you hear me talking to you my nigga." I said.

I heard Kia huff and puff through the phone. You can always tell when a woman's patience is running thin with you.

"I'm busy right now Reem..." Kia said with so much hurt in her voice.

Hurt that I couldn't comfort her through because I was in here until the white man decided to give me my freedom again.

"Busy doing what yo?" I asked then I turned around to all the noise that was going on in the pod.

I looked to my left and there were Hispanic muthafuckas sitting on the table betting on a baseball game in exchange for—.

"What Reem?" Kia asked saying my name with an attitude.

"Who the fuck is that talking in your background?" I asked holding the phone to my left ear tapping my right hand on my thigh.

"Uh...It's Nyla," Kia said as her voice started to crack which meant something was wrong.

"Kia you're really trying to play me like I'm a dumb ass nigga," I said chuckling but I was laughing to hold my composure.

"What are you talking about Reem?" Kia asked flabbergasted.

"I can name two reasons how I know that's not Nyla in the background. For one when you're nervous about something you always hesitate to tell me the truth. You get too caught up in questions and your brain doesn't think quick enough about what you'll say next. Number two I have a daughter yo...A fucking daughter Kia so I know the difference between a woman's voice and a man's voice and that my friend was a nigga talking in your background. So who the fuck is it?" I asked.

Kia got silent on the phone. I never heard her so quiet but I knew she was mute because she was thinking of something.

"You got Nyla around another nigga Kia?!" I asked and this time I yelled much louder than before.

I turned to my left where the prison guards would sit at their desk watching the cameras or doing paper work. Through the clear window one guard stuck out to me. Why? Because as long as I have been locked up I've never seen his face before. He looked mix and he was standing; smirking at me with his arms crossed like he could hear my phone conversation through the glass window.

"How *dare* you ask me some shit like that Reem?! You know I would never disrespect you or our child like that. You're too busy accusing me of doing something wrong when all I ever did was hold shit down for you, our child and everyone else around me yo. When are you going ask me how I'm feeling Reem? I mean really ask me how I'm feeling baby because my mental isn't what it used to be. I'm afraid that I will end up hurting—" Kia paused and I heard her take a few breaths.

I wanted to ask her who was she thinking about hurting but then I looked back up at the sign hanging above the phones and remembered that we were being recorded.

"Since you called me have you asked where me and Nyla are laying our heads at tonight? Have we eaten? Nah...you didn't ask not one question because you aren't concerned. When the real question is why does Nyla have this fucking phone in her bag and where did she get it from Reem?!" Kia said.

I knew I had to do something to get myself out of this situation.

"Man, I'm not about to be arguing on this phone—" I said trying to put all the blame on Kia.

But she just started laughing instead. Did I missed the joke? What the fuck was so funny?

"You see? Now we both know I'm not the one that has something to hide...It's you with the skeletons in the closet, Kia said then she exhaled deeply.

Though it was so much noise in the prison I was doing my best to focus on her background but I couldn't hear a sound anymore...Not even Nyla's voice.

"I have to feed my daughter or at least find something warm to put in her belly tonight. Goodbye Reem." Kia said.

I couldn't allow Kia to be upset with me...As a man I couldn't do that shit. All this animosity between us was killing me slowly. I would lose my mind if something happened to her...Especially on bad terms.

"All I'm saying is the voice in your background sounds familiar—" I said then I heard the dial tone.
Kia hung up on my sorry ass again. I slammed the phone down and I heard the door to the pod pop open which meant someone was about to come into this cell. No matter how much time I did I would NEVER get used to the sound of the doors popping, the door slamming or the tone of a guard yelling your last time. I mean some shit you never get used to, right?

"I need every inmate to go in your cell now!" The prison guard yelled while walking into the pod and looking at the Hispanics sitting on the table.

I noticed that this was the same guard looking at me through the glass smirking.

"Man, y'all just came in and did a headcount plus the game is coming on tonight," One of the Hispanic prisoners said jumping down off the table.

The guard took a few step towards him then stopped.

"GO TO YOUR FUCKING CELL!" He yelled again. Every prisoner did what they were told. If not that meant shut down and none of us wanted that. Which meant no phone calls, no visits and no commissary.

"Get the fuck out my face...Why don't you just go to the game and be in the crowd like everyone else?" The prison guard asked the Hispanic inmate.

"Because I'm in this fucking prison—" The Hispanic inmate said.

I walked up the cold steel stairs and headed to my cell. For some reason the Hispanic inmate and the prison guard followed behind me up the stairs as well.

"My point exactly...Maybe next time you will think twice about your actions now you know where you will end up," The prison guard said.

I entered my room which was at the top of the stairs and the Hispanic inmate looked at me when he said this shit.

"Fucking pig." He said while entering the cell on the right side of mine.

"What the fuck did you just say to me?" The prison guard reached the top of the stairs and walked into the Hispanic inmates cell.

I turned around minding my business and I clapped up my cell mate Goose. This was my Bunkie for the last three years. Goose sat up on the bed when we both saw a shadow standing in our door way but we didn't hear our door open up.

"Get out my nigga" The guard said looking straight at Goose.

"This is my cell though," Goose said pointing to his top bunk.

I stepped back and sat on top of the cold white table that was not even five inches away from our toilet. The toilet that me and Goose had to use with one another in the room. You think that's bad? Imagine when one of us takes a shit...We don't have any air fresheners we can't even crack our cell door. *They know* this prison food is fucking our stomachs up!

"For the next two minutes it's not...Go stand in the fucking hallway nigga," The prison guard said to Goose.

I looked down at the guard's name tag and it said Sanchez.

Goose looked at me waiting for the, *"okay,"* to leave out and I just nodded my head up and down. Goose left out, walking into the hallway and now it was just me and this guard Sanchez face to face.

"What I do? I don't have any contraband in my cell," I said looking around.

Sanchez started laughing.

"You guilty of something Reem? I never said shit about you having anything," Sanchez said looking back in the hallway then he took another step towards me.

This nigga looked like he could be Hispanic or something...I think he has the wrong cell because I'm blacker than a muthafucka. Ain't shit me and him have in common!

"You're the new prison guard...I'm not too fond of you," I said telling the truth. It was just something about this CO that rubbed me the wrong fucking way.

"That makes two of us...I heard you arguing with your shawty on the phone," Sanchez said putting his hands down in his pocket then he looked back at the prison phones that were hanging up on the wall downstairs.

From my cell you could see it with the door cracked open.

"That shit don't have anything to do with you," I said shrugging my shoulders.

"Relax playa..." Sanchez said putting his hands up and he laughed again. "I was reading up on your record and I read everything you and your shawty did down to the last detail," his pupils got large like he was getting excited off the shit I did in my past.

"I don't want to talk about that shit...I'm putting that life behind me once I get out of this prison," I said thinking about changing my life for Kia and my daughter Nyla. I got down off the table and laid flat on my cell floor so I could do some push-ups.

"Well I do want to talk about it my nigga! Shit...Y'all were making more money than doctors, nurses, lawyers and judges put together," Sanchez said and now I was the one laughing. I continued doing my push-ups not paying his ass any mind.

"What's your point my nigga?" I asked counting the amount of push-ups I was doing in my head.

"I know you still have bread waiting for you the moment you walk out this prison and I want half of what you got," Sanchez said walking back and forth while I was still working out.

My father always taught me the weakest shit someone could do is hurt you while your back was towards them. I hope he was right but I wasn't trying to look like no coward either.

"I don't have a dime to my fucking name" I said as I was still counting in my head.

"In this prison? Of course not, but I know a smart man like you put millions away for a rainy situation like this." Sanchez said while tapping me on my prison uniform with his right foot.

I felt like that shit was so disrespectful but he had one more time to try me like I was some punk ass nigga.

"Let's come to a common ground how does two million sound to you Reem? Because to me It sounds like I can quit this bullshit ass job for a while," Sanchez said still pressing the issue that DID NOT EXIST.

I don't have no fucking money! You think if I did my baby mom and my daughter would be out there in the streets trying to make a way. Like damn my nigga I don't know where he's getting his information from but he got it completely wrong.

"Nigga, I don't have any fucking money!" I said jumping up to my feet.

Sanchez smirked and walked backwards to the cell door.

"I was afraid you might say that...if I don't get what I asked for someone will get hurt." Sanchez said looking down at his fingers to see if their was any dirt in his nails.

"What the fuck can you possibly do to me?" I asked breathing heavy from working out.

"I never said it was going to happen to you and I'm not the one that's doing anything." Sanchez said turning his face up at the scene of my room.

I mean it wasn't no bachelor pad or no shit like that but me and Goose kept our cell pretty decent...For the most part.

"What the fuck do you mean by that?" I asked rubbing my hands together being discreet.

Sanchez smiled harder than he ever did before.

"You will know soon that I'm really the good guy here and I'm trying to help you out," Sanchez said. He looked back to see if anyone was listening in on the conversation then he looked back at me. "You have option A which is to just do what I ask nicely or option B..." Sanchez said rubbing the side of his face.

"What's option B?" I asked curious because it was obvious I didn't have option A; which was to give him any money. I was a broke nigga at the moment too. Which was something I wasn't proud of.

Sanchez sucked his teeth a few times then walked to the door like he was leaving out.

"You're a smart nigga Reem? Think about it...Kia and Nyla is it?" Sanchez said, bringing up my family as he looked back at me.

My eyes grew the moment I heard him say Kia's name, call it being in my feelings or whatever my nigga but my family was my number one priority.

"Muthafucka!" I yelled charging at Sanchez.

Goose heard me yell and came running to my aid getting in between me and Sanchez.

"Reem, chill out my nigga," Goose said holding me back from Sanchez.

"Yeah listen to your Bunkie...Chill out pretty boy before I throw your ass in the hole." Sanchez said smiling slamming my cell door closed even though it wasn't time to lock in just yet.

This nigga was acting like a bitch.

"What was all that about?" Goose asked letting me go.

I could hear myself breathing. I sucked my teeth, rubbing my right hand down my face and jumped back on the hard rock table in our cell room.

"Crazy part about that shit Goose; is I'm still trying to process what the fuck he said to me..." I said thinking but the only thing I saw flashing in my head was Sanchez's devilish smile that I knew was going to haunt me…

But will I allow another nigga to dictate my life? I know this is my first time meeting y'all *(yes you…You that's reading this right now)*. I think y'all know me better than that but we will get more acquainted soon.

"I need to find some money and fast when I get out of here. I can't put my family in jeopardy because of me," I said to Goose.
"If that conversation y'all had was about money then I'm confused as hell my nigga." Goose said scratching his overdue hair that needed a cut.

This nigga knew the days to get a cut and he still chose to let his hair wolf.

"Why are you confused Goose?" I asked curious.

"To be honest I don't even know why that prison guard is working here." Goose said then sat down on my bed. He looked out the tiny little window of our cell then back at me.

"You're saying it like having a job is bad my nigga," I responded calmly.

"Having a job isn't bad...But when your brother is loaded with bread that's where you raise suspicion. That prison guard has money Reem I guarantee it...His intentions is what you need to be worried about. There are about 1800 inmates in this bitch and you're the only one that nigga had a conversation with... Something is definitely wrong here," Goose said.

"Who is Sanchez's brother?" I asked confused.

"His name is Angel, do you know him?" Goose asked.

"Nah never heard of him..." I said.

Goose looked at me shocked because I didn't know anyone by that name.

"Well, while Sanchez was in here chomping it up with you I heard some shit in the other room," Goose said pointing towards the cell with a straight face.

"You always hearing some shit Goose..." I said smiling then jumped down off the table and I went to look out our cell window.

"Nah, on some real shit all them niggas are like fans of Angel and his drug business. Well I heard this nigga Mir got blood on his hands and Angel is going to take care of it. I think that nigga Mir is pretending to be blind or something like that." Goose said standing up off my bed.

When I heard Mir's name Goose automatically had my attention.

"Angel is plotting to murder Mir?" I said turning around.

Goose looked bothered.

"Slowly but surely...Angel is getting close to some shawty in order to get to Mir. I think her name starts with a K," Goose said. I just stared at him.

CHAPTER 5 KIA

"Back the fuck up my nigga," I said looking at the motel door as Angel took a step in my direction. I could hear the waves splashing in the bathtub that Nyla created in the distance.

"Kia...Relajate mi amor," Angel said holding his hands out.

I just gave him a mystified look.

"What did you just say Angel? I don't speak Spanish but I think you knew that already" I said. I looked to my left and saw the chair sitting under the table. I pull the chair out to put some distance in between me and Angel.

"I'm telling you to relax Kia," Angel said in a calm voice.

I shook my head no until I received some answers.

"Answer my fucking question Angel," I said keeping my voice at a minimal because my daughter was in the next room.

"Which is what Kia?" Angel asked confused.

"How the fuck do you know about my daughter? I never told you that." I said.

Angel just stared at me for a minute like he was trying to figure me out.

"Wild guess my love," he said dryly.

"Nah, you have to do better than that," I said.

Angel just shrugged his shoulders. I started tapping on the chair in front of me and reached in my back pocket.

"You know what...Just get the fuck out before I contact the police." I said while pulling out the phone Nyla possessed to receive phone calls from her father.

"Listen Kia...After I dropped you off at that random house I parked down the street and waited for you to come out. Once someone brought your child to the front door I thought you had a daughter. Now that I see the girly bookbag on the back of the chair my guessing confirmed that you have a daughter. I'm sorry I just didn't want to come off like a creep just because I wanted to look out for you." Angel said. Then pointed down at Nyla's bookbag on the back of the chair.

I stuffed the phone back into my pocket and ran my fingers through my hair.

"Look I'm sorry, understand that I am a mother first and I have to do whatever I feel is necessary to protect my daughter—Fuck! What time is it? Oh my God...Oh my God," I started to react differently.

I began looking for a watch that I didn't own to be on my wrist just so I could check the time. I started pacing the room back and forth. I was on a time schedule with the motel clerk, I just wanted to get Nyla together and suck Jason's dick until he exploded. If that's what I had to do to keep a roof over my child's head then it was necessary and I wont allow anyone to tell me differently.

"What's wrong Kia?" Angel asked dumbfounded watching me walk back and forth.

"I have to tend to my daughter but I made a *promise* to the motel clerk—" I said and my pacing increased from my anxiety...Anxiety of the unknown to be exact.

"It's done Kia," Angel said in his deep and mellow voice.

"I need to go before me and my daughter get tossed out in the rain," I said walking to the motel door to leave out.

Before I could reach the doorknob, Angel reached for my left hand pulling me back in his direction.
"I paid for your motel tonight...I'm assuming that you made an exchange with the clerk just to keep a roof over y'all head tonight. I'm not superman or anything in that nature Kia but I'm a damn good man. I covered the fees so there is no reason for you to do something that you're uncomfortable doing." Angel said looking down at my eyes like he knew what wicked sin I was about to commit.

"How do you know my motel wasn't paid for?" I asked confused but I didn't move a muscle.

My feet were still planted in front of him. I didn't know whether to smile or keep a straight face so I went with my second choice. Niggas don't do favors just for nothing...But I was confused about what exactly Angel wanted from me. I was a broken mother that didn't have anything to offer...I honestly was living day by day; protecting what I have right now which is my daughter.

"The look you have in your eyes I saw it growing up with my mother. My pops dipped on us when we were little boys but my mother she had our backs...She never gave up on us. My mother would only cry at night because that's the only time she felt safe. Though we never saw her cry physically we always heard the loud wailing throughout the night. My mother would sell her body to put food on the table but she kept her soul pure. I feel like you were in the same boat tonight with that motel clerk and I'm sorry for any hardships you're enduring right now Kia. I know how it is when a mother is trying to do her best and she is struggling to make a way.

"My mother went through exactly what you're going through...The expression of desolation and lost hope is all I saw in your eyes," Angel said reaching down for my hand as he caressed it.

If Reem knew what was going on right now he would throw the word disloyalty in my face so I dropped my hand to my side. I walked around Angel and sat down on the motel bed.

"I'm just an open book, huh?" I asked looking down at my hands.

"Let me do something for you...I don't want to overstep my boundaries but I want to help," Angel said turning to face me.

"I don't need any fucking pity Angel!" I yelled out jumping up off the motel bed.

"Who hurt you?" Angel asked me with a disgusted look on his face that I was now starting to question.

"Excuse me nigga?" I asked looking him up and down.

"How many niggas hurt you in your lifetime for you to act in such a nasty manner towards me? Since I met you I haven't asked you for shit...I just want to be there for you," Angel said with truth and sincerity in his voice. "How about you get your daughter dressed, put on her pajamas or something. Y'all pack every belonging and meet me outside at my range rover. I have a house not too far from this area and I live alone. You see them roaches going in and out that hole over there. This isn't a place for you and your child to be and I won't allow you to stay here Kia." Angel said walking to the motel door.

I felt so guilty for the way I was treating him but my gut feeling was telling me I was feeling this way for a reason...I just didn't know what it was just yet.

"Why are you doing this Angel?" I asked confused.

He opened up the motel door and turned back, looking me in my eyes.

"My wife would want me to do this...And it's just something about you Kia that I'm just drawn too. I will find out exactly what it is soon," Angel said and I just looked down at the motel carpet.

I guess the cleaning company didn't give a fuck if a customer saw the stains on the floor or not.

"Please come with me," Angel said pleading this time.

"I will meet you outside within ten minutes...Let me get my daughter situated first," I said pointing to the bathroom.

Angel smiled which seemed heavenly, he closed the door behind him and I walked over to the bathroom opening up the door.

"Nyla...Come on baby," I said reaching on top of the toilet for a towel. I shook the towel out just in case any roaches or anything were hiding inside there before I handed Nyla the towel.

"You just left me...Again," Nyla said shaking her head. She stood up in the tub, wrapping herself with the motel towel and entered the room.

"Baby I will never leave you ever again. Mommy just had somethings to take care of first...I'm sorry, okay?"

Nyla had her back towards me and didn't say a word.

"Nyla...When mommy asks you a question that means you need to be respectful and answer me, understand?" I said.

Nyla shrugged her shoulders then reached inside her book bag putting on a pajama set with socks.

"Well I think you need to be respectful and listen when I'm trying to tell you something important," Nyla said.

"What did you say to me?" I asked spinning her little ass around so she could look me in my eyes.

Nyla held her socks in her hands staring at me.

"Just put them on and put your uggs back on," I said pointing down to what was in her hand.

"Where are we going?" Nyla asked.

"Mommy and her friend are going to take you somewhere better than this and do you know why Nyla? Because you deserve it baby. Go grab your jacket out the bathroom and come on beautiful," I said.

Nyla didn't smile or anything, the expression was dull on her face. She got her belongings out the bathroom, grabbing her notebook off the table and threw her bookbag across her right shoulder. I opened up the motel door and we headed towards Angel's Range Rover. The raining had stopped and I felt like God was giving me a sign. I'm not a Christian or anything like that but I knew hints when I saw one.

"My name is Angel...What's your name?" Angel asked opening up the backdoor for Nyla.

"It's Nyla," my daughter answered the question as she hopped into the backseat.

"Nice to meet you Nyla," Angel said closing the back door. He opened up the passenger door for me and I got in.

I looked behind me to check on Nyla and she was yawning her little body away.

"Do you see the lights flickering in the motel office?" I asked as Angel started up his vehicle and pulled away frpm the parking lot.

"Nah...I don't know what you're talking about Kia" Angel said.

I turned my face because the flickering lights were pretty obvious unless Angel just chose not to give it any attention which was pretty weird to me. I looked down and saw some fancy ass all-black equipment.

"What is that?" I asked pointing to the wide box and I saw a mic attached to it.

"This right here?" Angel asked and now we were both looking at the same equipment. "You never saw a police scanner before?" Angel said laughing as he switched lanes.

"Are you a cop or something?" I asked and he immediately shook his head no.

"Far from one...I just keep this inside of my car so I can keep up with everything that's going on in the streets. I also have another scanner inside my home," Angel said being truthful.

"Sounds like you're a bit paranoid to me." I said looking out the passenger window.

"I'm untouchable," Angel said. He kept one hand on the wheel and used his free hand to turn on the police scanner.

"Which means what?" I asked not understanding his statement.

"Niggas out here can't touch me Kia...I'm like God," Angel said hyping himself up.

I just started smirking. One thing I would never do is undermine anyone especially a nigga that was too prideful.

"So how many brothers do you have?" I asked starting conversation.

"What?" Angel asked like he was getting offended.

"You told me the story of your mother struggling to make a way for you and others which I assume you have other brothers, correct?"

Angel cleared his throat; switching over into another lane.

"I have two brothers...I'm the only one that chose to take a different path in life while my brothers are out here doing their own thing. My mother is in Mexico right now and—" Angel said but my rude ass cut him off while he spoke.

"Where are your brothers?" I asked curious. I wanted to know what his brothers did for a living. I wanted to know their names...Just to see if one of his siblings caught my attention.

"Around," Angel said keeping his answer short and sweet.
He turned the corner, driving down the street where the houses looked like mansions. This was the type of environment that I would steal from just so my daughter could eat. I looked at Angel and he had his face balled up.

"What the fuck?" Angel said quickly pulling over and putting his vehicle in park.

I looked to my right and saw a huge white gate, I couldn't see anyone entering this property without knowing the numbers to the keypad. Angel was on some high tech living shit...Or maybe he was just too paranoid like I said. I saw Angel reach for something under his seat.

"You pull a gun out while my daughter is in the backseat of your vehicle," I said confused.

Angel looked in the backseat and sucked his teeth.

"Last week I got set up...I pulled up to my crib and someone was acting homeless. Just like this fucking person sitting outside my gate. I approach the muthafucka and they try to rob me at gun point," Angel said confiding in me.

But I didn't see what he was so afraid of until I saw him point forward.

"I usually have security outside my crib but I gave them the night off...Fuck! The one time I let them off for the night is when this weird shit happens," Angel said.
I squinted my eyes to see someone sitting outside his gate covered up shaking and rocking back and forth.

"That still doesn't give you a right to pull a gun out...My daughter could've saw you," I said.

"But she didn't see me Kia...Nyla is knocked out in the backseat. Look for yourself," Angel said while jumping out the car and I followed behind him.

"I don't give a fuck nigga...It's the principle of shit!" I yelled again slamming the passenger side door. "Where are you going? Wait—" I said looking at this person from a distance. The closer I got the more familiar the face became.

"Kia, get back in the car...I got this," Angel said walking ahead of me as he pointed for me to get back in the car.

"I think I know who that is—" I said in a low tone. Angel approach this person while aiming his gun.

"Why the fuck are you on my property muthafucka?" Angel asked with his deep Spanish accent but this person didn't budge they just continued to rock like a melody. "Answer the fucking question! Who are you?" Angel started yelling. He stuck out his right foot and kicked this person disgracefully that I became appalled by the second.

"Please don't hurt me...Please don't—" I was so sure this was a male until the eyes connected with mine and it was my sweet sister.

"Jada?" I asked running to her aid.

"You know who this is Kia?" Angel asked confused.

"It's my sister...Her name is Jada," I said looking at Angel as I held her in my arms.

"She looks like she needs to be admitted in the hospital," Angel said shaking his head.

"Jada...Jada baby look at me it's me. Your sister Kia...Look at me you don't have to be afraid," I said holding up her chin.

Jada was dressed in oversized clothes and she was sweating profusely like she was hot but shaking like she was cold. Her pretty curls dropped from her body heat and she was having a rough time keeping her eyes open.

"Kia, I miss you so much," Jada spoke as she opened and closed her eyes.

"Why are you on this side of town Jada? Aunt Tasha lives on the east side baby," I said.

I don't give a fuck if anyone judges me I was taught to be there for family no matter what and Jada is my sister...My blood sister I couldn't leave her on the streets like trash because in my eyes she was worth more.

"Kia, I need something...I need something so I can sleep throughout the night. Do you have two dollars or even five dollars I just need a taste of something," Jada started pleading but I shook my head no because I knew she wanted to buy heroin.

Jada hated the word no and she would go the fuck off when she couldn't have her way. "I NEED SOME FUCKING MONEY!" Jada yelled out then a few seconds later she started crying but I couldn't tell if the tears were sincere. I stood up on my feet and wiped the sweat off on my thighs.

"She's sweating bad...Kia I think your sister is withdrawing from drugs. She is a bit disoriented too...Shawty don't even know how she got from the east side to way over here," Angel said to me.

I looked back at the vehicle then looked at Angel.

"Can I put her in the car please?" I asked praying he would agree.

"You..." Jada said opening up her eyes more as she looked at who I was accompanied with. "Angel I know you got something for me. You always sell the good shit...Please just hook me up with something and I will suck your—" Before Jada could finish I pulled her ass up off the cold ground. She wiped her eyes and began sweating more.

"JADA!" I yelled out so she could stop talking. I kept a tight grip on her as we walked to the vehicle. After Jada spoke some truth, Angel wouldn't make eye contact with me.

"Sis...I'm fucked up, I'm fucked up...I'm cold and hot at the same time. If I don't get something quick I don't think I'm going to make it" Jada said and I looked over at Angel and he just had guilt written all over his face.

"Angel what is she talking about?" I asked confused. He opened up the backseat and helped me put Jada inside the vehicle.

"I don't know anything—" Angel said getting defensive.

I slammed the door and looked at him with more fire in my body then the devil himself.

"Jada called you by your first name my nigga...Do you sell drugs?" I asked and Angel exhaled deeply.

"Kia?" Angel tried to reach for me.

But I wasn't the type of bitch that needed comfort right now...I needed the truth. The fact that he was *acting* nonchalant about it was pissing me the fuck off!

"DO YOU SELL DRUGS?! OH MY FUCKING GOD...YOU SOLD MY SISTER DRUGS," I said getting a bit emotional thinking about how heroin took over my sister's life.

"How was I suppose to know that she was your sister?" Angel said.

I walked around to the passenger side and slammed my hands on top of the vehicle.

"I'm not superman or anything in that nature Kia but I'm a damn good man, huh? Isn't that what you told me Angel? That's bullshit...Now you know why I have my guard up when it comes to you my nigga," I said looking so turned off then I jumped in the passenger seat.

Angel entered the driver's seat.

"Kia it's not—" Angel tried to touch me again and I made a noise.

"Don't fucking touch me," I demanded.

"Mom, what's wrong with Auntie Jada?" Nyla asked looking over at Jada.

"Auntie Jada is just a little sick baby but I'm going to make sure she gets better," I said turning around to face my daughter then I looked at Angel. "Put the fucking gun away Angel my daughter is awake now." I said whispering to him.

Angel nodded his head and stuffed the gun under his driver's seat.

"Get the fuck off of me Angel," I said as he reached for me again but I wasn't in the mood.

"Man listen you coming at me and you won't even let me explain myself to you. You believe a crackhead over me?" Angel said not choosing his words carefully.

"That's my muthafuckin' sister nigga...Fuck is you talking about?" I said balling up my face.

"So I'm the only one with secrets now?" Angel said.

I wanted to know what he knew about me since he asked *that* question.

"I don't have time for this shit," I said leaning my head back into the seat.

"Kia..." Jada moaned my name from the backseat.

"Jada, I will take care of you just please be quiet," I said as I was getting annoyed.

"Kia" Jada said again. "Kia I need a hit of heroin so bad...If you give ten dollars I will tell you what Mir did to this woman," Jada said confessing that we knew Mir.

My heart started pumping like a muthafucka.

"Fuck," I said under my breath. I jumped up and looked back at Jada.

Angel looked at me with a balled up face.

"What the fuck did she just say yo?" Angel asked shaking his leg.

I shook my head no so he would just leave the subject alone.

"I heard the name Mir," Angel said and he was certainly right but I had to play along just to protect my baby brother.

"Like you said she's a bit disorientated," I said not trying not to pay Jada any mind.

"Jada what did you just—" Angel turned his attention towards Jada to make conversation with her.

"Angel, leave it alone she isn't thinking straight right now," I said pushing Angel back in his seat so he wouldn't look at Jada.

"I need all units out to creek wood motel...911 call came in that the motel clerk was found dead bleeding out behind the desk," The operator said on the police scanner.

The street light hit Angel's left hand and I noticed something strange.

"Angel...Why do you have blood inside your left hand?" I asked getting timid.

No wonder why Angel didn't want to notice the flickering lights in the motel office. It's Not because he didn't notice but because he murdered the motel clerk Jason.

CHAPTER 6 KIA

"Angel, I asked you nicely not to touch me." I said yanking away from him as I had Jada's right arm across my neck.

"Kia all I'm trying to do is help you," Angel said getting defensive. He aimed his key ring towards his Range Rover and pressed down on the button to lock his car doors.

I looked at Jada and she just had her head down staring at the rock passage that led to the double doors of Angel's house. Nyla was walking slowly in front of me amazed at the new scenery she engaged herself with. I was getting a pain in my stomach with every step I took towards the front doors. I knew that it was God telling me to get your damn child and your sister and get the fuck away from Angel or maybe I was becoming the paranoid one here. Jada was a hardcore drug addict and I don't know if I could trust her just yet. Drug addicts will go to any extent just to get drugs... Even if that means throwing Mir under the bus. I don't have both sides of the story and Mir is family at the end of the day. So I would go to any cost to protect my baby brother. Jada clearly wasn't thinking like me in this situation.

"I don't think it's safe that we stay here with you." I said turning to Angel as he walked up the stairs then he stopped and chuckled. "What's funny Angel?" I asked confused.

"Basically you just said in your mind you don't think that it's safe if y'all stay here. I honestly think you're speaking your own truth Kia... I would never put you, Jada, or your precious daughter in harm's way. EVER! I think you feel that way because you're hiding something from me." Angel said reading me like the back of his hand. I was guilty because I knew it was true and I wanted to do whatever I could so he would think otherwise.

"You know what? Nyla and Jada come on—" I said turning around heading back to the gate. Then Angel jogged down the stairs and stopped in front of me. Nyla's mouth dropped because she didn't want to leave, I know my baby was exhausted from moving around all night. I looked at Jada and she just continued to open and close her eyes like she was drifting away. Her arm was around my neck but her body temperature was now getting me hot as well.

"Whoa, whoa, whoa...listen Kia you don't have to leave I told you I would take care of y'all and that's my word yo. One thing I will let you know is I'm not a dumb nigga so please be cautious when it comes to me." Angel said folding his hands together but he looked me in my eyes when he said every word. I don't know if that was a threat but his body language made me fucking uncomfortable.

"Right this way...Nyla hand me your belongings, I will carry it for you." Angel said reaching for Nyla's bookbag. I turned and walked up the stairs following Nyla and Angel.

"I'm so fucking cold right now...Kia where are you taking me?" Jada asked confused looking around the neighborhood. Angel put his key in the door and the right side opened up. We all walked inside while Angel closed the door behind us. I looked straight ahead and started shaking my head.

"Fuck! It's impossible to get Jada up all them stairs." I said getting aggravated. My body was tired and I just wanted some needed sleep that was long overdue.

"Mommy you just cursed again." Nyla said looking at me like she was disappointed. Angel walked over to Nyla and bent down to her level so he could speak to her.

"Nyla, mommy is very sorry for her bad language. Tomorrow morning I will get you a swear jar and you will see the difference around here." Angel said making a promise to her. Nyla looked at Angel and started chuckling, seeing her smile made Angel return the friendly gesture.

"A swear jar?" Nyla asked confused but she continued to laugh. Angel nodded his head up and down as he stood up to his feet. He was still carrying Nyla's book bag on his back while jiggling his keys in his hand.

"Yes, whenever mommy or whoever speaks foul in your presence they have to put a dollar in the swear jar." Angel said looking at Nyla.

"A dollar Angel? Don't you think that price is a little too steep?" I asked. With the position I was in right now, I couldn't afford to give money away just because I said a bad fucking word. See? There I go again, let me try to watch my fucking mouth. Yeah, I don't think this is going to work. I will go in impoverishment in a day just because of the things that come out my mouth.

"Discipline Kia." Angel said to me. "There is an elevator down the hall to your right, but I honestly think it's best if Jada stays in one of the guest rooms down here." Angel said and I started to shake my head no.

"Hell—I mean no." I said correcting myself before my daughter says something about her swear jar. "I want all three of us to stay together." I said looking at Jada and my daughter. Angel took a deep breath and walked over to me.

"Kia...Nothing and I mean absolutely nothing will happen to Jada down here. Your sister is too weak to move around upstairs and suppose she falls down the stairs God forbid. I just want to make sure everyone in this house is safe" Angel said giving me the reassurance that I needed.

"Nice house by the way, I see you have expensive taste." I said smirking as I observed what was in my presence. The foyer was enormous and when you looked up there was a shiny chandelier sparkling down on you watching your sins.

"Is that your way of giving me a compliment and saying thank you?" Angel asked arrogantly because he knew this was his time to come off as a cocky nigga. Damn, the mortgage in this home would give me a heart attack right now. I couldn't imagine owning anything this expensive.

"Take it how you want." I said with a straight face. I rubbed my hand on Jada's face and she felt cold but the sweat beads wouldn't give my sister a break.

"I contacted my sister in law. She is a nurse and can help Jada." Angel said offering more assistance.

"What do you mean help Jada?" I asked confused.

"Your sister will start treatment and begin detoxing as soon as my sister in law arrives. Either Jada can start rehab in this crib or she can go to a rehab facility, your choice but I'm trying to do what's easier for you. My security around the house will be back tomorrow morning, so there will be more than two eyes looking after Jada. There is a guest room around this corner, it can be Jada's." Angel said.

As bad as I wanted to smile, I just held my composure. "Is it okay if I take Nyla into the kitchen to get some food? I promise your daughter is in good hands." Angel said pointing in the direction of another room in the house.

"How does that sound to you Nyla? Are you hungry?" I asked smiling at my daughter. She had her small hands on her belly and shook her head up and down confirming what I asked her. I didn't trust niggas around my child especially ones I didn't know too well. But it was evident that Angel just wanted to be a man and help me.

"Let me take care of Auntie Jada first and I will come to the kitchen with you." I said. Angel lowered his hand so Nyla could grab it and we all departed from one another. I turned the corner and I could see the room but Jada was making it so hard to use her feet. She was dragging herself and it was causing me to get winded fast. Once we reached the guest bedroom, I opened up the door and laid her on the bed.

"Kia I'm freezing, can someone turn the heat on in this bitch?" Jada asked but she had an incoherent speech. The room was dark and I traced my hands on the bedroom wall to find the light switch.

"How does a warm shower feel Jada?" I asked turning on the light. I looked around the room and Jada had half of her body on and off the king size bed. The marble headboard would compliment Jada's skin if she was sober. There was a marble dresser in front of the bed that I leaned back against to catch my breath.

"I don't need a shower...I need a fucking fix." Jada said getting out of her sweaty clothes. I walked over to help keep her balance. "I don't need your fucking help Kia. I can take my clothes off by myself." Jada said with an attitude. When she tried to take her pants off, she fell down. She slammed her hands on the bed from being frustrated. I walked in the bathroom that was connected to the bedroom and handed Jada a white robe.

"Look at me sis, you're going to kick this shit do you understand? No more drugs will be entering your body after tonight." I said putting my foot down. Jada looked at me like I was crazy as she snatched the robe from me. Her c-cup titties were bouncing while she was still dressed in panties.

"I'M GROWN! I DO WHAT THE FUCK I WANT—" Jada yelled again as she fell back down to the floor. I shook my head and walked back into the bathroom to wet a cold rag.

"With no money?" I asked but she heard me loud and clear.

"Look at the pot calling the kettle black." Jada said laughing in the bedroom. I rinsed the rag out and came back into the room walking up to her.

"Excuse me Jada?" I asked as I started wiping her face and chest with the rag. Jada sat on the edge of the bed with the robe open laughing like she has been holding in jokes all damn day.

"Bitch you're just as broke as I am. What do you think Reem is going to do when he finds out you and Nyla are staying in this big ass house? Girl, the house of a drug dealer?" Jada said snatching the rag out of my hand.

"Angel isn't a drug dealer Jada." I said wiping my hands off on my thighs. Jada jumped up off the bed and started cracking the fuck up like it was comedy day in this huge house we were now living in.

"Girl get your head out the clouds and open up your eyes. That Spanish muthafucka has sold more drugs than multiple kingpins combined. Angel looks and walks like a drug dealer. Damn, drugs that I need right now." Jada said with a straight face then she walked over to the door.

"Do you think he has anything in his room upstairs?" Jada asked biting down on her nails from being curious.

"We are guests in his house Jada and you will not do any dumb shit to get me and my daughter kicked out, do you understand?" I asked getting in her face and Jada shrugged her shoulders. "I said do you understand, my nigga?!" I asked again yelling louder this time.

"I heard you! Get the fuck out my face Kia!" Jada yelled pushing me out the way as she fell back on the bed with her eyes closed.

"Can I ask you a question Jada?" I asked leaning back on the bedroom door.

"What is it Kia?" Jada asked not wanting to engage in any more conversation with me.

"Who got you hooked on heroin?" I asked curious. Before I went into prison, Jada wasn't like this. Jada is educated and had a job. Out of me and Mir, she was the only one that graduated college. It's different when you hear stories about this shit but when you actually see it up close and personal it gets you angry. The type of anger that makes you want to get revenge. Damn, what happened to you Jada?

"We all share the same blood line." Jada said but I didn't know what she meant by that.

"Was it Angel that got you on drugs?" I asked and I swear to God I was holding my breath the entire time until she gave me an answer back. Jada quickly shook her head no but I still wanted to know who did this to her. "I need you to promise me one thing... Do not and I mean DO NOT bring Mir's name up in this fucking house. If anyone asks, you do not know that nigga and I will tell Nyla the same shit. I have to watch y'all back and I need y'all to watch mine also." I said. Jada sat up on the bed looking at me with her right titty hanging out her robe.

"What do I get for keeping my mouth closed?" Jada asked smirking.

"Jada we are all we got left in this world without mommy. Please don't fuck this up because you can't keep your mouth closed. We need to stick together and we will! I will be back, fix yourself up and I will bring you a hot meal back. Angel is not allowed to come in this room if I'm not in your presence. I'm just afraid of any conversation overflowing when I'm not around. I don't want you to say the wrong shit." I said taking a deep breath.

"I prefer sweets over food." Jada said winking at me.

"Another thing I love you to death Jada, I really do but I love my child more. DON'T YOU EVER let me hear again that my daughter walked into a room with a fucking needle sticking out your arm. I'm not judging you, but I don't want Nyla to get curious about the shit she sees. Please keep it the fuck away from her Jada." I said speaking some truth to my sister. Jada just tilted her head down in shame but didn't say a word back. I left out the room and closed the door behind me. I heard Angel and Nyla laughing in a distance. I walked towards the front door so I could try to get in contact with Mir. I walked outside on the porch and pulled the phone out my back pocket.

"Answer the phone...Please answer the phone." I said praying Mir would answer Aunt Tasha's house phone but it just went to voicemail.

"You calling your boyfriend, huh?" Angel asked coming outside behind me and I almost jumped out my skin.

"Nah, I was just..." I couldn't think straight for a minute because Angel startled the shit out of me. I bit down on my bottom lip and stuffed the phone back down in my pocket.

"So how many siblings do you have?" Angel asked cutting me off while I was speaking.

"Excuse me?" I asked getting caught off guard. Angel looked down at his hands then stared at me like he was memorizing something.

"I answered your question when you asked me how many siblings I had. Now I want to know how many you have Kia." Angel said.

"How many siblings do you think I have Angel?" I asked trying to take the attention off of me once again.

"Why can't you just tell me Kia?" Angel asked tilting his head to the side. I stepped down on the stairs and shrugged my shoulders.

"What if I say it's just me and Jada?" I asked and Angel turned his head while sucking his teeth.

"I would think that you're lying to me" Angel said. I looked down at his hands and decided to change the subject.

"Are you going to tell me why blood is on your hand?" I asked and Angel looked at me and smirked.

"Where?" Angel asked extending out both hands in front of me so I could look but the blood disappeared.

"You obviously washed it off when you took my daughter to the kitchen." I said pushing his hands from in front of me. "That operator on the police scanner, did you have anything to do with the death of Jason?" I asked and Angel didn't give me any eye contact when I asked him that question.

"Jason?" Angel asked confused like he didn't know who I was talking about.

"The motel clerk" I said gently pushing him on the right shoulder. Before Angel could answer me the front door opened up and Nyla came outside running to me with her bookbag on her back.
t
"Mommy I was looking for you!" Nyla yelled out.

"You was?! Did you eat baby?" I asked laughing embracing Nyla's touch as she fell into my arms. Angel looked down at me and Nyla and he started smiling.

"I wanted to wait to eat dinner with you and Auntie Jada." Nyla said.

"I will go make you and Jada's dinner." Angel said to me as she walked back in the house and closed the door behind him. Nyla sat down on the stairs and pulled a book out her bag.

"What's that baby?" I asked sitting down next to her.

"I told you mommy...I draw and write in this book" Nyla said shaking her head at me. Nyla opened up to her last drawing and the details on her drawings look so familiar. I gently took the book from her and studied the pictures.

"Baby, you're freaking me out right now. This picture looks like someone sitting outside the gate which is Jada I'm assuming, right? Then two people approach Jada one male and one female.

This is me and Angel, huh baby?" I asked and Nyla pointed to the picture with her index finger.

"Yes this is Auntie Jada. This is you mommy and this is Angel." Nyla said. I squinted at the picture when I noticed something.

"What's in Angel's hand baby?" I asked pointing to the object in his hand that was in the picture.

"A gun" Nyla said nonchalantly.

"What Nyla? Did you ever see Angel with a gun before?" I asked.

"Never." Nyla said which just confused me more.

"So why is Angel holding a gun in this picture in your book?" I asked.

"That's what I saw." Nyla said and I shook my head no.

"No baby. You were sleep when we stopped the car I saw you sleeping with my own eyes. Then you woke up when we put Auntie Jada in the car" I said and Nyla took a deep breath before she responded back to me.

"Mom I see things before it really happens. That's the best way I can describe it. I fall asleep but I draw what I see in my notebook while my eyes are closed." Nyla said. I flicked through the pages of her drawing when I noticed something else.

"HOLY SHIT" I said and my eyes were starting to water up. "Nyla what is this baby?" I asked pointing down to another picture she sketched out.

"A married woman with a wedding ring on. Dead on the floor with two men standing over top of her trying to get rid of her body." Nyla said. The details in her work look so surreal. The pain and the last breath that this woman endured dying on the floor, my daughter delivered emotion but this shit was dangerous yo. This shit was beyond dangerous.

"Nyla, who is standing right here holding the knife?" I asked pointing to one of the dark figures in the drawing.

"Uncle Mir. Mir killed this married woman." Nyla said and I looked back at the front door to see if Angel was listening.

"Put everything back into your bookbag. NOW NYLA!" I yelled and Nyla looked at me like she was broken again. She grabbed her notebook from me and stuffed it inside of her bag.

"What did I do mommy?" Nyla asked confused, I wiped my eyes and started whispering to my daughter.

"At the motel tonight you said sometimes you fake being sick around Aunt Tasha because he comes into—What Nyla? What did you mean by that? What male were you talking about?" I asked confused wanting answers.

"It's too late now mommy. You should of listened to me when I was trying to tell you" Nyla said grabbing her bag and she walked back inside of Angel's house leaving me in the dark sitting on the step.

-KASSANA WILSON

_CHAPTER 7 ᴋIA

"Nyla! Nyla baby where are you?!" I pulled back the silk covers on the queen size bed me and my daughter slept in the night before. I jumped up and my child was nowhere in sight. "Nyla! I need you to answer mommy back right now." I said lowering my thick body out of the bed. I turned to my left and the guest bathroom door opened up.

"I'm right here, I was using the bathroom." Nyla said standing up on her tippy toes to turn the light off then she entered back in the bedroom. I ran over to her and held her in my arms.

"DON'T DO THAT! DO YOU UNDERSTAND? YOU HAVE TO LET ME KNOW—" I started yelling and Nyla just looked completely disappointed in me.

"Mom, you were sleep—" Nyla said breaking out of my hug I had her in. I walked back over to the bed and sat down. I took the hair tie I had around my wrist and put my hair up in a messy bun.

"I can give two shits—I'm sorry Nyla." I said calming myself down as I put my hands on my hips.

"Sorry for what exactly? Yelling at me or just the cursing?" Nyla asked trying to get to the root of the problem. I took off the robe I had on and put on a t-shirt, sweatpants, and my boots.

"Cursing. I know I have to put money in your swear jar now." I said turning to face Nyla and she just smirked at me. That same shit reminded me of what I used to do when I was a little girl.

"My swear jar shouldn't be your concern right now. I think you have bigger problems coming your way mommy." Nyla said digging her feet into the bedroom carpet then she looked at me. "Remember you said last night on the stairs excuse my language. That all of this shit was beyond dangerous?" Nyla asked with a balled up face. The wrinkles she provided in her forehead reminded me of her father.

"Dangerous? I never said that out loud to you Nyla I was just thinking that in my head." I said thinking back to last night.

"I can read thoughts when good tension is interrupted." Nyla said and I kind of lost my breath for a second. The last person I wanted to come in contact with was my Aunt Tasha but I think Nyla needs to be evaluated by a specialist. My daughter's gift was out of my hands and it scared me more than anything. I was afraid for Nyla's safety not mine.

"What did you mean when you said bigger problems are coming my way Nyla?" I asked confused but I wanted to talk. I wanted to understand my daughter but the fact that I couldn't just frustrated her more than I knew. She walked up to the table and looked down at her notebook.

"Are y'all ladies awake yet?" Angel asked knocking on the bedroom door but he didn't wait for a response. He just walked in covering his eyes.

"You don't have to cover your eyes, we are dressed." Nyla said giggling. I don't know if Nyla was missing Reem's presence in her life but I felt like in just a short amount of time she connected with Angel.

"Buenos Dias Reinas. I heard some yelling going on up here and decided to check on you ladies. Nyla I see you were doing some morning drawing, huh?" Angel walked up to the table to look at Nyla's drawing and my heart deteriorated to my stomach.

"UH...YOU CAN'T SEE IT YET!" I yelled out. I ran over and stood in front of Angel so he wouldn't look at the picture. I turned around and closed the book and looked at my child who I tried my best to please. "Nyla go get your book bag baby." I said handing the book to Nyla and she took it from me gently and stuffed it down in her bag.

"Why not? I just want to take a peak." Angel said looking at Nyla's bookbag.

"It's not finished yet Angel." Nyla said shrugging her shoulders.

"I want to see when it's completed, deal?" Angel asked Nyla. He smiled at her then he walked over to the door.

"GET THE FUCK OFF OF ME!" I heard the frantic yelling of Jada downstairs which scared the shit out of me.

"Is that Jada screaming?" I asked looking at Angel. He responded back but with a question instead of an answer.

"What's going on with all the women screaming around here?" Angel asked confused as he walked out the room. Just from my guilt and my paranoia I was thinking of the absolute worst to be happening to Jada right now.

"Nyla! Book bag and shoes on now! Let's go!" I yelled out. Nyla threw her book bag on her back and slipped her small feet into her Uggs. I grabbed my daughter's hand and followed behind Angel. "Who is Jada downstairs yelling at?" I asked Angel but he didn't budge. He just walked down the stairs quietly like he was in a deep thought. The closer I got down the stairs to Jada's guest room, the more her yelling started to scar me with more guilt.

"I DON'T GIVE A FUCK HOW WEAK I LOOK BITCH, IF YOU TOUCH ME AGAIN I WILL CUT YOU—" Jada yelled more this time but once I walked in the room she calmed down a little. Angel entered the room and stood by a beautiful Puerto Rican female dressed in baby blue scrubs. Bitch looked like she got her body done in Dominican Republic.

"What's going on here?" I asked.

"Kia, this is my sister in law Teka remember I was telling you about the nurse that would start Jada on treatments so she could detox?" Angel asked sincerely. I looked at Jada and she was on the bed rocking back and forth. The more she moved the more she began to break out in a sweat.

"Nice to meet you Teka." I said extending my hand out. Teka returned the gesture but she didn't smile.

"Jada needs fluids in her body but she refused because of the needles." Teka said to me pointing to a machine that was next to Jada's bed.

"Uh, can you give me a minute with my sister please?" I asked nicely. Angel and Teka both removed themselves from the guest bedroom and closed the door so I could speak to Jada.

"Nyla...Go inside the bathroom and cover your ears please." I said letting Nyla's hand go so I could point to the bathroom. Nyla did what I asked and closed the bathroom door behind her. I grabbed the towel that was at the end of the bed and walked over to Jada.

"What the fuck are you doing Jada? Why are you making yourself look like a bigger fool my nigga? Start your treatments so you can get better. Aren't you sick of this shit yo? Don't you want to live better and do right—" I asked wiping Jada down with the towel but she fell back on the bed and started laughing.

"Live better and do right my ass Kia. Did you forget that you just did five years in prison beloved? Shit, was you doing right in your life? Bitch don't come in here preaching like you're all holy and what not. No one in our family is living right not even Aunt Tasha. Shit, there are skeletons in her closet that I tried to confront before, but you can tell by looking at me that I didn't get far by questioning her past. Now you want to talk about me sinning because I stick needles in my arm so I won't face fucking reality. That train has left the station for any of us to live right in life and you know it sis." Jada said shaking her head. Then she leaned up from the bed and put on her clothes from the night before. "I need to go. I have somewhere to be and I can't stay here." Jada said shaking because her body was cold.

"Not uh. Where do you think you're going Jada?" I asked standing in front of her.

"Anywhere is better than here...Plus I just need some fucking air." Jada said and I looked down at her lips shivering.

"Listen to me Jada...If I take you to go get some air will you come back here with me and start detoxing?" I asked helping Jada with her over-sized clothes. She hesitated at first then she nodded her head yes. I took a deep breath, walked over to the bathroom and opened up the door. "Nyla. Come on baby." I said. Nyla removed her hands from her ears and came back into the room. I walked over to help Jada walk and Nyla led us out the bedroom.

"Going somewhere?" I heard Angel asked while standing behind me which caused me to jump. I looked at Nyla who was just playing with her bookbag on her back and Jada was fighting between being hot and cold.

"I need to visit my Aunt and Jada needs some air." I said as I turned around to face Angel. I don't know how I was going to get to my Aunt's house, but I needed to find a way. Lord knows I needed to speak to my baby brother before it was too late. Angel and Teka were just standing side by side staring at me.

"Is everything okay?" Angel asked walking up to me then he looked at my sister. "Jada really needs to start detoxing Kia." Angel spoke softly but then Jada sucked her teeth.

"I promise she will start today Angel. I just want to make sure she's comfortable first." I said turning back around to head to the door.

"Sometimes you're going to have to be uncomfortable in order to get comfortable." Angel said but I continued to walk and so did Nyla and Jada. "There are three keys hanging up on the left side of the door, pick a car and it's yours." Angel said and I looked to my left and he was telling the truth. Angel jogged up to me and kissed me on my forehead. I began to get chills throughout my body that made my pussy jump. I knew I had no fucking business feeling like this. Feeling like what? A woman Kia? There they go the angel and the devil on my shoulders playing tug-a-war with my feelings.

"Angel I can't accept—" I said shaking my head no which was fucking stupid because now I actually had a way to get to my aunt's house.

"I would be heartbroken if you wouldn't accept it. Never feel like you're trapped in this big house. You can come and go as you please Kia, you're a grown woman." Angel said reassuring me. I grabbed the keys to the Benz and we walked out the door. After I put Jada and Nyla inside the car, I looked back up at Angel and he closed his front door leaving a mark on me that I couldn't express just yet.

"That nigga definitely has intentions for you. Kia you better find out what Angel wants from you before blood starts to shed. No nigga is going to give you one out of three cars just because. I'm telling you Kia you better open up your eyes." Jada said sitting in the front seat as she began to cough. I started up the car and pulled off heading to Aunt Tasha's house.

"It's something about that lady." Nyla said and Jada just started shaking her head.

"What about her Nyla? The bitch is a nurse.We all know that shit." Jada said staring out the passenger window.

"That's why I said it's something about her. I don't think Teka is a nurse." Nyla said and my eyes got bigger listening to my daughter speak.

"Here we go. Queen Nyla swear she knows everything." Jada said getting a tad bit annoyed with her niece.

"Well, we all know that you're a crackhead Jada and no one tells me I'm wrong when I say that." Nyla said and I was completely astonished. Jada's mouth dropped and she turned around in the passenger seat to confront Nyla.

"Kia, get your fucking daughter before I beat—" Jada said. I kept one hand on the wheel and used my other hand to pull Jada back around in the front seat. I looked up in the mirror so I could look at Nyla.

"Nyla, what has gotten into you lately? Your mouth is getting a bit out of control." I said as I made a left turn.

"Maybe your absent presence has her rebelling—" Jada said rocking back and forth in the front seat. Commenting on my parenting skills made my fucking skin boil because I was doing my absolute best when it came to Nyla.

"Jada, please just shut the fuck up! Do you have kids of your own? I don't think you do so please don't tell me shit about my own child. I can handle Nyla! Why don't you tell me why you're rebelling. Are you going to blame my absent presence on you being strung out on drugs?" I asked Jada and she looked at me like I destroyed the only integrity she had left in her body. The expression on Jada's face had me more guilty than before.

"Wow Kia. That's really a fucked up thing to say to someone." Jada said wiping her eyes. I reached out to touch her but she snatched away from me.

"Listen, Jada I'm sorry—" I tried to apologize but I knew Jada didn't want to hear nothing I had to say.

"Can you just drop me off at the police station please?" Jada asked which had me confused.

"Why do you need to go to the police station?" I asked turning down Aunt Tasha's street.

"Something to do with Uncle Mir and reward money." Nyla said from the backseat and Jada looked at me in shock.

"What is Nyla talking about Jada?" I asked.

"How the fuck would your daughter know something like that?" Jada asked staring at Nyla like she was the devil. I parked the car, turned the vehicle off and jumped out the driver's side.

"Stay in the car I will be right back" I said. Before I could close the driver's door Nyla started talking.

"Mom I think Jada should go in with you. I don't think it's a good idea that she waits in the car." Nyla said. I looked at Jada sitting in the passenger seat and she just continued to shake. I closed the car door and walked up the stairs to the front door. I knocked on the door but no answer. I reached down to open the door and it was unlocked.

"Mir!" I yelled out closing the front door behind me. "Aunt Tasha? Mir are y'all home?!" I yelled out again as I entered the kitchen. No one was around but there was an iPhone on the table that vibrated not even five seconds of me being in the kitchen. The phone continued to vibrate I picked it up and placed the phone to my ear.

"Mir it's JoJo. Make sure Jada takes all them drugs and she will overdose within twenty minutes. I have been doing my part making sure she doesn't show up at the station. Why aren't you responding back to me today? Hello I know you're there I can hear you breathing on the phone." JoJo said through the phone. Then I see the doorknob twisting at the back door. I hung up the phone and held it behind my back. When I saw his face my entire heart stopped beating and this was my first time being afraid of a nigga because I didn't know what to do or how to react.

"Damn Kia, prison has done your body right mamacita." JoJo said walking through the backdoor entering the kitchen. My hands started sweating and I backed up towards the counter so I could find someway to hide Mir's phone.

"JoJo..." I said nervously. "Have you seen Mir?" I asked confused.

"Nah...I haven't baby girl I was just about to ask you the same question." JoJo said walking up to me dressed in his cop uniform smiling. I placed the phone on the counter then I turned around and hid the cellar device behind a box of Cheerios.

"Well, if you see Mir can you please tell him to call me. It's very important." I said wiping my hands on my thighs and I left out the kitchen heading towards the front door.

"Ayo Kia. Have you seen Jada?" JoJo asked following behind me.

"Nah...I haven't heard from Jada since I got out of prison. I have to go I have my daughter in the car but it was nice seeing you JoJo." I said lying. I was trying to say whatever I could to get myself out of this situation.

"Can I see Nyla?" JoJo asked and I walked out the front door but I turned around to speak.

"Maybe another time JoJo...Nyla is taking a nap in the car." I said lying.

"I will stick around here and look out for Mir then." JoJo said walking up to the door. I ran to the car and I saw Nyla in the passenger seat.

"Baby where is Auntie Jada?" I asked breaking out in a sweat. I opened up the door and Jada was nowhere to be fucking found!

"She disappeared mommy." Nyla said shrugging her shoulders but she had her notebook in her hand.

"What is this Nyla?" I asked grabbing the book. It look like me and a cop having a conversation but there was something in my hand. "Is this supposed to be me and a cop baby?" I asked Nyla for confirmation. Nyla nodded her head up and down. I reached down in my pocket to look for the phone I took from

Nyla but I left it at Angel's house. Instead of finding the phone I found the key from the motel. I looked at Nyla and she had this petrifying look on her face as she pointed at something behind me. I turned around and it was JoJo licking his lips at me.

"Creek Wood motel. You know it was a murder there last night Kia? The clerk name was Jason or some shit like that. He was divorced but has a son with his ex-wife. During my investigation something clicked in my head that all the motel keys were hanging up I mean all of them except one. It's the same key that's in your hand right now. Either you tell me where Jada is or I will bring you in on evidence. You already did five years in prison so the judge will give you life with no hesitation when he hears this shit. Look at Nyla's face, are you ready to go back because you want to protect Jada? Your choice beloved." JoJo said to me. I looked down at this motel key in my hand. Some shit I had nothing to do with but I was being dragged down because of FAMILY. I looked at Nyla and she spoke in a soft voice.

"I told you it was too late mommy. You should of listened to me." Nyla said.

CHAPTER 8 NYLA

"I'm feeling sick to my stomach. I think I'm going to throw up JoJo." My beautiful mother held her stomach like every emotion she was feeling was twisting and turning in the pits of her belly. I looked over at JoJo and he was smirking at the pain my mother was in as in this shit amused him in a way. I sat in the passenger seat holding my book in my hands but I was observing each and every thing that was going on around me. JoJo walked off heading towards the front door.

"Bring your thick ass in the house then Kia so we can discuss this shit some more." JoJo said to my mother. I felt like I had to be my mother's back bone in this situation. Yes, I was young but I was wise and I knew what the fuck was going on. I jumped out the passenger seat and closed the car door. My mother looked at me and shook her head no.

"Nyla baby. Put the book down." My mom insisted but this book was the key in helping saving my mother's life.

"Mom, I can help you just let me bring my book." I spoke with more courage than other kids my age. I held on to this fucking book and I wasn't letting it go until she agreed with me.

"NYLA!" My mom yelled out my name like she was frustrated with me.

"Please mom—" I said looking my mother in her eyes. I think my mom was just afraid of the unknown and that's what scared her about my book. Little did she know, the shit that I encounter and the things I endure scare the living shit out of me too but does she ask me how I feel? Not at all. Staying out of prison and harms way has been the only thing on my mothers mind since we reunited. I feel it every time she holds my hands.

"Let the little girl bring her book Kia. That way she can have something to do while grown folks are talking." JoJo said waving my mom off. He opened up the front door, waiting for me and my mother to enter in behind him.

"JoJo, you don't know how dangerous that book—" My mother tried persuade JoJo and I felt attacked so I spoke over top of her. Why the fuck would she tell JoJo about my book when I was the ONLY ONE trying to help her ass right now?

"I thought you had to throw up mommy?" I asked entering the living room then I sat down on Aunt Tasha's love seat. My mom walked up the stairs and she stopped when she heard JoJo speak.

"Ayo, Kia stop playing with me just tell me where Jada is..." JoJo said pacing the living room. My mother stared at JoJo like she couldn't breathe then her beautiful eyes circled back to me.

"Nyla come up—" My mother waved her hand for me to come upstairs with her to the bathroom. Once I stood up off the love seat JoJo pointed to the furniture so I would sit back down.

"Nah, go ahead upstairs and throw up Kia. Me and Nyla will wait down here until you get back." JoJo said. He looked over at me and smiled. I swear something more horrific ran through the bones in JoJo's body.

"Don't talk to my fucking daughter JoJo don't even look at her, you understand me? This situation with Jada has nothing to do with my child." My mother said and I could tell that she spoke with such sincerity.

"Mom do you trust me?" I asked and my mom tilted her head to the side when I asked her that question.

"What Nyla?" My mom asked dumbfounded because she didn't expect that question to come from me.

"Tell me you trust me mommy" I said standing up off the love seat again without JoJo's permission. Having this conversation with my mother was the only thing that kept my heart pumping. It was like we were the only two in the living room right now finding common ground among us both. I needed to hear them words from her mouth though. I needed to hear that she believed in me because if not what the fuck was I doing all of this for?! What would any of this even mean if she didn't believe in her own daughter? If she didn't believe in me?

"How the fuck did we go from vomiting to having trust issues?! Kia go handle your business in the bathroom and come the fuck back downstairs yo." JoJo said getting irritated as he waved my mother off but he continued to pace the carpet floor.

My mother walked up the stairs silently and when I didn't hear what I was anticipating on I just dropped my head and looked down at my book in my hands.

"Nyla..." My mother said my name with honor. I lifted up my head and stared into her eyes. Her light brown eyes are my father's favorite feature of my mom and I could see why. "I trust you beloved." My mom said smiling at me revealing her hidden dimples then she continued up the stairs to go to the bathroom. Once I heard the door shut upstairs it was time for me to get down to business. I sat back on the sofa and flipped through my notebook.

"JoJo, you know my mom didn't hurt anyone at the motel last night. You're trying to frame her because you can't get what you want which is Jada." I said not making eye contact. From the corner of my eye I saw JoJo stop in his tracks. The pacing in the living room has come to a dead end.

"Damn Nyla you're smart." JoJo said.

"You have no idea JoJo. I said getting cocky as I continued to flip through my book.

"Perhaps I was trying to frame Kia. I would have a case because your mother still has the motel key in her possession. Which means she was there last night and disappeared as soon as Jason was murdered. So that would make Kia a suspect, don't you agree?" JoJo asked me but I didn't budge.

"My mom has a good heart JoJo. Don't do this to her." I said but I promise I wasn't pleading. Why? Because a shawty like me got a few tricks up her sleeve.

"Tell me where Jada is then." JoJo said walking over to me dressed in his cop uniform. That shit didn't phase me though.

"I'm not going to tell you a damn thing." I said still looking down at my book but I was smirking this time.

"I think you need to watch your mouth Nyla, you're only a little girl." JoJo said and I just shrugged my shoulders.

"How about we call this even because you have skeletons in your closet too JoJo." I said reassuring him. I looked up at JoJo and winked my right eye at him.

"What little girl?" JoJo asked stuffing his hands in his pocket but his face was balled up like nobody's business.

"You covered up a murder for someone which makes you an accessory after the fact." I said staring at JoJo. He removed his right hand from his pocket and balled up his fist. "What the fuck are you going to do? Punch me Killa?" I asked with a little hood slang to my vocabulary.

"YOU BETTER SHUT—" JoJo spoke in rage. I could see the veins popping out on his forehead. I shook my head and pointed to my temple.

"Sorry I got that wrong. You covered up four murders to be exact one in January, April, August, and November." I said telling the truth then I looked down at my book where I had my little fun facts.

"How the fuck—" JoJo lowered his fist and backed away from me slowly.

"The very last murder you covered up will hurt you more than you know if someone finds out. Me and you BOTH know who that someone is I'm talking about. Leave my mother and Jada the fuck alone JoJo before I start running my mouth—" I said and JoJo eyes became watery. I looked down and this nigga was pissing through his uniform pants.

"Something... There's something that ain't right with you girl." JoJo said running out the front door. I got up off the sofa still holding my book but I stared out the window watching JoJo disappear.

"No one will take my mother away from me again...Not if I can help it." I said to myself looking out the blinds in the living room.

"Nyla? What are you doing here?" My Aunt Tasha asked coming through the backdoor. I turned around and headed towards the kitchen. Aunt Tasha was dressed in her scrubs which let me know she just got home from work. "Let me guess your mother dropped your little ass off because she couldn't handle you, huh?" Aunt Tasha asked laughing creating her own jokes. She took off her name badge and sat it down on the counter.

"My mother is upstairs throwing up actually. She doesn't feel too well." I said telling the truth. I walked up to the table and traced the pattern design with my right index finger. I kept my book hostage in my left hand.

"Why are y'all in my house without my fucking permission?" Aunt Tasha asked pushing her purse back on the counter.

"Jada's house..." I said correcting her then I smiled.

"Excuse me Nyla?" Aunt Tasha asked with attitude then she walked over to me. "What the fuck is so important in this book that you have to keep carrying it around for?!" Aunt Tasha yelled out as she tried to snatch my book out of my left hand. I use my right hand to keep my book in my possession but Aunt Tasha wouldn't get the fuck off.

"GET OFF AUNT TASHA!" I screamed out.

"Let me see Nyla!" Aunt Tasha yelled out still fighting with me to get my book. Her hands touched mine and multiple flashes went off in my head like history. I saw all of her secrets that she kept hidden. Aunt Tasha kept them buried for a reason. The visions were so intense that I didn't notice tears coming from my eyes until they fell down on my shirt.

"Oh my God." I said softly. Aunt Tasha let me go and my back hit the kitchen wall. I wiped my eyes and held on to my book.

"What happened?" Aunt Tasha asked jittery. I shook my head so she wouldn't think anything of it. I walked over in her direction but she just looked afraid of me.

"Touch me. Touch my hands again." I demanded. I put my book in between my thighs and held my hands out in front of her.

"You're a crazy little bitch, just like your mother." Aunt Tasha shook her head no and refused to touch me.

"TOUCH ME! TOUCH MY HANDS NOW!" I yelled out. She hesitated again but she embraced me. The flashes were causing me heartache and suffocation.

"You did that to her. That was your fault." I said throwing Aunt Tasha hands off of me. I grabbed my book and I walked backwards trying to get away from her.

"What Nyla? What are you talking about baby?" Aunt Tasha asked nervously. She looked down at her hands confused then tried to walk over to me.

"No...Uh don't baby me now." I said under my breath.

"Nyla! Nyla baby where are you?!" I heard my mother's beautiful voice in a distance I was saved by the bell.

"Mom—" I tried to whisper as she came running down the stairs. I needed to get my mother's attention but she wouldn't focus on me.

"JoJo left?" My mother asked and I nodded my head yes. "Aunt Tasha...I really need to talk—" My mother walked passed me and headed to the kitchen when she noticed Aunt Tasha was home. I ran up to my mom and pulled on her arm.

"Mom no!" I yelled trying to put some space in between her and Aunt Tasha.

"What's wrong with you Nyla?" My mother asked perplexed as she looked down at me.

"We need to go now. Trust me please." I said whispering again. Aunt Tasha looked at me and started smiling but my mother didn't notice.

"Come in here Kia and Nyla so I can make y'all something to eat." Aunt Tasha offered pointing to the refrigerator. I squeezed my mother's right arm and gave her a look of panic.

"MOM WALK OUT THAT DOOR NOW." I said whispering loudly again. My mother agreed with me and headed towards the front door to leave out.

"Aunt Tasha I will call you later. Nyla isn't feeling too well." My mother said lying and Aunt Tasha left out the kitchen entering the living room with a look of concern on her face.

"Is everything okay Kia?" Aunt Tasha asked.

"Yes...Don't worry, let me handle my child first and I will give you a call once I'm done." My mother said as we walked out the house. We headed towards the car and before I got in the passenger seat I turned to look behind me and Aunt Tasha eyes were just peeking through the blinds. Her appearance gave me chills.

"What's wrong Nyla?" My mother asked me closing the driver's side door.

"Remember growing up you would tell me stories about grandma?" I asked closing the door behind me. I was too paranoid so I locked the car doors and placed my book under my seat.

"Yes I remember baby, why are we talking about my mother right now Nyla?" My mother asked me starting up the car.

"You told me grandma passed away—" I said softly and my mother pulled off making a right turn down the street.

"She had an accidental death. She was found at the bottom of the stairs with her neck broken. The detectives ruled her death as accidental and it was closed three days later." My mother said. Whenever she spoke about this particular death, I hear the wounds in her throat that gave me a great amount of pain because my mother was still hurting and not healing.

"That's not what happened to her. Well this is difficult for me to explain mom." I said taking a deep breath. My mother rubbed the side of my face with her hand but she didn't speak. "Uh, your mom isn't really your mom. Aunt Tasha is the mother of you, Mir and Jada. Y'all also have another sibling out there somewhere. I saw everything when I touched Aunt Tasha hands in the kitchen but when I tried to see what the fourth sibling looks like my vision didn't want to cooperate with me. Aunt Tasha gave her rights to her sister (the woman you thought was your biological mother) but since y'all were too young y'all didn't notice what was going on. Once Aunt Tasha saw that her sister was giving each one of y'all the perfect life growing up, she became resentful and enraged. Later on that night when no one was around, Aunt Tasha pushed her sister down two flights of stairs which resulted in her neck breaking. That's why the detectives ruled it an accidental death. Aunt Tasha didn't take y'all in because she felt bad after her sister died. Aunt Tasha took y'all in because all three of y'all are her children but she's just covering her tracks." I said putting the visions together when I touched Aunt Tasha hands. My mother swerved the car when she heard me say this and my heart started pumping fast.

"Are you okay mom?" I asked and my mother just nodded her head up and down but I knew she wasn't okay. I could feel the tension within this car.

"Where is the fourth child at?" My mother asked me taking a deep breath.

"Mom...I'm not sure. That's the first time my vision has become blurry like that. I'm sorry." I said apologizing.

"I can't believe this shit—" My mother's voice started cracking when she spoke. I turned to look at her and tears started rolling down her face. I saw my mother emotional before, but this time she was broken.

"That's not all," I said and I felt terrible giving my mother all this news at one time. "Aunt Tasha also has a secret with daddy that she's hiding." I said finally getting everything off my chest.

"What the fuck is going on with Tasha and Reem?" My mother asked me as more tears fell from her eyes.

"That's not my place to tell you mom. You need to talk to daddy." I said shaking my head because I knew exactly what it was and y'all think my mother is broken now?! Imagine when she finds out the secret between them two.

-KASSANA WILSON

CHAPTER 9 JOJO

"How the fuck does she know yo?!" I yelled through the phone as I switched to the right lane.

"Who baby? Calm down what are you talking about JoJo?" Tasha asked dumbfounded but she was calm as waves in the ocean.

"Your fucking niece Tasha! That's who I'm referring to." I yelled again into the phone. I had the cellular device up to my left ear as I pushed the gas pedal down in my patrol car.

"I think you're just a little stressed my love. Why don't you come over so I can get on my knees for you daddy. How does that sound JoJo? I will suck your dick until you bust in my mouth. You know I can get real nasty for you." Tasha said sucking her lips through the phone. I was not in the mood to get head right now. I'm a fucking cop and I just got intimidated by a little ass girl a few minutes ago. Someone was going to pay for this shit!

"I don't need my dick sucked Tasha I need some fucking answers!" I yelled again stopping at the red light ahead.

"You're not telling me what's going on JoJo so how do you expect for me to make it better baby?" Tasha asked and I just took a deep breath.

"Nyla knows that I was involved with covering up Bella's murder." I said to Tasha. I pushed down on the gas pedal and continued straight.

"What?" Tasha asked laughing through the phone. "That little girl doesn't know a damn thing JoJo." Tasha said as she continued laughing.

"You think this shit is funny yo?!" I yelled out hitting my steering wheel. I looked to my right and saw two black niggas standing on the corner at the stop sign. When my eyes connected with them, they turned around trying not to make eye contact. "Nyla even brung up my past. Some shit that I tried to keep buried she spoke on it! So that only means one thing." I said and Tasha sucked her teeth.

"Which is what nigga?" Tasha asked with more attitude than yesterday.
"You been running your fucking mouth yo and Nyla heard you speaking about me." I said. Me and Tasha been fucking around for two years now. Tasha knew what I did to Bella by a mistake. I mean since we being honest here let me just run the story down real quick.

Bella used to work at the hospital before she got murdered. Bella used to wear this rich perfume to work and the night I helped Mir cover up the murder, she was wearing it on her body. Somehow Bella's perfume stuck to my body and Tasha noticed when I got to her house. Mir doesn't know about me and Tasha's affair. Actually no one knows. We keep our business on the low. That night I walked into Tasha's bedroom and she ran up to me sucking on my neck. She tasted the perfume and gave me a funny look, yes she noticed but she didn't speak up on it until the next day.

Bella's body was discovered and Tasha saw it in the paper. She came home early one night and confronted me. When I didn't deny my involvement in Bella's murder, Tasha told me she knew already. I asked her how and she said that the scent I came in the house with was one of a kind. That scent belonged to Bella. I never told Tasha the whole story shit she still docsn't know that Mir really ain't blind.

"What muthafucka? I don't discuss what we talk about to anyone especially not to a little ass girl. I think you're just paranoid baby. Come over here and just let me taste you please JoJo. I want to feel your dick inside of me." Tasha said still trying to convince me to come over.

"I'm not fucking you bruh!" I yelled again turning the corner. One thing that I'm concerned about is how my anger grows and nothing or no one is able to put that flame out. I heard my phone beep and I took the phone away from my ear and it was a text from Angel asking me where I was. I replied back "Omw bro". I put the phone back up to my ear when I heard Tasha talk.

"Well, I'm backed up on bills JoJo so if I give you head can you at least give me money for the bills this month." Tasha said and I chuckled. I went through the yellow light before it turned red.

"Man, you must have lost your damn mind. I'm not giving you shit until you tell me how Nyla knows specific shit that she has no business knowing." I said telling the truth. "Either you do something about this shit or I will." I demanded.

"Go ahead and hurt that little bitch. I don't like her smart ass anyway." Tasha said and I just started shaking my head because I was kind of disappointed in her ass.

"You and I both know I'm not talking about harming little shawty...I'm talking about hurting you Tasha with information I have against you." I said and I heard Tasha gasp on the phone like she was stunned.

"What the fuck are you talking about JoJo?" Tasha asked as she started getting out of character again.

"Remember the night your sister accidentally fell down two flights of stairs breaking her neck? Who the fuck did you call to come save you to make that look unintentional?" I asked and Tasha hesitated to speak.

"JoJo—" Tasha spoke but I cut her off.

"My father helped you Tasha. Didn't he?" I asked. I didn't give a fuck about my father going down because he always treated me like an outcast out of my brothers. I was kind of hoping Tasha declined my offer this way I could take both of these muthafuckas down anyway. Shit, this was going to be payback to my father for treating me the way he did when I was younger.

"JoJo please don't do—" Tasha tried to plead with me.

"Get that shit done Tasha." I said and my phone was beeping. I took my phone off my ear and it was Mir. I clicked over so I could answer his call.

"I've been calling you all day my nigga where the fuck you been?" I asked Mir as I turned down Angel's street.

"I had to take care of some shit JoJo. Why do you sound like you're in a panic my nigga?" Mir asked and I just stayed quiet. I slowed down in my patrol car when I started approaching Angel's house. "Man fuck that. Anyway, did you find Jada?" Mir asked me.

"We can't touch Jada. At least not yet Mir." I said.

"Why the fuck not? Our freedom is on the line." Mir said reminding me of shit I knew already. Who wanted to know that they were close to going to jail? Shit, NOT ME! Worst feeling is being a cop then getting incarcerated. Do you know what them muthafuckas in the county would do to me? That would be like a field day to them niggas.

"Your niece knows." I said pulling into the drive way of Angel's house. There were two wrestler looking niggas standing in front of the gate. Angel always had himself an entourage of security. I rolled my window down, putting in the code to get let in. A few seconds later, the wide gate opened up and I pulled up parking behind Angel's Range Rover. Angel usually had three vehicles outside his home but I only saw two.

"Nyla?" Mir asked confused as I put the phone back up to my ear. "How the fuck would Nyla know something like that?" Mir asked but he was talking slowly.

"I think your niece is smart yo." I said. I had too much shit on my mind so what I actually wanted to say was coming out of my mouth totally different.

"What nigga?" Mir said chuckling.

"Like I think Nyla can read people meaning she knows the past and she knows what you're thinking that little bitch is dangerous." I said shaking my head as I turned my patrol car off and took the key out.

"Watch your mouth when you're talking about my niece yo. You're telling me that a ten year old is dangerous JoJo? Do you hear yourself right now my nigga? You're speaking like Nyla has visions or some shit. If she's that fucking talented maybe she should audition for Disney Channel." Mir said laughing thinking this shit was hilarious.

"MUTHAFUCKA THIS IS NOT A GAME!" I yelled out and I could feel my heart pumping fast right now. "I'm serious. You wasn't there when she was talking to me my nigga. Nyla knows some dark shit about me. Secrets that I never told a soul. There she was, bringing up skeletons while kicking her little feet smiling down at her book. Your niece made the hairs on the back of my neck stand up. Goose bumps are on my arms from talking about her now. It's like when she looks at you, that little girl is sucking the life out of you with her eyes alone." I said thinking back to that encounter I had with Nyla in Tasha's living room.

"So what the fuck are we supposed to do with Nyla?" Mir asked but the tone of his voice sounded like this conversation was boring him.

"This is not just my life we're talking about Mir." I said but I stopped talking because what I was going to say next might scar Mir for life.

"Answer my fucking question JoJo and stop beating around the bush. What do you want to do with Nyla?" Mir asked again and this time he put some bass in his voice.

"Drive-by and make her death look like an accident." I said. I turned my head and I see three men exiting out of Angel's house dressed in all-black just observing everything that was going on outside. I turned my head in the opposite direction so I could focus on this conversation with Mir.

"DRIVE-BY JOJO? REEM AND KIA WILL HUNT YOU DOWN AND YOU KNOW IT—" Mir started yelling like what I said to him was disrespectful. Was it inconsiderate? Maybe but I didn't give a fuck.

"Why you sitting out here? Come in the house nigga I need to talk to you about something." Angel said tapping on my passenger side window. I hung up on Mir without responding back to him. Angel's presence scared the fuck out of me. I hopped out the car, holding my phone and keys in my hand. I opened up the trunk to pull out a duffel bag.

"Is it bad?" I asked following Angel up the stairs.

"Nigga, does it matter? Come on." Angel said waving for me to follow behind him. We walked passed his security, entering the house. Angel stayed quiet as we continued to walk. Angel was my blood brother and we have another brother named Sanchez. He was a prison guard. We turned the corner and I saw a guest room set up like a hospital room. Shit made my stomach turn. To be honest it reminded me of a room for Jada but shit what the fuck do I know?!

"This looks like a hospital room...Who the fuck is sick?" I asked peeking in the room seeing all the machines and gadgets.

"Treatment room nigga. I have a few people living with me now." Angel said as we walked into his huge living room. He walked over to the bar and motioned for me to come over.

"You running a shelter my nigga?" I asked and Angel picked up a glass taking a swig of his liquor. He offered me one and I shook my head no. "Names?" I asked and Angel put his glass down on the counter.

"What JoJo?" Angel asked staring at me. I handed him the duffel bag and he sat it down next to his feet.

"You said you have a few people staying here, right? I want to know their names." I said acting like the older brother even though I was the baby out of both my brothers. I sat my phone and keys down on the bar counter and looked around the living room. There has not been a woman's touch in this home since Bella been gone. God rest her beautiful soul...I guess.

"Maybe, my guest will come in while you're still here then I can introduce y'all to each other." Angel said focusing on what my eyes were looking at. "I spoke to dad earlier. He asked about you." Angel said calmly as he poured himself another drink. I hated my fucking father so I didn't give a fuck about his concerns.

"What did you want to talk about Angel?" I asked curious and my brother tapped my shoulder like he forgot to tell me something.

"So remember I told you that word has been going around that this nigga Mir murdered Bella?" Angel asked and I shook my head up and down.

"Yeah. I don't know who Mir is though." I said denying any attachment to Mir. See Angel is my blood brother but Mir was like a brother to me as well. I don't give a fuck what y'all niggas say, yes I was playing both sides. I know they say loyalty before anything, but to be honest I was more loyal to Mir than I was to Angel. I believe it was my envy towards my brothers because I felt the same way towards Sanchez.

"I didn't say you knew him personally JoJo. Damn what are you getting defensive for?" Angel asked balling up his face then he looked at me suspicious. I didn't answer his question because I didn't want my nervousness to show. "I also heard that two people were involved with the murder of my wife." Angel said and I started breaking out in a sweat.

"Uh...What do you mean by that?" I asked playing stupid because the second person involved in the murder was my ass.

"Exactly what I said nigga. Mir may have murdered my wife but he wasn't alone and I want to know who the other nigga is before I retaliate." Angel said putting his liquor down then he rubbed on the side of his face.

"I'm going to find out for you my nigga. You know Bella was like a sister to me." I said lying. I didn't care too much for that bitch and I will explain some more the next time y'all muthafuckas hear from me.

"That's what I have you on payroll for JoJo." Angel said to me and I looked down at the duffel bag by his feet. "Damn yo...This shit is eating me alive everyday yo. You sure you don't know nothing about this nigga Mir?" Angel asked and I could see the broken emotion all over his face. A part of me enjoyed it though.

"I never heard of Mir but I will have more info on him this week. That's my word Angel." I said lying clapping up my brother.

"I thought you said you didn't know Mir my nigga?" Angel asked with veins popping out his forehead and neck. I looked at him dumbfounded and started walking backwards.

"I don't bro." I said lying again but it looked like Angel wasn't believing my bullshit.

"WHY THE FUCK IS HE CALLING YOUR PHONE THEN?" Angel asked getting aggressive holding up my phone and there it was.

Mir name popped up as an *incoming call* on my phone screen. I turned around when I heard footsteps behind me and I see three security men pointing their guns at me.

CHAPTER 10 KIA

"Nyla...Go play over there where I can see you. I'll be over there as soon as I get off the phone," I said. I was parked behind Angel's range rover with the driver's side window down as I was talking to Nyla.

"Who are you on the phone with mommy?" Nyla asked me. She was kicking her feet back and forth staining her boots up while anticipating an answer from me.

This is why Nyla always had to get new footwear because she didn't know how to take care of shit. Honestly how can I blame a *little girl*, right? Because when me and Reem was out here robbing muthafuckas we took Nyla shopping every few days. My little shawty was spoiled. Whatever my baby grabbed in the store we didn't hesitate to purchase. Damn, crazy how everything I had just got taken away from me. Instead of buying her something new to put on her feet I will just go in the house run a rag under some hot water and soap to get the stains off her boots.

"Nobody important baby...Just go do what I asked you to do; please Nyla," I said while holding the phone up to my right ear.

Nyla turned to walk over to the steps but then she turned back around giving me a surprised look.

"Why are you looking at me like that?" I asked Nyla, still talking to her out from the driver's side window.

"Just leave it alone..." Nyla said looking at me but she started fumbling with her bookbag on her back.

"What Nyla?" I asked balling up my face.

My child walked back over to me and looked me in my eyes when she spoke.

"Whatever you're doing right now to get back at Tasha...Leave it alone mommy before you end up hurt—" Nyla said but I didn't make out what she said completely because someone spoke on the phone.

"Ms. Graves? Sorry to have you waiting for so long it's busy in this police station today," The detective said picking up the phone to talk to me.

I took the phone away from my ear to give Nyla my attention real quick.

"Nyla...Go over there," I said pointing for her to go over to the front door and play.

Nyla shook her head at me and walked away. Once I saw that it was some distance in between us both I put the phone back up to my ear.

"Is everything alright down there?" I asked concerned.

"I have a police officer on my force that's missing...He has been missing for the last three hours," The detective said confiding in me. I rolled up the driver's side window and took the key out the ignition.

"I'm pretty sure everything is copacetic," I said trying to reassure him about his officer. I got out the car and gently closed the car door shut then turned my head to look at the gate and I saw two security men dressed in all-black just standing still looking like store mannequins. I looked up at the front door and there was another security guard with black shades on looking down at me with his hands folded together.

"Nah, I can't track him down...His body camera isn't on and I can't locate his patrol car. This is unusual and this shit isn't like him at all," The detective said through the phone. I turned my head because I didn't want anyone to read my lips while I was on the phone with law enforcement.

"I'm sorry for dumping my worries out on you. Uh, what can I help you with...It's Kia, right?" The detective asked changing the subject.

Before I spoke I turned to check on Nyla and she was just jumping up and down the stairs.

"There is a case down at your station that was closed over two decades ago, due to no evidence of foul play detectives ruled the death accidental. This case means everything to me and I want to know if you can help me—" Before I could finish speaking the detective rudely interrupted me.

"Help you reopen the case Kia? If no evidence was found during that time then that case will remain closed," The detective said and my stomach just got fucking tight. The way he responded back to me was like he was trying to keep something hidden and covered.

"What if I have substantial evidence to prove that this death wasn't accidental at all?" I asked then turned to look at Nyla again and she was poking at the security guard at the front door to see if he was real and if he would move.

I honestly think that my child wanted a reaction out of this security guard but he didn't budge. I took the phone away from my ear and made a noise to get her attention. Nyla looked at me and moved away from the security guard then I put the phone back up to my ear to talk.

"Goodluck trying to prove it Kia." The detective said to me and I knew my gut was accurate. There was something not right about this detective I just spoke to. You could hear how nervous and determined he was about this case staying closed.

"Fuck!" I yelled out and I hung up the phone on him. In my eyes I had the evidence but how the fuck would I look taking my child down to the station and telling detectives, *"Nyla had a vision and she saw what really happened that night."*

Them muthafuckas are going to put my child in a mental hospital and I refuse to allow that to happen. Damn, I just felt like I was in a lose-lose situation. I wanted justice for what Tasha did to my mother...Because that wasn't right at all. *I know y'all reading this shit like Tasha is your real mother but fuck that!* The only person *who loved us* and took care of us was Tasha's sister and for that reason *she will always be my mother,* in my eyes even if she didn't birth me and my other siblings.

I put the phone in my back pocket and I saw Teka dressed in her nurse uniform storming out the house looking like a sad puppy. She rushed passed Nyla without speaking, heading to her car.

"Teka! Do you have a second to speak to me real quick?" I asked.

Teka stopped in her tracks and wiped her face.

"Are you okay? You look a bit emotional" I said staring at her face turning red. It was like she'd just endured something upsetting inside of Angel's house. I looked at Nyla and she sat down on the stairs, watching me and Teka talk.

"Uh—I'm fine...What's bothering you?" Teka asked lying to me as she cleared her throat.

"I know you don't know me Teka...Well don't know me at all for that matter and maybe I'm foolish to even ask you something so personal right now but I will hate myself if I didn't try..." I said trying to figure out the right words to say.

"Spit it out Kia" Teka said calmly. She looked out the corner of her eye to the security standing at the front door then she looked over at the gate. The way she was moving just seemed as if she was afraid of something...Or someone.

"If I give you blood samples are you able to test that for DNA results," I whispered. I figured if that detective wasn't going to help me reopen this case then maybe testing my blood with Tasha's blood would be step one in the process. If results come back that Tasha is my biological mother then these niggas are going to have to look into this case.

"You know I can...How soon do you need this done?" Teka asked shaking her head up and down.

"ASAP Teka, when I get the blood I will let you know...And please just keep this between me and you," I said tapping her on the shoulder. I gave her a genuine smile then turned to walk to my daughter but I heard Teka speaking while my back was turned.

"Now that you asked me for a favor...I'm going to ask you for one and I need you to keep this between me and you," Teka said lowering her voice.

I turned back around and walked up to her. "Whatever you and Angel got going on make sure it doesn't come with secrets Kia—" Teka said looking up at the house making sure Angel wasn't watching or listening to her.

"I don't—" I started shaking my head while I spoke but she cut me off. Teka grabbed me gently by my arm and pulled me behind a car to speak in private.

"Uh no...Listen to me Angel has a heart of gold BUT when that muthafucka feels like he is being betrayed life will end for you. He would rather you be honest with him from the jump than to find some shit out in the long run. No matter how much love and feelings he may have for you loyalty means everything to that nigga. He will forget about you faster than he knew you...I'm warning you because I just saw some shit inside of Angel's house that will scar me for life. If your sister, daughter and yourself are going to be living here please make sure it's worth it Kia," Teka said and a tear dropped from her right eye. Emotion that I wanted to question I knew she would just twist it around to make it sound sincere like Angel was a child of God.

"Are you saying that Angel is dangerous Teka?" I asked confused.

"What are y'all out here talking about?" Angel asked coming outside smiling.

Teka wiped her face and walked away to her car. I took a deep breath and walked towards the stairs.

"Nyla, come on baby," I said reaching down for her hand. Nyla embraced my touch and stood up from the stairs. I looked at Angel and he just gave Teka a death stare that I didn't understand.

"Hey Angel," Nyla said poking Angel on his side while she walked passed to get inside the house.

Angel smiled at Nyla as he tickled her neck and she exploded with giggles. My hand was still attached to Nyla's hand. I looked behind me and Angel was still standing on his porch eyeing Teka down. I don't know what's going on but I was going to mind my business.

"Nyla baby...I have to ask you something," I said as we entered the kitchen. I leaned back on the kitchen island that was centered in the middle of this room.

Nyla took her bookbag off her back and placed it down on the white tile floor.

"Are your visions ever wrong about something or someone?" I said while turning around to put the car keys down on the table then turned to give Nyla my undivided attention.

"When you were in prison mom I would hear and see things which made me write inside my notebook. Once I got back with you I see more than I ever did before. I have vivid visions, I can hear thoughts and I know how someone feels just by looking in their eyes," Nyla said tilting her head to the side as she looked at me.

I reached out my right hand holding her chin to straighten up her face her. My daughter was beautiful nothing about her should appear crooked.

"Are you saying I made your gift stronger Nyla?" I asked creating wrinkles in my forehead and Nyla picked up her bookbag then threw it on her back again.

"You damn sure didn't make it weaker mommy," Nyla said winking at me.

"Your mouth Nyla..." I think tapping my fingers on her lips and she nodded her head up and down. It was completely quiet in this kitchen and I wanted my daughter to talk to me. "Can you tell me what I'm feeling now?" I asked holding my hands out.

Nyla licked her bottom lips and reached out to touch my hands. The expressions she delivered within ten seconds was nowhere compared to someone that was bipolar.

"You're feeling guilty! You can't do this to daddy!" Nyla yelled out looking at me with tears in her eyes. The pressure she had on my hands just got tighter and tighter by the minute.

"What Nyla?! What is your problem?" I asked confused when Nyla threw my hands down.

"You belong to my dad," Nyla said pointing at me.

"I don't belong to anyone Nyla...I'm not anyone's property but I'm confused on what you mean by all of this," I said.

Nyla looked at me and shook her head, she always presented me with that body language whenever she felt disappointed in me.

"You have feelings for Angel," Nyla said wiping her eyes and my mouth dropped.

"No-no-no-no I don't," I said putting my hands up denying what she said to me.

"I felt it...I saw it when I touched your hands and I also saw something else," Nyla said. The more she wiped her tears, the more they came running down her face.

"What did you see Nyla?" I asked walking up to her and she stepped back from me. Nyla looked down at her hands and then she looked at my belly.

"What happened to the baby mommy?" Nyla asked and my eyes began to water.

"WHAT?!" I yelled out and my breathing was starting to increase.

"Who's having a baby?" Angel asked with a straight face entering the kitchen.

"Uh, I don't—" I began stuttering. I turned so Angel wouldn't look at me while I was wiping my face. I didn't want an ounce of emotion to be discussed in this fucking kitchen.

"I'm taking a nap...I'm feeling a little light headed—" Nyla said softly as she tried to walk out the kitchen. I turned around to look at her but she wouldn't give me any eye contact.

"I can have the chef make you whatever you want to eat Nyla," Angel said. He walked up to the island and picked up some grapes that were inside a bowl on the table.

"No, thanks...Maybe you should get the chef to make my mom something to eat I'm pretty sure she will enjoy it," Nyla said rudely walking out the kitchen.

"Nyla!" I yelled out but she disappeared out my sight.

"Is something wrong with her?" Angel asked confused chewing on his grapes.

"It's been a long morning...She will be alright," I said running my hands through my curly hair.

"Where's Jada?" Angel asked looking around when he noticed she was nowhere to be found.

"Like I said it's been a long morning but she will be here soon," I said lying. Truth was I didn't even know where my sister was but it sounded like the truth so that's what I gave him. Sue me if you don't like it!

"Can I ask you something Kia?" Angel asked swallowing his grapes then he walked over to me. He was dressed in an all-black polo suit with timbs on his feet. His hair was pulled back into a messy pony tail but the rough look was suitable for him...Spanish hood nigga at its finest! LITERALLY.

"I'm listening...Do you mind?" I asked looking down at the grapes. Angel waved his hand for me to eat them. I grabbed two and put them in my mouth.

"Where is Nyla's father? I never asked you if you were in a relationship or not," Angel said leaning on the Island.

I chewed and swallowed the grapes then wiped my mouth with a napkin.

"Nyla's dad is in prison...As far as my relationship status I'm single," I said lying. But honestly was I really telling a fib? Reem is in prison and as far as me and him that was never discussed. What can Reem do when he gets out of prison? He has a record just like me which means he can't provide for me or his daughter. He told me he had some niggas he trusted that would take care of me and Nyla and he couldn't even stand on his word. Maybe Nyla was right...I do have feelings for Angel but I was slowly getting over Reem as the days passed by.

"I'm just a single parent raising my daughter alone," I said putting the napkin down on the counter.

"You're not alone Kia...I'm here too and I would love to help you with Nyla," Angel said walking up to me holding my hands and rubbing on them.

"I don't know about—" I said breaking away from him. Yes, I was feeling Angel but I didn't want my daughter to be mad at me because I decided not to be with her father anymore. This shit was becoming a headache. Damn if I do...Damn if I don't.

"I really like you yo like something about you just makes my heart smile. I love the way you're with your child and I adore every flaw you try to cover up but I notice them and that's what makes you so fucking beautiful Kia," Angel said walking back up to me and he kissed me softly on my forehead. "Do you and the father of your child still speak?" Angel asked looking me in my eyes.

"I—I like you too Angel," I said disregarding the question he asked me about Reem. Angel turned around and looked at me smirking. He picked up a few more grapes out the bowl and tossed two of them into his mouth.

"One thing that makes me uncomfortable is being lied to...What makes me uncomfortable isn't the truth it's the person I turn into when a muthafucka can't be honest with me," Angel said and he looked at me when he spoke. The way Teka felt outside was the way I was starting to feel...And I was starting to sense that I was attracted to a monster. I rotated around the island and I was about to bust my ass and slip on the floor.

"What the fuck" I said looking down at the tile floors and I saw blood. I started backing away tracking more blood in the kitchen. Angel looked at me arrogantly and walked around to see what was on the floor.

"I need someone to come in here with a fucking mop and a bucket! I thought I told y'all niggas to clean this shit up!" Angel yelled out and a few seconds later two security guards came running in the kitchen doing what Angel instructed them to do. Both of these niggas were scrubbing everything down. The smell of bleach was starting to suffocate me.

"Who's blood is that Angel?" I asked wiping my eyes.

Angel pulled up a chair in front of me and grabbed my foot.

"Did you hurt someone?" I asked softly and he didn't answer right away. He pulled my boots off my feet one by one. A security guard walked over to Angel with a black trash bag.

"I murked my own brother JoJo...He was a cop. *He lied to me,* about knowing the muthafucka that murdered my wife," Angel looked me in my eyes when he spoke.

The way he carried himself was very casual. I thought back to the conversation I had with the detective and quickly put two and two together...The detective was worried about officer JoJo.

"You *murdered* your own brother because he kept Mir a secret?" I asked confused.

Angel snapped his fingers and the security guards left out the kitchen making everything look spotless even taking my boots because they were evidence.

"Damn JoJo," I said under my breath.

Angel got up from the chair and looked at me.

"You knew my brother Kia? And speaking of Mir...What do *you know* about the nigga and please don't tell me you don't know shit," Angel asked and I just swallowed the spit in my mouth.

CHAPTER 11 MIR

I was staring at my closet by the front door of my bedroom for a good thirty minutes; contemplating on so many things but something behind the doors of this closet, would change my world if anyone found out exactly what I was concealing.

"Ayo Mir!" I heard the faded voice of a woman in a distance from the hallway of my bedroom. I looked at my door just to reassure that I had a lock on it. Knowing my ass wasn't really blind I didn't want a muthafucka just walking in on me while counting money or having my drugs on a scale. Shit would blow my whole cover.

"Who is it?!" I yelled out though I was familiar with the voice already. I jumped off my bed and stuffed my money into my duffel bag thenreached for another bag and stuffed my drugs into it before the voice got closer.

"Stop playing yo...Open up the door!" The yelling seemed as if this person was standing right in front of my face. The pounding of the fist increased with every passing second. I threw both of my duffel bags under the bed and took a deep breath.

"Jada?" I asked playing dumb I just didn't want to get caught up. I leaned back on my bed to grab my black shades. I slid them onto my face and walked up to my bedroom door, unlocking it.

"I need something Mir...I need it bad," Jada said entering my bedroom. I closed the door behind her and just looked at my older sister up and down through my shades. Jada was still dressed in the same oversized clothes for the last three weeks. I looked down at her pants and she had a small red stain revealing itself and I knew she was on her period. Jada was more concerned about heroin than she was about buying herself some pads or tampons.

"What the fuck are you talking about Jada?" I asked as I watched her pace the brown wooden floors of my bedroom. I looked down at her run down air force ones that were turning yellow and bent in every shape possible.

Jada was making faces that she thought I couldn't see but I could...She just didn't know it.

"You know what I need Mir...I need some dope nigga. Look at me yo don't do this to me I swear if you just get me a little high like *I'm floating on the clouds,* I won't ask you for shit else. Kia has been trying to get me to detox since last night but I just continue to get more sick. I'm fucking sweating like I weigh more than two hundred pounds and it's not even hot outside" Jada said scratching her arms.

I see Jada eyes operate from me to under my bed. I moved away from her and stepped in front of my bed discreetly just to prevent anything from occurring. In Jada's head I was blind which meant I couldn't see shit so I didn't know if she was going to be sneaky and go under my bed taking advantage of me.

"Look, look, look, look Mir just give me a little bit and I swear I will clean myself up...I will get these open sores checked out on my body. I will straighten up my hair and go find a decent job," Jada said while pulling up her sleeves and she tried to touch me.

I loved my sister but I didn't want her touching me in any way. I pushed her hands out the way and started waving like I couldn't see. Jada just looked at me sucking her teeth and nodded her head up and down. Seeing my sister in that condition made my stomach turn but I couldn't blame anyone but myself.

"Damn sis...What the fuck happened to you Jada?" I asked her. She looked at me with more fury than a prisoner. Her face balled up in portions that I didn't know existed on her beautiful face. I could tell from her demeanor that shit was about to get ugly.

"Muthafucka, you're what happened to me!" Jada yelled out pointing at me with her right index finger. I examined her finger up close and personal while in my face and the skin was starting to peel from it. I didn't budge or speak on it. My ass was blind and I was sticking to that shit! I didn't want her to think otherwise.

"I didn't even know what heroin was Mir until YOU gave me two thousand dollars to try it...Why did you ask me to try it? Why couldn't you ask a crackhead on the street?" Jada asked walking away from me and up to my bedroom window. I pushed the shades further back on my face and stood in place.

"You told me you needed the money Jada so I did you a favor," I said speaking low. Jada looked at me and started shaking her head. I reached behind me to feel for the bed. You know, Playing dumb and shit. Once I felt it I sat down on it.

"Family doesn't do shit like that...Family is suppose to support and be there for one another. You could of just gave me the money instead you're asking me to try your dope! Now I'm fucking addicted nigga. I would of never thought I would have been in this place three years ago...Now look at me and it's all because of you," Jada said emotional pulling at her clothes.

Jada was right I could've chosen a random muthafucka off the street but instead I asked my sister. Why? Because lil mama needed the money and I figured if I scratch her back then she would scratch mine but I NEVER thought my sister would be hooked on it the way that she is. This shit was foul yo and I was that foul nigga for doing this to my own flesh and blood.

"I didn't put a fucking gun to your head and force you to try it...I just wanted to know if it was good or not," I said looking in the opposite direction like that's where Jada was standing. I knew she was over there at the window but I needed her to believe that I was blind just as much as I did.

"I was backed up on rent muthafucka...I needed that money and you knew that. As quick as you gave me that two grand it was gone in three hours tops. I lost my apartment and I never went back once I tasted that drug. I got high with muthafuckas in the alleyway...Muthafuckas that couldn't even tell me their last name. As bad as I want to recover from this shit it has taken over my entire life. I don't matter to you or the next nigga I bump into down the street.

"My own niece don't even respect me she looks at me like I disgust her in every way possible. Which may be true but I would rather Nyla do that shit behind my back than do it in my face. I'm just asking you Mir for one hit and I will leave you the fuck alone," Jada said turning from the window then stepped towards me.

I wiped the side of my face from the guilt I was feeling. JoJo instilled it in me to give Jada that bad dope but I couldn't yo...I damaged my sister enough and whether she witnessed me murder Bella or not I wasn't knocking off my fucking sister for freedom.

"I'm not giving you shit Jada," I said rubbing my hands on my thighs. "Let me ask you a question...Did you tell someone that you witnessed a murder?" I asked and Jada's face turned red like she was about to vomit. I stood up from my bed and Jada ran up on me crying.

"You know! You know! You know that—" Jada just continued yelling. She pushed me down to the bed and started hitting me.

I don't know if it was the fact that I knew she was plotting against me or if it was the drugs making her react this way but this little bitch hits like a nigga. I grabbed her arms and flipped her over on the bed, now I was standing over top of her.

"OH MY GOD! MIR YOU'RE NOT BLIND!" Jada yelled out. The surprise look she gave me sent chills throughout my body...It was priceless. I didn't even notice that my shades fell off my face until I saw them next to her on the bed playing camouflage. I could feel my breathing getting heavy, veins popping out my head and neck. It took me a good few minutes to understand that I was pinning Jada down on the bed making eye contact with her.

"Shut the fuck up Jada," I whispered covering her mouth with my right hand but she just continued to fight me aggressively.

I looked back at my door that was shut but it wasn't locked. I thought I heard someone downstairs and I didn't want Jada to draw any attention to them.

"OW! Fucking crackhead—" I yelled out when Jada bit down on my finger. Once I let her go she used her left hand to scratch my face. Jada tried to run towards the bedroom door to leave out but I caught her and threw her against the dresser. I heard a quick snap then her head hit my bedroom window.

"Auhhh—" Jada made a noise and then she never moved or spoke again. I ran up to her trying to comfort her because I didn't mean to do this shit purposely. I grabbed her head into my hands and her head was bleeding rapidly. I touched her neck and I couldn't find a pulse.

"Jada...Jada baby get up," I said shaking her as tears fell down my face. The more I shook her the more I felt like I was making it worst because my sister wasn't showing no signs of life. "Fuck I didn't mean to do this to you," I said and I heard someone running up the steps. I laid Jada down gently and ran up to my bedroom door locking it. I grabbed some of my dirty clothes out my hamper laying them down on the floor so I wouldn't track anymore blood.

"UNCLE MIR! ARE YOU IN THERE?" Nyla yelled out banging on my door. Damn, why did everyone want to fuck with me today? All I was doing was minding my business. I grabbed Jada and dragged her over to the second closet by my bed. Then I opened it up and laid her down inside as the banging on my bedroom door continued to occur.

"Hold on Nyla..." I said out of breath. I ran back over to the spot where Jada was and cleaned up her blood the best I could. I grabbed a towel and laid it down to cover the spot until I got Nyla out of my room. I used the other dirty shirt to wipe the blood off my hands.

"What are you doing in there?!" Nyla yelled out again getting impatient.

"Putting on some clothes...Give me a second," I said putting every bloody belonging back inside the hamper. I took a deep breath looking back at my room to make sure everything was in place besides this towel on the floor. I ran over to my bed grabbing my black shades as I put them on my face to give off the impression that I'm blind. I nodded my head giving myself the okay to open up the bedroom door.

"Hey Nyla, come in" I said opening up my door.

Nyla gave me a blank stare and entered my room. I turned my head when I heard more footsteps coming up the stairs.

"Mir...I have been looking for you all over and I've been calling you. Why don't you pick up the phone?" Kia asked entering my room and looked around like she suspected something. I reached out my hands like I couldn't see and walked back over to my bed. "Mir did you hear something? Like someone screaming and yelling? Maybe it's just the neighbors," Kia said making up conclusions in her head.

"Uh—" I said stuttering feeling sick to my stomach because of what I just did.

"What happened to your face Uncle Mir?" Nyla asked walking up to me. I reached out my hands to pretend that I was trying to feel for her. Kia stood back in a distance still checking out my room.

"I was trying to find my remote, I lost my balance and fell down on the floor cutting my face," I lied holding the side of my face where Jada dug her nails in my skin. Nyla looked at me and backed away from my hands. Kia looked at her like she was concerned for her daughter.

"Something about the smell in this room," Nyla said shaking her head then she pointed around with her right index finger.

"Wha—What Nyla?" I asked getting up off my bed because I didn't want what I just did to be revealed.

"I don't smell anything baby," Kia said looking down Nyla.

"Neither do I," I said cosigning with my sister. Nyla looked at me and sucked her teeth.

"It smells like Auntie Jada," Nyla said doing a complete 360 then she rubbed on her temple.

"Mir, speaking of that...Have you seen Jada?" Kia asked me and I shook my head no. Nyla looked down at the towel on the floor so I took the initiative to move over and step on top of it so she wouldn't observe anything. "Mir, do you know you have a towel on your floor? I can get it up for you if—" Kia said offering her assistance. When I see her coming in my direction I held my hands out and shook my head no.

"I dropped some ketchup earlier...I know I have a towel on my floor," I said trying to persuade her. Kia looked at Nyla then she looked back up at me.

"Do you have something to tell me Mir?" Kia asked me.

"What you mean Kia?" I asked confused.

"Tell me the truth Mir," Kia said getting a little loud when she spoke.

"I don't know what you're talking about," I said shrugging my shoulders. Kia tapped down on Nyla's right shoulder and she headed to the bedroom door.

"Nyla, go tell him to come upstairs," Kia said and I balled up my face.

"Him? Who the fuck is him?" I asked getting defensive. Nyla looked at me and left out my bedroom disappearing into the hallway.

"The doctor...Tasha said that she couldn't afford to get you into any programs. She also said that she couldn't pay someone to help you get around so I hired a doctor. His specialty is working for the blind—" Kia said looking down at her fingers to check for any dirt.

"Kia—" I said exhaling deeply.

"Right up here doctor!" Kia yelled out towards the hallway and I knew it was over for me. Either Kia really knew the truth or she just wanted me to see a specialist.

"KIA!" I yelled out and Kia gave me her full attention. "I'm not really blind..." I said in a low tone but I was one embarrassed ass nigga. I took off my shades and threw them back on my bed. I was so afraid to look my own sister in her eyes.

"I had a fucking feeling that you weren't blind...Why are you pretending to be something that you aren't Mir?" Kia asked walking up to me and she caressed the scratches on my face.

"For my protection..." I said gently pushing her hand down from my face.

"What did you do Mir? Tell me the truth—" Kia said and my gut was telling me my sister knew way more than I expected her too. I took a step away from her and looked down at my wooden floors.

"JoJo...JoJo" I said under my breath. Kia walked up to me and lifted up my chin so I could look at her.

"What about JoJo?" Kia asked.

"I spoke to him earlier about a situation and I called him back a few minutes later. Someone picked up his phone saying he was JoJo's brother but this nigga JoJo never told me he had any other siblings. The bad part is when someone answered his phone I heard JoJo screaming like he was being tortured in the background. I'm worried something might've happened to him

Kia," I spoke with so much passion that I was getting goose bumps when I mentioned JoJo's name.

"You need to tell me the truth so I can help you Mir" Kia said looking me in my eyes. "Tell me what the fuck you did and tell me why JoJo *was* after Jada," Kia said and I shook my head no.

"You said WAS Kia...You're talking in past tense, what happened to JoJo?!" I asked yellingand getting a bit aggressive.

Nyla ran back in the room then she stopped in her tracks when she looked at me.

"Something isn't right..." Nyla said and I pointed to my eyes.

"Obviously, I'm not blind Nyla...I just told your mother the truth," I said looking at Kia.

"Nah, I knew that already but it wasn't my truth to speak on. It was yours Uncle Mir. When I say something isn't right I mean...Something is off in your bedroom," Nyla said looking around.

Kia walked up to her child.

How the fuck would Nyla know that about me?

"What's wrong with your daughter yo?" I asked getting fearful. I was starting to think what JoJo said about my niece on the phone was really the truth.

"Don't talk about her like she's a fucking freak or something," Kia said covering Nyla ears when she cursed. "Talk to me baby...What do you feel Nyla?" Kia asked removing her hands from her ears.

I was fearful of Nyla. She could blurt out *all* the skeletons in my closet...Literally.

"Nyla, go downstairs bruh," I said pointing for her to get out my room. Kia snapped her neck at me. I was about to question if she was possessed by a demon. I knew Kia didn't play when it came to her daughter but damn this was a little irrational.

"NO! STAY HERE AND TELL MOMMY WHAT'S WRONG," Kia said holding Nyla's face as she raised her voice a bit. Nyla removed Kia's hand from her face and walked over to my closet by the door

"Get the fuck away from my closet Nyla!" I yelled out walking up to Nyla and Kia extending her hand out to block me from touching her daughter.

"Don't speak to my daughter like that Mir before I come over there and fuck you up," Kia said pushing me back aggressively and she pointed to me like she knew what my soul was about.

I could tell Kia wasn't playing any games but I wish Nyla would just mind her damn business.

"There *is life and death* in this room...And you're the cause of it Uncle Mir," Nyla said looking straight at me. She looked around the bedroom one more time then opened up the closet door...revealing my secret.

"Shhh, shhh it's okay lil mamas," Nyla said picking up my daughter I had hidden in my closet. Kia's mouth dropped as she looked at me and she appeared to be more disappointed than finding out I wasn't really blind.

"Mir? Why the fuck do you have a baby in your closet?" Kia asked folding her arms across her chest. I looked at Nyla as she rocked my sweet child in her arms. I was completely speechless at my niece that words couldn't explain how I felt...

"Wha- What is wrong with your daughter Kia? How the fuck would she know something like that when this baby didn't make any noise since y'all set foot in my bedroom?" I asked looking at Kia.

Nyla looked up at me and smirked but I didn't understand what that gesture meant. I walked up to Nyla and gently grabbed my daughter out of her arms. I looked down at her face as she was sleeping in my arms and she reminded me so much of her mother.

"Who's baby is that Mir?" Kia asked me but I continued to rock my child as my mouth stayed shut. "Nyla said it was life and death in this room Mir which means the baby must be life but somewhere else in this room is death," Kia said walking over to the closet by my bed.

"Kia...What are you doing bruh? Get away from my closet door," I said nervously and Kia grabbed the closet door handle.

In a few seconds she was going to see our dead sister laying on the closet floor...

CHAPTER 12 KIA

"Kia!" Mir yelled out my name. He walked up on me while holding this yellow beautiful baby in his protective arms. I squeezed the closet door handle tighter about to open it then Mir jumped in front of me. I took a step back and just studied my brother. "Ayo! Kia...Wait yo, just wait! There's something that I need to tell you. Mir started to raise his voice more when I tried to move over to see what he was hiding inside the closet.

"Make sure you're being honest with me when you open up your mouth and speak," I said. I turned to my side and Nyla was walking around Mir's bedroom with her right hand on the wall. I'm not sure if she could hear or feel things while her hand was maneuvering from one side of the room to the other side.

"I am death..." Mir said looking at me with a disheartened look on his face.

"What nigga?" I asked confused turning my right lip up.

"Nyla said it's life and death in this room, correct? The baby was life and the death is going to be me." Mir said shaking his head to the words that just came out of his mouth. Then Mir looked over at Nyla and they both made eye contact with one another. "I think your daughter was speaking my death into existence," Mir said still looking Nyla in her eyes.

"Nyla, is that what you meant when you were speaking about life and death?" I asked distancing myself from Mir a little then I walked up to Nyla. She looked at Mir and this expression on her face just appeared of dejection for her uncle. I know she loves Mir dearly but I wonder if she loves him enough to cover up for him just because she feels like she owes him something. When I say, *"owe,"* I mean that Nyla may feel like since I was locked up and Mir was watching her back that she's indebted to show loyalty.

"I don't know everything but I can say that the vibe is still definitely off in this room," Nyla said then she played with her bottom lip with her right hand. Nyla looked at Mir then she looked up at me with a blank stare on her face. Nyla has always been the type to prove her point so it was hard to explain why she was shutting down so quickly now.

"That's why I want to check this other closet right here," I said pointing to the closet that Mir was standing in front of.

"Man, Kia ain't shit in that closet but dirty clothes," Mir said looking back at the closet door then he looked down and kissed this beautiful baby on her cheek.

"Dirty clothes? But your hamper is over there in the corner," Nyla said pointing by the dresser as she observed the entire room.

"I know that shit Einstein—" Mir said looking at my daughter and Nyla looked back at Mir and stuck her tongue out at him.

"Mir, watch your fucking mouth when you're talking to my daughter," I said looking back at him and he just shrugged his shoulders.

"All I'm saying is that it's more laundry in this closet...Opening up this closet is just going to make you mad because of the stench of my clothes." Mir said trying to convince me and I just nodded my head up and down. I looked down at the baby in his arms that he seem to adore excessively since she has been in his presence.

"Mir, tell me wassup my nigga...Why do you have a baby hiding in your closet?" I asked and Mir looked at Nyla.

"Nyla, can you take the baby and go wait in the hallway please?" Mir asked walking up to Nyla.

"Just tell—" I said putting my hands up but Mir turned to look at me cutting me off.

"I swear on mommy's grave I'm going to tell you everything yo that's my word." Mir said handing the baby off to Nyla. He walked over opening up his top drawer and pulled out an object. "Take this pacifier Nyla," Mir said passing the pacifier over to Nyla. She gently took it from Mir and looked back at me to see if I was alright. I nodded my head giving Nyla the okay and she disappeared with the baby into the hallway. Mir looked at me nervously rubbing his hands together, I was one person that wasn't too fond of awkwardness like my nigga you have a mouth! Open it up and talk damn yo.

"The baby Mir...Who's fucking baby is that?!" I asked raising my voice a little as I pointed into the hallway.

"Charlie is her name and that's my daughter Kia—" Mir said softly looking down at his hands and I just turned up my face. I NEVER HEARD OF MY BROTHER HAVING A CHILD! Shit, I didn't even know he was fucking around with anyone.

"What the fu—" I couldn't even finish talking because he cut me off to explain.

"Listen to me please! I was messing with this shawty name Bella for more than a year. When she told me she was pregnant with my child nothing could ruin what God has blessed me with because I was finally happy. I was grateful to have a child of my own but I was more appreciative that my child would always have a piece of Bella within herself. During the course of our relationship Bella kept coming to me bitching and arguing about stupid shit every other day. Either I took too long to answer my phone when she was calling or I didn't text back right away. It went from petty disagreements to her actually accusing me of fucking other bitches. Bella's father left her a house in Margate and that's where we lived at.

"Two weeks after giving birth to Charlie my entire life changed forever. I came in the house with JoJo and we were drunk to the point I was falling and tripping over everything when we entered the house. Bella walked up to me carrying Charlie and she just kept screaming at me how I was a no-good ass nigga and how dare I come home at 3 in the morning from fucking random bitches. I told JoJo I would be right back, that I was taking Bella outside on the porch to talk. I was hot from the drinking and I needed some air anyway.

"Bella laid Charlie down on the couch protecting her with pillows so she wouldn't move. Once we got out on the porch Bella started attacking me yo like on some real shit. Punching me going the fuck off Kia! I was trying to calm her down and defend myself at the same time. Everything happened so fast and Charlie's crying made my adrenaline rush more. I grabbed Bella by her hair and threw her down on the front porch. I didn't know how tight I was squeezing Bella around her neck until I actually removed my hands and she didn't have a pulse. I was distraught and broken...Broken exactly how I was when we lost mom, remember that Kia? I screamed for JoJo to come and help me and as my best friend that nigga got rid of Bella's body for me. It was 3am and we're outside arguing but we made sure no one was around to see anything. The next day her body was discovered but I needed Bella far away from me as possible every time I looked at her I just got sick to my stomach. I know I was wrong Kia but at the time I needed to defend myself and shit went too far…

"I took everything that could be traced back to me and got rid of it. I took my daughter Charlie and hid her in my room when Aunt Tasha went to work that night. After that JoJo created fake documents from doctors and presented it to Aunt Tasha and everyone else to believe that I was blind from glass getting in my eyes. Which was a lie. I figured the cops wouldn't look for a blind nigga and at the time it was a perfect cover story," Mir said exhaling deeply and he wiped the tears that was falling from his eyes. I looked at him quietly for a second and folded my arms across my chest.

"How does Jada fit into all of this?" I asked confused.

"JoJo told me that Jada was a witness and—" Mir said clearing his throat and I cut him off to speak.

"Do you know that shit for a fact or you just decided to take JoJo's word because that's your best friend?" I asked with an attitude. We never take the word of a muthafucka over our own family! THAT'S LAW and Mir knew better than that. I'm not sure if JoJo being a cop scared Mir but he should of done his homework with this shit.

"What you mean Kia?" Mir asked confused.

"When did you murder Bella?" I asked and Mir's eyes got more watery and he dropped his head to the floor.

"I didn't murder—" Mir began to say and I shook my head no.

"I don't know if denying what you did is making you feel better my nigga but you need to face reality. You murdered that woman because you were drunk Mir. It is what it is end of story but stop saying you didn't because that's not the truth. So when the fuck did you strangle Bella?" I asked getting more aggressive as I began to talk.

"January 8th..." Mir said looking at me and I ran up to him with my fist out.

"You fucking idiot Mir!" I yelled out.

"What yo?! Why are you hitting me?" Mir asked dumbfounded putting his hands up in front of his face to stop me from hitting him.

"You don't remember Mir? Jada was in the hospital that entire week so how the fuck was she a witness to anything you or

JoJo did? Doesn't make sense my nigga...Sounds like JoJo is the one lying here" I said pushing him back and he fell against the bed. I remember calling back home from prison and hearing Jada overdosed and was in the hospital. That night I had trouble sleeping thinking about Jada...That is a day I will never forget. Her little ass was admitted the night before so how was she a witness?!

"Fuck, fuck, fuck, fuck..." Mir said under his breath sitting up on the bed like he was thinking.

"What's wrong Mir?" I asked getting closer to him. Mir appeared more jittery than before and you could tell from the look in his eyes that something heavy was weighing on his mind.

"I need to call JoJo." Mir jumped up off his bed and searched around for his phone. I moved out of his way and I could see him sweating now. Mir finally found his phone but his breathing was increasing quite a bit.

"Put your phone down," I said to him and he looked at me with his face was balled up.

"What yo?" Mir asked still putting the phone up to his ear.

"Do as I say...Trust me," I said and Mir lowered his phone.

Truth was I didn't want Mir to get caught up more than he already was. I was also trying to hide that JoJo got murdered and he would never see him again.

"Does anyone else know about the baby Mir?" I asked and Mir placed his phone on his bed and started shaking his head no.

"Nah...Just me and JoJo," Mir said running his hand down his face to get the sweat off.

"You and Charlie stay in this room...Don't come out until I come back tonight. You need me and I'm not going to leave you abandoned. Believe it or not I need you just as much Mir but I need you to be fucking honest with me. I'm your sister, do you understand my nigga? I'm not your enemy...Nyla where are you?!" I yelled out looking at the bedroom door.

A moment later Nyla walked back in the room smiling down at the baby. "Nyla! Sweetie come in here...This is Charlie, this is your baby cousin. We will get more acquainted later but right now give Mir back his daughter," I said pointing to my brother.

Nyla nodded her head up and down and gave Charlie to Mir.

"I can't do this alone Kia," Mir said holding Charlie and looked at me like he was about to have a panic attack.

I walked up to Mir holding his arms pushing them closer together so he could squeeze Charlie. I wanted Charlie to feel how fast and heavy her father's heart was beating this way...She could feel the beating heart of someone that loves her. Also Mir would understand who he was doing all of this for which is his daughter. I looked at the two of them bonding as he rocked Charlie in his arms.

"Is there anything else you need to tell me?" I asked making sure he didn't keep anything out. "Are you sure?" I asked Mir again.

"Uh..." Mir said nervously then he nodded his head letting me know we were good.

"I will be back tonight make sure you and Charlie's clothes are packed because you can't stay here anymore. Don't leave out this room until you see my face, understand?" I asked looking back at Mir as I headed towards his bedroom door to leave out.

Nyla followed behind me looking down because she didn't want to leave Charlie.

"I got you sis," Mir said confirming that he understood the rules. I walked out his room with Nyla holding her right hand. We went down the stairs and out the front door heading to my car. I lowered my head to grab my car keys out of my pocket until I heard someone speak.

"Where the fuck do y'all think y'all going?" The voice was so unapproachable. Nyla dropped my hand and I looked up and it was Tasha...AKA my real mother. I sucked my teeth and hit my temple trying to laugh shit off.

"Um...Nyla lost her earring and we came back here to see if it might have fallen out," I said pointing back to the house.
Nyla gave Tasha an unsettling look as she stood behind me but looking at Nyla she looked like she was ready to go off at any minute.

"That's funny," Tasha said looking down at her nails smiling like she had something up her sleeve.

"What's funny?" I asked biting the inside of my lip playing with my car keys in my hand.

"Nyla doesn't wear earrings Kia and you know that...So what are y'all really doing here?" Tasha asked and I stayed quiet.

"Three babies, three babies, three babies," Nyla said counting her fingers.

"What Nyla?" I asked looking down at her confused as she continued to repeat the same thing.

"You will tell your truth soon because you will be forced to." My daughter said to me as she stared at my belly then looked me back in my eyes. "Mir just told his truth and Tasha I think you need to tell yours," Nyla said giving her direct attention to Tasha.

"Tasha? Little girl who the fuck are you talking too and when did you start calling me by my first name?" Tasha asked as she started getting defensive.

"Three babies? What does that mean Nyla?" I asked rubbing my hands together as I looked at Nyla but she continued to keep her eyes on Tasha.

"Should I tell my mom Tasha or do you want to tell her?" Nyla asked pointing at Tasha with her right index finger.

"Tell me what?" I asked lifting Nyla's chin up to look at me but she pulled away.

"That little bitch doesn't know—" Tasha said disrespectfully waving my daughter off like she wasn't shit.

"WATCH YOUR FUCKING MOUTH TASHA!" I yelled out getting in her face and she stood in place just staring at me with her scrub uniform on.

"Why do y'all muthafuckas keep saying my first name without saying, *"Aunt,"* first?" Tasha asked scratching her temple.

"You know better than that," Nyla said smirking at Tasha and I shook my head. Tasha moved from in front of me to get in Nyla's face.

"Say one more thing to me and I'm going to fuck—" Tasha said lowering down to get to Nyla's level to speak. Nyla waved Tasha off and looked at me with sorrow in her eyes.

"Daddy got Tasha pregnant two nights before y'all both went to prison mommy. Tasha couldn't depend on daddy to help provide for the child so she got an abortion two weeks later and daddy thinks that she had the baby while he's incarcerated," Nyla said in a low and soft tone. I looked at Tasha and she just appeared petrified. She started rubbing her hands on her thighs and backed up away from me.

"YOU FUCKED MY MAN AND YOU GOT PREGNANT BY HIM?!" I asked yelling with more emotion than I was born with.

"Ny-Ny-Nyla why would you lie to your mother?" Tasha asked stuttering but her body language and behavior was giving me all the validation that I needed.

"I can prove it mommy—" Nyla said trying to make me believe her but I already did, I always have. She turned to walk back towards the house but Tasha ran in front of her like she was a damn kid herself.

"Don't walk your little ass back in my house!" Tasha yelled out to Nyla.

"Come on Nyla we need to go baby," I said reaching down to grab Nyla's hand. I looked back at Tasha and she just looked distressed. I turned towards my car, unlocking it so me and my daughter could get inside.

"KIA! KIA! DON'T WALK AWAY FROM ME," Tasha yelled out pointing at me but I wasn't paying her ass any mind.

"Mommy I'm sorry that you had to hear that," Nyla said closing the passenger side door.

I put my car key into the ignition and wiped my eyes so my daughter wouldn't see how broken I was about to become.

"It's not your fault baby...Maybe God was telling me to open up my eyes to see the truth," I said forcing a smile but a blind man himself could see I wasn't happy. My phone started ringing in my back pocket. I pulled it out, tapping on the button and put it up to my ear. "Hello?" I said with so many mixed emotions running through me.

"Hey Kia...Where are you Mi Amor?" Angel asked in his Spanish accent through the phone.

"I'm leaving the store, I'm on my way back home now," I said lying. I heard Angel chuckle into the phone then he hung up the phone on me.

"You should of never lied to him mommy," Nyla said soft spoken opening up the passenger door.

"What you mean Nyla? And where are you going?" I asked watching her exit out the vehicle. She touched all around the car then ducked down low. I looked around from inside the car to see where she went and I jumped when I heard her little ass tapping on my window with her fingers.

"This is why I said you shouldn't of lied...Angel can track where the car is," Nyla said while holding up something in her hand.

When I turned to look it was a small black box and a red light flashing which was a tracker.

CHAPTER 13 ANGEL

I was sitting in my black leather chair in my office. I exhaled deeply because the room still had Bella's scent after all this time. I used my right index finger to trace the picture frame sitting on my desk...Even though I was attracted to Kia and my feelings for her wouldn't rest. I just couldn't help but think about Bella's *smile*...That smile that would light up a room from a distance. Or the way her voice sounded like a melody on her darkest nights. Yes, my wife was in a grave now but my heart still belonged to her beautiful soul whether she was living or not.

"Ayo! My man...Come here for a second," I said as I saw one of my security men walk pass my office door that was wide open.

I leaned back in my office chair looking down at my phone. Kia was calling me but I didn't pick up, I just let my phone ring.

"Do you need another shot of patron boss? Cause I can get that for you right away—" Chino offered his assistance looking down at my shot glass on the corner of my desk that was empty.

I looked at the glass and shook my head no with a slight smile but honestly how happy was I though? Amazing how we go through life holding emotions in but having two young brothers it was my job to be the man of the house since my mother was struggling. There was a story behind my silence and intentions behind my smile that I didn't even understand yet but I would warn any muthafucka to be cautious when it came to me. I didn't have time to cry about shit I had to hustle and pick up whenever my mother lack because she was too prideful to ask for help.

My mother was too afraid to apply for section 8 or food stamps. She always thought once she went to the office asking for a little bit of help that they would deport her back to Mexico. So she worked for a cleaning company, getting paid under the table but it wasn't enough to take care of us including herself. My mother would apologize to me and my other two brothers every morning then cry herself to sleep at night. I never understood why my mother was so apologetic when the sun came out in the am until I walked in the bathroom one morning ya know?

Crust and shit still in my eyes and there she was. My mother sucking a man's dick for fifteen dollars. There was sorrow in her saliva, pity down her throat and shame in her eyes. Nah, my mother wasn't proud of what she became but she made sure we had a meal everyday so fuck you if you have something to say about the way she got her money. That fifteen dollars got us white rice, corn beef and a gallon of Tampico juice.

"Nah...I'm good on the liquor my nigga. I need for you to find out how many people live in Kia's aunt house and I want the names also," I said moving my phone to the side and I tapped on my desk with my right hand.

"Did something happen Angel?" Chino asked standing straight in front of my desk with both of his hands folded.

I looked at my phone and sucked my teeth a few times back to back. Kia doesn't know that I have a tracker on her car which showed me that she was parked in front of her aunt's house. The real question is why the fuck was she lying about being there?

"It makes my fucking blood boil when a muthafucka lies to me...I just want the truth and I will go from there," I said looking at Chino. I didn't want to make any final decisions until I knew every fucking thing! "Before you go Chino...Find that blind nigga Mir and bring his ass to me untouched," I said.

Chino nodded his head up and down walking out my office. I was looking down at Bella's picture missing her beauty. If this muthafucka is the one that murdered my wife, I swear to God I will never be sane again. I heard my phone ringing once again and I checked the caller ID...It was Kia. I just looked at it and nodded my head up and down.

"*Kia...Kia...Kia baby,* what are you hiding from me and why? I really like you yo but if you lie or betray me in any nature I will murder you like I murdered my own brother JoJo," I said to myself looking at the phone while it was still ringing. I was the type of nigga that didn't like to assume, sometimes I have to tune you out in order to collect my own thoughts.

I like to have all my ducks in a row before I open up my mouth. I put my head down on my desk and my mind was racing like traffic. My thoughts were getting too loud in my head that I was starting to get a headache.

"Boss?" Chino said coming back into my office speaking in a low tone. I elevate my head on my desk and I see Chino holding something in his hand. "The little girl that lives in the house left her book bag in the hallway...I will leave it in here with you," Chino said. He walked up to me laying Nyla's bookbag down on top of my desk then he left out of my office again.

Nyla's bookbag was open and something caught my attention which was like a coloring book but it wasn't no ordinary shit...Lil shawty sketched out everything by hand and it looked like some real life shit. I flipped through the pages and one of the drawings stood out to me.

"This looks interesting..." I said looking down at Nyla's craft. There were too men in the room, one sitting at the desk and the other nigga standing in front of the desk. The muthafucka standing up is pointing to something in the corner and the nigga sitting behind the desk is looking at what the other dude is pointing at. This entire drawing on this page just screams, *"tension."*

"Boss?" Chino said again knocking on my door to get my attention.

I jumped as I was startled and stuffed Nyla's drawing back inside her bookbag trying to play it off like I wasn't snooping. I placed her bag by the side of my desk and changed the subject.

"Did you find out the information on Kia's aunt that fast my nigga?" I asked running my hand down my face. Chino looked at me confused for a second and shook his head no.

"Nah boss I came here because...You have a guest," Chino said turning his head to the side but since I was inside the room I couldn't see what he was looking at.

"Guest? Who the fuck is it?" I asked giving him a dumbfounded look.

"Your brother...Sanchez," Chino said moving out the way and Sanchez walked in the room smiling at me. I nodded my head so Chino could leave and Sanchez closed the door behind him.

"Wassup my nigga?" I asked relaxing back in my office chair.

"Ain't shit...Still dressed in my uniform just getting off work," Sanchez said looking at himself up and down in his correctional attire.

"You need some money or something cause you know I got you if—" I said reaching down in my bottom draw to give him a stack of money. Sanchez walked up closer to me extending his hand out to stop me.

"Yeah my nigga I need money but I want to earn it on my own Angel. I need to put in that hard work so I can feel like I'm deserving of the shit I get. I'm sick of coming over here with my hand out like a needy muthafucka! Let me work Angel...I can do this," Sanchez said looking me in my eyes begging for a position that I refused many times before.

"You are working nigga you're a correctional officer," I said pointing at his uniform that he was dressed in.

Sanchez shook his head no and pulled up a chair that I had in the corner of my office. Now we were sitting face to face...Only thing giving up some fucking distance was this desk between us.

"You and I both know that's not what the fuck I'm talking about muthafucka," Sanchez said leaning forward in the chair giving me a sharp look. I smirked at him and folded my hands together.

"My nigga I'm not putting no drugs in your fucking possession! I told you whatever you need Sanchez I got you but I want you as far away from this shit as possible," I said making sure every word was solid in that hardheaded dome of his. I pulled out money from my draw and placed it on the desk.

"I can't work for you Angel but JoJo comes here twice a week with a fucking duffel bag full of cash. Muthafucka I'm your fucking brother why can't you put me on too?!" Sanchez asked raising his voice.

"You have a job already Sanchez! Why are you willing to risk everything you worked hard for just for extra money?" I asked and Sanchez looked at the money I had sitting on my desk and sucked his teeth.

"I just want to be important to someone bro, I want a muthafucka to look me in my eyes and know that I mean business...I want to respected—" Sanchez said and I cut him off to speak.

"You're a correctional officer Sanchez, muthafuckas do respect you," I said pointing to him.

"Them niggas don't respect me Angel! I dread going to this fucking job every morning because it's the same routine every damn day...Arguing with a fucking inmate to make their bed up, to stop banging on their cells doors for attention. They want to see the nurse for simple shit like the sky being blue just to get out of their pod and if you don't put their medical slip in they want to get aggressive. Some of them niggas just mess with you because they're fucking bored. All they have is time...Time to sit and think so they mess with us correctional officers. If that sounds like respect Angel then I might need your hearing because evidently I'm missing something!" Sanchez yelled getting hype jumping out of the chair.

I waved him off and continued to act civil...I mean why not? That's my brother at the end of the day I didn't want any bad blood between us.

"I said no my nigga what don't you understand?" I began to speak and Sanchez started pacing my office back and forth. I never noticed how sharp his fade looked until now...Shit maybe I need to hit up his barber to get a shapeup.

"JoJo—" Sanchez said under his breath and I just started shaking my head.

"What about him Sanchez? Damn why are you always comparing yourself to JoJo?!" I yelled out and now this nigga was starting to irritate the shit out of me. I slid the money across my desk trying to get Sanchez's attention but he continued to run his mouth which is one reason why I can't put this nigga under my wing.

"JoJo is a cop and he moves weight for you. I'm a correctional officer, why can't I do the same yo? All three of us are brothers we should be getting money together," Sanchez said looking straight at me as he stopped pacing the floor.

I pointed down to the money and he shook his head no. I shrugged my shoulders and put the money back in my desk.

"I wish you would look out for me like you look out for JoJo" Sanchez said and little did he know the truth about our baby brother.

"Muthafucka what?! You have food in your belly? Your wife is happy and comfortable? I just upgraded your house, correct? You're well taken care of, is that right my nigga?" I asked standing up out my office chair. Chino walked in to see what all the yelling was about and I nodded my head letting him know we was good in here and we were going to be whether Sanchez liked it or not. Chino gave me a look then exited out my office and I gave my attention back to Sanchez.

"What does that have to do—" Sanchez said getting all timid.

"ANSWER MY QUESTION MUTHAFUCKA!" I yelled out slamming my hands on my desk.

Sanchez stuffed his hands down in his pockets. I could see by the expression on his face that he was holding his tongue from saying some slick shit to me.

"You right Angel," Sanchez said agreeing with me but the tension was still unsettled in this room. He walked back up to the chair and sat down biting the inside of his mouth.

"You and Teka don't have to work...Y'all choose to have careers with 401k. I always tell you Sanchez the two of you can quit at any time and I will take care of you," I said sitting back down in my seat.

"Nah, fuck that Angel you just don't want to hear the truth which is...You treat JoJo better than you treat me," Sanchez said with a dumb ass look on his face.

"Nigga you sound stupid! I treat JoJo better because he was moving weight for me and you wasn't, really my nigga? Muthafucka I'm keeping your hands clean and you're still standing in my face bitching like a fucking female yo!" I yelled out and Sanchez just looked down at my carpet floor.

"Did something happen earlier?" Sanchez asked and I just gave him a look.

I began to feel myself getting nervous and I was the type of nigga that didn't get nervous about shit and I put that on my mom! I wanted him to spit out exactly what he was thinking. I mean damn, did he know that I murdered JoJo? This was the first time I ever murked a family member before let alone my own brother but that muthafucka crossed me.

"What are you talking about Sanchez? I swear it's always something with you my nigga...Take this money and get the fuck out of my face before you really make me mad," I said feeling a bit guilty that I just took out our baby brother. I reached back down in the desk pulling out the money and I tossed the bread in his lap.

"Teka called me in a panic earlier saying she just left your house," Sanchez said checking out the money.

I just wanted to know if Teka ran her mouth about what I did to JoJo...This was a secret I needed to keep from my mother and Sanchez. This shit would break their hearts yo but how else was I suppose to handle a disloyal muthafucka?!

"Did she say anything else?" I asked rubbing my hands together.

"Nah, but she was nervous as hell though and her speech was fucking up while she was talking so I didn't understand too much," Sanchez said putting the money in his pocket then he looked up at me. "Why was Teka over here in the first place?" Sanchez asked.

"I hired her to be my in-home nurse," I said tapping my fingers on the arm of my chair.

"Nigga ain't shit wrong with you...You want to fuck Teka or something?" Sanchez asked and his little insecurities were starting to reflect.

"Muthafucka, watch your mouth Teka is your wife so that makes her blood automatically...I would never do any disloyal shit like that and you know that fool," I said grilling him plus Teka wasn't even my type...That bitch had too much plastic surgery done she was beginning to look distasteful.

"I have a few people staying with me and one of my guest shoots heroin. Teka is starting treatments helping shawty detox...That's what I hired your wife for nigga. Any infidelities y'all got going on don't got shit to do with me" I said and Sanchez chuckle but he wasn't laughing forreal.

"Oh, you being funny Angel?" Sanchez asked and then he sucked his teeth. "Me, you and JoJo need to have a talk," Sanchez said.

"Nigga, have a talk about what? Your ass is starting to give me a fucking headache," I said rubbing my head.

"Have you seen or talked to JoJo?" Sanchez asked me directly.

"JoJo is closer than you think Sanchez..." I said staring back at Sanchez. What I said was the truth JoJo was cut up into pieces in my backyard. Blood or not that nigga had to be dealt with! I told that nigga NOT to lie to me yo I've been telling him that since we were kids.

"What that mean Angel? Let me call this nigga..." Sanchez said taking his phone out of his pocket. He tapped a few buttons on his screen then held it up to his right ear.

Suddenly, JoJo's phone starts ringing in my pocket. I forgot I never got rid of it because I needed information on Mir. I took the phone out of my pocket and turned it off. I quickly let it drop down to my feet and kicked it smooth under my desk.

"His phone just keeps ringing...Oh shit, did you hear that Angel?" Sanchez asked confused taking the phone off his ear.

"Hear what Sanchez?" I asked playing dumb.

"I thought I heard a phone going off...I'm just going to call this nigga again he's probably getting some pussy right now," Sanchez said sucking his teeth then he tapped another button placing the phone back up to his ear.

"JoJo isn't going to answer you Sanchez," I said telling the truth.

"Why the fuck not? Oh! Because he only answers to you right, Angel? Since I'm not on your level," Sanchez said being fucking smart and I punch down on my desk.

"Why the fuck do you have to make everything a fucking competition muthafucka?!" I asked balling up my face and Sanchez put his phone back into his pocket. He turned his attention to the side of my desk.

"You have a little girl living in the house too?" Sanchez asked.
I swear to God yo this nigga must be bored or some shit always talking about stupid shit...I don't understand why this nigga is still in my presence. Sanchez has his own crib, go the fuck home and go fuck your wife.

"Yeah, her name is Nyla...Kia which is Nyla's mom and Jada is the aunt. Those are my three guest that now live with me," I said grabbing Nyla's book bag and her book fell out with her drawings.

When I grabbed it the drawing was the same one I mentioned before...Only difference was I was the nigga behind the desk and Sanchez was the nigga standing in front of my desk. I was confused on what me and Sanchez were looking at because he was pointing in the drawing.

"What the fuck?" I said putting Nyla's book down on my desk.

"Kia...Does she have a boyfriend?" Sanchez asked scratching his temple standing up from the chair.

"Nah, she told me she was single..." I said still looking down at the drawing that Nyla created BEFORE TIME.

"Are you sure about that Angel?" Sanchez asked but my eyes were glued down to this book. "Was JoJo here Angel?" Sanchez asked another question and my head jumped up so quick you would think muthafuckas were doing a drive-by.

"Why are you asking me that?" I asked confused and Sanchez turned his head and I followed to where he was looking at.

"Those are, *cop keys*...over there on the table, right? Those are JoJo keys..." Sanchez said pointing to JoJo's keys in the corner on my office table.

That's what we were looking at on Nyla's drawing but how the fuck did a ten year old predict something like this?!

-KASSANA WILSON

CHAPTER 14 ANGEL

"What type of shit is this yo?" I asked myself as I stared down at Nyla's drawing. Every detail was so on point my nigga, that everything that was on this drawing in front of me happened exactly that way.

"What's your problem Angel?" Sanchez asked looking at me like he was missing something which he was. If he knew what I knew right now then that nigga would be tongue tied as well. I closed the book and I just shook my head.

"Something just caught me by surprise...That's all Sanchez," I said clearing my throat.

"Well am I right?" Sanchez asked waving me off and I just looked at him.

"Right about what yo?" I asked standing up out of my office chair.

"Those are JoJo keys...Matter of fact let me see," Sanchez said in a low tone. He walked over to my office table and picked up the silver keys that belonged to JoJo. "This nigga JoJo always losing something...Ayo! JoJo where you at? Stop playing my nigga I need to talk to you!" Sanchez yelled out. He squeezed his right hand with JoJo's keys still inside then he walked to the front door of my office and opened it up chuckling.

"Aye Sanchez—" I said calmly rubbing my head looking down at my carpet floor.

"JOJO!" Sanchez yelled out again walking into the hallway.

"Ayo Sanchez! I yelled out following behind him but Sanchez still thought shit was a game.

Little did he know JoJo was not alive. When we were younger JoJo and Sanchez used to hide around the house trying to find one another. Either JoJo or Sanchez would leave something behind like a shoe, sock or remote which was a clue that the other person was close to finding you. Only difference is now we are grown ass men and JoJo wasn't *playing* the game anymore...He was completely out of the game forever because he couldn't be loyal to me.

"JOJO COME HERE MY NIGGA! STOP PLAYING SO MUCH!" Sanchez yelled out still standing on his two feet in the hallway. I knew deep in his heart that Sanchez was waiting for that moment for JoJo to run up to him and start playing but how the fuck was I suppose to tell one brother that I murdered my other brother?!

"Sanchez...SANCHEZ! Lower your muthafuckin' tone in my house yo..." I said raising my voice a bit. I grabbed Sanchez by his navy blue uniform shirt and pulled him back into my office.

"What is your problem Angel? Where is JoJo?" Sanchez asked balling up his face. He started to straighten out his shirt that I wrinkled up and he stuffed JoJo's keys into his pocket. I leaned back against my desk and shrugged my shoulders.

"Nigga why are you asking me? I don't *see him* around here...Do you?" I asked being funny looking around my office.

"How far could the nigga go without his car keys? Where is his patrol car? I didn't see it parked out front," Sanchez spoke like he was in a panic as he pointed to my office window.

"Did you forget that JoJo also owns a Chrysler and not just a patrol car?"

"Nigga, all I want to know is why is JoJo keys in the corner of your office but he's nowhere to be found," Sanchez said scratching his head then he looked around my office again like he was observing for clues.

"He left out in a hurry—" I said and Sanchez started shaking his head no. He walked passed me behind my desk rubbing his hands together.

"None of this shit is adding up...Oh shit," Sanchez said and I heard him bump against my desk.

"You good Sanchez?" I asked looking at him funny as I spun around to see him getting up off the floor.

"I'm straight my nigga...Uh, I just hit my knee on your desk," Sanchez said rubbing on his right knee then a few moments later he came back over to me.

Me and Sanchez were standing right in front of one another quiet but it was more tension in this room than before. His eyes were glued to me like secrets.

"I have been calling you! Why haven't you been picking up your phone?!" Kia asked yelling as she walked into my office. I turned my head and I see Chino holding Kia by her right arm. "Nigga get your fucking hands off me!" Kia yelled out trying to push Chino off but that big nigga wouldn't budge.

"Let her go Chino...She's good" I said waving him off. Chino nodded his head up and down then he left out of my office. Kia balled up her face as she folded her arms across her chest. She looked behind her and rolled her eyes at my security which made me smirk a little.
I enjoyed her presence though...Even if her ass seemed to be bothered. I turned my attention back to Sanchez and before I could speak Kia started snapping again.

"Angel I'm fucking talking to you—" Kia said dropping her arms and came up to me. I rubbed my lips together and pointed to my brother.

"Kia, this is my brother Sanchez...Sanchez this is Kia the woman I told you that is now living here," I said introducing them to one another.

"Oh, so it's just the two of you left now...It's very nice to meet you Sanchez," Kia said under her breath. Kia extended her hand out to Sanchez and he returned the gesture.

My eyes grew to the boldness of her speech which caught me by surprise. Sanchez lowered his eyes to the words that came out of her mouth. Kia was trying to give a hint to Sanchez that JoJo was dead.

"Just the two of us left now? What is she talking about—" Sanchez asked dropping his hand from touching hers and he looked at me.

Before I could explain his phone started ringing. Damn, that was right on time because I couldn't even make up an explanation for that shit coming out her mouth. I walked up to Kia and whispered in her right ear.

"Don't do this Kia...Just keep your mouth closed," I said to her and she didn't say anything nor did she look at me.

"Hello? What happened Teka? I'm on my way yo!" Sanchez yelled out in a fright on the phone. He took his phone away from his ear and put it back into his pocket.

"Everything good Sanchez?" I asked giving him a look and he just rubbed his hands together but the look on his face...You could tell he was getting overwhelmed about something.

"I need to meet my wife at the hospital something happened...Once I get all the details I will call you bro," Sanchez said to me clapping me up then he turned his attention to Kia. "It was a pleasure meeting you Kia...I will be seeing you and *Nyla* real soon. Believe that..." He spoke low when he shook Kia's hand. He looked back at me giving me a head nod then disappeared out of my office.

"Did you tell your brother my daughter's name?" Kia asked nervously then she wiped her hands off on her thick thighs.

"Yeah I did briefly in conversation...Why?" I asked leaning back on my desk.

"The way he said Nyla's name...I don't know, It's something about your brother that gives me the chills...His entire presence is cold," Kia said looking around my office and I smiled.

"Sanchez? Nah, that nigga might be hardheaded as hell but he's a cool muthafucka," I said rubbing my lips together. "Let me ask you something Kia...Where were you?" I asked looking down at my hands and I could hear Kia breathing deeply now. Body language always tells a different story I'm telling ya!

"I was at the bodega across the street from my Aunt Tasha's house...The car was still parked in front of her house when me and Nyla decided to walk to the store," Kia said looking at me in my eyes.

"Who lives with your Aunt Tasha?" I asked and Kia scratched her head with her right index finger then stuffed her hands down in her pockets.

"Uh...She lives by herself Angel," Kia hesitated to say. I bit down on my lip and shook my head.

"Are you telling me the truth?" I asked walking up to Kia. I used my right hand to caress her chin.

Kia looked me in my eyes and the expression on her face was calling my name. After a few seconds she nodded her head up and down with my hand still attached to her chin.

"Where is Jada?" I asked and Kia sucked her teeth.

"I can't find her anywhere!" Kia yelled out and I could see she was getting a bit emotional.

"Your sister just disappeared Kia? She needs to start detoxing or she won't make it much longer on those streets," I said dropping my hand from her chin.

"You don't think I know this shit already Angel?! I'm scared yo...I'm scared that I'm going to get a phone call that Jada is dead but what the fuck am I supposed to do if she won't let me help her?! I failed her once...I can't fail her again," Kia said with tears in her eyes.

"CHINO!" I yelled out looking at my office door. I looked over at Kia and she was rubbing her eyes with the back of her hand.

"Yes boss?" Chino asked standing outside my door.

"Check the video cameras in my other office from this morning...Print the picture out of Jada and you tell my little niggas on the block to search for her and don't rest until they find her. We need to get little shawty to detox as quick as possible," I said giving him clear directions. Chino nodded his head and left out of my office. "Come here yo," I said opening up my arms so I could embrace Kia. She fell into my arms, her presence and touch gave a nigga like me butterflies.

"I'm trying to be the best mother possible to Nyla while trying to do right by my own sister" Kia said squeezing me tighter then she turned her attention to something else. "Wha—What are you doing with that Angel?" Kia asked breaking herself out of my embrace. She looked over at my desk, backing away from me still wiping her tears.

"What are you talking about yo?" I asked confused with my hands still out.

"THAT! WHY DO YOU HAVE NYLA'S BOOK?" Kia yelled out. She ran over to my desk grabbing Nyla's book and reached down to get her bookbag.

"Chill out mamacita! Chino brung me Nyla's book bag, he said she left it abandoned in the hallway. I was closing it up and the book fell out her bag—" I said and Kia was starting to go bananas.

More tears were falling from her eyes, the veins were popping out from her neck and forehead. She zipped up Nyla's bag and walked to the front door of my office.

"What did you see Angel? What the fuck did you see?!" Kia cried out to me.

"The real question is...What can Nyla see?" I asked and Kia turned around carrying Nyla's bookbag on her back.

"Please don't touch her shit anymore unless you ask first," Kia said wiping her face and she sniffled. "It's not safe," Kia said under her breath but I didn't comprehend what she just mumbled.

"It's something about Nyla that you're not telling me...Isn't it?" I asked concerned and Kia's chest was pumping up and down from her adrenaline running.

"Angel! Just the nigga I needed to see," The feminine voice said. I turned my head and Teka came running into my office dressed in her nurse uniform.

"What are you doing here Teka? Sanchez left out of here in a panic saying that he needed to meet with you," I said thinking of Sanchez just storming out of my office.

Kia continued to wipe her face. I pointed to the chair in front of my desk so she would take a seat. Kia walked over to the chair and sat down without speaking.

"I know...I know...I called Sanchez to get him out of your house so I could speak with you in private. Do you mind?" Teka asked looking at Kia with a straight face. Kia got out the chair and I shook my head no.

"Chill out Teka...She can stay I want Kia here," I said nodding my head and Kia sat back down in the chair.

"I didn't run my mouth about the incident with JoJo if that's what you're thinking," Teka said whispering.

I smirked and walked up to Teka.

"I know you didn't baby...I trust you. What is it that you need to speak with me about?" I asked rubbing the side of her face with my hand then I kissed Teka on the cheek. Kia looked up at me and bit down on her bottom lip but I knew she wasn't cool with what I just did. I didn't mean any disrespect by it...That's just how Spanish people show love and gratitude.

"About Bella," Teka said and I took a step back.

"You sure you want me in here Angel? It's not a problem I can wait in the hallway," Kia said pointing to the door of my office and I turned my attention to Kia.

"You don't have to go mi amor," I said to reassure Kia that she didn't have to leave.

"Well, Angel..." Teka said in a low tone but I could see how nervous she was to talk to me.

"Come on with that beating around the bush shit Teka be straight forward with me my nigga because I always keep it one hundred with you. ASI QUE DIME NINA!" I yelled out slamming my hand on my desk. Teka and Kia both jumped from the frustration I just let out.

"I was the first nurse on scene when Bella came to the hospital because she still had a weak pulse but she wasn't stabled," Teka said.

I walked around my desk to sit down in my chair but I was shaking my head.

"You're telling me shit I already know Teka!" I yelled out sitting down. Kia was looking around pretending that she wasn't listening to what Teka was telling me.

"I know this is a sensitive subject for you Angel but my nigga she was family to me as well! Everyone is still grieving over this!" Teka yelled out trying to raise her fucking voice back at me.

"WHAT THE FUCK DO YOU HAVE TO SAY TEKA?" I yelled out getting aggravated. My apologies but hearing Bella's name still cut me deep...That was one pill that I just couldn't swallow. When muthafuckas bring up her name it makes shit harder for me to deal with.

"Oh my God...This shit is making me so uncomfortable," Kia said under her breath.

"There was a lot of traffic going on in the hospital so I only stayed with Bella for a few minutes until other patients arrived. Well the nurse that took over for Bella ran a few test before she flatlined and Bella..." Teka said rubbing her fingers through her hair and she took a deep breath.

"What about Bella?!" I asked raising my voice.

"Bella *gave birth* to a baby girl a few weeks before she was murdered. I decided to take a look at her medical records and there it was," Teka said shaking her head.

"My wife couldn't have kids Teka..." I laughed because this shit had to be a joke. "We always spoke about adopting kids because she couldn't give birth so I know that isn't true. I think you have your charts switched up with another patient," I said waving Teka off and she ran up to my desk and pointed to me.

"I know how to do my fucking job Angel and I do it damn well. What am I gaining coming here with this type of information? I'm trying to help you muthafucka!" Teka yelled out and I just leaned back in my office chair. "Two detectives came down to the hospital asking for medical records for Bella so they could reopen it...I wanted to see what they were so curious about then I did my own digging into Bella's case," Teka said.

"Reopen Bella's case? I thought them muthafuckas were down at the station working on her case already!" I yelled out standing up from my chair.

"Your brother...JoJo closed Bella's case. It was closed three days after her murder," Teka said.

I couldn't believe that sneaky muthafucka yo. Every time I asked JoJo were detectives any closer to finding out who did this to Bella that bitch ass nigga always told me they had six detectives trying to solve her case.

"Look Angel..." Teka said pulling something out of her scrub pocket. There were four folded up sheets of papers. I unfolded them but I still didn't understand what this meant...My ass was a thug I didn't know shit about the medical field. Kia must of had enough because she walked towards my door to leave out.

"What the fuck is this Teka?" I asked and she pointed her index finger to the top of all four papers.

"Bella was very fertile these are records from the abortion clinic that run back three years ago...Bella had four abortions then a few weeks before her murder she gave birth to baby girl name Charlie. I think I know where Charlie is Angel..." Teka said.

Kia stopped in her tracks and turned back to look at me. I wonder why this specific part caught her attention so much...I looked down under my desk and I didn't see JoJo's phone...Sanchez must of took it when that nigga said he bumped his knee on my desk.

CHAPTER 15 KIA

"I'm not feeling so well..." I said turning up my face as I held my stomach.

"What's wrong Kia?" Teka asked dumfounded turning from Angel's desk then she gave me her undivided attention. Angel looked at me and rubbed on his chin hair.

"I just need..." I said taking a deep breath then I paused. I was having too many fucking mixed emotions that things out of my control was starting to control me. I just didn't know what I would do if Teka revealed this dark secret that was meant to be kept hidden.

"I just need some air Teka I'm feeling a bit nauseous," I said wiping my head just to put on a performance but little did I know that I was really sweating on my forehead.

"Kia, come here...Why did your mood just change so fast?" Angel asked removing his hand from his chin. He stood up from the desk and looked at me extending his hand out so I could walk over to him.

I shook my head no and held my stomach tighter. Teka exhaled deeply and walked over to me.

"I'm going to take her outside so she can get some air Angel...It is a bit hot in here. I can get my pressure cuff out of my trunk so I can check her numbers." Teka said while placing her left hand around my waist and she used her right hand to touch from my head down to my neck to feel for a fever. I still had Nyla's bookbag on my back as I tried to head to leave out of Angel's office but he came around the desk speaking.

"Hold on...Tell me where Charlie is!" Angel yelled out.

Me and Teka entered the hallway heading towards the front door but Angel's tone increased a bit as he was becoming agitated. "

Ayo, Teka tell me where Charlie is yo!" Angel yelled out again.

As Teka's left hand was still around my waist we turned to face Angel...But my guilty ass couldn't look him in his eyes. Damn my own brother murdered Angel's wife and had a child with her. I couldn't face Angel anymore especially when I knew all about it. I was just trying to get out of the house as quick as possible.

"My nigga hold the fuck on let me take care of Kia first and I will be right back in," Teka said reassuring Angel.

"Make it quick..." Angel said calmly.

I heard footsteps then a moment later the movement stopped. I looked up like I was peeking and Angel walked back into his office. Teka turned back around and we both walked out the door. I looked behind me and I just couldn't believe I made it out with all of these secrets weighing my body down.

"I know Kia..." Teka said still holding me as we walked down the stairs and headed to her car.

"What are you talking about Teka?" I asked confused and she started grinning.

"You're not feeling nauseous Kia...Something is bothering you about what I said, isn't it?" Teka asked trying to get some secrets out of me. Teka walked to the trunk of her car and pushed the button on her key ring.

"Lately, I just been feeling a little sick to my stomach," I said which was the truth.

"Are you really going to stand here in my face and lie to me?" Teka asked and her trunk popped open. I licked my bottom lip and looked around before speaking.

"If you know so much Teka why didn't you call it out while we were inside of Angel's office?" I asked and she pointed to herself then she pointed to me.

"At the end of the day us girls have to stick together...I don't give a fuck about Angel. I witnessed too much shit with that muthafucka but Bella is a different story I loved her deeply and so did that nigga. Maybe having Charlie in his life will make him see that he still has a piece of Bella as well," Teka spoke like she was sincere and that was something I couldn't question but Charlie was my brother's daughter...Not Angel's. A few seconds later the front gate opened up and a black Tahoe truck drove in like a madman. The tires came to a screeching stop and the driver's side door came flying open.

"Are you playing games with me yo?!" The familiar voice yelled out.

I moved over to see who it was and it was Sanchez wobbling out of the truck still in his work attire.

"Fuck!" Teka yelled out slamming her trunk closed shut. Teka maneuvered from the back of the car to the front of her vehicle.

I looked at security at the gate and they were standing in place but speaking on their radios.

"Get the fuck over here Teka! Didn't you just ask me to meet you down at the fucking hospital?" Sanchez asked with his face balled up. I moved out the way as Sanchez was trying to chase Teka. I wasn't trying to get involved in anymore shit...I had enough fucking drama in my life.

"I...I..." Teka started stuttering then she looked at me but baby girl I couldn't save you. This relationship involved two people and I was minding my damn business.

"I— what Teka? Stop fucking stuttering and just tell me the truth. You were never at the fucking hospital in the first place. What the fuck did you lie for, huh?" Sanchez asked running around the car but Teka moved twice as fast.

"Baby, it's not what you think..." Teka said running around the vehicle holding her hands out. Sanchez was in shape but his ass was getting winded pretty quick.

"You wanted me to leave so you could have Angel to yourself? That's what the fuck we doing now Teka? You cheating on me with my fucking brother now yo?!" Sanchez yelled out and Teka just dropped her head like she was disappointed.

"WHAT?! SANCHEZ DO YOU HEAR YOURSELF NIGGA?!" Teka yelled out again keeping her distance around the car.

"Teka, you have yet to explain why you're here..." Sanchez said breathing heavy then he bent over holding his knees so he could catch his breath.

"I work for Angel baby," Teka said pointing behind her to Angel's house. Sanchez shrugged the shit out of his shoulders...For a moment there I thought he pulled a muscle in his back.

"You think I give a fuck about that shit? Let me ask you something Teka...Is your patient inside that house?" Sanchez asked concerned and I looked back at security at the gate and they were still over there talking. Teka hesitated to answer Sanchez question so his ass got louder. "IS YOUR FUCKING PATIENT INSIDE OF THAT HOUSE?!" Sanchez yelled out and the veins were popping out on the side of his neck from frustration.

"No Sanchez! She's not here at the moment—" Teka said finally telling the truth but Sanchez was right and wrong in this situation. He was right because Teka shouldn't of lied to him BUT this nigga was wrong because he was running around this fucking car chasing her like a fucking female.

"Who's to say that this patient of yours really exist baby girl? Get your shit yo we will talk about this at home," Sanchez said pointing back to his truck and Teka shook her head no.

"I'm not leaving Sanchez I have to—" Teka said trying to plead with Sanchez but rejecting him just pissed him off even more.

"Have to do what Teka?! You want to fuck Angel...Don't you or do you want to fuck JoJo?! Which one of my brothers?!" Sanchez asked.

See what I mean? Only insecure muthafuckas act like this...I messed with a few in my lifetime to know a broken nigga can NOT be healed. It's only so much reassurance a woman could give to a nigga.

"What is wrong with you Sanchez?!" Teka yelled out looking around because she was embarrassed. Shit, I would be too!

"GET YOUR SHIT SO WE CAN GO HOME!" Sanchez yelled out running around the car. Teka finally gave up she didn't even run anymore. She allowed Sanchez to get a hold of her. He grabbed Teka by her right arm and pulled her towards his truck.

"LET ME GO SANCHEZ! YOU'RE HURTING ME!" Teka screamed out trying to push Sanchez off her arm.

The front door came flying open and Chino came running out the door and down the stairs.

"Chino, stay the fuck out of this my nigga," Sanchez said to Chino as he continued to pull on Teka.

"You know I can't ignore this Sanchez...Let her go and leave the property before your brother comes outside and you know that shit won't be pretty," Chino said getting in between Teka and Sanchez.

"Nah fuck that! Come outside Angel! I have a few questions for my big brother!" Sanchez yelled out stumbling again still holding on to Teka's arm. Chino removed Sanchez's grip from Teka then she started to rub the side of her arm.

"Sanchez...Just go home baby you're making a fool of yourself," Teka said pointing to his truck so he would leave.

"This is too much fucking drama," I said under my breath running my fingers through my hair. Sanchez neck turned in my direction rapidly like I was talking about his mother or something.

"What bitch?" Sanchez said walking up to me with more aggression than a few minutes ago.

"Come on Teka," Chino said gently pushing Teka back.

"Who the fuck are you calling a bitch?" I asked looking at Sanchez and he smirked at me.

"You muthafucka...I would advise you to keep your fucking distance away from me before we have a problem," Sanchez said whispering to me and I started chuckling.

"You're a weak ass nigga," I said and Sanchez walked towards his car but when he heard me speak he stopped in his tracks.

"Say another fucking word to me," Sanchez threatened me getting closer to my face.

"Leave her alone Sanchez!" Teka yelled out standing behind Chino's back.

"Bruh, just get the fuck out of here you're attracting the wrong attention," Chino said to Sanchez as he took a deep breath.

"Get the fuck out of my face...Punk ass Mexican," I said to Sanchez and he looked at me up and down. I never realized how red his eyes were until he was standing directly in my face.

"I'm not Mexican bitch...I should go tell Angel about you and Reem," Sanchez whispered to me so I was the only one that could hear him. I felt like my heart stopped pumping for a second.

"Wha—What?" I asked stuttering backing up away from him.

"Wassup with y'all bitches stuttering every time y'all get caught?" Sanchez asked laughing at his own joke. "Don't act scared now Kia...I'm the CO for Reem's pod and I know that he's the father of little Nyla...I also know that the two of y'all are still in a relationship," Sanchez said to me and he looked up at Angel's house. I looked up to see what had his attention and it was Nyla staring down at us out the window. Sanchez winked at Nyla and that shit made me sick to my stomach.

"What do you want from me?" I asked and I mouthed the words "I'm sorry" to Nyla as she looked at me out of the window. I know my child felt a bit uncomfortable especially at that age.

"I will tell you when the time is right...Until then learn to mind your fucking business," Sanchez said to me and he hopped in his driver's seat starting his car back up. He slammed his car door shut and rolled down the window. "I will see you at home sexy," Sanchez said looking at Teka as he blew a kiss to her. Chino said something into his radio and walked back into the house.

"What did Sanchez say to you?" Teka asked me and I shook my head because I didn't want her to know about my baby dad.

"Why do you put up with that shit Teka?" I asked her as I changed the subject.

"It's not as bad as it seems Kia...Sanchez isn't a bad guy. I guess he's trying so hard to just fit in with Angel but he has a bad way of expressing that," Teka said shrugging her shoulders then she rubbed on her arm.

I looked down and I could see some bruising starting to appear from Sanchez grabbing on her. I looked up and Nyla wasn't in the window anymore.

"Can I ask you something?" I asked and I made sure to lower my tone when talking to her. "Inside of Angel's office you said that you know where Charlie is...Do you really know?" I asked curious and Teka nodded her head up and down.

"I checked Bella's medical history and found a birth certificate...The dad's name is Mir I believe. I forgot his last name but he signed as Charlie's father" Teka said still rubbing on her arm.

"Fuck...Stupid ass move Mir," I said under my breath and Teka looked at me perplexed.

"What did you say Kia?" Teka asked balling up her face.

"I said...So you didn't know Bella was pregnant?" I asked playing dumb knowing that's not what I really said.

"Bella worked in the ER with me...Sometimes different shifts and no one knew. I don't know how Bella covered up that pregnancy and birth for so long but she did a damn good job keeping secrets," Teka said dropping her hands to her side then she stuffed her hands in her pockets.

"I know that I have asked you for a lot Teka but please don't go back into Angel's office and tell him what you told me about Mir," I said whispering checking my surroundings.

"Do you know who Mir is or something?" Teka asked me looking at me suspicious.

"I'm begging you Teka..." I said walking up to her holding her hands but she pushed me off of her.

"What do you expect me to do Kia?!" Teka asked yelling out and I just looked around the premises to make sure no one was seeing this commotion going on.

"Tell Angel that you got your information wrong and you're at a dead end," I said whispering and Teka just exhaled deeply.

"This will be a big break for me and Sanchez," Teka said slapping her hands against her thighs.

"What?" I asked confused.

"If I go back and tell Angel what the fuck I know then maybe he will welcome Sanchez with open arms in this business. I'm tired of these fucking demons that my husband are fighting...Angel has treated JoJo so much better than Sanchez and I can't bare to see this shit anymore. I know Sanchez acts the way he acts because of his jealousy toward his brothers and I have the key to bring him out of his misery and you're telling me not to do it Kia? Fuck that! I have to," Teka said turning around walking towards the stairs so she could go in the house to speak to Angel but I ran behind her.

"Please Teka... I thought us girls had to stick together," I said in her left ear and she stopped in her tracks.

"You're right but my husband comes first girl," Teka said winking at me. Nyla came running out the house and she ran up to me. Teka turned back around walking to the front door.

"Nyla, go back in the house baby grown folks are talking," I said pointing back to the front door.

"Teka don't go and run your mouth," I said ignoring Nyla in my presence.

"What the hell? Why not...I mean what are you hiding Kia?" Teka turned back around and crossed her arms across her chest. Nyla kept tugging at my shirt so she could get my attention.

"NYLA! GO IN THE HOUSE! I'M TALKING!" I yelled out at her but I didn't mean it I was just worried about Mir getting more caught up than he already was.

"Bend down to my level..." Nyla said. I took a deep breath and lowered down so my daughter could speak privately in my ear.

"WHAT THE FUCK" I said getting back up after Nyla told me about a vision she had.

"Make it your last time yelling at me when I'm trying to help you," Nyla said to me and she pointed to my back.

I took off her bookbag and handed it to her. Nyla smiled at me and skipped up the stairs humming a song.
"Bye Teka..." Nyla said waving at Teka then she entered the house leaving me and Teka alone again.

"What the hell is your daughter so happy about?" Teka asked looking at me with an attitude. I smiled when I saw the look of discomfort on Teka's face.

"I think the real question is what are you hiding Teka?" I asked smirking and Teka just looked bothered as she tried to read my body language.

"What Kia..." Teka said in a low tone nervously.

"You weren't really born a woman...Were you? That's why you keep getting plastic surgery Teka?" I asked her and I looked down at her private part and winked at her. "How big are you girl?" I asked sarcastically.

-KASSANA WILSON

CHAPTER 16 ANGEL

"Where are you going Teka?" I asked walking out of my house. I see Teka wiping her eyes as she headed to her car. She continued to walk while I was speaking. "Ayo, Teka I know you hear me talking to you," I said jogging down the stairs. I looked over at Kia, she had her hands stuffed down in her pockets smirking at Teka but I wanted to know what the fuck was so funny.

"I have an emergency down at the hospital Angel...I will call you later," Teka said walking over to the driver's side of her car. I followed behind her and sucked my teeth.

"Nah, my nigga it's always something with you. Just tell me where Charlie is Teka," I said and I could feel my hands sweating from the unknown. If Bella did give birth to my child I needed to act fast and find her.

"I had the wrong information Angel," Teka said opening up her car door and I slammed it shut with my right hand.

"What the fuck is that supposed to mean Teka?" I asked confused gently moving her out of the way. Teka looked at Kia then she started fidgeting with her hands like she was nervous.

"All I know is Bella gave birth to a baby girl name Charlie but I'm not sure where she is at the moment Angel," Teka said but she was looking at Kia the entire time...As if Kia was coaching her to say the shit that she was saying.

"Didn't your little ass just come into my fucking office crying about how good of a job you do? Now all of a sudden you can't locate Charlie?" I asked balling up my face and I took a step back. Teka continued fidgeting with her hands and she spoke in a low tone.

"It's not like that Angel...Please just trust me," Teka said trying to whisper like she didn't want Kia to hear us having a conversation.

"Well, explain to me how it's like Teka cause right now I'm fucking confused," I said and Teka maneuvered back to the door of her car.

"Angel..." Teka said taking a deep breath. "Let me go back down to the hospital to get more information on Charlie...I swear I will let you know everything once I have my ducks in a row" Teka said nodding her head up and down but who the fuck was she agreeing with? NOT ME. She opened up the door of her car and slid inside. A few moments later she started up her vehicle and I tapped on her window as she pulled it down.

"Let me ask you something Teka," I said. Teka looked over at Kia then she gave me her full attention. "Did another nigga sign Charlie's birth certificate?" I asked out of curiosity and Teka hesitated to answer at first then she shook her head no.

"No, no, no, no why would you ask me something like that?" Teka asked confused but I didn't answer her question. Kia sashayed over to me and winked at Teka.

"Teka girl...You may want to get some looser work pants...I think the ones you have on are a bit close to revealing something," Kia said but I figured she was talking about Teka's pussy in case she popped out of her work pants.

I just kept my nose out of their business because that didn't have shit to do with me. Teka didn't respond back to Kia she just busted a U-turn and headed towards the gate to leave out. Kia walked ahead of me to enter back inside the house.

"Kia...How are you feeling?" I asked and Kia stopped in her tracks and looked at me.

"I'm fine...What are you talking about?" Kia asked confused and I just looked at her briefly for a second. I walked up to her and rubbed my hand on her right cheek.

"In my office you were feeling nauseous or did you forget that?" I asked and Kia tapped on my left shoulder and started chuckling but I didn't find anything funny about this.

"Oh! I'm feeling much better, I think I just needed some air," Kia said turning around walking back into the house and she turned to look at me. "I'm going upstairs to check on Nyla I will be right back down," Kia said trying to reassure me as she headed towards the stairs.

"Chino?" I said as I saw him walk down the hallway. When he heard me call his name he headed in my direction.

"What's good boss?" Chino asked holding out his hands in front of him.

"Did you get the names of the muthafuckas living in Kia's aunt house?" I asked whispering as I looked up the stairs to make sure Kia wasn't listening to me.

"Don't worry I'm on it...I was just on another call," Chino said and I rubbed my chin hair.

"With who?" I asked curious.

"I will get that information right to you..." Chino said ignoring my question. He turned to head to the back of the house but I continued to talk. I wondered why this nigga disregarded my question like that.

"Did them niggas find Jada yet? Shawty really needs to detox as soon as possible," I said and Chino turned back around and pointed at me.

"Every nigga is out here on the streets looking for her...Relax boss we got this," Chino said. I nodded my head up and down and walked into the kitchen.

"Nyla...Your mother is looking for you. She just went upstairs—" I said pointing behind me. I looked at Nyla as she was sitting at the island eating a club sandwich with a bottle of water by her plate.

"I just needed something to eat...You don't mind do you?" Nyla asked swallowing what she had left inside her mouth. I shook my head no and started grinning.

"This is your home too Nyla," I said and I meant every word. Nyla picked up her bottled water and took a few sips. "Can I ask you something mi amor?" I asked walking closer to Nyla and I leaned back against the counter.

"Go ahead and ask...I think I may have an answer for you," Nyla said picking up her sandwich and she took another bite.

"Why do you always carry that notebook around? What are you expressing with each picture on every page?" I asked curious and Nyla started shaking her head no. She got up from her seat and reached in front of her to grab a paper towel.

"I don't think you would believe me if I told you," Nyla said while wiping her mouth.

"Try me—" I said and before I could finish speaking Nyla cut me off.

"I see things Angel...I see situations before they occur and I know how someone feels all the time even from a distance," Nyla said putting the paper towel down by her plate then she picked up her water again.

"You know what a dream is right, baby girl? Sometimes we dream and it's called déjà vu," I said thinking that she may have the two confused and she started chuckling...The laugh she delivered reminded me so much of her mother Kia.

"I'm very well educated on that word Angel but I don't have Déjà vu...I know dark secrets...Secrets that would make you very uncomfortable every time you see my face. You're letting my family stay in this beautiful home and I don't want to ruin that for them. So whatever secrets you have, keep it away from me...Just make sure you don't touch my hands," Nyla said taking a few more sips then she put the bottle down on the table.

"Touch your hands? Why not?" I asked leaning up from the counter.

"If you touch me...I see everything," Nyla said looking me up and down.

"There was a picture inside your notebook with two men inside an office—" I said and she put her right hand up in the air cutting me off to speak.

"You and your brother Sanchez, right?" Nyla asked. She looked at me like she was trying to figure me out. "Sanchez was pointing to car keys on your office table...That key belonged to your baby brother JoJo. I drew that picture two hours before that situation occurred Angel. I have to go...I know my mother is worried about me," Nyla said walking towards the door to leave out but I jumped in front of her.

"Wait, Nyla don't go!" I yelled out grabbing her hand. Nyla eyes started rolling to the back of her head and her body started shaking.

"OH MY GOD...OH MY GOD IT CAN'T BE," Nyla said falling down to the floor with tears filled in her eyes but I don't know what the fuck just happened.

"What the hell are you talking about Nyla?" I asked stepping back away from her because her little ass was starting to creep me out.

"Touch my hand again please," Nyla said crawling over to me on the kitchen floor. I shook my head no and she got up slowly from the floor. "You know what I'm talking about Angel...Lopez club, red silk sheets, intoxication...April 2008. Why—Why would you do that?" Nyla asked wiping her eyes and I continued to shake my head no.

"What are you talking about Nyla I didn't do anything" I said denying everything she just said.

"Nyla...You didn't hear me calling you? What are you doing?" Kia asked walking into the kitchen with a confused look on her face.

"Mom...I need to talk to you, please," Nyla said running up to her mom as she grabbed on her arm.

"Sorry Angel I know she was probably talking your ear off," Kia said chuckling and I forced a smile but I was standing in my own home terrified right now.

"Mom please," Nyla said whispering to her mother but her eyes were glued to me the entire time.

"What's wrong Nyla?" Kia asked embracing Nyla while looking down at her.

"Papi...Angel Papi where are you?" I heard the familiar voice in a distance. Then a moment later the voice got closer.

"Papi where is JoJo?" My mother asked me walking into the kitchen not even acknowledging Nyla and Kia.

"Tell the truth...Just tell the truth," Nyla said under her breath. My mother looked at Nyla but she didn't pay her any mind.

"Be quiet Nyla," Kia said to her daughter.

"I don't know Mami...I haven't seen JoJo all day. Mami this is—" I tried to introduce my mother to Kia and Nyla but she just waved me off.

"That's not what I came over here for...I had a dream about fish Angel and I'm not talking about a new born baby," My mother came up to me and caressed my cheeks.

I'm a grown ass man and I was embarrassed that she was doing this in front of guest.

"So what does that mean?" I asked and my mother took a step back from me and smiled.

"You have a child out here already Papi...For many years now. My dreams are never wrong Angel," My mother said and my heart dropped to my stomach.

"Lopez club, red silk sheets, intoxication...April 2008. Why...why would you do that?" Nyla repeated the same thing when it was just me and her in the kitchen but I didn't know what it meant. Kia looked down at Nyla and then the two of them looked at me.

CHAPTER 17 KIA

"Nyla baby...What are you talking about?" I asked looking down at my golden child. Her beautiful brown eyes were stuck on Angel like glue. I used my right hand to lift her chin to look at me. When her eyes landed on me my entire body got cold. "What does that mean?" I asked removing my hand from Nyla's chin and she continued to stare at me like she was deaf and didn't hear me talking to her.

"Mami, I'm not sure what you're referring to but let me introduce you—" This was take two for Angel but it was pretty clear that he failed again. His mother wasn't concerned with exchanging conversation with me and my daughter. She treated us like our presence bothered her...She couldn't even look me in my eyes.

"Do I look interested in meeting your little negro amigos Papi? Ahora camina tu preciosa madre al carro." His mother said turning her face up at Angel and she turned to leave out of the kitchen.

Excuse my language when I say this but I didn't know that bitch from a hole in the wall...I didn't know why she had a problem with me. Or maybe she just didn't like black people...but I wasn't offended. Being in prison for five years you encounter so much racial shit that it goes in one ear and out the other. I was bunking with this white chick for two years and she used to tell me stories about her great-great grandfather being apart of the KKK. Was I uncomfortable? Fuck yes! Does this shit make me angry? You're damn right it does but if I reacted to ignorance I will end up right back in the system with 3 hots and a cot.

"I'm not Spanish but I heard that smart shit your mother just said—" I said putting my right hand up. Angel looked down at Nyla like he was timid then he came up to me to speak.

"My apologies Kia I'm not in the business of making anybody uncomfortable so I will take care of this. I don't know what has gotten into her...Madre let's go," Angel said rubbing on my shoulder then he turned around pointing to his mother. There were two ways to get to the kitchen and I heard small footsteps behind my back and I knew it was my daughter. I turned to see what she was doing and she was walking away from me.

"Nyla...Come here I'm not done talking to you," I said following behind Nyla as we entered the hallway. Nyla took a deep breath and continued walking.

"Now you see me mom?" Nyla asked with her voice cracking. Her feet touched the stairs and then she turned around to face me.

"I always see you Nyla...Aye, what is your problem baby? I'm trying yo I really am and you're making it hard for me," I said reaching out to touch her but she took another step up the stairs.

"Why can't you just listen to me?" Nyla asked but I could hear it in her tone that she was very frustrated with me. She turned back around and skipped up the stairs by two. I continued to follow behind her even though she was running away from me. "I'm just trying to help you," Nyla said but I couldn't understand her because she was speaking low. We reached the top of the stairs and Nyla walked towards the bedroom. I was so exhausted going up all them fucking stairs...I wish I was young again.

"I do listen to you Nyla and I'm sorry if you don't acknowledge me doing my best with you but you're a mystery baby...a beautiful mystery which in a way terrifies me. I'm not sure if that's a good thing or bad thing just yet. I feel like whenever I'm close to putting the pieces to the puzzle together another piece is waiting to be attached," I said closing the bedroom door. Nyla jumped up on the bed that we shared together and she started chuckling and laid back on the bed. "Am I amusing you in some way Nyla?" I asked crossing my arms across my chest.

"You don't even know, do you?" Nyla asked in a smart tone as she sat up on the bed.

"Is there something I'm supposed to know?" I asked confused dropping my hands to my side. Nyla got down off the bed and grabbed her bookbag out of the closet.

"You're the puzzle...You're trying to put pieces together in your life so don't try to switch it around on me like I'm making this universe hard for you...I wasn't the one that got locked up and disappeared for five years mom. So you remember that when you start pointing fingers," Nyla said and my eyes blew up.

My child was only ten years old...I know she wasn't a dummy but I didn't expect for her to talk to me this way. Nyla sucked her teeth and unzipped her bag like she was searching for something.

"You always fall down in a hole and I'm the only person putting my hand down to get you out of your problems. You never even said thank you...All you do is yell at me and push me to the side so you can keep your secrets hidden" Nyla said getting emotional then she pulled out her notebook...the notebook that I grew to hate because them drawings held more weight than I could ever imagine.

"Secrets?" I asked confused walking over to her and Nyla looked up at me and smirked.

"Please don't act surprise now mom...You know just as well as I do that your secrets are darker than Angels," Nyla said flipping through the pages then she stopped when she heard me talking.

"Angel? What does he have to do with this Nyla?" I asked.

"I don't want to talk about that right now," Nyla said and a tear dropped from her right ear. I tried to touched her face and she just backed away from me. I took a deep breath and just remained calm.

"What do you want to discuss right now?" I asked and Nyla wiped her face and continued flipping through her book. A moment later she turned away from me like she didn't want to be in my presence. "I'm talking to you why do you keep turning your back on me?" I asked grabbing her right shoulder gently turning her around. She had her book in her hand and threw it down on the bed.

"Let's talk about this mom," Nyla said pointing to the bed. I looked at the drawing and I immediately got sick to my stomach. I knew exactly what the drawing was but I needed more understanding.

"Nyla...Nyla...Nyla what the fuck is this?!" I yelled out stuttering with tears rolling down my face. I grabbed her book so I could rip up the drawing but Nyla ran up to me taking her art from my arms.

"Remember I mentioned three babies mom? Uncle Mir having his daughter Charlie was baby number one. Aunt Tasha getting an abortion was baby number two and you..." Nyla said shaking her head like she was the mother and I was the child. She started humming and she traced her picture with her right index finger.

"Nyla, you don't know what you're talking about," I said sitting in a chair next to the bed as I wiped my tears.

"Are you ever going to be honest with me mom? You know what I'm capable of...I saw the truth already when I touched your hand," Nyla said in between humming then she looked up at me and shrugged her shoulders.

"Who purchased a phone for you?" I asked changing the subject.

"Tit for tat, huh?" Nyla asked nonchalantly then she stuffed her notebook back inside her bag. "Uncle Mir...He came in my room one day and handed me the phone. He said it was a gift from my dad and a few hours later I started receiving phone calls from the prison. I knew Mir wasn't blind when he handed me that phone...I never said nothing to no one because one hand washes the other. I was allowed to speak to my dad secretly whenever he called so in return I kept my mouth closed and played along to Uncle Mir's antics. Was it foolish of me? Maybe so...But I didn't hurt anyone during the process but you did," Nyla said looking at me then she walked over to the closet placing her bookbag back inside.

I knew Nyla was covering for Mir but I didn't want to be the fool to accuse her without facts. My daughter was loyal and I will always commend her for that even though I don't agree with it.

"How did I hurt you baby?" I asked getting up from the chair and I walked over to her. Nyla looked at me up and down while pointing to my belly.

"The third night in prison you made a stick out of notebook paper, toothpaste and water...you let it get hard overnight. The next morning you took the stick hiding it underneath your clothes while you went to go take a shower. During your shower you used that stick to end your pregnancy...my sibling fell out of you onto that prison shower floor. You stayed in bed for the next few days and traded commissary for pain medication—" Nyla spoke in a deceiving way.

I mean I would never hurt my daughter but she knew too much...She just knew too fucking much and I wanted her to close her mouth!

"NYLA! STOP IT!" I yelled out covering my ears. I leaned back on the bed and continued to rock back and forth...That's the only way I knew how to deal with my anxiety. I took a deep breath and removed my hands from my ears, shit maybe it was time to face the truth. "What else was I supposed to do yo?! I already had you out here living with Aunt Tasha! I couldn't give her the responsibility of taking care of another child so yes I got rid of it," I said and Nyla jumped up and down.

"YOU WEREN'T THINKING ABOUT ME WHEN YOU MURDERED—" Nyla said pointing to me with tears in her eyes. I jumped up from the bed wiping my face and I stood my muthafuckin' ground. I was the fucking parent and she was the child...it was time she started acting like one.

"Watch your fucking mouth...I didn't murder anyone I wasn't even a month pregnant at the time. I couldn't live with doing five years in prison with two children Nyla. I'm sorry I just couldn't! That was a decision I will have to live with for the rest of my life but at the time it was necessary. The moment I got arrested I knew I couldn't take care of that baby growing in my belly. If I did go through with that pregnancy my child wouldn't even know my name...my face...my touch.

"That would be another relationship I had to repair because of my foolish decision. You think I don't care about what I did in that shower? I hated myself for years for doing that shit Nyla...I was mourning a loss that your father never knew about. You were being raised by someone else and that alone was hurting me so imagine having that baby, I would have to worry twice as much and I couldn't go through with it," I said telling the truth.

Nyla started pacing the bedroom floor back and forth wiping her face.

"That could have been my little brother or sister..." Nyla said balling up her fist.

I understood her frustration completely but I wish she would understand where I was coming from. I ran up to my daughter and I embraced her. Oh yeah! Nyla tried to break out of my arms a few times but I didn't let her go.

"What I did had nothing to do with you...I didn't want to be in prison struggling worrying about two kids. I will promise to listen to you and put you first from here on out. I love you wholeheartedly baby. You're my first love...And I couldn't imagine life without you. I don't know where life is going to take me but I promise I will never do that shit again I was just in a bad position in my life. Do you understand Nyla?" I asked holding her with my left arm and I wiped her beautiful face with my right hand. A few moments later Nyla finally nodded her head up and down. "Do you forgive me?" I asked curious and she smiled at me.

"I forgive you scrub," Nyla said kissing me on my cheek. We shared a moment of laughter together and that name was something I used to call Nyla before I went to prison...Amazing how she still remembers after five years. Once the smiling and the laughter stopped the room became quiet...It seemed small again even with my daughter in my arms. I looked down at her as she rubbed on my right arm.

"You said something about the Lopez club and silk sheets? What does that mean baby?" I asked and when the bedroom door opened up she jumped out my arms.

"Sorry to interrupt...Can I speak to you for a minute?" Angel asked peeking in the room without knocking first but this was his house so could I really complain about that?

Nyla gave me a kiss and walked over to the closet and I knew she was getting her bookbag. I closed the bedroom door and followed Angel into the hallway.

"I see your madre doesn't like black people, huh?" I asked leaning back on the hallway wall. I turned my head and I never noticed the picture in a gold frame hanging on the wall with four people. It was three Spanish boys which appeared to be Angel, JoJo and Sanchez. Then it was a Spanish girl which didn't look like Angel's mother, I just figured it was a female cousin because that couldn't be his sister...Angel said he only had two siblings which was JoJo and Sanchez.

"Nah, it's not like that...She was just a little drunk," Angel said. The way he looked at me held substance like he saw me for me. Reem loved me but he couldn't hold a conversation looking me in my eyes. Angel was different...His eyes danced with my brown eyes and it made me feel like a woman again.

"Well, that saying must be true then, huh?" I asked.

"What saying?" Angel asked with a straight face walking over to me biting his lip.

"It's always some truth when a drunk person speaks," I said.

"Chill out Kia...I will make her apologize to you," Angel said grabbing my right hand and I shrugged my shoulders.

"I'm not owed an apology Angel," I said and Angel licked his lips.

"I'm pretty sure she offended you though Kia," Angel said and I looked at myself up and down.

"I have thick skin...I shook it off the moment she said negro," I said and Angel stuffed his hands down in his pockets like he was uncomfortable. "So is what your mother said really true?" I asked.

"I already told you Mami she was drunk," Angel said I smirked and shook my head no.

"That's not what I'm talking about Papi," I said and I started blushing when I caught myself.

"Papi, huh?" Angel said getting cocky.

"I meant to say Angel..." I said smiling and Angel rubbed the left side of my cheek.

"Nah...Go ahead and say Papi I like when you call me that," Angel said.

"Your mother said you already have a child out here and she said it wasn't a newborn so she can't be talking about Charlie," I said and Angel looked as if he was about to break out in a sweat.

"Uh, huh—" like I said she's drunk...I have to take this call," Angel said hesitating to speak then he reached down in his pocket to pull his phone out while it was ringing.

"What time?" Angel asked putting the phone up to his ear then he distanced himself from me down the hall. I kept my eyes on him like I was infatuated by the type of nigga he was. I lowered my head when he turned around and caught me staring at him from behind. A few seconds later my phone starting ringing in my pocket.

"Hello?" I said putting the phone up to my right ear.

"Sis?" Mir said on the other end of the phone.

"Hey dad," I said playing it off when I see Angel end his call and head back in my direction.

"Dad? What the fuck are you talking about Kia...We don't even know our father," Mir said dumbfounded on the phone.

"What is it dad? I'm kind of busy right now," I said lying. I was just trying to play it cool cause Angel was back in my face.

"Are you role playing Kia? Cause I'm not with the incest shit girl this feels a bit weird," Mir said and he was aggravating me because his dumb ass wasn't catching on to what I was trying to do. Though I couldn't really blame Mir because I didn't even tell him about Angel yet...It was like I was playing both sides of the fence.

"NEITHER AM I DAD...WHAT DO YOU HAVE TO TELL ME?" I asked smiling at Angel as I raised my voice and rolled my eyes while being on the phone. Angel gave me some space and he pulled his phone back out walking down these huge hallways he owned.

"Um...I'm still a little confused but I need help with Charlie. She has been crying for the last two hours and I think she's running a fever. Sis I need you immediately...Aunt Tasha gets off in thirty minutes," Mir said confiding in me.

"I will be right there dad," I said hanging up the phone on him.

"Going somewhere?" Angel asked looking up at me and he put his phone back into his pocket.

"Mom!" I heard my beautiful child yell out the word that made my heart skip a beat. I turned around and I saw Nyla smiling rushing towards me but Chino came out of nowhere and she bumped into him falling down to the floor.

"Whoa...Slow down kid!" Chino said helping Nyla up off the floor with his right hand. When I see the smile disappear off her face and her eyes roll to the back of her head I knew something was wrong. I ran over to her and Angel followed behind me to check on Nyla. "Are you okay?" Chino asked and Nyla let go off his hand immediately.

"That look..." Angel said with his mouth wide open.

"What look Angel?" I asked playing dumb.

"Uh Is Nyla, alright?" Angel asked shaking his head as he changed the subject.

"Yes...I'm going to lay her down she just hit her head," I said lying. Chino walked off but he just stared at Nyla and she kept her eyes on him. I grabbed Nyla's hand and walked into the bedroom. I locked the door and pulled Nyla into the closet so we could talk in private...I was too paranoid.

"What did you see baby?" I asked whispering. Nyla rubbed on her temple like her head was hurting her and I offered assistance to massage her temple.

"Chino..." Nyla said like she was out of breath and then she closed her eyes.

"What about Chino baby?" I asked grilling her.

"Chino is your fourth sibling mom," Nyla said opening up her eyes and she just stared at me.

—KASSANA WILSON

CHAPTER 18 KIA

"Kia...Can I come in?" Angel asked knocking on my bedroom door. I turned my head to look in the direction of the bathroom to make sure the door was closed. Nyla was in the tub relaxing, I think Nyla felt like she had too much weight on her shoulders trying to help me through situations that I was getting my own self in. I had a heart to heart with my only child and ran her a hot bath. I didn't have much money...So maybe this would make up for it.

"It's your house Angel you can do as you please," I said turning to look back at the bedroom door. My wet curly hair was falling down my shoulders while I was wrapped in a pink towel. Angel walked in the bedroom closing the door behind him as he rubbed his right hand on his chest. He appeared to be stunned by my appearance like a cat had his damn tongue.

"This is your home too Kia," Angel said reassuring me. He looked at me up and down while shaking his head no and turned to the side. "Damn, I didn't mean to intrude I can wait in the hallway—" Angel said pointing back to the door so he could leave out but I disagreed.

"Angel, it's fine come here," I said flirting in a sense. Was my daughter in the next room? Yes she was but damn I was feining to be craved by a nigga...THIS NIGGA. Who I adored but was terrified of also. I wanted to take Angel's breath away without even touching him and while I was standing in this huge bedroom just wrapped in a towel I was accomplishing the goal. It felt amazing but damn I wanted more...I wanted to feel goose bumps on my skin. I wanted a nigga to give me a compliment when I least expected it.

"You're putting on clothes I don't want to make you feel uncomfortable—" Angel said and this time he turned completely around giving me respect but I didn't want that shit! I was now staring at his back but I wanted him to look at me and see that I wasn't perfect but damn I was trying.

"You never seen a naked woman before?" I asked dropping the towel down to my ankles. Only thing I was feeling guilty about is my daughter walking in here and seeing what I was doing but other than that I was completely fine putting on this performance.

"Are you being funny?" Angel asked with his back turned to me.

"It's just a question...So turn around and look at me," I said and a few seconds later Angel turned around and his Spanish face turned red like he chewed on something hot...Or maybe it was just my naked ass standing in front of him.

"Uh...Damn, Kia this is kind of—" Angel said wiping his forehead then he turned his head so we wouldn't make eye contact. I reached down on the bed, grabbing my panties and I slipped it on.

"Kind of what? Awkward?" I asked smirking at him. Angel looked at me then he shared a smile and shook his head up and down. I picked up my bra and shirt and slipped it on. Angel stood back in a distance just admiring me...It felt like heaven.

"I just came in here to check on Nyla...How is she feeling?" Angel asked. I sat down on the bed grabbing my pants and put them on.

"She's feeling much better, I put her in a hot bath to relax her a bit" I said pointing to the bathroom. As soon as I stood up Angel walked over to me and placed a mellow kiss on my lips that made my pussy wet.

"What was that for?" I asked biting down on my bottom lip. Angel stepped back and stared at me like I was a math problem.

"I'm still trying to figure it out..." Angel said. I slipped my feet into my boots and I sat back down on the bed.

"Can I ask you something?" I asked.

"I'm all ears mi amor," Angel said waving at me.

"In the hallway when Nyla was looking at Chino...You said something about that look in her eyes, what did you mean by that?" I asked confused. I just didn't want Angel to know the truth about Nyla...I wanted to keep that life as far away from him as possible. Angel shrugged his shoulders and rubbed his hands together.

"Uh...She just appeared to be distressed," Angel spoke nervously.

"It seems like you saw that look of distress in her eyes before, have you?" I asked concerned and he came over and sat down next to me on the bed.

"Nah...Nah I mean—Is it hot in here or is it just me?" Angel asked getting up from the bed and he wiped his forehead again.

"I think it may be both," I said chuckling but Angel didn't think my joke was funny. I changed the subject and took a deep breath. "Chino seems like a good nigga—" I said and Angel looked at me and smirked.

"You like my security now, Kia?" Angel asked jokily but if he knew what I knew...Then that nigga wouldn't of said it.

"Nah...Nothing like that I'm just an observer and he seems to be loyal to you. How long have you known Chino for?" I asked trying to get more information on my fourth sibling.

"For about five years...I took him under the wing when he was sixteen years old," Angel said biting the inside of his mouth. I got up from the bed and started pacing the bedroom floor out of tenseness.

"Five years, huh? So that means he must know your mother too, right? Did you ever get acquainted with his mom?" I asked and Angel just balled up his face at me.

"Why are you so curious about my security guard Kia?" Angel asked stuffing his hands down in his pockets.

"Uh, just starting conversation...That's all," I said lying and now I knew I had to take a different route because this wasn't going to be easy. I heard the vibration of my phone going off on the dresser. I walked over to it and it was a message from Mir telling me I needed to come over right now. "Fuck" I said under my breath putting my phone down in my pocket.

"What's wrong?" Angel asked concerned.

"I just have an emergency right now...I have to leave out but I won't be too long," I bent down grabbing Nyla's Uggs and I knocked on the bathroom door before entering.

When Angel saw that I was going into the bathroom he moved back towards the dresser so he wouldn't see anything. I respected that.

"Nyla come here baby put on your boots we have to go," I said winking at her and she nodded her head up and down. Nyla was dressed in her pajamas but she was standing at the sink brushing her teeth.

My phone went off again and it was Mir. I exhaled deeply and put the phone back into my pocket entering the bedroom.

"Is that your dad blowing you up again?" Angel asked and this nigga caught me by surprised that I was completely confused.

"Huh? My dad?" I asked dumbfounded. I grabbed my car keys off the dresser and snapped my fingers so Nyla would come on.

"Wasn't you speaking to your father on the phone in the hallway?" Angel asked raising his right eyebrow.

"Yeah, yeah...He's in a nursery home and his nurse just contacted me saying it was urgent that I get down there," I said waving him off lying. I had to come up with something quick to cover my ass.

"What nursery home is he currently living in? I donate to every one in the city and I may know him," Angel said and my heart sunk to the bottom of my stomach.

"I'm not too familiar with the name I only been there once before—" I said lying. Truth was I didn't know what nursery home it was because I didn't know my damn father...None of my siblings did. Good thing the attention was off of me when Nyla entered the bedroom.

"Nyla, how are you feeling? You took a hard fall in the hallway" Angel asked looking at Nyla and she just looked at him with a blank face.

"I'm feeling much better than you..." Nyla said in a smart tone.

"Nyla, what is your problem?" I asked looking at her. Angel opened up the door to leave out and we followed behind him.

"It's all good Kia...Girls will be girls," Angel said.

"Niggas will be niggas," Nyla said and my mouth dropped. My daughter was only ten I didn't want her to have that mindset throughout life and I don't know what I could do to change it.

Angel was leading us down the stairs and I gave a look of concern to my child. Once we hit the front door to leave out Nyla opened up her mouth again. "You know you were wrong Angel" Nyla said I didn't know what she was talking about but I wanted her to stop. I think Nyla would say anything when it came to Angel because I wasn't with her father anymore.

"That's enough Nyla...Go to the car and wait for me inside I will be right there," I said. Nyla shrugged her shoulders and walked over to the car. I walked down off the porch and Angel started talking.

"Kia?" Angel said my name. I stopped in my tracks and looked at him. "Is there something about Chino that I should know about?" Angel asked stuffing his hands into his pockets and my heart was beating so fast I felt like Angel could hear it.

"Why are you asking me that?" I asked.

"Yes or no?" Angel asked grinning.

"I will see you later," I said disregarding his question. Angel turned around to walk back into the house.

"Make sure you tell me the name of the nursery home when you come back and tell your father I said hello," Angel said and it was something...It was something about the way he said that shit that made the hair on the back of my neck stand up. My phone started ringing again as I headed to my car and I pulled it out.

"I'm on my way...I can't talk right now," I said with the phone up to my right ear. I sat in my driver's seat and started up the car.

"Kia, Kia, Kia..." Mir sounded like a scared child...I remember this a few times before when we were young kids. Every birthday Mir would get toys, bikes and video games but the little nigga wasn't intrigued by that shit. You know? You give a muthafucka that shit now they would stay in their room all day and play but not Mir...Not my brother he was different. He started asking for animals like cats, turtles and dogs but they never lasted with Mir. I always wondered why every animal he received disappeared within a week until one day I walked into his room to tell him dinner was ready. Mir was doing open heart surgery on the dog he got for his birthday but he wasn't using the right utensils.

He had blades and duct tape. My mouth dropped when I walked into his room and he started panicking when he got caught. The dog was bleeding out all over his bedroom floor, I asked him why did he do it and he said it was an accident. Mir said his dog was broken and he was trying to put him back together but the look he gave me you could tell this nigga enjoyed having victims. I helped him bury the dog so he wouldn't get his ass whooped by our mom. The way he is panicking on this phone right now...Is the same way he sounded when he murdered them animals but he never got caught.

"I know Mir I said I was coming," I said rushing to get off the phone. I made a U-turn while he was yelling in my ear.

"SOMETHING HAPPENED!" Mir started screaming into the phone.

"What the fuck are you saying right now?" I asked confused. Nyla looked at me and started shaking her head.

"Charlie...Charlie isn't breathing!" Mir screamed into the phone. "It was an accident, I swear—" Mir tried to convince me but I didn't even accuse him of anything YET. It is kind of crazy how this nigga keeps having accidents all of a sudden. Before I could leave out the gate a truck pulled in and blocked me from exiting.

"Who the fuck is this?" I asked putting the phone on my lap. Even without the phone on my ear I could still hear Mir crying and panicking on the phone. The lights of this truck was beaming into my car that me and Nyla had to raise our hands over our eyes to see.

"Bitch! Where is he at?!" Someone yelled out swinging my driver's side door open but I couldn't see who it was until I turned my head.

"Don't you see my daughter in here muthafucka? And didn't I tell your Mexican ass to watch your mouth when you speak to me?" I asked looking at Sanchez.

"Tell the truth before I tell my brother! WHERE THE FUCK IS HE AT?!" Sanchez asked grabbing me by my shirt. I pushed him off of me and balled up my face.

"Kia I need you..." Mir said sobbing into the phone.

"Where is who nigga? I don't know who you're talking about," I said truthfully.

"Something is about to happen mom..." Nyla said rubbing her temple.

"Reem...He was released from prison two days ago!" Sanchez yelled out to me with his veins popping out on his forehead.

CHAPTER 19 MIR

"MIR IS SHE BREATHING?!" I looked down and Kia was yelling through the speaker phone. I looked over at Charlie's small body stretched out on the center of my bed and she wasn't responding to me.

"I don't know—I don't know Kia!" I yelled out panicking. I started pacing my bedroom back and forth, I wiped my forehead and didn't notice how much I was sweating. I could even feel the sweat dripping on my back.

"What the fuck do you mean you don't know Mir?!" Kia yelled out again through the speaker phone. "Did you try giving your daughter CPR?!" Kia asked and the tone of her voice was making me overthink consequences. I stopped in my tracks and walked over to my daughter.

"I'm not sure if I did it right Kia," I said breathing heavy as I wiped my forehead off.

"You did CPR on them animals you split open when we were younger...But you can't do the same to your own child, your own flesh and blood?" Kia asked but you could tell it was some attitude mixed with disappointment in her voice.

"I call you to ask for help and you bring up my past muthafucka?" I asked looking down at my phone as I balled up my face.

"You need to call 911 Mir I'm only a few minutes away," Kia said and I couldn't wait until she arrived here in a taxi cab.

"I can't fucking call the cops! Damn, don't you listen to anything I fucking say Kia or do you just worry about yourself? If I call the cops them muthafuckas will put two and two together about Bella's murder and the truth about Bella having a baby will be surfaced. I'm too deep in to get caught up Kia and you know it," I said dropping down to my knees and I crawled closer to my bed...Afraid to look up because I didn't want to come face to face with reality.

"Listen, Mir in order to save Charlie you need to call 911 or try to give her CPR or your child will not make it. SAVE HER LIFE NOW!" Kia yelled out. I took a deep breath and swallowed the dried up spit in my mouth. I used my index and middle finger giving Charlie compressions in the center of her chest. Her eyes were still closed but she was barely breathing right now.

"I got a pulse...I got a pulse Kia, now what the fuck am I supposed to do?" I asked jumping up off the bed. Charlie's chest would pump up and down slowly every few minutes.

"Put Charlie in the recovery position," Kia said. I walked back over to my child and I did as I was told. "What happened anyway?" Kia asked. I grabbed the phone taking it off speaker and held it up to my right ear. I knew I had to think fast in order to save myself.

"I caught Aunt Tasha harming Charlie yo..." I said lying and shit became so quiet on the phone.

"WHAT?!" Kia yelled out.

"I came in my room and she was holding Charlie's face down until she passed out...Why would she do that to my fucking daughter?!" I yelled out trying to put on a phenomenal performance like I was receiving the academy award winner for best actor.

"That's odd Mir," Kia said like she didn't believe me.

"What's odd Kia?" I asked fidgeting with my right hand in my pocket.

"When you initially called me the first time YOU SAID that it was just an accident like you did something to Charlie," Kia said and my heart sunk to my belly.

"Uh—Uh, I mean I was just trying to cover for Aunt Tasha but I knew I would feel much better after telling you the truth," I said lying and exhaling to give the impression that what I was saying was solid.

The truth was I couldn't stop lying if I wanted to...I was the type of nigga that was too afraid of consequences but continued to react no matter where life took me. I wonder if I will receive a life lesson from the shit that I'm doing and the pain and heartbreak that I'm putting the people that I love through. Kia told me she needed me but it was like when I needed her where the fuck was she at?! The anxiety I was overwhelmed with was nothing compared to the secrets that I wanted to keep hiding. I was ducking off in the house so much because I knew this nigga Angel was after me.

I was too afraid to walk these streets until I knew that it was safe so I waited, waited and waited until the last minute. Usually JoJo would drop off anything I needed but the time was going on twenty-four hours and my best friend was still nowhere to be found...It wasn't like JoJo. I felt like Kia knew something but her telling me the truth about the one person that I trusted with my life would having me cutting my own flesh and blood up like my old animals *(I'm talking about Kia)*. I was afraid of what I was going to do without JoJo and I wasn't talking about no homo shit...

Nah y'all muthafuckas know I don't rock like that. I meant I'm not sure if I knew how to function without him if it came down to it. That nigga could tell me to jump and I would say, *"How High,"* without a doubt. I didn't have shit to give Charlie but a damn pacifier. I ran out of formula, diapers and wipes. Charlie was beginning to go on two hours with her crying and the headache I was receiving was unbearable. I just wanted her to stop crying and I'm not sure if she was hungry, sleepy or needed her diaper changed but at that moment I'm going to be honest. I

DID NOT WANT MY CHILD ANYMORE...I WANTED HER GONE. I reached for my pillow on my bed and held it down on her face and small fragile body until she didn't move. Once I saw that she was laying still on my bed I panicked. It was like I left my body when I was making her suffer. I came up with a lie and said that Aunt Tasha harmed Charlie but she was working...

I was a narcissist and I couldn't help the lies coming out of my mouth. Was I sorry for what I did to my daughter? I was only sorry of getting arrested if I got caught but she's alive and breathing I mean barely but it is what it is. I must admit...It felt good and if it came down to it I would do it again. My daughter isn't safe with me. My heart and my mental state knows that.

"God gave you another chance...You need to find out what your purpose is before someone finds it for you Mir," Kia said hanging up the phone but I didn't know what the fuck she meant by that.

I stuffed my phone into my pocket and grabbed my black shades. I looked back at Charlie still laying on the bed with her beautiful eyes still shut. I ran out my room and went to Aunt Tasha's bedroom but her door was locked. I was trying to find some perfume that I could rub on Charlie so Kia would believe my story...If she didn't before. I put my shades on and went downstairs. My breathing was becoming more and more intense. Aunt Tasha would leave a bottle of perfume on the kitchen table so she could spray herself quickly a few times before heading to work. I entered the kitchen and before I could search for it Aunt Tasha came in through the back door so I had to act like a blind nigga again.

"What the fuck is that noise?" Aunt Tasha asked walking in putting her purse on the table. I didn't reveal my secret to her yet so I just stretched my hands out like I was looking for something. Ya know? Playing stupid to the bullshit. I heard Charlie crying in a distance and I was just praying to God that she would just shut the fuck up...Before I suffocate her again and this time I wasn't going to revive her.

"What noise? I don't hear anything—" I said lying.

"It sounds like a baby crying," Tasha said looking up at the ceiling so she could hear better...My room was right on top of the kitchen. I knew I had to think quick so I wouldn't get caught up in this bullshit.

"That's my television in my room...I have the volume up loud," I said lying. Aunt Tasha looked at me up and down while grinning. She pulled a chair from under the table and sat down in the seat. I reached out for a chair and even though I wasn't really struggling to find stability she was smiling watching me.

"Have you seen Jada?" Aunt Tasha asked. She put her left foot on her right thigh kicking off her nurse shoe and she began to rub her own foot. That's when I noticed a bandage wrapped around her right hand but I couldn't speak on it because then she would know the truth.

"Seen Jada?" I asked dumbfounded pulling out a seat as I sat down and thank God the crying of Charlie stopped but why all of a sudden?

"My fault Mir...Let me rephrase that because it's obvious you can't see shit. Have you heard Jada's voice around here lately?" Aunt Tasha asked being funny and I shrugged my shoulders.

"Should I have?" I asked being calm because I wasn't going to let this bitch get me out of character.

"It's been too fucking quiet and I haven't heard a peep from her in a few days...There has not been any reports of heroin overdoses in the hospital so maybe her little ass is dead in an alleyway somewhere," Aunt Tasha said stuffing her left foot back into her nurse shoe.

"I told you before to watch your mouth when you speak about my sister Aunt Tasha," I said and she started chuckling.

"Or what muthafucka?! What can you possibly do to me? I say what the fuck I want in my damn house. It seems like I'm the only one concerned about your feined out sister anyway...Shit is disgusting, I don't know how Jada became a product of her environment," Aunt Tasha said shaking her head and I jumped up from my seat hitting the table.

"YOU'RE NOT THE ONLY PERSON THAT CARES ABOUT JADA!" I said pointing in the opposite direction on purpose.

"So I'm guessing you care Mir? Your ass can't even see nigga...Your sister has been out of prison for a few days now and I see that she's already driving around in a luxury car while me and my Toyota are paying the mechanic's shop a visit every other week—" Aunt Tasha said getting up from the table and she reached inside her purse grabbing her Newport's.

"Wait, Kia is driving around in a luxury car?" I asked. I reached back for the chair sitting down confused. I knew Kia had some type of transportation but how the fuck did she bounce back that quick? Yeah, she was definitely keeping secrets from me.

"Nigga, you heard me when I said it so why would you ask me again? I guess she's up to old habits again robbing muthafuckas out of their items and money...It's only a matter of time before Nyla is back living under my roof again," Aunt Tasha said shaking her head. She walked over to the stove and lit her cigarette up again inhaling deeply.

"How many times we have to tell you that this house isn't yours?" I asked smirking. She exhaled and nodded her head up and down.

"You want to bet? How about I just put your ass out and maybe then we can see who house it is handicap," Aunt Tasha said grinning at me. She took a step towards me then the crying began again. "What the fuck is that crying noise?" Aunt Tasha asked looking up at the ceiling and I could tell she was getting a bit suspicious so I walked into the living room to block her from going upstairs and seeing Charlie.

"Uh, fuck—" I said when I heard the cries getting louder. I stood in front of her and she exhaled deeply trying to get passed me.

"Get out of my way so I can go up my stairs nigga!" Aunt Tasha yelled out. I turned my head and I see some Spanish nigga at the back door looking through the window.

"Someone is at the door," I said and Aunt Tasha looked at the back door then she stepped away from me with the cigarette still in her hand.

"Which is true but he didn't knock on my door..." Aunt Tasha said looking at me questionably and it was too late to try and cover my ass. She exhaled her cigarette smoke and just stared back at me like she was thinking about something while walking over to the door.

Then she reached down on the handle opening it up and walked out on the porch. I walked into the kitchen so I could hear what they were talking about. I leaned against the wall to look out the window and the guy was pure Spanish wearing a suit with a badge on his hip...I figured this nigga was a detective. So much shit was running through my head I thought he was coming to ask me questions about Bella until I saw he kissed Aunt Tasha on her right cheek.

"What happened to your hand Tasha?" The detective asked her.

"I got cut at the hospital by another nurse...She was rushing down the hall too fast with tools and didn't see me in front of her," Aunt Tasha said looking down at her right hand then she put the cigarette back into her mouth. "What are you doing here? You know you're not suppose to be at my house," Aunt Tasha said blowing out smoke.

"I received a phone call from someone about reopening your sister's case," The detective said and Aunt Tasha just stared at him like he was fucking stupid.

"What?" Aunt Tasha asked dumbfounded. "That case can't be reopened it's closed...Me and you both know that," Aunt Tasha said pointing to him and he just bit the inside of his mouth.

"Not quite," The detective said.

"What the fuck is that supposed to mean?" Aunt Tasha asked tossing her cigarette so she could focus on this conversation.

"I tried to be as *convincing* as I could on the phone to let this person know that no matter what we couldn't reopen up the case. But once new evidence touches my police station we have to make that case our first priority even if it's closed...It gets reopened because the evidence doesn't lie," The detective said.

Aunt Tasha tapped her right hand against her thigh like she was nervous which was something I didn't understand. We knew it was an accidental but the way she was reacting her body language was telling a different story right now.

"What was the phone call about exactly?" Aunt Tasha asked whispering.

"To prove that your sister's death wasn't accidental," The detective said.

"What the fuck...What's the name of the person that called this tip in?" Aunt Tasha asked worried.

"I'm not too sure, my mind was preoccupied with something else but when I go back to the station I will trace the cell phone," The detective said trying to reassure her.

"Your mind was preoccupied with *something else,* huh?" Aunt Tasha asked bothered.
"Does anyone know the truth about you and your sister?" The detective asked.

"As far as—" Aunt Tasha stopped and she rubbed her hand on her pussy...And he quickly nodded his head up and down. I wondered what that was all about but I knew for a fact they were speaking in code.

"Nah...That secret is kept hidden," Aunt Tasha said shaking her head no.

"I think you just made a mistake," The detective said and Aunt Tasha raised her eyebrows.

"Which was what nigga?" Aunt Tasha asked. The detective reached down to touch her right hand that was covered with the bandage.

"What's the name of the nurse that cut your hand at the hospital?" The detective asked her.

"Teka," Aunt Tasha said without hesitation.

"FUCK!" The detective yelled out and now he was the one that was starting to panic.

"What's wrong?" Aunt Tasha asked confused.

"I don't want you to be concerned—" The detective said putting his hands up to calm her down.

"Well, it's a little too late for that—" Aunt Tasha said.

"Chill the fuck out I got this...I'm trying to locate my son he's been missing all day let me get everything sorted out and I will give you a call," The detective said to Aunt Tasha. He stepped down off the porch and she followed behind him. I heard something in the living room but the conversation between these two muthafuckas was so intriguing...I guess I wasn't the only one with secrets.

"I don't know why me mentioning Nurse Teka spooked you in some way but you just remember that if I go down then so do you muthafucka...I know what you did so don't forget that," Aunt Tasha said poking the detective in his chest.

I heard another noise and I leaned up off the wall and I saw that the front door was wide open which was fucking confusing to me. I closed the front door shut and ran up the stairs. My closet door was wide open, Jada's blood was still on my wall and floor but she was gone and so was my fucking child!

"WHAT THE FUCK!" I yelled out. I turned to run back down the stairs. "No, no, no, no..." I said panicking more than I was before. I must have been running so fast because I bumped into someone and fell back against the stairs.

"I thought you was blind nigga?" I heard the familiar voice in a distance. I looked up and it was Reem...No one told me that this muthafucka was home.

CHAPTER 20 TEKA

"Girl, why don't you just be honest with the nigga? Me and you been through this while you were transitioning..." Zori said fixing the white sheets on the hospital bed. I was refilling the top cabinets with small, medium and large gloves.

"Well, now shit is different Zori," I said without looking at her.

"What do you mean by that?" Zori asked. She spoke like she was confused on the shit I just said when it was clear as day.

"Venting to you about my transitioning is reassuring...Reassuring to the fucking point where I covered my tracks and I didn't worry about what I was doing behind Sanchez's back. But now a bitch like me is worried and I think I have every right to be," I said with a straight face. I closed the cabinets and turned around to face her.

"So what's the problem now Teka?" Zori asked patting the bed down with her right hand. I looked down at the black gloves covering both her hands then I looked up at her and balled up my face.

"The fucking problem is that you're NOT the only person that knows my secret!" I yelled out then I stopped and took a deep breath. I had to remember that this was still my job and I had to keep my composure.

"You told someone else that you're a man?" Zori asked with her left eyebrow raised. I looked out the room and ran up to close the curtains shut so no one would get curious about our conversation and listen in on it.

"First of all bitch watch your mouth...I'm not a man, anymore. I guarantee that I'm more woman than three nurses in this unit put together," I said as stern as I could but while whispering. Zori thought her little joke was funny but if I popped her ass upside her head how funny would shit be then?!

"You still have a dick though, don't you Teka?" Zori asked looking me up and down. I exhaled deeply and went over to the counter leaning back against it. Me and Zori were still on the clock but I just needed a muthafucka to vent too right now.

"Is the sky blue?" I asked being sarcastic.

This chick really hesitated to answer my question like she was thinking of what response she was going to give me first. Zori nodded her head up and down and took her black gloves off tossing them into the trash next to the hospital bed. "Alright then bitch...You just answered your own question. Some woman—" I said and Zori ignorant ass cut me off to speak.

"So a woman confronted you about your secret?" Zori asked and I shook my head no.

"Nah...It was the woman's daughter—" I said and Zori wiped her hands off on her pink scrubs.

"How the fuck would a child know that?" Zori asked and I started to scratch my neck for a quick second.

"Zori?" I asked dumfounded.

"Yeah Teka girl...Wassup?" Zori asked without looking at me.

"I said the woman's daughter...I never said if it was a child, teenager or if she was damn near grown. So how did you know I was referring to a little girl?" I asked confused and suddenly the room curtain came flying open.

It was Nurse Libby...Some Italian bitch that never thought she could do any wrong. She could tell you that 10+11=44 and if you disagreed she would rip you apart just to prove a point. Her ass done got into it with several patients in this hospital and been on thin ice but do you think she stopped skating yet? Fuck out of here...The board called her in to talk about possibly terminating her if she had another incident...And let's just say her ass ain't leaving this hospital any time soon.

"Nurse T?" Nurse Libby asked. She had the curtain in her right hand looking at me and Zori like we were doing something wrong. Little shit intimidated Zori so she quickly walked over to the sink to wash her hands like she was doing work.

"Yes?" I said and the look on my face was screaming annoyance. Zori turned off the sink water, grabbing two paper towel sheets.

"I have to go...I need to check on my patients," Zori said walking passed me and Nurse Libby.

"Wait, wait...Zori come back here," I said going after her but Nurse Libby stepped in front of me letting Zori get away. I stepped back and just balled up my face so the bitch knew that she was getting on my nerves.

"Let Zori go do her job...There is a detective waiting to speak with you up front," Nurse Libby said. I moved the curtain out the way and left out of the unoccupied room.

"Did he say what he wanted to talk to me about?" I asked and Nurse Libby followed behind me.

"I didn't ask...It's not my business to ask questions." This prissy bitch said folding her arms across her chest. She walked like she had a stick stuck up her ass.

"Well, aren't you Ms. Goody two shoes? All y'all nurses are always in someone else's business but as soon as a muthafucka waves their badge...Suddenly it's not, 'YoUR BUSineSs." I said with a little humor in my voice but she didn't think it was funny. "What the fuck happened to the nurse code around here?" I asked and she shrugged her shoulders.

"Well, maybe you wouldn't have to worry about cops if only you kept yourself out of trouble" Nurse Libby said smirking as we continued walking to the desk.

"You're filled with fucking assumptions, huh?" I asked and she tapped me on the arm. I looked to my right and I see a Spanish detective with a tooth pick hanging out his mouth.

"I will tell you what...If the conversation looks like it's getting too heated I will pull you away and just say your patients are waiting on you...I'll think about it I wouldn't want to be a sinner like you," Nurse Libby said pointing to the detective then she walked away chuckling. I started shaking my head because I couldn't stand that bitch.

"Can I help you?" I asked clearing my throat.

"Nurse Teka?" The detective said taking the tooth pick out of his mouth. He turned around to throw it out and then came back over to me. "Can we step inside this room for a second? This conversation won't be too long. You're married, huh? What's the name of the lucky guy that put that ring on your finger?" The detective asked checking out my wedding ring. I stuffed my hands down in my pockets and took a deep breath. I started walking to a vacant room and once he entered in behind me I closed the curtain shut.

"Sanchez...My husband name is Sanchez," I said and the look he gave me sent chills up my spine.

What muthafuckin' cop shows up at your job to ask you about your wedding ring?! I don't know what it was about him...But he looked like he was trying to figure me out in a way. Me and Sanchez got married in our living room...We always told his brothers that we went to Vegas and got married but that was a lie. I didn't want to go through the process of Angel taking control of the wedding which meant hiring a make up artist, someone helping me get dress and etc.

I was too afraid of my secrets being revealed like the make up artist seeing a feature on my face that only a man has. I didn't want anyone helping me get dress and my dick fucks around and make an appearance. I just told Sanchez that I was dealing with insecurities which in a way I was but I decided to handle everything on my own. I paid this lowlife to make our fake marriage certificate because my real name isn't changed yet for personal reasons.

He also got me a fake driver's license and a passport. My mother did not support me transitioning but as time went on she accepted it. She asked me to NEVER change my name because she named me after my grandfather that passed away and I made a promise to her that I would never touch what she created me with. The only thing that was off limits was my name, shit I was taking full advantage of my plastic surgeries.

Next surgery I needed was to remove my penis but when it came down to my operation I always reneged because I actually like my dick. I honestly think I was bigger than my own husband but shit that's neither here or there. If it wasn't for the promise I made to my mother life would have been different for me...I just wished she would've asked me this BEFORE I married Sanchez. *Now* my husband doesn't even know he's married to a man.

Oh, for y'all nosey muthafuckas that's worried about how I'm working at the hospital as a female...Let's just say I have the connect. If you need the hook up don't be afraid to hit me up just don't tell my husband about me sis!

"Listen, your other detectives came down here already for Bella's case—" I said. I forgot I was getting questioned because I was so stuck on my past.

"Speaking of Bella...Who was in the room when she gave birth?" The detective asked.

"Dr. Jacobs but he transferred to another hospital in Pennsylvania. Nurse Humia was also in the room but she passed away a few weeks ago from lung cancer," I said being honest.

"How close was Dr. Jacobs, Nurse Humia and Nurse Bella?" The detective asked but something made me smirk. Usually when detectives come to ask questions they either have another partner with them OR they pull out a notepad and pen to write everything down to, *"help the case."*

"They were pretty close I guess...They always ate lunch together. If you walked into the room while they were speaking they would stop completely until you left out and they always met up in the parking lot behind the hospital," I said walking over to the cabinets in the room to closed them.

"You worked around Bella when she was allegedly pregnant?" The detective asked and I turned to look at him. I raised my right eyebrow and exhaled deeply.

"Allegedly?" I asked confused. "We worked different shifts sometimes but I would see her when I was coming into work or vice versa," I said and he walked around the hospital room tracing the bed with his right index finger.

"Did you actually see her belly when she was pregnant?" The detective asked but I didn't understand what he was getting at.

"What is this about detective?" I asked biting down on my bottom lip.

"Someone created a fake birth certificate for Bella...I'm not too sure that this child on record is actually her own flesh and blood. I don't know if it was Dr. Jacobs or Nurse Humia but isn't it a coincidence that they disappeared as soon as Bella was out of the picture?" The detective asked me smiling.

"Nurse Humia had lung cancer...She didn't choose to disappear" I said giving him more attitude than before.

"Maybe not...I guess the guilt was eating at her, what you think?" The detective asked me but none of that was any of my business.

"I think I need to get back to work," I said walking towards the curtain to leave out.

"Before you go Teka can I just get the complete spelling of your first and last name? I also need your birthday," The detective said and I'll be damn NOW he pulls out his pen and notepad for information on me.

"FOR WHAT? I DIDN'T DO ANYTHING," I said getting loud turning around to face him.

"Just following up on my investigation," The detective said smirking.

"I wasn't involved in anything so I refuse to give you what you're asking for. I have to get back to work," I said pulling the curtain open and he cleared his throat following me into the hallway of the hospital.

"Teka...Did you cut another nurse last night?" The detective asked and I exhaled deeply and slapped my right hand against my thigh.

"Oh, come on! It was an accident!" I yelled out and I calmed down when I saw people looking at me...Even Nurse Libby who saw that I clearly needed her help.

"Did you help clean up the blood?" The detective asked with the notepad and pen still in his hand.

"Why?" I asked balling up my face.

"Nurse Tasha, right? What did you do with her blood after you were done cleaning it up?" The detective asked stepping closer to me. Actually, Kia told me her Aunt Tasha worked at the hospital and she also asked me to test her blood for a favor. I don't know what the test was for because I didn't ask questions but since Kia knew my secret I had to go along with this shit. I pretended that I was rushing to a room and Tasha ran into me cutting her right hand. I offered to clean up her wound and during my plan I took her blood to the lab like I was told...But my question is why the fuck was this so important to the detective? I know Tasha wasn't pressing charges on me for a little ass cut.

"Wouldn't you like to know," I said smirking and someone touched me on my lower back.

"Nurse Teka? You have a patient waiting for you in the next room" Nurse Libby said pointing to room 206 on the left.

"See? I have to go..." I said moving around him to get to the room. Nurse Libby smiled and walked back to her station.

"Teka...Please don't make this shit hard on yourself," The detective said.

I entered the room and closed the curtain shut. I walked straight over to the file on the counter without looking at my patient...I was going to be completely honest I wasn't even focus as I should be right now.

"How are you doing? I will be your nurse for the evening...My name is Nurse—" I said opening up the tan folder and before I could finish reading I heard someone speak.

"Pablo?" The voice was familiar and raspy.

"Shay?" I said with my eyes wide open then closed the folder and threw it on top of the counter. "Uh, my name isn't Pablo anymore" I said whispering looking back at the curtain then I looked back at Shay. She was dressed in an all-black fitted suit.

"Clearly I can see that...I mean damn—" Shay said shaking her head and she hopped down off the hospital bed observing me.

"Why are you here?" I asked confused, I haven't seen this woman in fifteen years but I could see that nothing has changed.

"I get headaches on and off every day...Sometimes they go away and other times the pain increases," Shay said rubbing her temple. I rubbed my hands on my scrub uniform from being nervous because her eyes were glued on me and I still remember this look.

"I can schedule a MRI and we can go upstairs to the lab—" I said pointing to the hallway. Shay walked up to me and put my hand down to my side.

"I want something else," Shay said licking her lips.

"What is it that you want Shay?" I asked backing away from her.

"I want your big ass dick in my mouth like you used to do in high school...I bet I can make you bust in two minutes," Shay said rubbing her right hand on my private part and it caused me to jump.

"I'm married," I said as I shook my head no.

"You think I give a fuck about a ring? You think that's going to stop me? We were both in relationships in high school and you still continued to fuck me behind my boyfriend's back," Shay said. Every time she walked closer to me I stepped back.

"We aren't in high school anymore and we damn sure aren't teenagers...Things have changed," I said putting my foot down. Was I into niggas in high school? You damn right but I was popular and I played football. Shay was the cheerleader and I felt like my image would look better if I fucked around with her. Yes, I fucked Shay...She also could make my toes curl in seconds SO COULD HER BOYFRIEND.

"Are you ready to go partner?" Someone asked walking into the hospital room. It was the detective that was questioning me a few minutes ago.

"Yeah, my headache went away...Like I said it comes and goes..." Shay said winking at me. She put her hands on her hips and there it was her fucking gold badge. She was the partner of this muthafucka.

"By the way Teka..." The detective said and Shay was standing behind him smirking.

"What the fuck do you want now?" I asked shaking my head.

"Did you know that I'm the father of JoJo, Angel and Sanchez?" The detective said then he walked away. Damn...I never knew my husband's father was a fucking cop.

CHAPTER 21 REEM

"Nigga, help me up." Mir said laying back on the stairs. I looked to my left and the back door was open, from a distance it sounded like people outside talking but I didn't pay it too much mind. I turned my attention back to Mir and he extended his right hand out to me but his eyes were looking in the opposite direction.

"What you mean help you up? You can see nigga..." I said assuming and Mir sucked his teeth. His right hand was still reaching my way yet disappointed by my lack of help.

"Reem, if I could see then I wouldn't of asked you to help me up muthafucka. I gave you my word that I was blind damn you think I would lie about some shit like that?" Mir asked with some base in his voice. He started shaking his head, I hesitated at first but I didn't have all the facts so who the fuck was I to tell someone that they didn't have a disability. I heard the story about what happened to Mir when I was inside of prison...It wasn't my place to question that unless shit seemed sticky.

"My bad nigga...I'm just dealing with a lot. I will walk you upstairs to your room." I said grabbing his right hand. He stood up and I put his arm around my neck. I maneuvered for him to turn around so we could walk up the stairs.

"I would appreciate it Reem you know it's hard getting around the house when you don't have any help." Mir said and before we reached the first step he stopped me in my tracks. "Can you hand me my shades please? Shit boosts my confidence when I have them on." Mir said using his left hand to point around the floor signaling me that they fell around here somewhere. I removed his arm from around my neck searching around for the black shades. A second later I found them camouflaging and I put them on Mir's face. The moment I did that he started to smile...But it was a smile that made you think. Something was wrong with this nigga.

"Let me ask you something." I said. I grabbed Mir's arm again, placing it back around my neck and we walked up the steps. "Why were you running down the stairs like that if you can't see?" I asked and Mir used his left hand to scratch his face before answering my question.

"Running down the stairs? Uh...Oh, I thought I heard someone in my room. Don't get me wrong I'm not a scary muthafucka but the fact that I can't see it was kind of hard to confirm what I was hearing in my room...So my ass ran down the stairs." Mir said trying to laugh it off so I shared a chuckle or two with him.

"Have you seen Kia and my daughter Nyla?" I asked as we got to the top of the stairs. Mir removed his arm from around my neck and he stepped in front of me. He used his right hand to feel on the cold creek walls to get to his bedroom.

"Seen?" Mir asked confused and I didn't want him to take offense to what I was saying.

"My fault my nigga...Have you heard from them?" I asked following Mir to his bedroom.

"They pop up at the house sometimes—" Mir said and I reached my hand out cutting him off to speak.

"Wait, Kia and Nyla aren't staying here with y'all?" I asked confused. Kia didn't have any money so where the fuck was her and my daughter living at?

"Nigga, didn't you just hear me? THEY POP UP SOMETIMES. It's a challenge keeping up with them but I guess you knew that already." Mir said entering his room and I entered in behind him. I turned to my left and started to observe the little shit that I did see. Mir had his sneakers lined up from Nike, Jordan's down to his timbs. Funny how everything was in order down to the fucking color details. Mir sat down on his bed, I guess he imagined what I was doing because he was so quick to change the subject. "Does Kia know that you're out of prison?" Mir asked patting his right hand on his bed.

"What you think?" I asked getting smart then I stuffed my hands down in my pockets and looked around while standing in place. "Where is Tasha at?" I asked and Mir started smirking.

"Nigga, you and Tasha don't get along, why the fuck are you worried about where she's at?" Mir asked. Shit, if only he knew what I knew then he wouldn't question why I was so worried about her.

"Uh— Just making conversation...That's all." I said lying waving him off with my left hand. I smiled and walked forward a little bit when something caught my fucking eye. "Is that blood Mir?" I asked confused checking out the closet from a distance. Mir jumped up off his bed and started shaking his head back and forth but you could tell that this nigga was panicking.

"Where?" Mir asked. He used his right hand to maneuver his way to his closet. "Nah, uh...A friend of mine got Nyla a kitty for helping out around the house. Well, this muthafucka didn't tell me that he gave my niece a pregnant cat. Earlier, I came back in my room from getting something to drink and I hear this cat purring in my closet. The cat gave birth to three kittens and I guess that's where the blood came from, funny huh?" Mir asked breaking out in a sweat then he started laughing.

He pushed his glasses back on his face and closed the closet door so I wouldn't see the blood anymore.

"Where is the cat and kittens at?" I asked and he slapped his right hand on his thigh.

"Oh! My friend took them to the vet to make sure everything was copasetic and shit." Mir said waving me off then he walked over to his bed sitting down. It was pretty tensed in this room until outside noise interrupted us. "Who's outside blowing their horn?" Mir asked pointing around the room. I walked over to the window and saw that it was my cab honking his horn with his engine running.

"My cab...I'm about to go over to my mom's crib to get situated. Before I go let me ask you a quick question Mir." I said walking over to the door to leave out then I stopped in my tracks and turned around. "Do you know a nigga name Angel?" I asked and Mir wiped his forehead and stuttered.

"Uh— Angel? Nah, bro never heard a name like that since I was in kindergarten it was this kid in my science class that—" Mir tried to give me his childhood story that I didn't give two fucks about.

"While I was locked up, did you do something you weren't supposed to do? Something that could put Kia and my child in danger?" I asked. Mir stood up from the bed wiping his hands off on his pants.

"I'm not too sure I understand what you mean Reem, sorry." Mir said shrugging his shoulders.

"Just be honest with me my nigga." I said getting frustrated and my cab driver started beeping his horn again.

"How much trouble can a blind nigga get in? Let's be serious right now." Mir said pointing at himself while chuckling but what the fuck was so humorous right now?

"Did Kia ever mention Angel's name?" I asked wanting answers and he shook his head no.

"Kia knows my enemy?" Mir said something under his breath but he was mumbling so I didn't understand what he said completely.

"What Mir?" I asked balling up my face and he shook his head no.

"By the way Mir, my daughter is allergic to cats and I never said that blood was in your closet. You just assumed that it was." I said and I looked at Mir. He trembled just standing in place. I jogged down the stairs heading to the door. I noticed traces of blood on the floor throughout the front door and my gut was telling me that this blood didn't have shit to do with cats and kittens.

"3001 Lincoln drive..." I said hopping in the backseat of the yellow cab. He nodded his head and pulled off. I ran my hand down my face and just stared out the window.

"I know that look...That look of questions." The cab driver said looking at me through the mirror. I sat up in my seat and gave my attention to him.

"Excuse me nigga?" I asked balling up my face. He nodded his head up and down then continued to focus on the road.

"In the pit of our stomachs, we have that feeling that shit is about to get real but we just don't know exactly when. So we pace our self...We stress, we cry and most importantly we overthink until that time actually comes. We beat ourselves up trying to prevent a situation from happening when God blocks all that shit that we try so hard to be blind to. That's his way of showing us the truth...Even when it hurts. I was in a relationship with this beautiful black woman who was so good at hiding secrets from me. Everything was good until coming home every night turned into coming home every four or five nights. That's where my stress and overthinking kicked in at because I wanted to be blind to this shit ya know?

"I didn't want to think that she was cheating on me or treating me like an option. One night I pull up in my taxi to pick some niggas up from the club and I'm honking my horn. I would of pulled off but I needed every fare I could possibly get because somehow money was starting to disappear from out my crib. One of the niggas told me to stop beeping the horn and just pull into the alleyway and wait for a minute. I flashed my lights and there she was...The woman that could do no wrong in my eyes shooting up heroin in an alleyway with three muthafuckas that were old enough to be her damn father. That shit made me sick to my stomach that's when I realized not only was I an option...but I was an option because of drugs. Everything slowly started to make sense. The coming home every few days, money disappearing and I was blind to the shit." The cab driver said getting emotional.

He used his left hand to wipe his eye as he made a left turn. I watch the red numbers on the meter going up...And I was afraid of where this conversation was going with this stranger.

"Where is your shawty at now?" I asked concerned.

"To be honest...I wish I knew my nigga. I always leave the key under the mat just in case she ever wants to come home. I mean she comes and goes but she always appears when I'm out riding in my Taxi. I asked her how did she get hooked on to heroin and she said her brother introduced her to the drug. During her addiction she gave birth to my daughter. I didn't even know she was pregnant because the drugs stopped her growth but I was blessed even through her uncertain circumstances. You know I didn't judge her I just wanted my child." The cab driver said stopping at the red light ahead.

"Where is your daughter at now?" I asked. Talking to this nigga made me think about my own child Nyla.

"I can't track her down...Before I went to work one day she was pregnant then when I got home that night she told me that she gave birth already. I asked her where the baby was and she said she took our newborn baby to the hospital without my fucking permission. I went down to the hospital wanting to fight every muthafucka that came my way even the security guards but I still left out of there with no answers." The cab driver said.

"The hospital can't tell you anything?" I asked getting frustrated like this was my situation we were speaking on.

"Everybody covers for everybody in that facility and they will deny that my baby mom was ever pregnant. No one ever believes a drug addict, they basically laughed in my face. I got the cops involved but no surveillance video was found with my baby mom on the video so they dismissed my assumptions...I think them nurses in the hospital kidnapped my daughter." The cab driver said. Then he reached down for something.

A second later he flipped over a picture to show me through the clear window in between me and him. "This is my baby mom...Her name is Jada and she's addicted to heroin." The cab driver said.

CHAPTER 22 TEKA

"Baby?!" I yelled as I walked through the front door. I closed the all-white door behind me while locking it. I played with my tongue inside my mouth as I headed towards the kitchen. Around this time Sanchez would probably be walking around in the kitchen with his polo boxers on. I would always catch him eating a bowl of cereal or biting into a sandwich that contained too much mayonnaise. Too each his own, right? Who the fuck am I too judge?.

"Sanchez, baby where are you?" I asked I walked into the kitchen and Sanchez was no where to be found but my kitchen light was on then this muthafucka gets mad when the light bill comes. This is why the bill be so fucking high because he just enters rooms in the house without turning the fucking light off! Whew child, let me get back into character. I flicked the kitchen light off and proceeded to walk upstairs.

Even the damn hallway light was on and I bet you every dollar in my pocket Sanchez wasn't sleep he was either in the bed playing the game or watching television. I turned the hallway light off and opened up the bedroom door.

"So you didn't hear me calling you when I came in the house nigga?" I asked balling up my face. Sanchez sat up on the bed balling up his face. He had his PS4 controller in his right hand laying in the bed with his Polo boxers on. Now you see what I mean?! Why the fuck was all these lights on if you're in one room throughout the house?. Sometimes I didn't understand Sanchez logic...I was afraid that I would never understand it and that was a hard pill to swallow.

"The volume on the game was too loud—man, fuck that don't come home with all that attitude girl." Sanchez said pausing his game then he sat his remote down on the king size bed that we shared together. I kicked my crocs off my feet. I laid my purse and car keys on the dresser. "Why are you home so early anyway Teka? I thought you were pulling a double." Sanchez said looking at me and I shrugged my shoulders.

"I had another nurse cover my shift...I just wanted to come back home and be with you." I said giving him a smile but y'all muthafuckas reading this know that was a lie. The only reason I was home early was so I could be around to prevent Sanchez's father from getting in contact with him. If the truth came out that I was really a man I'm not too sure how life would turn out for me. Therefore, I had to do what was necessary to keep this secret as far away from Sanchez as possible.

"So did you think about what I said?" Sanchez asked sitting up on the bed. I took off my nurse badge and placed it on top of the dresser as well.

"Which was what Sanchez?" I asked dumbfounded. Sanchez started shaking his head then he reached for his bottle of Hennessy on the table by the side of his bed.

"I swear Teka anything I say to you goes in one ear and out the other yo." Sanchez said tilting his head back to take a huge gulp of the liquor. I figured Sanchez would drink to cover up what's really bothering him but every time I tried to ask...He would changed the subject. I just want that nigga to know that he can't drown his problems in a liquor bottle...You will have to deal with whatever demons are on your shoulders.

"Sanchez with all the shit that's going on at work I can't even concentrate on anything else. I apologize mi amor...What is it that I was supposed to be thinking about." I said trying to be nice.

"You were going to tell Angel that you quit...You don't want to work for him anymore." Sanchez said and I put my hands on my hips.

"Sanchez, baby we need that money." I said shaking my head no. Sanchez took another guzzle of his liquor and jumped up from the bed.

"What the fuck do we need the money for Teka? Please answer that question for me...Huh? What are you so quiet for?!" Sanchez yelled out and I could see the veins popping out on his forehead and neck. I backed up away from him but he continued to walked towards me like he wanted to attack me. Truth was I needed Angel's money for my surgery to get my dick removed. Was I going to say that shit to Sanchez though? Absolutely not y'all got me fucked up.

"Angel, doesn't look at me like a fucking man Teka and do you know how much that shit hurts baby? That he would allow JoJo to work for him but I can't?! What the fuck is wrong with me, huh Teka? Nah...FUCK THAT! Until that muthafucka sees me for who I really am YOU will not be working in his home. Fuck whoever is addicted to heroin in his house...Put they ass in a real rehab if he really wants to help." Sanchez said toning his voice down a bit as he waved me off but I could see it was passion in everything that he was saying right now.

"Sanchez, this is a personal problem between you and your brother I don't have anything to do with it." I said shrugging my shoulders. Sanchez started chuckling and pointed to me.

"You don't have anything to do with it? Are you my wife?!" Sanchez asked yelling and I dropped my head down to the carpet floor. "I ASKED IF YOU'RE MY FUCKING WIFE?!" Sanchez yelled out again. He used his right hand to grab my chin so that I could look at him while he was speaking.

"Yes baby you know I am." I said forcing a smile. At this moment Sanchez was still holding on to my chin but he was just staring at me.

"So that means as my wife anything attached to Angel you will not associate yourself with Teka. Do I make myself clear?" Sanchez asked still looking me in my eyes.

"Loud and clear Sanchez." I said rubbing my lips together. Sanchez let me go and he walked back over to his side of the bed and picked up his bottle of liquor. I know what y'all muthafuckas are saying reading this...Sis leave his ass he is mentally and emotionally abusing you. Just mind y'all fucking business because me and my man are good over here!

"Fuck his money...You will not get another dime from that muthafucka. Even if we have to struggle we will until that nigga allows me to hop on board with his drug business." Sanchez said without looking at me but his attention was on his liquor the entire time. "One more thing stay the fuck away from that bitch Kia." Sanchez said putting the bottle down and he sat on the edge of the bed. I rubbed my nose and just looked at him.

"Why? Do you know something that I don't Sanchez?" I asked.

"Just do what I say...Understand?" Sanchez asked. He waved for me to get out of his way because I was standing right in front of the TV. He picked up his controller and took the game off pause. "Get out of them clothes...I need my dick sucked." Sanchez said with his eyes glued to the game.

"Sanchez, not tonight baby I'm not feeling so well." I said trying to get out of fucking tonight.

"All of a sudden?" Sanchez asked looking at me with his right eyebrow raised.

"You know what? Don't even worry about how I feel Sanchez...You want to get pleased? I will do my job and satisfy you." I said extending my hands out to him. I walked into the bathroom that was connected to our bedroom and took a deep breath. I closed the door locking it behind me as I started shaking my head. I got out of my nurse uniform and threw them clothes into the hamper inside my bathroom.

I grabbed my silk robe putting it on but I didn't tie it just yet. I used my right hand to grab my dick just to make sure I was tucking it inside my butt. My ass was pretty fat from surgery so my dick played camouflaged. My titties looked perfect thanks to my plastic surgeon...I even sucked my doctors dick to make my breast more defined and perky. A good blow job will get you what you want ladies! TRUST ME.

I tied up my robe and took the bun down that I had in my hair. I allowed my hair to fall down my back and shoulders being care free. I walked out in the bedroom and Sanchez looked at me like he was in love again. I forgot a rubber band so I walked back into the bathroom.

"That's what the fuck I'm talking about with that fat ass! I swear to God I love watching you walk away just so I can watch that ass giggle!" Sanchez yelled out. I grabbed the rubber band off the sink and slid it onto my wrist.

"Did anyone call you tonight baby?" I asked looking in the mirror just staring at myself.

"Nah...Why do you ask?" Sanchez asked getting curious.

"Oh! Uh...Just asking." I said lying and I smiled when I realized his father didn't try to get in contact with him.

"Anything special happen at work tonight?" Sanchez asked as I came out the bathroom.

"Nah, same shit as every night...Actually something did happen." I said shaking my head then I stopped.

"Which was what baby?" Sanchez asked. He grabbed the remote and turned the television completely off. I was standing in a distance from Sanchez but I could still smell the liquor coming from his pores.

"This new nurse shadows me at work and she just confided in me about something quite disturbing but I know you will look at me funny if I tell you what she said." I said crossing my arms across my chest.

"Why the fuck would I look at you funny Teka when her situation doesn't have anything to do with you, right?" Sanchez asked looking at me dumbfounded and just laid back on the bed.

"Right, right, right well...This new nurse name Zori told me she has been married to her husband for a few years now—" I said but Sanchez interrupted me.

"So what? Everyone gets married nowadays." Sanchez said shrugging his shoulders.

"Nah, it's not about the marriage just listen because shit gets wild when I say this. Zori said that she's transitioning from a male to female. This is a secret that her husband doesn't know about and she thinks that she will get caught up soon." I said as I sat down on the end of the bed.

"What type of shit is that yo?!" Sanchez yelled out and he looked very uncomfortable as he jumped up on the bed.

"You see what I mean? I can't stand muthafuckas that's always hiding shit especially from their significant other. I told Zori this was something that should have been discussed before the dating stage that way her husband could of made a decision if he wanted to ride that shit out or not. What she did was completely wrong and I don't agree with that bullshit." I said but y'all know I was lying…

The story I told was completely about me but I just wanted to see how Sanchez would react to the news and he was very disturbed. "How would you handle it?" I asked curious. I looked down at my hands and started playing with my finger nails.

"Teka, I think you know me by now baby girl. There wouldn't be anything to talk about yo and that's real shit. The fuck I look like being with another man when I'm a damn man myself. If Zori was my wife…Well I can't say wife cause that muthafucka is a nigga." Sanchez said. I looked up at him and he held his stomach like he was about to throw up.

"Pull some shit like that and someone will end up missing…With they dick cut off that's word to my mother." Sanchez said and I got up off the bed because now I was the nigga feeling sick. The fuck? Did I just refer to myself as a nigga and not a bitch?

"So you would murder your wife? What about all the love you have for her? That would go out the window?" I asked rubbing on my belly and Sanchez bit down on his lip giving me the death stare.

"Without a question…You know how distressing and disloyal that shit is Teka?" Sanchez asked and I shook my head yes because I did understand but I don't think I deserved to be punished for it. Sanchez got up off the bed and walked over to me. I was starting to break out in a sweat thinking the worse right now. I used both of my hands to cover and protect my private part that way Sanchez wasn't walking over to me to grab my dick or anything.

"Thank God I don't have to worry about shit like that with you because you always keep it real with a nigga. Now come over here and give daddy some head." Sanchez said planting a kiss on my lips then he slapped my ass. When he turned his back towards me I took a silent deep breath and wiped my forehead because I felt like my back was against the wall a minute ago.

"The best part of my day is when you bust in my mouth..." I said walking over to Sanchez. I wanted to change the mood up and forget what we were just talking about. I told Sanchez when we were dating that I had Vaginismus and I showed him proof. Of course I wrote the doctors note...Y'all know I'm phenomenal when it comes to that lying shit. Basically it's a condition involving a muscle spasm in the pelvic floor muscles. I even went to the extreme to tell Sanchez if he did try to fuck me in the pussy (something I don't have) then I could be rushed to the emergency room for severe bleeding and pains.

He never encouraged it after I gave him a lying ass sob story. Me and my husband do fuck though...I just get fucked in my ass but I make sure that all the lights are turned off. My dick is held tightly in one of my hands when he's giving me back shots. I told Sanchez he couldn't rub or grab on my pussy because it's painful to deal with sometimes and that muthafucka believed me.

Just because I felt bad for hiding this secret from Sanchez I allowed him to have other sex partners but under three conditions. These bitches CAN NOT suck your dick, they CAN NOT get fucked in the ass from you and USE A FUCKING CONDOM. You see? My husband gets pussy...It's just under different circumstances because I don't have one. I can see the bitches reading this dropping their jaws...Mind your damn business because I guarantee I throw it back better than you in the bedroom sis!

"I love when you talk dirty like that Teka." Sanchez said licking his lips at me. I got down on my knees and pulled out his dick. All I did was lick the head for five seconds and he stopped me. "Hold on baby." Sanchez said moving me out the way and I fell back on my ass. He stood up, pushing his dick back into his boxers and picked up his phone.

"Who is that Sanchez?" I asked confused getting my dumb ass up off the floor.

"My father." Sanchez said looking at his phone.

"YOUR FATHER?!" I yelled out panicking and I ran over to him.

"Yes...What's wrong with you girl?" Sanchez asked puzzled but he was still staring at his phone.

"Babe just put your phone down...Don't you want me to suck your dick, huh? I know how you like it when I swallow your dick down my throat daddy." I said trying to persuade him not to answer the phone. When I saw that my plan wasn't working I snatched his phone out of his hand. I ended the incoming call and held the phone behind my back.

"Give me my phone girl why did you decline the call?" Sanchez asked confused.

"Why weren't you honest with me?" I asked staring at him.

"What yo? How did your attitude just change from submissive to aggressive like that?" Sanchez asked scratching his head. "Why weren't you honest with me Teka?" Sanchez asked smirking. The fact that I didn't know what he was talking about had me a little fearful right now.

"Uh—Huh? What are you talking about?" I asked backing up away from him.

"Why didn't you tell me that you were bipolar?" Sanchez asked cracking a smile then he started chuckling.

"You think this shit is funny Sanchez?" I asked pushing him and he just gave me a puppy dog look. "You told me you don't speak to your father..." I said reminding him of what he said to me in the past.

"I don't speak to him" Sanchez said shrugging his shoulders.

"So why the fuck is he calling you?" I asked and he started smirking.

"I mean I would know but you took my phone crazy" Sanchez said.

"You still laughing about this shit?" I asked getting annoyed and he could see it on my face. Sanchez exhaled deeply and he walked over to the bed...His dick was bouncing back and forth.

"Is all this really worth getting upset about baby?" Sanchez asked and he waved for me to come over to him. "Tell me what's really bothering you" Sanchez said leaning up on the bed caressing my thighs as I stood in front of him.

"I don't like being lied to...Everyone lied to me my entire life." I said. Was I being truthful? I think y'all can answer that question. Sanchez extended his right hand out so I would give him the phone. I handed it to him and he kissed my belly through my silk robe. He looked down at his phone while tapping something then he smiled at me.

"Look Teka...I turned my phone off and I won't touch it for the rest of the night, will that make you feel more at ease?" Sanchez asked putting his phone down on the table then he stood up.

"Honestly, I don't think you need to speak to your dad anymore Sanchez." I said trying to be an instigator in this situation just because I didn't want my dark secrets to be revealed.

"What made you just say—" Before Sanchez could continue talking I interrupted him.

"Is your dad in communication with Angel?" I asked.

"The two of them muthafuckas are like best friends or some shit—" Sanchez said walking to the bathroom to get some tissue.

"You see baby? Angel is treating you like an outcast...He's close to JoJo and y'all father but that nigga leaves you out of the loop. Why? Because both JoJo and your father are cops and you're a correctional officer? You don't need to be around muthafuckas that think they are better than you." I said instigating some more and it felt good at the moment.

"Teka?" Sanchez said my name while coming out the bathroom.

"Yes Sanchez?" I asked turning around to face him.

"How did you know my father was a detective?" Sanchez asked with his left eyebrow raised.

"Huh? Uh?" I asked stuttering.

"JoJo is a cop...Me and you both knew that already but I never disclosed my father being a detective to you. I never really spoke about my father around you let alone what his career is." Sanchez said which was a great point and I knew I had to think quick on my feet.

"Oh! I heard Angel and JoJo mention it one time when I was walking past Angel's office." I said lying then I smiled as I rubbed my temple. There was an awkward silence in the bedroom until the front door bell went off alarming both of us.

"Who the fuck is at my door at this time?!" Sanchez yelled out getting frustrated...Shit, sometimes I think this muthafucka was the bipolar one. I went up to Sanchez and placed my hands on his bare chest.

"I got you baby...Lay down and relax. I will take care of it, maybe it's a concerned neighbor with all the yelling going on." I said and Sanchez nodded his head up and down while walking back to the bathroom. When I saw that his attention wasn't on me anymore I ran over to grab his phone. "Make sure them boxers are off by time I get back upstairs." I said hiding the phone as I left out of the bedroom. I powered his phone back on as I headed down stairs to the front door. Once the phone came on I went to his father's contact name and sent him a pleasant message.

Text Message:

Don't call my phone no more my nigga I don't have anything to say to you. You weren't there for me or my brothers growing up, so I think we should keep it that way muthafucka. Just a friendly reminder if you come near my wife Teka again I will make life hard for you and anybody else you truly love.

Text Message Delivered.

I deleted the text and I blocked his number. My heart was beating so damn fast, I ran in the kitchen quickly. I looked around and needed a quick hiding spot. I grabbed the box of Cap'n Crunch cereal and threw Sanchez's phone inside the box. I wiped my hands off and proceeded to the front door.

"Who is it?!" I yelled out but it was no answer. I hesitated at first but I swung open the front door. "An—Angel?" I asked stuttering. He smirked at me and walked in my house without my permission.

"You look like you seen a ghost beloved...How are you?" Angel asked observing me. I closed the door and looked back at the stairs to make sure Sanchez wasn't coming downstairs.

"I was fine until you rung my doorbell what are you doing on this side of town?" I asked making sure my silk robe was tied completely tight. Angel looked down at my hard nipples and smiled.

"Well...You didn't call me to give me any information on Charlie so I decided to pop up on you." Angel said looking around the house and then he grinned.

"At this time Angel? It's a bit late..." I said shaking my head.

"My brother upstairs?" Angel asked and I shook my head yes.

"Yes...He's in the bed." I said pointing back to the stairs.

"Tomorrow I will have all the information—" I said walking back to the front door and Angel looked at me like I was crazy.

"You always got excuses Teka...I tell you what tomorrow you better have every medical record and information on Bella and the baby." Angel said walking behind me like he was checking me out. "Are you hitting the gym doing squats? Your ass is getting fatter girl." Angel slapped my ass with his right hand so fucking hard that it was starting to sting.

"You know that was very inappropriate your brother is right upstairs...I think you need to go, have a good night Angel." I said getting stern. I opened up the front door and Angel started chuckling.

"TEKA?! WHAT'S TAKING YOU SO LONG GIRL?!" Sanchez yelled from upstairs.

"Angel please leave." I said pleading with him and he closed the front door closed.

"I'm not leaving just yet...Open up your robe and show me your body." Angel said and I swallowed the saliva down my throat because it was going to be a long night.

CHAPTER 23 ~KIA

"This isn't going to end good...This isn't going to end good at all." I said turning my high beams on as I continued driving down the street. I decided to take a short cut just so I could get to my destination a bit faster. My daughter was fumbling with her hands silently just staring out of the passenger window.

"MOM! STOP THE CAR!" Nyla yelled out leaning up in the passenger seat. I looked in her direction and pressed down on my breaks immediately.

"What the fuck?!" I yelled out as my chest hit my steering wheel. I saw a short figure with a hoodie on holding something in both arms. Nyla tapped my arms and took her seat belt off. She hesitated to speak at first but cleared her throat.

"Is that...Auntie Jada?" Nyla asked focusing on this person standing inches away from my car. I squinted my eyes and rubbed on my bottom lip. I didn't want it to be my sister only because I was afraid of how I was going to react. I was trying to get her clean and she decided to run away to feed her drug habit. I mean I know I should be the last one to judge because I did some selfish shit in my life too but I was so tired of meeting my sister under these fucking circumstances.

"I'm not too sure baby but whoever it is...Isn't alone." I said referring to what this person had in their arms. I put my vehicle in park and took my seatbelt off. "Stay in the vehicle Nyla, I will be right back." I demanded and Nyla shook her head no.

"Mom, I can help—" Nyla insisted and I scratched the right side of my face.

"Whew, child." I said shaking my head and took a deep breath. It was time for me to stop being afraid for my child and allow her to do somethings on her own. "I know you can Nyla and who am I for stopping you for wanting to help? I will not hold you back anymore, come on." I said getting out the car and I walked over to this person who was backing up away from my high beams.

"HELP ME!" I heard a familiar voice yell out to me sobbing.

"JADA?!" I asked with my heart pumping now as I ran towards her. No matter how bad I wanted to be upset with her I couldn't.. I just wanted better for my sister and me being frustrated with her wasn't going to give her that. "Sis, what the fuck are you doing out here like this? Is that blood on your clothes? Your head is bleeding Jada." I said taking the hood off her head and I saw that she was bleeding from the back of her cranium. It wasn't a lot but when I tried to see how bad the damage was she pushed my hand out of the way.

"I'm fine Kia!" Jada yelled out with attitude but I wasn't understanding where it was coming from.

"Auntie...Auntie Jada." Nyla said looking at her confused...And that was something Nyla never did before, well not in my presence.

"I need to take you to the hospital." I said assisting her back to my car but she wouldn't budge. Jada had more emotion on her face than a toddler. Whatever she had in her arms she was now hiding it from me as she started to pace back and forth in front of my car.

"NO! I CAN'T GO THERE—" Jada yelled out and now she was freaking out. Nyla looked at me but didn't say a word she appeared to be in disbelief. Jada was covered in blood as well as dried up blood, her hair was all over the place, she was crying and sweating and her neck was red like someone was trying to strangle her.

"Why can't you go to the hospital Jada?" I asked confused and she turned her back towards me.

"I—I just can't...Alright?" Jada asked like she wanted me to change the subject. I was puzzled on how she cried out for help then was giving me attitude...Unless she was afraid of something OR someone. Nyla looked at me and started shaking her head. I walked over to Jada and turned her ass around to face me but what I didn't expect was a baby in her arms.

"Jada...Jada why is Mir's child in your arms?" I asked taking a step back way from her. Jada swung her arms so fast I thought she was about to drop the baby.

"This isn't Mir's daughter Kia...This is my child! Her name isn't Charlie!" Jada yelled out. She held the baby in her left arm while pointing at me with her right index finger.

"I'm not sure if your high right now Jada but—" I said and Jada balled up her face and I knew she was about to snap.

"Bitch, do I look high right now?! I know exactly what I'm saying and this child belongs to me...I BIRTHED HER! I don't know how she got in the arms of that muthafucka but she is mine!" Jada yelled out. Nyla rubbed her hands together but she had a bit of sadness on her face...Damn my child should not being seeing all of this right now especially at her age.

"Jada, let's all take a deep breath and think about—" I said putting my hands out and she sucked her teeth.

"Think about what my nigga?!" Jada yelled out again with her face still balled up then she started chuckling like something was funny. "Oh! I know what the fuck it is... You think I'm crazy, huh? You think just because I shoot up heroin that I'm incompetent of thinking clearly?! Well I tell you what Ms. Know it all...I haven't been high since the day we left Angel's house and after the shit I went through I will not think about using again. Do I get tempted? Yes of course I do yo but I'm ready Kia...I need to get clean so I can be a mother to my child." Jada said rocking the baby in her arms as she pleaded with me. I took a deep breath and pointed to the baby.

"Jada, just give me Charlie." I said in a soft tone and Jada came up to me and shoved me. I laughed to hide my frustration because I wasn't about to be out here in the streets fighting my sister like she was a stranger. Nyla got in between us and pointed for Jada to back the fuck up.

"DIDN'T I TELL YOU THAT'S NOT HER FUCKING NAME YO?!" Jada yelled out then she spit on the floor. She was moving back and forth in place but causing herself to sweat even more, I guess her adrenaline was rushing. "You don't think my daughter is safe with me, huh?" Jada asked wiping her forehead with the back of her right hand. I looked down at my own child and shook my head.

"It's not even like that Jada—" I said trying to get her to understand me but she shook her head and sucked her teeth.

"Well, tell me what the fuck it's like then Kia." Jada said shrugging her shoulders.

"I think you're just being a bit paranoid." I said with a straight face.

"If you been through the shit I've been through then you would be paranoid too." Jada said moving back and forth frantically. Right now I didn't know if she was high or just nervous...It's fucked up when you can't tell the difference.

"What the fuck are you talking about Jada?" I asked confused. Jada touched the back of her head with her right hand and made a face like she was in pain. I walked up to her wanting to examined her wounds. "And where did all this blood come from...What happened to you?" I asked placing my hand gently on her neck.

"Mir...Mir tried to murder me." Jada said looking me in my eyes.

"Uh...No, no, no." I said tilting my head to the side and I backed up from her.

"Yes he tried to murder me Kia but God told me it wasn't my time to go just yet. I'm here for a reason. I don't know what that is exactly but I'm not living to overdose. My purpose is bigger than that and I have another chance in life." Jada said as she took two steps towards me then stopped.

"Mir has a problem and you know it Kia. I know you saw it when we were kids because I have seen a dark side to him as well. Mir is getting worse and I think him taking a life makes that muthafucka heart skip a beat...In a good way. I noticed he wasn't blind, his vision was very clear and when I tried getting away he threw me into the window. Something cracked...I'm not too sure what it was but it wasn't anything broken on my body. Thank God I learned to slow my heart rate down exceptionally, that was a bad habit I picked up on while doing drugs but it came in handy.

Mir reacted too quickly without doing his due diligence because he thought I was deceased but here I am" Jada said wiping the tears coming down her face. My blood was boiling but how the fuck was I suppose to get even when family was HURTING family?! Nyla looked at me then motioned her head towards the baby and I knew what that meant. I walked up to Jada and looked down at the baby in her arms.

"May I?" I asked and Jada shook her head yes. Jada placed the baby in my arms and wiped the sweat and tears from her face.

"Touch me." Nyla said holding her hands out while speaking to Jada.

"What?" Jada asked smirking because she thought Nyla was playing a game since she was only a child.

"Touch my hands...Please." Nyla said extending her arms out more than the last time. Jada finally gave in and touched Nyla's hands...A moment later Nyla pulled away from Jada . She was about to fall but Jada caught her just in time grabbing her right arm before Nyla hit the dirt.

"What did you see Nyla?" I asked and Nyla eyes blew up and she scratched her head.

"What the hell is going on?" Jada asked confused. I continued to rock the baby in my arms as she was sleeping and I hushed Jada so she could listen. You comprehend a lot better when your mouth is closed shut.

"Shhh, Jada...What did you see?" I asked giving my full attention to Nyla.

"Remember the towel that was on the middle of Mir's floor in his bedroom?" Nyla asked looking at me but with an expression of guilt more than revelation on her face. "Underneath that towel was blood...Jada's blood. She is telling the truth...Before we came in the room he stuffed Jada in the closet to cover up what he did. Noticed when you mentioned Jada being in the hospital when he committed Bella's murder he became agitated and sweaty. That's because Mir was feeling guilty about what he did to Jada." Nyla said and Jada's mouth dropped when she heard her niece speak the truth.

"Life and death. You said it was life and death in his bedroom." I said looking at Nyla. She looked down at the sidewalk and stayed silent, Jada was just grilling my daughter.

"Something is wrong Nyla...I can see it all over your face." I said to her and Jada walked over to me looking Nyla up and down like she was an animal in the circus.

"Is Nyla a psychic or some shit yo?" Jada asked balling up her face but I didn't answer the question.

"Nyla...You knew exactly what you meant when you said life and death." I said to her because I wanted my daughter to be truthful.

"No! Sometimes my visions confuse me mom." Nyla said scratching her head then she looked at the baby in my arms. "I didn't know how deep it was until I held Charlie...I mean Auntie Jada's daughter in my arms and I touched her hands." Nyla said using her right hand to touch the baby and she started to caress her soft skin.

"So this really is your daughter Jada." I said with a face full of fault and apology. I honestly thought my sister took this baby and was going to sell her just for some heroin. Damn, I need to stop thinking so negative.

"I told you I was telling you the truth." Jada said nodding her head up and down.

"What did you see when you touched Jada's daughter?" I asked and Nyla looked at Jada and swallowed saliva down her throat.

"I saw the quick flash of a fast delivery, a visit to the dope house to pick up heroin so Auntie Jada couldn't feel anymore pain because she just gave birth at home." Nyla said in a low tone as she spoke with her eyes closed like she was trying to remember.

"Then a trip to the hospital, she left her newborn in the waiting room and Auntie Jada disappeared. Uh, I saw the sorrow of a cab driver...That was heartbroken when he noticed he would never see his child again." Nyla said opening up her eyes with discomfort on her face. I gave Jada back her daughter and used my right hand to tilt Nyla's chin up at me.

"So you knew that Jada was probably dead in his bedroom closet? Fuck, the closet door that I should of opened up but I took his word for it that it was just dirty clothes in there. If you knew this why didn't you call his ass out when I called you back in the room with the baby?" I asked and Nyla eyes got watery. "That's why you were confused saying Jada's name when you got out the car just now...Because you thought she was dead and you wasn't even going to tell me, were you?" I asked and a tear ran down Nyla's right eye.

"Mom..." Nyla said sobbing. I let her go and she started wiping her tears then Jada spoke. Nyla watery eyes were stuck on Jada the entire time she was speaking.

"It was loyalty, family is always loyal to family. Nyla felt like she owed her uncle Mir loyalty so her mouth was sealed shut. Yes, I'm hurt but I get it...While your mother was locked up, I was on these streets shooting up and you even caught me once or twice with a needle sticking out of my arm inside the house. Aunt Tasha was always working double shifts at the hospital and your dad was doing time just like your mother. Who else did you have left? Your Uncle Mir...The nigga that watched your back, clothed you, fed you, made sure you got to school every day...Day in and day out from the moment your mother went to prison from the moment she was released. I should have been there too and I'm sorry Nyla...So you knew that Mir could see this entire time, didn't you?" Jada asked balling up her face looking at Nyla. It may seem like we were double teaming my daughter but I promise that wasn't the case.

"Ease up off her Jada...She already feels bad." I said and Jada redirected her energy towards me.

"You should feel bad too muthafucka for leaving me." Jada said shaking her head and I raised my eyebrows.

"Bitch, what the fuck are you talking about?" I asked dumbfounded.

"You should have been searching for me...You left me alone with that nigga." Jada said.

"That nigga you're referring to is STILL our brother." I said pointing to her and myself. "I told your ass to stay in the car with Nyla but you still disappeared. You know dopefiends gonna do whatever they can just to get they next high. What the fuck did you expect me to do? Send an entire search team out looking for your ass just to find you high as fuck in a vacant building with other crackheads?! You will not make me look like a damn fool and you won't turn this around on me." I said. I looked down at my daughter and helped her clean the tears off of her beautiful face.

"Them words hurt like bricks being thrown at your body but I deserve that Kia." Jada said walking pass me and I pulled her back to face me.

"Listen, Jada I was wrong...I'm just—I don't know I'm sorry for what you had to go through but I'm trying my best to be there for everyone including you and my own child. Damn, sometimes I feel bad because I had to put other muthafuckas before my child when she should come first. I want to help you...But you have to help me help you Jada, it works both ways." I said making sure she understood where I was coming from. I looked down at her child in her arms and never in a million years did I expect my sister to become a mother. "What's my niece name?" I asked smiling and Jada shared a curved smile with me.

"When I gave birth to her, I named her Rose. Even though I was married to my drug addiction, having her made my heart blossom in a form that I didn't know existed. My sweet baby Rose." Jada said. She rubbed her nose against her daughter's nose and I watched as Rose smiled in her sleep. A mother's bond is unconditional...Nyla used to love skin to skin when she was a newborn.

"Come on so I can get you and Rose checked out." I said walking to the car and I opened up the backseat for Jada.

"Can't we find another alternative? I can't go to the hospital Kia." Jada spoke like she was shaken up and intimidated. "I know I was wrong for just dropping my newborn off in the emergency waiting room but I just wanted to get high and come back for my child. When I went back to the hospital every nurse and physician I spoke to said they didn't know what I was talking about. They had no clue that was an infant was left inside the hospital. So I left without a fight...I scored more drugs and went back home and got more high than before." Jada said. I looked her in the eyes and she had more shame than me when I was robbing muthafuckas. Jada slid in the car with her daughter tightly in her arms. I hopped in the driver's seat and Nyla got in the passenger seat leaning her head against the window silently.

"So how the fuck did Mir assume that Charlie...I mean Rose was his child?" I asked confused putting my seat belt on.

"I think me and you both know the answer to that question. Something funny is going on at that hospital but who am I to accused a qualified hospital full of expert muthafuckas in the medical field? These niggas went to Yale University...Howard University, shit you name it. I graduated from, *'Get High,'* university so whatever I said didn't matter because I am a drug addict." Jada said cracking a smile trying to make light of the situation but something needed to be done about this shit.

"Jada—" I said shaking my head and she just took a deep breath.

"It's okay...Let's just go to Aunt Tasha she's a nurse she can look at my wounds," Jada said waving me off through the mirror. I turned around and shook my head no.

"Absolutely not. We will go back to Angel's house, you and Rose will lay low. It's about time Mir is dealt with...I need some time to think so it's best if we all stay away from Tasha's house," I said.

"Why are you just calling her Tasha without saying Aunt first?" Jada asked looking at me.

"I guess you didn't get the memo," I said mumbling under my breath.

"Huh?" Jada asked confused and I shook my head to change the subject...I wasn't ready to open up that closet full of skeletons just yet. I looked over at Nyla and she was quiet as a mouse.

"Nyla...Come on baby, what's wrong?" I asked looking at her. Nyla looked at me and dropped her hands. "Why are you so quiet...What did you see?" I asked because I knew my daughter better than anyone else.

"Mom..." Nyla said sniffling. I motioned for her to look at me and she did. "Uncle Mir held a pillow down on the baby, he was trying to suffocate her," Nyla said in a low tone but Jada heard it.

"SEE WHAT THE FUCK I'M TALKING ABOUT KIA? SOMETHING IS WRONG WITH THAT NIGGA!" Jada yelled from the backseat and I heard her daughter make a noise from the commotion. My phone started ringing, I reached down in my pocket and pulled it out.

"Hello?" I asked without looking at the contact name.

"Kia? It's Teka...Remember Tasha's blood that you asked me to test? I picked up the results from the lab to see if it was a match to your blood." Teka said taking a deep breath and I knew shit was about to go down.

"That's my mother, right? Just break the news to me already," I said shaking my head and Jada tapped me from the backseat to see what was going on. I shook my head no because my attention was with this phone call right now.

"No baby...Tasha isn't related to you beloved," Teka said then she hung up the phone.

CHAPTER 24 TEKA

The only thing on my mind this morning was the fact that Sanchez saved my ass last night. When Angel asked to see my body my husband came down stairs just in time before I opened up my robe. Sanchez said he was worried about me when I didn't come back upstairs right away. Angel tried to play it off and say that he was concerned about JoJo...That's why he came over to the house that late. Crazy part is me and Angel BOTH KNOW what happened to JoJo but I had no choice but to keep my fucking mouth shut...Angel terrified me in a way I couldn't explain. I walked through the double doors into the hallway and there this muthafucka was again. Sanchez's father standing in the hallway popping on watermelon flavor chewing gum with his hands stuffed in his pockets.

"The other nurses will be back from their lunch break in about ten more minutes...If you care to wait." I said holding my patient's file in my right hand. I assumed he was here to visit someone else besides me. I wanted to continue walking, I had so much on my mind I couldn't take the thought of being interrogated right now.

"Nah..." The detective said popping on his gum as he looked both ways down the hall.

"Nah? What nigga?" I asked stopping in my tracks and I turned around to face him.

"I don't care to wait because you're exactly the nurse I was looking for," The detective said smirking at me. I tapped the tan folder against my right thigh and started shaking my head.

"Why the fuck do you keep coming down to my job? I answered all your dumb ass questions...I don't have anything more to offer you," I said shrugging my shoulders. The detective laughed as he circled around me and took a step back. His arrogance reminded me of Angel, his smile reminded me of JoJo and whatever front he was putting on to hide his pain reminded me of his middle child Sanchez.

"Damn, why are you giving me so much attitude Teka? I'm just trying to get acquainted with you," The detective said chuckling and I just closed my mouth. It was quiet for a second because a doctor spoke over the intercom for two nurses to report to the critical unit in the ER.

"Acquainted for what muthafucka? I don't know you and I would like to keep it that way." I said balling up my face walking away but he started to speak again.

"My name is Julio," he said following after me. "You're married to my son...So I'm like a father figure to you now. I mean it's obvious you didn't have a nigga in your life to teach you discipline or guidance," Julio said and the words that came out of his mouth made my knees buckle. My fingertips became butter and my file folder fell on the floor.

"Wha—What the fuck do you mean by that?" I asked startled because he caught me off guard. I bent down to pick up my paper work and then I looked up to confront him. My eyes were stuck on him like glue. I was kind of worried that Shay might of revealed my secret when she left out of here last night...I mean after all Julio was still her partner.

"Which part offended you Teka?" Julio asked me.

I turned back around walking towards the elevator and I pressed the button to go up. Since my back was turned towards him I took the opportunity to get that expression of secrecy off my face. I took a deep breath and was praying in my head for this fucking elevator to come as fast as possible.

"By the way...What did you tell my son?" Julio asked. He popped on his gum and walked up behind me. I heard the double doors open up on the elevator and It was a rookie nurse pushing out a patient with a broken leg in a wheelchair. I held the elevator door open as I entered inside...So did this muthafucka. I decided I wasn't going to be the victim here nor was I going to be the only one to feel uncomfortable...Two can play that game.

"What son? Oh! You mean the three sons that you abandoned when you left their mother?" I asked without looking at him. I pressed the number three button and held on tightly to my file folder. I must of hit a fucking nerve because Julio cornered me in the elevator getting in my face.

"Listen, you little bitch...I don't know what that muthafucka Sanchez told you but I left because—" Julio tried to justify his wrong doing but I gave him more attitude looking him up and down.

"Honestly, my nigga I don't give a fuck," I said shrugging my shoulders again.

"I need to get in touch with my son," Julio said and the elevator doors opened up.

I walked out on my floor and it was more commotion on this floor than it was downstairs. I turned to see a few nurses in the same color scrubs laughing and talking. Then I saw other nurses walking in and out of their patient's rooms actually doing their damn job...Shit I wish I could but this muthafucka was in my way right now.

"I know you hear me muthafucka," Julio said whispering as he stood in my face. He tried to smile so other nurses wouldn't think that it was a situation going on right now.

"That's not my problem...You see my husband has daddy issues and as long as I remind Sanchez how you upped and left him and his brothers he will always have a vendetta against you. So please just leave us alone...It's obvious that my husband doesn't fuck with you." I said walking down the hall to the office that me and other nurses shared together.

"Sanchez isn't the only one that has daddy issues," Julio said as I opened up the office door. I looked at him and I could feel myself breaking out in a sweat.

"What the fuck are you really saying muthafucka?" I asked and he just smiled at me as I threw down the file folder on the desk. He crossed his arms, still chewing on his gum as he started to observed the office we were in.

"Oh...Me and you both know," Julio said. I leaned back on the office desk while he stayed in a distance a few feet in front of me. I scratched my head with my right middle finger giving this nigga a message.

"Did Shay say something to you about me?" I asked and at this moment...Bitch, at this very moment my heart was pounding like a muthafucka. Julio stayed quiet but his eyes stuck to me like he was putting a puzzle together.

"That look of fear in your eyes is mysterious...Ya know? It makes me wonder what you're really hiding," Julio said with a straight face.

"Sanchez—" I said extending my right hand out so we could just end this conversation for good now.

"Nah, I'm not talking about Sanchez anymore," Julio said and I tilted my head to the side looking at him confused as kindergartner.

"Well, what the fuck are you talking about?" I asked putting my hands in my scrub pockets.

"You're covering for Nurse Humia and Dr. Jacobs...Aren't you?" Julio asked and I looked at this muthafucka like he was crazy.

"Excuse me? I didn't have anything to do with Bella's murder." I said poking my bottom lip out as I shook my head no.

"Bella's murder? I never said you were involved with that...All I did was mention a nurse and a doctor by name and you bring up Bella? Why is that?" Julio asked rubbing his right hand on his goatee beard.

"I have a job to do now if you don't mind—" I said leaning up off the desk. I walked passed him but he grabbed my left arm aggressively.

"Bella, never gave birth to a child...Did she Teka?" Julio asked and I yanked away from him as forcefully as I could.

"FUCK YOU!" I yelled out and Zori stopped in the hallway and she turned to look inside the office at me and Julio. The tension was real and so was the quietness...Zori cleared her throat and walked away but the look on her face told a story I wouldn't understand because I wasn't good with shit like that.

"You gotta have what I like first in order to do that...Enjoy your day muthafucka," Julio said looking me up and down smiling. During this conversation Julio threw shots at me like he was saying shit WITHOUT really saying what he wanted to say. Shit like that created fear in my body, ya know? I was always afraid of the unknown. I entered the hallway, walking in the opposite direction and Zori jogged up behind me with papers in her hand.

"Girl...What the fuck was all that about? That detective came up here twice in two days to pay you a visit," Zori said. She turned around to look at Julio entering back on the elevator with a natural smirk on his face. I looked down and she appeared to have goosebumps on her arms. I didn't question what she was afraid of...Because it would come out sooner or later.

"Questioning me about Bella," I said shaking my head and Zori tapped my shoulder as we both stood in place to talk to one another.

"Everyone knew Bella in this hospital...Why is he just questioning you?" Zori asked. I looked down at the papers in her hands then I looked at the goosebumps on her arms. I scratched my forehead and licked my lips.

"Speaking of questioning...You never answered my question," I said and Zori chuckled but she wasn't really laughing.

"Teka Girl what the hell are you talking about?" Zori asked looking around without giving me eye contact.

"When I was confiding in you about the woman Kia and her daughter...You mentioned that the daughter was only a child," I said reminding her of the mistake she created during our conversation.

"So what bitch...What's the problem?" Zori asked pushing me playfully.

"The problem is Zori I never disclosed whether the, 'daughter,' was a child or not." I said looking at her and she just started coughing then she cleared her throat.

"You didn't say that?" Zori asked confused as she started scratching the left side of her head. "Damn, if I'm not mistaken I swear you said that the daughter was only a child," Zori said and I knew for a fact that wasn't the truth.

Zori appeared to be uncomfortable so I smiled to ease the tension between us even though I wanted the truth...But I'm a liar my damn self so I was only getting what I deserved, right or wrong?

"Did anyone check Bella's medical records?" I asked changing the subject but I needed to know because this shit was important.

"Nah...Not that I know of, why?" Zori asked shrugging her shoulders. I waited until a nurse walked passed us in the hall to speak...I didn't want everyone to know what we were talking about but Bella's records disappearing was suspicious to me.

"I was looking for information on her and everything is gone," I said telling the truth.

"What do you mean it's gone Teka?" Zori asked balling up her face.

"What the fuck do it sound like Zori?! GONE, DELETED, NEVER EXISTED! Someone in this hospital got suspicious and deleted EVERYTHING attached to Bella. Her personal visits to the hospital are blank...Bella could of got sick a million times when she was alive but no one would know anything because her entire file was erased." I said getting loud and I heard someone speak behind me which caused me to jump like a little bitch.

Thank God neither one of these muthafuckas noticed my reaction with my scary ass.
"Something wrong?" Nurse Libby asked looking at Zori but she didn't respond back to her. "Why aren't you at the nurses station? Your pathetic ass patient has been hitting the button like a wild animal in a zoo...Go handle that before I rip the hair out of

my head Zori" Nurse Libby demanded giving strict orders to Zori which she followed like a dumb ass. Libby didn't run this fucking hospital and I don't know why Zori was so afraid of her ass. Zori nodded her head and walked away to tend to her patient.

"Teka—" Nurse Libby said to me but I put my index finger up because my phone was ringing. Libby had the game fucked up I wasn't Zori and I wasn't taking orders from anyone! Fuck out of here.

"Hello?" I said as I answered the phone walking away. I turned back around and saw Libby still standing in place with her hands on her hips...Her dumbass would be standing there all day fucking with me. I do what I want around here.

"Nurse Teka? Its Dr. Jacobs...You asked me to call you?" Dr. Jacobs said and excitement overpowered the fear I had running through my blood when Julio was in my presence.

"Oh! Yes! It has been a while Dr. Jacobs," I said. I entered the office and closed the door behind me.

"Please don't remind me...I hear your voice and I get homesick all over again. I missed working at the hospital with your guys." Dr. Jacobs said. I looked over at the wall and saw Bella and Humia's picture hanging up side by side.
"I wanted to say I'm sorry about Nurse Humia, I never got to give my condolences...I know that you, Bella and Nurse Humia were all close" I said and I heard Dr. Jacobs clear his throat through the phone.

"What did you want to speak about that was so urgent Teka?" Dr. Jacobs asked not even acknowledging my condolences.

"I don't know how to say—" I said freezing up and Dr. Jacobs started to laugh.

"Just speak...That's what we have a mouth for," Dr. Jacobs said. I held the phone tightly up to my right ear and tapped my fingers against the office desk procrastinating on what I wanted to say.

"When I ask you this I'm going to need you to be honest and transparent with me please," I said pleading. "You're not being recorded and I put that on my life. I'm actually on the clock alone inside the office so whatever you say is strictly for my ears only. Understand?" I asked making sure we were on the same page.

"It depends on what you're asking me Teka" Dr. Jacobs said standoffish.

"Did Bella give birth to a baby name Charlie?" I asked crossing my fingers that I would get the truth.

"Listen, Teka—" Dr. Jacobs said and I just exhaled deeply.

"Please just tell me the truth...My life is on the line here," I said. Dr. Jacobs remained quiet for a minute or two but I guess that guilt was starting to eat at him just like Julio said when he questioned me last night.

"Bella didn't give birth...She wasn't allowed to have children," Dr. Jacobs confessed.

I felt like I couldn't breathe. Why? Because Angel said the same shit when I went to his office and I didn't take his word for it. I was so wrapped around trying to prove to Angel that this baby name Charlie really existed when I was actually blind to the truth.

"Why not?" I asked shaking my head as I had the phone up to my ear.

"Bella had untreated chlamydia which caused her infertility and the amount of abortions she had over the years didn't help either. She waited too long to be put on medication and that process caused sterility," Dr. Jacobs said and I guess high saditty bitches do have dirty secrets...LITERALLY.

"I checked the records in the system and there was a fucking birth certificate for—" I said because Bella fooled everyone with this shit. Dr. Jacobs took a deep breath and he cut me off to speak.

"Bella pleaded with me that she needed a baby but she didn't go into detail until I gave her what she asked for and now I realized how big of a fucking fool I looked because of it. For five months Bella asked for this favor and I couldn't resist. Everything about her ass was captivating. She would even flirt with me and my heart would stop pumping when I saw how much I mattered to her...Well I only mattered until she got what the fuck she wanted. Bella would compliment me every day on a new tie I wore to work or she would switch out other nurses just so she could work with me.

"Our lunch break she would put a napkin on my lap and lick her lips like *my* presence was turning her on. One night I went into my office to submit documents from the previous day and there she was...Bella walks into my office, slams the door behind her and sticks her tongue down my throat. At that point Bella had me exactly where she wanted me...Under her spell. I finished up in my office and I entered the waiting room. There was an abandoned newborn baby just laying in the chair...Waiting for comfort. So yes I did it! I mean why the hell not? Who the fuck would be stupid enough to leave a newborn baby sheltered like that. So I took the baby girl and I went back to an operating room.

"I sent another nurse out to bring Nurse Humia and Nurse Bella to me. While I was waiting, I paid the security men in my hospital to erase all the footage so if police came into my emergency room they wouldn't have any evidence. That baby didn't exist because no one could PROVE that she did so that was case closed. Bella came in the room and I laid the baby girl in her arms. That moment was remarkable because Bella's smile lit up the entire room. Nurse Humia was my alibi just in case some shit went down and she also kept her mouth closed. I forged a fake birth certificate as well as blood tests for Bella and Nurse Humia signed off as my delivery nurse," Dr. Jacobs said.

I couldn't believe this shit. Due to their foolishness I was dragged into their mess because it looked as if I was apart of it.

"You took an innocent child that did not belong to neither one of you just because you had a crush on Bella? I'm sorry my nigga but are you a doctor or a dummy?" I asked but he didn't answer my question. "I can only imagine what that mother is going through because of the shit that y'all caused," I said feeling sorry for the mother of the baby he took.

"I'm sorry...I truly am sorry. Sometimes I can't sleep at night knowing what I did. I thought that maybe if I took that baby for Bella then she would pursue me more but I was wrong...Dead ass wrong. The very next day Bella came into work and expressed to me how grateful she was to have me as a friend. Can you fucking believe that?! Me? A fucking friend?! After *everything* I did for that bitch. I sacrificed my entire career kidnapping a newborn baby for her and she calls me a friend!" Dr. Jacobs yelled through the phone and his entire attitude turned into frustration and livid anger.

"I'm confused...You said that you were sorry for what you did but you're mad because Bella called you a friend?" I asked trying to get a good understanding.

"I'm mad because she came into work the next day bragging to me about how this baby was going to change the life she shared with her man," Dr. Jacobs confessed again sounding regretful but was this muthafucka really sorry for what did? "I did all of that bullshit and Bella had a man at home that *entire* time," Dr. Jacobs said.

"You didn't know Bella was married to her husband Angel?" I asked because everyone knew she was married...Well at least that's what I thought.

"Husband? Angel?" Dr. Jacobs asked sounding confused. I turned around to look at Bella and Humia's pictures hanging on the office wall again. "Bella told me she wanted a baby so her man wouldn't be in the streets anymore...I think she said his name was Mir. Bella having a husband was *never* mentioned in our conversations before, shit that girl never wore her wedding ring to work...Looks like she was playing all three of us." Dr. Jacobs said and my eyes blew up when I turned back around...Angel was standing outside my office door just staring at me.

-KASSANA WILSON

CHAPTER 25 TEKA

It always seems like the wrong people save me at the right time because I needed saving when I was working my shift. I couldn't even finish my phone conversation with Dr. Jacobs because when I turned my body Angel was standing outside the office door just staring at me. I ended the phone call without warning Dr. Jacobs...I didn't want to be caught up in this shit more than I was already. Before I could utter a word to Angel that's when Zori came in the office grabbing me by my arm. Zori told me that she needed help with giving medication to a patient...

She didn't know the amount of milligrams to give. I think y'all muthafuckas already know what happened next. Me and Zori didn't have a conversation for more than five minutes before Nurse Libby came and found her. Libby told Zori she needed to go to the nurses station to condense paperwork. After Zori walked out the room, Libby just stared like she had a personal problem with me.

I didn't understand what it was, Libby was a tough bitch. But I couldn't figure her out and the look in her eyes made me question my entire existence. It was something about Zori that

Libby didn't want me to know but that was the last thing on my mind. Right now I needed to confront Angel because I was tired of being taken advantage of.

"Where is Angel?" I asked as Chino opened up the front door to Angel's house.

"Last time I saw him he was in his office," Chino said responding back to me. He opened up the door wider and moved out of the way. I walked in and stared him down. The expression of worry and curiosity was written all over his face.

"In the back?" I asked and Chino nodded his head up and down. He closed the door and walked beside me escorting me to Angel's office. I stopped in my tracks and looked around the house when something caught my attention. "Y'all got a baby living in the house now?" I asked confused and Chino continued walking while chuckling. I followed behind him and bit the inside of my mouth.

"What are you talking about girl?" Chino asked stuffing his hands down in his pockets.

"I thought I heard a baby crying...I may be wrong though," I said rubbing on my right ear thinking that it may be all in my head.

"Yeah I think you're hearing shit," Chino said clearing his throat.

"Nigga I said I *may be* wrong...I never said I was wrong," I said correcting him.

"I don't hear—" Chino said but I cut him off when I reached my destination...Angel's office.

"You can go Chino I won't be long," I said.

Chino stood in place for a few seconds then he walked away. I knocked on the door but I didn't wait for an answer, I just invited myself in...The same shit Angel did when he came to my house last night.

"Angel—" I said closing the office door behind me. Angel stood up from his office chair startled. He walked over to me and hugged me tightly.

"Teka—" Angel said in my right ear but I pulled away from him. I took a deep breath and stepped back giving us some distance.

"Wait! Angel I came here to explain some shit to you so please just let me do that," I said holding my hands out. Angel rubbed his right hand on top of his low ponytail and walked back around to his desk.

"Let me go first...I want to apologize—" Angel said and I gave him a puzzled look because I wasn't expecting that.

"Wait, you want to apologize to me?" I asked dumbfounded. Angel shook his head up and down while sitting back down in his chair.

"You think I'm too prideful to apologize? When I'm wrong best believe I'm wrong. I don't have any problem saying sorry to you," Angel said leaning back in his leather chair just staring me in my eyes. "I just want to say I'm sorry for asking you to expose yourself and opening up your robe last night. My mind was all over the place with Bella and the baby Charlie. I was overwhelmed and unfulfilled then when I saw you...Teka you distracted me from my thoughts. The robe covering your body was the only thing holding me back from a good time so I wanted it off your skin. I will admit I had a few drinks no it does not make it acceptable but thank God Sanchez came down stairs. When you said no the first time I should've just left your house without pressing the issue," Angel said being remorseful.

"Uh—Whew!" I just exhaled deeply because this muthafucka caught me by surprised. All the years I have known Angel this nigga has never fixed his lips to enlighten when he was wron. Now even though I was honored; it was new to me.

"What's wrong Teka?" Angel asked when he noticed how speechless I was.

"I just...I just didn't expect that from you," I said being truthful...Damn, was I being honest for the very first time? I must admit it did feel good.

"Why did you think I showed up at your job? I was just coming to apologize in person but, I knew I didn't have the time when another nurse pulled you out of the office," Angel said tapping his right hand on his desk.

"I really need to talk to you about something important," I said changing the subject.

"I'm listening," Angel said calmly. I pulled up a chair in front of his desk and took a seat.

"Remember I told you that Bella had a baby girl name Charlie?" I asked starting off the conversation.

"Yes! Did you find Charlie?!" Angel asked getting excited in his chair and this was something that I was afraid of.

"Not exactly...Bella had a baby girl named Charlie but, Bella wasn't the one that birthed that baby," I said. Angel chuckled and scratched his chin.

"Teka, you lost me here," Angel said confused.

"Bella had a bond with this Doctor that used to work down at our hospital but, when Bella showed up murdered he transferred to another infirmary," I said. I paused before I spoke again. "During shifts Bella would plead to this doctor that she wanted a baby," I said and Angel squinted his small eyes at me.

"So that muthafuckin' doctor got my wife pregnant?! Is that what the fuck you're telling me right now?! Where is Charlie?!" Angel continued to yell as he jumped up out of his chair. I stood up and backed away from him shaking my head no.

"No Angel...You were right about your wife. Bella couldn't have children—" I said and Angel pointed at me.

"But you just said—" Angel tried to catch me in a lie but I cut him off to speak.

"Listen to me please...At one point Bella could have children but she was getting abortions and not telling anyone about them which means she was pregnant before. Then she contracted a STD and waited too long to get treated which caused her to become infertile. The doctor that used to work at our hospital knew what Bella went through and he wanted to help. Plus Bella wasn't letting him go that easy," I said being serious but Angel thought I was being sarcastic when I wasn't.

"What the fuck is that supposed to mean yo?" Angel asked with his eyebrows raised.

"I know Bella was your wife Angel but that woman had secrets...Dark secrets and if you want the truth you have to listen to what I say with an open mind," I said trying to calm him down but he just nodded his head up and down. I knew he wasn't trying to hear me.

"Bella would compliment him, flirt with him until she had that doctor exactly where she wanted him. Bella tonguing the doctor down put the icing on the cake for her and she didn't even know it yet. During our phone call the doctor told me he was leaving out of work and someone left their newborn baby abandoned in the waiting room so he took that baby. He gave that baby to Bella and she named baby girl Charlie.

"The doctor paid the security men working in the hospital that night hush money. It seemed as if Bella gave birth. The fact is that the doctor covered his tracks so no one would suspect a baby being kidnapped. I mean why would you? It's a hospital...It's supposed to keep us safe," I said in a low tone.

"What's the name of this fucking doctor?" Angel asked walking around his desk and I swallowed the spit in my mouth before answering.

"I gave him my word that I wouldn't say anything...I figured I would tell you because you deserved to know. I know this shit is fucked up Angel I was hoping this information would bring you reassurance and ease in some way," I said looking at him in his eyes while I spoke because I was being sincere.

"Little do you know Teka you just made shit a lot harder for me...Either you tell me who that doctor is or I will find out my damn self," Angel said. I walked up to him and I held his hands inside of mine.

"I'm sorry I gave him my word and I can't rebuttal on that," I said shaking my head no. Angel squeezed me by my arms and the pressure became intense every time a word left his mouth.

"YOU'RE LOYAL TO A MUTHAFUCKA THAT WAS A SIDE NIGGA TO MY WIFE? I HAVE DONE EVERYTHING FOR YOU AND YOU'RE TELLING ME YOU DON'T OWE ME SOMETHING AS SMALL AS A FUCKING NAME YO?!" Angel yelled out as he continued to squeeze me tighter.

"Angel you're hurting me," I said as my eyes watered up but he still didn't let me go. "Angel—" I said as calm as possible then he pushed me roughly against the chair and I knew my thigh was going to bruise up because of it.

"What the fuck is the doctor's name?!" Angel yelled out again as he started pacing his office floor back and forth. I rubbed my hand on my thigh and kept my mouth closed. "Let me ask you this are you telling me the whole story Teka?" Angel asked. He stopped in his tracks and looked at me.

"Wha—What are you talking about?" I asked stuttering as I faced him from a distance.

"Did another nigga sign that birth certificate even though it wasn't Bella's baby?" Angel asked curious.

"Uh—" I said rubbing my head and Angel walked towards me.

"Was it the doctor?" Angel asked and I shook my head no. "Was it someone else?" Angel asked.

I hesitated at first because what I said next out of my mouth could determine how life would turn out for me.

"No Angel..." I said lying. Angel smirked and got in my face...So close that I could smell the buttery toast and pork sausage that he had for brunch.

"You know firsthand how I get when someone lies to me Teka, don't you beloved?" Angel asked looking me up and down. I nodded my head fearfully as my hands began to tremble. "NOW GET THE FUCK OUT MY OFFICE!" Angel yelled out causing me to jump. He walked back over to his desk and I just looked at him uncertain about what was next. But, you see that's the thing with Angel you always had to watch your back because the thoughts in his head was dangerous beyond words. So you never ask questions you just do what you're told.

"But Angel—" I said in a soft voice.

"You're dismissed," Angel said without looking at me. I wiped my eyes and walked out of his office heading to the front door.

"Teka?!" I heard someone yell out my name but I continued to keep up with my pace.

"I can't talk to you," I said turning my head and I see Kia rushing towards me with a glass of wine in her hand. "I have to go..." I said turning back around anticipating this fresh air that was about to hit my nose when I got outside.

"Wait I need to talk to you!" Kia yelled out.

I reached down to open the front door but she pushed my hand off the doorknob. I looked at this bitch like she was crazy.

"Are you sure that the results are right?" Kia asked whispering to me. She looked around to make sure no one else heard what she was asking me. Before I opened up my mouth to answer her I heard the same distant crying that I heard when I first walked in this house.

"Why do I hear a baby crying?" I asked confused closing my eyes and rubbing my temple.

"Uh— I don't hear anything," Kia said looking at me up and down. I opened up my eyes and I watched as she took a sip of her wine. Kia was dressed in a oversized t-shirt that I assumed belonged to Angel cause this bitch didn't have any money. She had on dark blue ankle socks on her feet and her hair was wet and curly like she just got out of the shower. Damn, Kia was effortlessly beautiful...Something I desired to be without trying.

"Mhm...Who told you that Tasha was your mother in the first place?" I asked looking at her body...A body that I wished I had.

Kia turned around and there was Nyla holding a book in her hands standing at the top of the stairs. Kia gave Nyla a half of smile then looked back at me.

"It was your daughter wasn't it? I see it all over your face Kia. How would your daughter know something personal like that?" I asked whispering. Nyla looked at me from the top of the stairs smirking, I assumed she found some humor in that damn book of hers that she was carrying around. Then she looked at my pants and shook her head like she was disgusted. What the fuck was wrong with this child? The look she gives me really intimidates the living shit out of me.

"Did you double check the results?" Kia asked. I looked back up at Nyla but that little devil disappeared. I took a deep breath and gave my undivided attention back to Kia.

"I read the results off the papers and then I called you to deliver the message. Our system is pretty accurate so it seems to me like your daughter may have been lying to you," I said moving out of the way so I could finally leave this fucking house. Kia made a noise and stood in front of the door.

"I know my child better than anyone and she wouldn't lie to me. You see that's the difference...My daughter doesn't hide anything from me but you on the other hand...Whew, child you will go to the extreme to tuck your dick in your ass so muthafuckas won't know that you were born a man," Kia said laughing. Then she took another sip of her wine. "Does Sanchez know about your secret?" Kia asked looking down at my scrub pants that I had on.

"BITCH, DON'T YOU EVER FUCKING THREATEN AGAIN" I said getting a bit loud as I stood in her face. I don't know if she was drunk or just bored but she started laughing then removed herself from in front of the door.

"Muthafucka don't you ever mention my daughter again...You hit a nerve and I will hit two of yours. You see how this works nigga? I mean I can still call you that right? After all that is what you are Teka..." Kia said smirking cracking boy jokes on me.

"What do you know about Mir?" I asked changing the subject.

"Bitch I don't know anyone by that name," Kia said getting defensive and that's where she messed up at.

"Listen Kia I'm not your enemy and I don't give a fuck who that nigga is but right now I'm trying to help you and myself. I saw how you reacted inside of Angel's office when I said something about locating the baby Charlie. I also saw the look of fear in your eyes when I said that he signed the birth certificate," I said and Kia started to look nervous. "I don't give a fuck about the relations that the two of y'all have together but I don't know how much longer I have to live now," I said being truthful. I looked back down the hall to Angel's office and then I lowered my head in shame.

"What are you talking about?" Kia asked confused.

"I lied to Angel to save you..." I said and Kia turned up her lip.

"Correction you lied to Angel because I know your secret beloved," Kia said and yes that was the truth.

"I found out Mir and Bella were in a relationship and I lied to his fucking face about it. If Angel could slaughter his own blood brother into pieces. What the fuck do you think he will do to me when he finds out I was lying about Mir? Whoever that nigga is to you tell him to be careful because Angel don't play." I said and my phone started to ring and Kia just stared at me. I took my phone out my pocket and I opened up the front door walking out on the porch.

"Hello?" I said with my phone up to my right ear.

"Teka...It's Zori. I need to tell you the truth," Zori said and I rubbed the side of my face misunderstanding her.

"The truth about what girl?" I asked.

"Remember you called me asking for the results to the DNA test for Tasha?" Zori asked and I nodded my head up and down.
"Yeah what about it Zori? I already told Kia what the results said so if that's what you're calling for it's over with" I said walking down the stairs.

"Actually it's not over Teka...Tasha *is* the mother of Kia." Zori said and I stopped at the bottom of the stairs.

"Bitch, the results said that the two of them weren't related." I said smirking thinking she was playing with me because Zori was a goofball.

"Libby typed it up professionally and told me to say that to you," Zori said and I balled up my face.

"Why? Why the fuck do you always do what Libby tells you to do Zori?" I asked getting frustrated.

"I have to Teka...Libby is my mom and she was trying to protect her sister." Zori said and now she was confusing me even more while revealing secrets.

"Libby has a sister?" I asked confused.

"Tasha is her sister..." Zori said and I took the phone away from my ear.

"I think you owe me and my daughter an apology." I heard someone say and when I turned around it was Kia standing on the porch with tears in her eyes.

"WHAT THE FUCK IS GOING ON IN THAT HOSPITAL?" I asked myself.

CHAPTER 26 KIA

"What the fuck are you staring at?" Jada asked me with an attitude. I was staring in her room while standing in the hallway with my arms folded. It was obvious she caught me.

"Oh, so I see we starting this shit again," I said rolling my eyes. I checked my surroundings and entered her room, closing the door behind me. Angel doesn't know that Jada returned to the house and he damn sure doesn't know that there's a baby living under his roof either.

"Starting what shit again?" Jada asked looking at me confused. She wrapped a white towel on her head and tightened up the towel around her body. I looked around the room and saw her daughter Rose sleeping peacefully on the bed that she was now sharing with her mother. "What the fuck are you looking at Kia? So you're judging me now, huh?" Jada asked with more attitude than before. She caught me looking at the track marks on her arms from doing drugs but I wasn't judging her...

Honestly, I was thanking God that my sister was safe and back home with me. Once we got back in the house I took care of that cut in her head, the bruises would have to heal on their own. Jada still refused medical treatment and begged to me that she was fine so I left her alone.

"You're always being defensive...I don't know why you have this wall up like I'm your fucking enemy," I said shaking my head while looking at her. Jada shrugged her shoulders and kissed her baby girl on her forehead while she slept.

"You knew I was in Mir's closet and you didn't say shit to him! You were going to let me die, wasn't you?" Jada asked getting emotional. I took a deep breath and pointed at her face because it was quite obvious that she wasn't going to let this shit go.

"Bitch—See, I'm trying my best to respect you but a muthafucka like you makes it beyond hard. Let me correct you cause I know you been through a lot of shit last night so maybe you're not thinking straight. Nyla knew you were in the closet when she touched your daughter hands...I didn't know anything until I ran into you last night" I said telling the truth.

"Why the fuck didn't Nyla speak up then?!" Jada yelled out as she came towards me. I put my hand out to remind her to keep her fucking distance. I wasn't going to put my hands on my sister but I didn't have any problem defending myself if it came down to it. Jada sucked her teeth and waved me off.

"You even said yourself why she didn't call Mir out...She's loyal to him. No, that doesn't make it right Jada but I know my child didn't mean any harm by keeping her mouth closed" I said. I moved back and leaned against the wall. I looked over at her daughter who was still sleeping peacefully during this commotion.

"Your fucking daughter—" Jada pointed her index finger at me with rage and I stood up off the wall.

"Whoa! Wait a minute...Watch your fucking mouth when you speak about my daughter Jada," I said looking Jada in her eyes.

She turned her back towards me and sat down at the edge of the bed.

"Please don't let me remind you of that again. Nyla saved your fucking life! I know she feels unpleasant about keeping her mouth closed but I will not continue to make her feel like she's being attacked," I said and I could feel my energy shifting and I had a problem with that.

"So you're just going to let Nyla off the hook that easy?" Jada asked shaking her right leg and she started fumbling with the towel that was covering her body.

"Why does everything have to be a fucking argument with you yo? My child made a mistake and she looked you in your eyes and apologized for it Jada, what else do you want from her?!" I yelled out. I looked back at Rose sleeping, I shook my head and lowered my voice.

"Leaving me in that nigga's closet was a mistake to you?!" Jada yelled out jumping up off the bed. Jada was dealing with bigger demons than I could help with and I felt like she was taking her frustrations out on my child and it wasn't fair.

"My daughter made a wrong decision out of love. You have every right to feel how you feel sis but if I put the same energy towards my child our relationship will start to sink. I'm not saying our ship is the best but trusting one another keeps the two of us afloat. I allowed our ship to sink for five years...I can't take that risk anymore. At Nyla's age I need her to trust me which means if I keep pointing the blame at her she will shut down and not tell me a damn thing and do you know what will happen next?

"As she gets older she will confide in other niggas and other women that don't have her best interest at heart and a lot of shit can go wrong. I could find messages in her phone that would break my heart, I can wake up one morning and my child decides to run away and I'm sorry but that's not the life I want for us. WE ALL WE GOT! I have to keep my child close to me and if I'm wrong for that then so be it Jada." I said just giving her a sincere look.

As bad as I wanted to help Mir I knew I couldn't...Because what he did to Jada was completely unforgiveable. It would take another dark secret for me to really wipe my hands with him. I know I'm always the bitch preaching 'family over everything' but, to be honest what other choices did I fucking have left?! I turned around to leave out of Jada's bedroom until I heard her exhale then she spoke in a low voice.

"Kia...Tell me about her," Jada said. I lowered my right hand from the doorknob and turned back to face her.

"About who?" I asked confused.

"Nyla...Is she *normal?*" Jada asked and I just twisted up my face.

"Is she normal? What kind of question is that?" I asked giggling because I felt like she was referring to my child like a creature or some shit.

"I don't mean it in a disrespectful way...I mean Nyla isn't like us Kia. She's special and whatever gift God gave her will come in handy if it didn't already. Is your daughter psychic?" Jada asked.

That was a tough question...Why was it a tough question? Because I didn't know truthfully what I was dealing with. Sometimes I was afraid of what Nyla would do or say next.

"I will tell you about Nyla when you tell me about your daughter Rose. Damn, sis I didn't expect you to have a child out here in this world," I said changing the subject. I just didn't want my daughter to be the main event right now because Nyla's gift was hard to explain and I wasn't ready for it.

"That was quite fucking offensive" Jada said to me. I extended my hands out and shook my head no.

"You know I didn't mean it like that—" I said trying to justify what I said but, she just smiled at me. She walked over to the bed and rested her body next to her child.

"I know Kia...A lot of muthafuckas say that doing heroin messing up with your mental but honestly I thought it made my memory better. I remember like it was yesterday, I was pulling a double shift at work because I needed extra money for the rent that month. The next day my boss came in and said that the state had to do budget cuts and even with me pulling a double I wasn't going to make the rent. I was in a dark place...A vulnerable place because I just wanted to keep a roof over my head. I was heading out to lunch that evening and this cab driver walks in my direction with a dozen of red roses. In my head I'm like all these bitches got it good at this job with random phone calls from their husbands just to say, *"I love you."*

"Or coming into work with a warm meal for lunch and then there was a bitch like me struggling to make it. So when I saw this nigga holding a dozen roses I became envious. I just wanted to be that girl that had a nigga's attention and I just wanted to feel special. Turns out Kia...I was that girl. The cab driver came into my job to give me the roses and I couldn't stop smiling. I took a cab every time I had to work but, at that time I was so stuck in my head I wouldn't pay attention to anything, ya know? Only thing I was worried about was making enough to pay my bills. So by time I would get to work I would pay the cab driver and bounce. We never had a conversation until that day he walked in with the roses. He said I always noticed you...

"My silence in the cab was attractive to him yet peaceful and something about that nigga standing in front of me sweep me off my feet. It wasn't enough to keep me focused in life though. We started dating for a while and during the course of our relationship I ended up pregnant. I got addicted to heroin and I was trying my best to cover it up so he wouldn't judge me" Jada said as tears started falling from her eyes.

I wanted to console my sister but, I was getting a bit emotional over here in the corner too.

"It became rough Kia...I lost my apartment because I didn't have the money to pay bills. I would go inside his home while he was out driving the cab at night and I would steal or take valuable shit in exchange for drugs. Once I gave birth to Rose I couldn't go back to him. That heartbreak on his face was something I couldn't live with because I caused him unbearable pain. He deserved better and I couldn't give that to him. What the fuck could a heroin addict give to a man working his ass off?!

"I gave up looking for Rose but he didn't...He searched high and low but I couldn't bear to hear him crying and losing sleep because of me so I left. Last time I saw him I was in an alleyway getting high with strangers. When he saw me, tears started dropping from his eyes," Jada said.

I took a deep breath and I pointed to the track marks on her arms.

"I asked you before how did you get hooked on to heroin but you wasn't specific...I'm guessing it was from friends or strangers —" I said assuming. Jada gave me a face like I was tripping and shook her head no.

"Neither...Mir got me hooked on heroin while you were locked up. I was in need of rent money, Mir said that he would give me the money but I needed to test his product first. I did and I been like this ever since Kia. I didn't know how bad shit could be until my life changed for good," Jada said.

I swear to God I could faint from what I just heard her say. I continuously blinked my eyes and rubbed my right hand through my hair.

"I have to go—" I said turning around as I opened up the bedroom door. As soon as my back turned towards my sister tears fell down my face. This muthafucka Mir was disappointing me more and more as the days came.

"Where you going Kia?" Jada asked alarmed as she sat up on her bed.

"Get some rest Jada—I'm not feeling too well. Please keep that baby quiet until I talk to Angel," I said without looking at her because I didn't want her to see me crying. I closed her bedroom door and headed to the stairs. I wiped my eyes and I could feel my breathing increasing every time I walked up the stairs.

"Kia?" Angel asked as I reached the top of the stairs. I looked back and gave a fake smile as he was coming out of his master bedroom. "Is your father alright?" Angel asked concerned but I was confused.

"My father?" I asked dumbfounded. See, this is why I can't lie because it was so hard keeping up with the story telling. "Oh! Yes...My father is doing much better. I hate to see him in these uncomfortable situations", I said. Here I was lying again...But I was lying because Mir put me in the situation to lie but that shit was going to stop today.

"Mhm, come here beloved...Is everything okay?" Angel asked. He walked up to me and gently grabbed on my right arm. I nodded my head up and down yet I gave him a look of worrisome. This muthafucka looked so good right now but I knew I had to focus. He was dressed in a white wife beater shirt and black Nike basketball shorts. His hair was curly as it fell down his shoulders and back. I guess that was the Spanish in him.

"I have to talk to you about—Wait, what's wrong?" I asked. I noticed Angel was concerned with me but he had an anxious look on his face.

"Teka told me some information and now it has my head all over the place," Angel said. He let me go and walked back into his bedroom, I followed behind him. Everything in his room was black from the silk covers on his bed to the paintings, curtains and dressers. It was so comforting in this space though.

"Wh—What did she say? Did she say something about me?" I asked in a nervous voice.

"Nah...Why would she be talking about you?" Angel asked dumbfounded. He poked out his lip and just stared at me while I was dressed in his oversized T-shirt.

"I'm just asking—" I said. Angel came up to me smiling, he used his right hand to caress the side of my face then he planted a soft warm kiss on the center of my forehead.

"Boss, I think there's a baby in the guest room," Chino said knocking on the door. When he saw Angel kissing my head he cleared his throat and turned around.

"Jada is back...She's in the bedroom with her baby," I said finally telling the truth. I walked up to the door and closed it so I could speak to Angel in private.

"I didn't know your sister had a baby Kia," Angel said smirking at me and he rubbed his hands together.

"Shit, that makes two of us," I said under my breath as I looked down at his carpet floor.

"Huh?" Angel asked confused. He walked over to his bed and sat down looking at me. "Teka will no longer be Jada's nurse

I'm going to hire someone else—" Angel said changing the subject and I walked up to him shaking my head no.

"That's not what I wanted to talk to you about Angel," I said and I could feel myself sweating at this point.

"What's on your mind beloved?" Angel asked with his right eyebrow raised. I held his hands inside of mine and I squeezed because I didn't want him to let go.

"You're still looking for Mir, right?" I asked. "I know where you can find him...And you're right he isn't blind," I said.

"I heard you and Jada speaking about that nigga downstairs...So that's y'all brother, huh? You knew who he was this entire time Kia," Angel said snatching his hands away from me and jumped off the bed. At this point I felt like I was going to end up like JoJo...I needed Nyla to save me NOW!

CHAPTER 27 REEM

"I know you hear me talking to you yo," I said with the phone up to my right ear. I was outside on the steps of my mother's house. I've been knocking on the front door but I guess neither my brother or my mom was home yet.

"What Reem? I'm fucking busy right now," Tasha replied back to me with a little base in her fucking voice.

"Busy? You ain't doing shit Tasha...Stop playing with me," I said adjusting my left leg on the steps. I turned my head to my left and I see a young boy on a scooter and a little girl riding her bike. The little shawty on the bike reminded me of my daughter Nyla and I couldn't wait to hold my baby in my arms again. Her embraces kept my heart warm.

"Take heed to what I said my nigga," I spoke into the phone still watching the kids play down the street.

"Take heed about?" Tasha asked confused.

"You getting smart with me yo?!" I said while raising my voice a little.

"All I did was ask you a question Reem," Tasha said lowering her voice.

"I think you need to take a look in Mir's closet as well as your front door," I said being blunt.

"So you were in my house and you didn't bother to speak to me?" Tasha asked and I just started shaking my head.

"Man, fuck all that just do it," I said giving her clear directions.

"I wouldn't be too surprised if I saw blood," Tasha said but, she spoke as if that shit didn't frighten her what so ever.

"Blood? So you saw it too Tasha?" I asked sitting up on the step.

"Nah...What I'm saying is something is wrong with Mir. Something has been off with him since he was born," Tasha said whispering into the phone like someone was listening to her.

"Why the fuck would blood be in the closet of a blind nigga?" I asked confused because clearly shit wasn't adding up for me.

"This isn't the first time there has been blood in my house. Mir cut himself by accident a few times when I was working. I would come home and find drops of blood on my kitchen floor. No one is here to really direct him around the house so he injures himself at times...It's no biggie though," Tasha said but, I didn't know if she was trying to be sarcastic or not.

"Does Mir have any friends that come over to your house?" I asked. I turned my head to the right just watching cars drive back and forth.

"The only friend he has is JoJo but..." Tasha spoke but then she paused.

"But what yo?" I asked turning up my face.

"JoJo has been missing for almost a week now," Tasha said exhaling deeply. "It's not alarming for JoJo to disappear...That muthafucka leaves without a trace all the time then he resurfaces without question," Tasha said. The way she spoke about JoJo seemed as if she knew him more deeply like on a fucking tip.

"Something isn't right with Mir...I can feel it Tasha," I said shaking my head.

"I have to tell you something Reem" Tasha said hesitating to speak.

"What is it Tasha?" I asked.

"Let's talk about Nyla," Tasha said calmly.

"My daughter? What the fuck does my child have to do with any of this yo?" I asked standing up on the steps.

"Kia knows about me and you," Tasha said breaking the ice.

"WHAT TASHA?!" I yelled out in frustration.

"Our affair and the baby...Kia knows," Tasha said.

"How would Kia know something like that Tasha? I was careful! You were careful! Who the fuck did you run your mouth to muthafucka?" I asked clenching my jaw together.

"It didn't come out of Kia's mouth...It came out of Nyla's. I saw it with my own eyes," Tasha confessed and now I was a bit more confused than five seconds ago.

"How the fuck would my daughter know something like that?!" I yelled out again wanting answers.

"Because she's special Reem," Tasha said but, it sounded like she chuckled when she finished speaking or maybe I was so enraged that I was hearing shit.

"You're calling my daughter slow muthafucka?" I asked getting defensive.

"Nyla is far from that...I was saying special as a compliment. Nyla has a gift that we aren't blessed with and soon she will become dangerous. I don't think Kia understands how powerful y'all daughter is just yet," Tasha said and I sucked my teeth because it sounded like some 'Sabrina the teenage witch' type shit and I didn't believe in spiritual shit like that.

"Get out of here with that bullshit Tasha...I'm telling you right now. If I lose Kia and Nyla because you didn't want to keep your mouth closed I will fucking kill you with my bare hands," I said and I made sure every word I said stuck to her like a bad decision because it was a threat.

"I'm telling you the truth—" Tasha said but I cut her off.

"Just like you told me the truth about the baby...You told me you had a miscarriage but the truth was you got an abortion, right?" I asked getting angry all over again and I felt myself tearing up.

I know I was wrong for fucking Tasha but damn I loved her and I knew why. I was looking for a mother and sex came along with it unannounced. Her love kept me grounded and I'm not saying I don't love Kia. I love that bitch to death but, Tasha was a story I couldn't put into words.

"How did you know—" Tasha asked in shock but, I saw my mother approaching the house and I just hung up the phone without warning.

"Mom, let me help you," I said offering my assistance.

I used my right hand to put my phone in my back pocket and used my left hand to wipe my emotional eyes. I skipped down the steps and took the grocery bags out of my mother's hands. I kissed her on the cheek and she gave me a half of smile. I haven't seen her in five years and this was how she made me feel welcomed. Now you see why I was looking for a mother in another bitch? Chill, it gets deeper than this...Let me proceed.

"Thank you son...My hands were going numb," My mother said shaking both of her hands from carrying the bags. She was dressed in her work uniform with a black cardigan hanging on her neck and shoulders. She walked up the steps to her front door and pulled her keys out of her work uniform pocket.

"I've been out here almost an hour...Jason didn't hear me knocking on the door?" I asked.

My mother opened up the door and allowed me to walk in behind her then she closed the front door and headed to the kitchen.

"Jason..." My mother spoke in such despair.

"Why did you say his name like that mom? Is he working?" I asked confused. I put the bags up on the kitchen table and started taking the groceries out.

"Jason isn't working baby...Jason was found murdered at his motel job behind his desk," My mother said pulling out a chair and she sat down like she was out of breath. The gray and black hair was revealing the truth about her age as it was pulled back into a ponytail.

"WHAT THE FUCK?!" I yelled out dropping the bananas I had in my hand down on the kitchen floor. I took a breath, picked up the bananas and I put them on the kitchen counter.

"Watch your language in my house boy—" My mother demanded respect and I just started shaking my head.

"Why didn't you tell me this mom?!" I yelled out again and I pointed up to the ceiling because that's where Jason's bedroom was. "That's my brother!" I yelled out again and my mother rubbed her right hand on her chest and shrugged her shoulders.

"I'm barely making it with the bills in my household Reem. I'm sorry, I couldn't afford taking three buses just to see you in prison. You were already behind bars and I didn't want to break your heart telling you about your brother. I thought it was better to morn alone then to drag you into our wretchedness," My mother spoke with such humor it was kind of questioning.

"We are family...We were supposed to be family. You should of told me what happened to Jason!" I yelled out again and I wiped my eyes because I could feel myself getting emotional once again. My mother stood up from the chair and continued to take her groceries out of the bags.

"I'm not going to tell your ass again to watch how you talk to me," My mother said calmly. I walked over to the wall and leaned back against it catching my breath.

"Did the cops find out who did this to him?" I asked and she just poked out her bottom lip.

"No son...They didn't," My mother said grabbing the half gallon of milk then she walked over to the fridge. "Help me take my socks and shoes off. My feet feel swollen." My mother said putting the milk inside the refrigerator then she walked back over to her chair sitting down.

"So they closed his murder case?" I asked walking over to her. I pulled off her work shoes and proceeded to do the same with her socks.

"I didn't have money to hire private investigators... Somethings are just better off baby." My mother said trying to switch the subject. I balled up her socks, stuffing them into her shoes and put them against the wall.

"You could of continued to fight to get justice for your son mom!" I yelled out and she pointed at me and got loud this time.

"I didn't want to have a target on my back because of who he was—" My mother said finally speaking some truth.

"Let's be honest here mom...You just didn't want to be seen defending a pedophile," I said.

The look she gave me was pretty obvious that I struck a nerve.

"Excuse me muthafucka?" My mother asked balling up her face.

"Keep it real...Ever since Jason had to register as a sex offender you disowned him. You looked at him differently since that one mistake," I said moving over to the counter. She got up from the chair and she took a step towards me.

"You call fucking a sixteen year old a fucking mistake?!" My mother yelled out with tears in her eyes. I looked down and I could see how bad her feet were getting from working all day.

"That bitch told Jason she was legal! That wasn't his fault and he tried so hard to prove his innocence but you made him do it," I said looking back up at her. "You made him take the plea deal and register as a sex offender," I said calling her out on her truth.

My mother threw her hands up in the air and walked back over to her chair to sit down.

"I knew it was only a matter of time before someone snatched him away from me. From the moment his face was flashed all over the news down to picking up the morning paper. I knew he would have enemies from everywhere. So to be honest Reem...I wasn't surprised when the detective came here and said that he was found murdered.

"I honestly thought Jason deserved what he had coming to him. I told that boy...I told him to stay away from them little girls but temptation dragged your brother in like a sinner. After your grown ass brother had sex with that child I couldn't love him anymore...I didn't want a damn thing to do with him," My mother said looking at me while she spoke and a tear dropped from my right eye.

I felt guilty that my brother had to die alone; that shit wasn't fair and she knew it.

"Did you have a funeral for Jason?" I asked and I was praying she did. If nothing else she could do right by her youngest son by giving him a proper burial.

"No...I got him cremated and told the mortician to do whatever he pleased with Jason's ashes," My mother said shaking her head.

I knew if I wasn't in prison none of this shit would of went down.

"Ashes to ashes...Dust to dust," My mother said extending her right hand out like she was sprinkling something but I know she was being funny because she smirked.

"You think this shit is funny?!" I yelled out charging at her but, then I had to remind myself that she was still my mother. I had to stay in my place but regardless of what my brother did that was still my flesh and blood.

"You better plant your ass right there in that seat and don't you move. I wasn't the only one ashamed of Jason...Shit, did anyone know that he was your brother? Did anyone know that I was even your mother Reem? We all were ashamed of one another. So don't turn your nose up at me like I was the only one in the fucking wrong here!" My mother yelled out then she started coughing.

She was right I never claimed her nor Jason because I was ashamed of them but that didn't mean my love for them changed. I showed my mother exactly who Kia was when she was pregnant with my child but, I would always make up excuses. I told Kia my mother passed away and I was raised in the system. The truth was my mother was on drugs and my brother was labeled as a pedophile. I was doing whatever I could just to impress Kia...

Even if that meant lying to her. I told Kia I'm not sure if I had other siblings because the system lost all of my records. I had a brother Jason but, I always kept him a secret. My mother would always ask to meet Kia and I would say shit like she's out of town right now or she's not feeling good. I wanted to keep my personal life as far away from Kia as possible. My mother was sober now but she still disappointed me in some way I just couldn't put my finger on it yet.

"Jason is dead, you were in prison and I was left by myself out here! Who the fuck was going to protect me?" My mother asked and I wiped my face.

"You were wrong mom...End of story" I said walking away but she cleared her throat and began talking.

"Nah...Let me tell you about a person's wrongdoings since you want to be so damn quick to point the finger at me because I'm not the only one with secrets," My mother said. I turned back around to face her.

"I know what I did was wrong mom. I shouldn't of been robbing and stealing from people you didn't raise me that way. I prayed about forgiveness every night and I served my prison time ten toes down—" I said and she shook her head and extended her right index finger out to shush me.

"This isn't about you Reem," My mother said. "Do you remember the job I had before I got hooked on drugs?" My mother asked me and I nodded my head up and down.

My mother working that job got me everything I wanted as a teenager. New sneakers every week, money in my pocket when I went to school and a new stereo for my bedroom. When she started using drugs I started rebelling because I was so fucking angry at her...Truth is I don't ever think that anger went away. My mother started heroin and we lost everything...That's when I met Kia and my lies started. I was denying my mother and Jason.

"You were a maid for this Spanish family in Ocean City...You had to clean the entire mansion twice a day," I said thinking of the past.

My mother smiled and nodded her head up and down.

"This mother had four children, three boys and a girl all of them were teenagers. One night I was cleaning up the kitchen in the mansion so I could get back home to you and Jason. All three brothers were in the living room playing the PlayStation and the mother was in her bedroom calling around to see if anyone saw her daughter Tatiana. I was more concerned about getting my ass home so I can feed you and your brother. I just finished mopping the kitchen floor, I said goodnight to the boys and I grabbed my pocketbook. I headed to the front door and as soon as I opened up that door there were two detectives dressed in suits looking for Tatiana's mother.

"One of the brothers went to go get the mother and that's when they said that Tatiana was found murdered...She was stabbed to death. That was a family situation and I was only a maid so I stayed in my lane. The best I could do was give my condolences...I went on my way to the pizzeria so I could get you and Jason some take out for dinner. While waiting for the food I asked to used the bathroom inside the pizza place. I didn't know the bathroom was occupied until I walked in and I saw a young girl covered in blood trying to get rid of evidence. That's when I put two and two together," My mother said staring off into space when she spoke.

"You assumed that the girl in the pizzeria bathroom murdered Tatiana?" I asked and that's when my mother looked at me.

"No baby...I know she did. Tatiana carried around this notebook all the time and I never knew why. She would get this look in her eyes that scared the shit out of me when she touched someone's hands. The girl in the bathroom had Tatiana's book and she begged for me not to say anything. When she turned back around I saw that book and Tatiana's chain on the bathroom sink. The girl was stuffing Tatiana's belongings into her bookbag," My mother said then she pointed to me. "Now you see Reem...If you're going to judge me for the way I loved Jason. You need to judge yourself for the way you love Kia...Cause Kia murdered Tatiana when she was a teenager," My mother said and my heart sunk to the bottom of my stomach.

CHAPTER 28 –KIA

"How could you do that to me yo?" Angel asked balling up his fist. I took a step back away from him because I didn't know what was about to take place. I tell y'all one muthafuckin' thing I was shitting bricks right now...Angel's energy was terrifying and his whole existence intimidated me at this very moment.

"Excuse me?" I asked and I could feel my forehead breaking out in a sweat.

"You sat in my car and watched me get emotional as I spoke about the murder of my wife. You knew exactly who this muthafucka was and you're just now telling me this bullshit!" Angel yelled out and I was moving backwards so rapidly I didn't notice I backed myself into a corner in his bedroom.

"Angel—" I said using my right hand to wipe my forehead.

"Nah yo...Wait—You wasn't really feeling sick the night Teka came into my office with information, were you?" Angel asked looking me in my eyes and that's when I knew he was putting two and two together. "Of course you wasn't Kia...You wanted to distract me so you could protect your reckless ass brother." Angel said and he nailed it because that was the truth. I was trying to cover for Mir...Like I always do when he gets into trouble.

"Angel...That's my brother. Mir is my flesh and blood yo I couldn't betray him like that." I said looking down at his bedroom floor. Angel was the type of nigga you couldn't put into words when it came down to describing him. I was just praying I would see my daughter's beautiful face one last time just in case he did harm me for lying. I know what I did was wrong but what the fuck else was I supposed to do?!

"That nigga has always been your brother, correct? So why all of a sudden are you throwing him under the bus?" Angel asked walking up to me and I jumped.

"It's time for me to wash my hands with my brother...I can't save him anymore. I've been saving that muthafucka since we were kids up until now but things has changed. When he tried to kill Jada that's when I knew Mir had to be dealt with. It's time for him to stop hurting people, he crossed the line and he doesn't even know it yet. Let me just say something to you...I don't regret being loyal one bit because I was raised on that type of shit." I said looking Angel in his eyes. He nodded his head up and down then he smirked at me.

"Being loyal to Mir might have just caused you your life Kia." Angel said and my heart sunk to my stomach. Angel used his right hand to caress my cheek then he turned his back on me. "You see what I did to JoJo? I mean that muthafucka was my own flesh and blood but he lied to me! That shit makes my blood boil when a nigga can't be honest with me. I gave him chance after chance and it was evident he wasn't on my side. So I had to make that shit clear to him and whoever else! Brother or not...JoJo had to be dealt with and now that nigga is swimming with the fishes." Angel said turning back to look at me. I could feel myself getting more emotional than usual and maybe because I knew I had to face consequences.

"So—So you're going to murder me like you did JoJo?" I asked as a tear dropped from my right eye. Angel walked up to me and used the back of his hand to wipe away the emotion.

"Nah...I'm not going to hurt you Kia. Nyla needs us. But let me make this fucking clear don't you ever lie to me ever again. Next time there won't be anything to discuss, you understand Mami?" Angel asked and I nodded my head up and down. Angel walked over to his bed and leaned back against it.

"Yes...I understand." I said in a soft tone. I turned to leave out of his bedroom and then he began to speak.

"Kia?" Angel asked. I turned around to look at him when he called my name. "Why did Mir murder Bella?" Angel asked with despair on his face and I knew his heart still belonged to Bella that was something he couldn't deny even if she wasn't living on this earth anymore.

"Before you take him out Angel, I think you should ask him yourself." I said hoping Mir's confession would bring him closure. Angel pointed to his phone over on the nightstand and nodded his head. He didn't even have to open up his mouth. I ALREADY KNEW WHAT HE WANTED ME TO DO. I went to the dial pad on Angel's phone and called Mir's number blocked.

"Hello?" Mir answered the phone dumbfounded because the number came up unknown.

"Mir—" I said and I felt like it was a knot in my throat.

"Kia! Bruh where the fuck you at?!" Mir yelled out. He grew comfortable when he realized it was me on the phone. Angel walked up to me while I was on the phone and placed his right hand on my back...That shit gave me the chills.

"I—I, uh got tied up you know how Nyla gets. Someone—" I said and Angel shook his head no and I could see the look in his eyes that he wasn't playing. I shook my head, closing my eyes and I started talking again trying to come up with a false story. "I mean I'm going to pick you up. When I beep the horn just come outside and get in the car." I said opening up my eyes and Angel nodded his head up and down while removing his hand off my back.

"Nah, why can't you come in the house?" Mir asked and it seemed as if he was getting suspicious because I was stuttering on the phone. Angel rotated his index finger around multiple times signaling me to wrap it up.

"Because Mir I just can't...Please just do what I asked." I said pleading. I was stuck between a rock and a hard place. I wanted Mir to get what he deserved but damn as his older sister I was feeling guilty about me setting him up right now.

"Where did you get a luxury car from Kia?" Mir asked and I wonder where this question came from during our conversation.

"I will be there soon, alright?" I asked on the phone. I took a deep breath and Mir just made a noise on the other end.

"I know that I fuck up sometimes but I just want to say thank you for always having my back...I love you sis." Mir said and my eyes began to get watery again because Mir had no fucking idea what was about to come his way.

"Yeah...I know you do." I said and I hung up the phone. I placed the cellular device back on the night stand and headed towards the door.

"It's done Angel." I said with my back towards him and I quickly wiped the tears falling from my eyes. "I'm going to go check on my daughter now." I said as I continued walking into the hallway.

"I will have my niggas pull up and beep the horn. Mir will come outside because he will think it's you in the car." Angel said telling me his plan that I despised terribly. "You know Kia, we all got secrets and some secrets are so dark and dishonorable that we don't think we can be forgiven for the skeletons hiding in our closet." Angel said following me into the hallway of the house. I turned around and he just smiled at me.

"Wait, you have secrets Angel?" I asked confused. I'm pretty sure he committed sins throughout his life but Angel didn't look like he was hiding anything.

"You wouldn't even imagine...But, I feel like me and you have a secret in common." Angel said and I just looked at him in a perplexed way.

"I'm not too sure that I understand what you mean Angel...But, Nyla is waiting for me." I lied pointing down the hall to my room. I was becoming a bit uncomfortable for a reason I couldn't explain yet. I walked into my room and Nyla jumped up on the bed that me and her shared together. Her notebook dropped from her right hand and she ran over to me.

"Mom—" Nyla said in a low tone.

"Why are you whispering baby?" I asked bending down to speak to her.

"I think we need to get out of this house." Nyla said whispering again grabbing on my hand. I gently removed her hand and I walked over to the bed picking up my pants to put them on. Nyla looked out the bedroom door that was wide open and started shaking her head. "Mom you need to listen—" Nyla spoke again and I cut her off.

"And go where Nyla? Mommy is trying to do right by you but I don't have the funds to just pick up and leave honey." I said buttoning up my pants and I turned around to look at her.

"I don't think you understand how broken your mind, body, and soul will get when the truth comes out." Nyla said in a low tone as she fumbled with her fingers. She appeared to be worried about something out of her control.

"Is this about Angel? I told you Nyla I'm not interested in him so you don't have anything to worry about." I said lying. I walked up to my daughter and kissed her on the forehead.

"It's deeper than that mom and if you heard what I just said you would try to understand that." Nyla said and I just paused for a second. It was something she wasn't telling me but she was speaking in code.

"I already told Angel about Mir so—" I couldn't finish talking because she cut me off.

"What I'm saying has nothing to do with Uncle Mir." Nyla said getting frustrated.

"Kia?" Angel said my name. He knocked on the door and stepped in the room. Nyla ran behind my thighs and just peeked at Angel.

"What's wrong Nyla?" I asked looking down at her but she didn't answer me.

"Hey baby girl..." Angel said to Nyla but she didn't speak back. She just cuffed my legs like I was leaving her forever.

"Nyla, get back up in the bed and lay down I will be right back baby." I said and Nyla grabbed my shirt.

"Mom you need to listen to me before it's too late—" Nyla said. Angel cleared his throat and I pointed to the bed because I didn't want to make him wait.

"Nyla I'm not going to repeat myself again" I said. Nyla shook her head, she reached for her notebook and jumped in the bed. I walked over to Nyla and I kissed her gently on the cheek then I turned around walking into the hallway. Angel grabbed me around my waist and embraced me quickly. His lips touched mine as he squeezed my body.

"What was that for?" I asked backing away from him. I looked back at the bedroom to make sure Nyla didn't see what Angel just did.

"I missed your lips." Angel spoke like me and him had history together which was puzzling. I don't know if he was confusing me with his wife that passed away but this was a red flag for me.

"Angel, me and you never—" I couldn't finish talking because Angel cut me off to speak.

"Everything alright with Nyla?" Angel asked rubbing his lips as he changed the subject. I cleared my throat and nodded my head up and down.

"Uh...I think she just had a bad dream. Do you need to speak to me about something?" I asked wanting to just get away from him right now.

"I need you to come downstairs. I hired another nurse to take care of Jada I want you to meet her." Angel said pointing to the stairs. I turned and I saw Chino jogging up the stairs heading in our direction.

"Angel, I need to bend your ear for a second." Chino said to Angel.

"Go ahead Kia, I will be down in a minute." Angel said standing next to Chino. I walked passed Chino and he just stared down at me like he knew something. I continued down the stairs and minded my business.

"Hello beloved...You must be Kia, right? I'm Humia I will be the nurse taking care of Jada now." Nurse Humia said extending her hand out to me. Humia was beyond beautiful and young. Her scrubs were tight as hell but her figure was nice. Her teeth were white and straight while her curly hair was tossed up in a bun. She had on a gold necklace and two gold bangles on her right wrist.

"It's nice to meet you. Thank you for looking after my sister." I said after observing her for a second. But, her energy...Nah, her energy just alarmed me for some reason she just seemed sneaky. I gave Humia a half smile and knocked on Jada's bedroom door. "Jada, are you decent?" I asked waiting for her to respond back to me.

"Yeah girl!" Jada yelled out and Humia started laughing from Jada's response.

"You must have sisters?" I asked walking into Jada's room and Humia followed behind me.

"Nah...I'm the only child unfortunately." Humia said. Jada was dressed in a robe holding her baby girl in her arms.

"Jada...This is your new nurse Humia, she will be taking care of you." I said introducing them to each other. Jada looked Humia up and down then she looked at me.

"What happened to—" Jada spoke but I quickly cut her off.

"She's not working here anymore." I said referring to Teka.

"So that means you're stuck with me kid." Humia said jokingly. She smiled while shaking Jada's hand. Humia grabbed a chair from out of the corner and place it beside Jada's bed.

"You look pretty young how did you become a nurse?" Jada asked Humia.

"Money got me here. My mother wanted me to follow in her footsteps and be better than her so here I am today." Humia spoke like she wasn't satisfied with her career path. Jada was rocking her daughter in her arms. Humia was just staring at Rose to the point her eyes started watering as if she was thinking about something. I don't know what it was about Rose but it got Humia very emotional.

"Do you have kids? Seems like you have a connection with infants." I said being funny. Humia cleared her throat and wiped her eyes.

"Uh, I was close to having one but I didn't want my mother to be disappointed." Humia said shrugging her shoulders then she smiled.

"Sounds like you have some secrets, huh?" Jada asked kissing Rose on her cheek then she place her down on the bed. She surrounded her with pillows so she wouldn't fall.

"I was in love with this nigga Jason when I was younger. I always told him that I was older than what I was which was a fucking lie. I was sneaking around my mother's back whenever she was sleeping or at work. I would let Jason sneak into my bedroom from the window or we would meet at the local library. A week before this incident happened I found out I was pregnant with Jason's child and I knew I had to get rid of it but, how? I didn't have $300 to get an abortion and I wanted to hide the baby from Jason so he wouldn't look at me differently.

"I couldn't break my mother's heart...Nah yo I couldn't do it so that's when I started plotting. I called Jason and asked him to come over but, he had to stop by the sex store and pick up some handcuffs first. Jason wasn't suspicious about my demand because he always gave me what I wanted. That night I overslept on purpose because I knew my mother would come barging in my bedroom and that's exactly what she did. I was sleeping on his chest wearing just panties and a bra. My left hand was still cuffed to the bed as I was laying on his chest so it looked like Jason was holding me captive when honestly he had a heart of gold.

"I started crying and I told my mother that Jason took all of my clothes off and raped me. I also told her that he knew how young I was and still took advantage of me. Of course I was lying but I couldn't live with my mother being disappointed with me. So I chose to lie just so my mother would still look at me like her little princess. The cops were called and they took pictures of me as well as my hand being cuffed to the bed. They took Jason out my house in handcuffs, he had to register as a sex offender and he also had to do jail time. The court granted me a settlement and that's how I got into nursing school." Humia said and my heart started pumping rapidly.

"Where is Jason at now?" Jada asked intrigued.

"He was found murdered behind the desk at his motel job." I moved backwards towards the dresser and a few items fell on the bedroom floor.

"What's wrong Kia?" Jada asked looking at me with attitude because I was dropping shit on the floor. I shook my head so she wouldn't think anything was wrong and picked up the belongings off the carpet. A few seconds later Humia started chuckling.

"Why is your crazy ass laughing?" Jada asked balling up her face while looking at Humia.

"I heard Jason's brother was released from prison...But, what's funny is I never knew Jason had a brother named Reem." Humia said laughing. Jada looked at me and her mouth dropped. Now I could feel my heart rate increasing. Reem told me he was raised in the system and he didn't have any family.

CHAPTER 29 HUMIA

"Why the fuck do you keep calling me? If you're not calling for a cab then leave me the fuck alone." Tywan said on the other end of the phone.

"Don't you dare speak to me like that Tywan!" I yelled through the phone. I was sitting on the end of my mother's couch waiting for her to return home. This was my daily routine to spend Sunday evenings with her every week.

"What do you want Humia? I'm busy." Tywan said and I could tell his ass wasn't being truthful with me. He never was truthful with me until my feelings were involved.

"You're not fucking busy so please don't lie to me. When a muthafucka lies to me, it puts me under uncontrollable pressure...Pressure you wouldn't understand." I said shaking my legs while sitting on the couch.

"Man, what do—" Tywan started to put base in his voice but that shit didn't scare me not one bit.

"She should have been mine. You gave that bitch a gift that she didn't appreciate!" I yelled out and the adrenaline running through my body was causing me to get a bit emotional.

"She? Who are you talking about Humia?" Tywan asked dumbfounded because I didn't say any names that would catch his attention.

"You gave that bitch Jada a baby and you loved her more than me muthafucka." I said continuously shaking my legs as I looked around my mother's living room. She had pictures of me smiling throughout the entire living room but wasn't shit too appealing to put a curve in my lips right now.

"We still on this shit Humia?" Tywan asked annoyed. "I was in a relationship with Jada. Me and you were never together." Tywan said which was the truth but I wish it wasn't. Me and Tywan fucked one night and after that night. That one lonely night of him laying the pipe down on me I wanted to be committed to him. But, this muthafucka yo...This muthafucka said he only fucked me to get his mind off his girlfriend Jada.

I was an option and when I realized that shit that's when my entire world came crashing down. I began to stalk the bitch he claimed to love so much, I just wanted to know if she was on the same level as me. I was driving myself insane trying to find out what she looked like, what she sounded like, if she had a better job than me ya know? Shit like that. One evening, I took my lunch break early and pulled up to his apartment. From a distance I see a woman wobbling walking into the home. I didn't think anything of it because she looked like a bum. Wearing dreadful oversized clothes and her sneakers were turning yellow.

Her hair was in shambles just like her life was so I assumed that this bitch was a relative of his until I got out of the car and peeked through his window. Here she was giving birth at home sweating like she was high on heroin. I tried to be as discrete as I could glancing through these windows. Something caught my attention I see multiple pictures of Jada and Tywan hanging on shelves including the table. I was completely disgusted that he was more interested in loving this crackhead than he was loving me. I returned back to work while her bum ass was giving birth on the living room floor.

I prayed that entire ride back to work that maybe the umbilical cord would get stuck around the baby's neck and he/she would suffocate and die. Shit, that would be a reward to me. Not even an hour into me being back at work, Jacob called me into a room and he hands over the newborn baby to Bella. I knew exactly who that child was and even though Bella didn't give birth to the little bitch, I knew she would be safe with Bella so I kept my mouth closed.

I was outside smoking a cigarette and Tywan didn't even see me. He came up to the hospital saying that his girlfriend abandoned their newborn baby in the waiting room. That night was heartbreaking for me yet hilarious. Jada didn't deserve to be pregnant, so I didn't feel bad that we kidnapped their baby! Tywan should of chose me instead of her.

"You were in a relationship with a fucking heroin addict Tywan! I can't believe you would choose a crackhead over me. Them track marks down her arms are very distasteful." I said jumping up from the couch and I shook my head.

"Wait—You saw Jada?" Tywan asked easing up a bit and my heart was racing more than usual. It was racing because he was still concerned about this bitch and not me!

"Don't fucking change the subject...Why the fuck do you even care about that whore!? She didn't care about you and y'all child." I said and Tywan exhaled deeply into the phone.

"Jada will always have my heart. I know she is facing some difficult demons right now and I pray to God she doesn't let the devil win. I forgive Jada for everything she has put me through. I forgave her the moment she upped and left me." Tywan said sounding so fucking forgivable that it was making my stomach turn.

"Why couldn't your heart belong to me?! I would have done anything for you Tywan! Why can't you see that nigga?!" I yelled out again. I looked back at the front door when I heard a noise. I didn't want my mother to walk in and see me pleading for a nigga's love. "I wanted your baby but you kept denying me FOR THAT BITCH!" I yelled out again. I turned from the front door when I noticed it was just a false alarm.

"I don't love you Humia. I never have beloved." Tywan said. I held the phone up to my right ear as I clenched my left hand tightly together. Rage was a fucking understatement for me right now.

"That was supposed to be our child Tywan...I wanted your baby." I said breathing heavy and then I heard this disrespectful muthafucka laugh.

"But I didn't want yours Humia." Tywan confessed.

"I think you need to apologize." I said smiling while holding the phone up to my ear. I walked up to a picture of me hanging on my mother's wall and I started to trace the frame with my index finger.

"Or what Humia? What could you possibly do to me?" Tywan asked getting cocky and little did he know I was not the bitch to be fucked with.

"FUCKING APOLOGIZE TO ME TYWAN!" I yelled through the phone. My eyes were watery but yet my crazy ass was smiling.

"What exactly am I apologizing for beloved?" Tywan asked confused but he knew what he did to me! He knew being with that bitch would hurt me.

"For—For loving Jada when you should have been loving me and you're apologizing for not having your first child by me." I said stuttering and Tywan was laughing even more this time.

"Are you fucking delusional Humia? I knew something was wrong with you the night I told you our affair was a mistake but, now you just seem a little off." Tywan said trying to call me a fucking mental case.

"I'm warning you muthafucka! You better tell me you're sorry for breaking my heart if you don't I put this on my father's grave that I—" I couldn't finish speaking because he interrupted me.

"Do you even know your father Humia?" Tywan asked.

"Are you being funny nigga?" I asked wiping my eyes and I turned around taking a deep breath. Tywan wanted me. That nigga was just playing hard to get right now and even if he wasn't playing I was going to make him pay FOR NOT WANTING ME! Ya hear what I'm saying?

"I'm not apologizing to you Humia. I gave you dick one time and now you're acting fanatical." Tywan said getting arrogant and I just shrugged my shoulders before I spoke.

"Every day this week I need you to pick up the newspaper from your local corner store Tywan." I said giving him a warning as I came up with a plan in my head then I smiled again.

"What the fuck is that supposed to mean Humia?!" Tywan yelled through the phone but I could tell he was panicking. "WHAT DOES THAT MEAN—" Tywan yelled out again and I just hung up the phone. I swirled in the living room like I was young again dancing in ballet class. I started laughing and I fell back on my mother's couch. I scrolled through my call log, tapping on a name then I placed the phone up to my ear.

"Humia?" Dr. Jacobs said my name like he wasn't expecting my call. I mean he wasn't but damn nigga sound happy that I was blessing you to hear my voice.

"Jacobs I need a favor." I said placing my right leg on the couch.

"Is everything alright Humia?" Dr. Jacobs asked.

"Nah...But, I swear to God it will be." I said laughing into the phone and I could hear him on the other end clearing his throat. "Can you get me a bag of dope with fentanyl in it?" I asked whispering and Dr. Jacobs just gasped. I overheard this nigga name Chino running his mouth in the aisle when I was food shopping. He mentioned Jada's name and said that she needed an in-home nurse.

I felt like God was blessing me because now I could be more closer to her than I thought. Funny thing is Jada has no clue about me or who I am. That bitch is just naive and dumb as a deer stuck in headlights. I walked to the other aisle and introduced myself. I told Chino I was a nurse looking for work and here I am about to kill a bitch just to get Tywan's attention. Niggas run their mouth like females and now my ass was employed to take this bitch out.

"Fentanyl? You know that shit is deadly, right? The smallest quantity can—" Dr. Jacobs was about to teach survival class 101 and I swear I didn't give a fuck about any of it.

"Listen smart ass, I know you're a doctor and all but I didn't ask your ass for a fucking lecture. I asked for a favor because you owe me one. Now can you get it for me or what?" I asked getting annoyed. I changed my position on the couch to get more comfortable.

"What do you have up your sleeve Humia?" Dr. Jacobs asked with a bit of fear in his voice.

"I'm trying to get my man back." I said rocking back and forth on the couch. I paused for a second and started to hum.

"Your man? You're talking about Tywan? Humia was that nigga even your man to begin with?" Dr. Jacobs asked confused but, he didn't understand the love that me and Tywan shared so I expected that but I also fired back.

"Did Bella belong to just you Jacobs? Nah. I don't think she did so me and you are in the same boat my friend. Oops! I mean was in the same boat beings though my situation is still alive and your situation ended up murdered." I said smiling. I laid back on the couch and stuck my feet up in the air.

"You know your words can cut real deep Humia." Dr. Jacobs spoke like his feelings were hurt. "Ever since Bella died—" Dr. Jacobs began to speak but I cut him off.

"Bella didn't die someone murdered her so correct your sentence and start again." I said exhaling deeply.

"Ever since Bella got murdered, you became a totally different person Humia." Dr. Jacobs said and that my dear was definitely true. I will never be the same again.

"Are you going to give me the fucking fentanyl OR WHAT JACOBS?! I DON'T HAVE TIME TO PLAY GAMES WITH YOU!" I yelled out as I sat up on the couch.

"Sounds like you're trying to make someone overdose why can't you just use morphine?" Dr. Jacobs asked and I just started shaking my big ole head.

"Because I'm a fucking nurse. I have to make this shit look like an accident. A heroin addict isn't going to backtrack to something like morphine muthafucka. It's not strong enough and since muthafuckas think I died of lung cancer, it's kind of hard to get my hands on any medication at this point. So are you going to fucking help me?" I asked tapping my left hand on the edge of the couch. Dr. Jacobs made up this lie telling everyone I passed away from cancer. I asked that nigga what was his motive behind the fib and he said he was just trying to protect me. If the cops ever found out that we kidnapped a baby, he wanted all the blame to be on him because he loved Bella. I wasn't going to argue with that but, it was so fucking hard to find a decent job because of this lie he created.

"Of course I will help you—" Dr. Jacobs said finally giving in. Before I could respond back the front door opened up. My mother came walking through but, she didn't see me. I hung up the phone and stood up forcing a smile on my face which wasn't hard to do.

"Humia?" My mother asked saying my name as she closed the door behind her.

"Yes mom...You know I'm here every Sunday." I said walking up to her and I placed a kiss on her cheek. She smiled and I gently took the roses out of her hands that she was carrying. I walked back into the living room and placed the roses on the glass table. My mother would go to the flower shop and pick up roses after church.

"Who were you just talking to?" My mother asked looking down at my phone in my hand. I waved her off and sat my phone next to the vase on the glass table.

"I was speaking to this administrator about enrolling into their program so I can pick up more patients." I said lying. My mother took off her sweater and sat down on the couch.

"Why aren't you working down at the hospital anymore?" My mother asked kicking off her shoes and I knew I had to think quick on my feet.

"Oh, mom it's too overstaffed plus my hours end up getting cut every week." I said lying again and I sat next to her on the couch. Her eyes were observing me for a few seconds then she scratched the back of her head.

"Hand me the phone so I can call and speak to your boss—" My mother said and I jumped up off the couch. Everyone believed that I was dead right now and I couldn't have this lie being exposed because the real truth would come out.

"NO! MOM! I mean...I like the position I'm in right now. I have a decent amount of patients that I take care of and I have a set schedule." I said calming myself down as I lied again. My mother gave me this look that made me uncomfortable then she nodded her head up and down. I looked over at the roses sitting on the table and I could feel my heart pumping right now. "Did you go out to eat with Mrs. Ester?" I asked changing the subject.

"I did...And it was amazing until—" My mother said then she paused.

"Until what mom?" I asked confused.

"When you realize that a person's lie can change your entire life. Then you think about making it right but, at that time it's a bit too late." My mother said without looking at me.

"I see Mrs. Ester been talking to you about her court cases again, huh?" I asked delivering a fake chuckle.

"Ester told me she had a case with two boys that have been sitting in adult prison since they were sixteen." My mother said then she turned her head to look at me.

"Sounds horrible unless they did—" She shook her head while cutting me off to speak.

"This young lady told the police that those two boys raped her at a party. Without any evidence the cops took her word for it and put them two in jail. A month later they been bumped up to prison just because the judge said so. Now these little boys are sitting in prison with grown ass men until the judge feels like he wants to take it to trial." My mother said and I stood up from the couch because I was getting hot. "Ester told me she knew that the young girl was lying." My mother said standing up too but I didn't know what her intentions were. I rubbed my neck then scratched my head.

"How did Ester know the accuser was lying?" I asked and I swear I was breaking out in a sweat. My mother smiled and walked up to me.

"The same way I should have known all them years...Jason never raped you when you were a little girl, did he Humia?" My mother asked and that smile disappeared off her face.

CHAPTER 30 CHINO

"How is Jada holding up?" I asked as Humia walked out of Jada's room. Her bedroom door was cracked open and I watched as Jada laid on her side getting her beauty rest.

"Can you let go of my arm please?" Humia asked looking at me. I didn't even notice I was grabbing her left arm.

"My fault girl." I said putting both of my hands up in the air like I was surrendering.

"Jada is fine, she just needs to rest. I will do her evaluation when she wakes up." Humia said rubbing her hands against her thighs like she was nervous. I looked down at her pocket and I noticed something that caught my attention.

"What's that?" I asked biting the inside of my mouth. Humia fearfully looked around and stuffed both hands into her pocket.

"Huh? What are you talking about Chino?" Humia asked dumbfounded but I had a feeling in my gut that she knew exactly what I was talking about.

"That little piece of plastic that was hanging out of your scrub pocket." I said pointing to her right pocket. Humia smiled and waved me off like I was speaking nonsense. "I could be wrong but since I been living on this earth I would admit to being wrong one time...Maybe twice if I count that last time but, I know what I just saw" I said circling around her then I looked into Jada's bedroom watching her inhale and exhale beautifully.

"I—I—I don't know what you're trying to get at Chino." Humia said and I turned my attention back to her.

"Is that dope in your pocket Humia? I hired you to wing Jada off that shit not to—" I said quietly but I put some base in my fucking tone. I didn't completely see what was in her pocket but if it got my attention like this. Then it couldn't be good.

"Dope? I'm fucking offended that you would even accuse me of something so horrendous like that!" Humia yelled out but, what startled me was the smile she delivered while she spoke. Anyone else would have been quite upset of accusations that I presented but she smiled like she won the lottery. Shit made me a bit uncomfortable. I'm going to explain why because any muthafucka that can show a personality like she just did doesn't have anything to lose. Everything becomes a game to them. I'm not even going to lie I was a bit on edge but I had to remind Humia that I was the nigga in charge.

"All I did was ask you a question...Lower your voice when you speak to me bitch before me and you have a problem." I said stepping to Humia and at this point I was all in her face.

"Are you threatening me Mr. Security guard, huh?" Humia asked jokily. She smiled at me then she used her right hand to rub on my dick. I moved her hand off of me aggressively and shook my head. Damn, this bitch was crazy and I never seen anything like it in my life. I had another feeling that this was only the beginning. If she was capable of showing signs of split personalities. What the fuck else was her mental ass capable of?!

"I see you have a few funny bones in your little body so let's play a game. Since you have a smart mouth let's see if you can tell the difference between a joke and a threat." I said. Humia chuckled and reached for the doorknob to enter Jada's room again.

"I don't have time for this." She said. I quickly moved and grabbed Humia by her nurse scrub top.

"Nah, come here yo." I said spinning her ass around to face me. When her eyes connected with mine she just smiled. A lot more than before. "If anything happens to Jada and I'm talking about the smallest mistake you bring her way, Humia you won't have to worry about this job or any other nursing job ever again. I mean what I say my nigga I always do. Now you can proceed. Get the fuck out of my face." I said. Humia poked her bottom lip out like a child. She swirled around back into Jada's room while humming. Why the fuck did I hire that bitch? That was the only thing on my mind right now.

"Everything good my nigga?" Angel asked walking up on me from behind. I took a deep breath moving to the side as I clapped him up. I turned my head and watched Humia rock back and forth in a chair just watching Jada sleep.

"I wish I could answer that question and keep it real with you Angel." I said to him. He looked into Jada's room to see what had my attention then he tapped me on my right shoulder.

"What's bothering you Chino?" Angel asked.

"Something...It's something about Humia that makes the hairs on the back of my neck stand-up." I said whispering then I moved away from the door. Humia stopped moving in the chair and she just looked at me while smiling again. But as long as her eyes were on me she continued to hum. Angel followed behind me but he just looked at me perplexed. That's because he didn't have the same encounter as I did with Humia.

"Let me found out that you're scared of a female now Chino." Angel said chuckling but I didn't find shit funny.

"Muthafucka, when have you ever known me to be timid of anyone especially a bitch?" I asked putting on the tough guy act. "I'm just saying...I think the bitch is sneaky and hiding secrets Angel." I said rubbing the side of my right face.

"Why the fuck did you hire her Chino? I told you I was searching for another nurse for Jada but you insisted that you knew what you were doing." Angel said balling up his face and I returned the favor.

"Nigga I do know what I'm doing." I said looking at him in his eyes.

"So why are you so against Humia?" Angel asked concerned but I didn't answer the question because Humia was a bitch you couldn't put into words. So I didn't even try. "Do you want me to go in there and—" Angel took my silence as approval and walked towards Jada's room. I gently grabbed his right arm and pulled him back over to me. I looked around then I looked upstairs to make sure no one heard me speaking.

"Nah, I got this I'm going to wait until she slips up. A bitch like that is definitely bound to get caught up." I said and Angel just rubbed his hands together.

"How do you know?" Angel asked.

"Because it's something about her." I said and Angel just stood silent but he looked at Jada's bedroom door like something had his attention. "Let me ask you a question." I said and Angel turned back to face me.

"I'm listening my nigga." Angel said.

"Does Jada have a man?" I asked and I felt myself getting a bit uncomfortable asking about her. Angel looked at me like he was repulsed but I didn't understand why.

"Why nigga you got a soft spot for that drug addict?" Angel asked and I started shaking my head.

"That's a fucked up thing to say Angel." I said and Angel tapped me playfully on my arm.

"Muthafucka you know I didn't mean it like that my mind runs faster than my mouth sometimes—" Angel said but I cut him off. I moved over to Jada's room so I could watch her sleep one more time.

"I can't keep my eyes off of her yo. But, she doesn't pay me any mind." I said which was the truth. She hardly comes out of her bedroom. Angel will have his chefs bring her food to her bedroom whenever she's hungry so it's hard to even talk to her. Only chance I get of seeing her beautiful face is when her bedroom door is cracked open and still I feel like I'm doing something wrong because of how I'm watching her from the hallway.

'You know her ass got a daughter, right? Yo...Crackheads hide everything when they doped up. That was a big ass secret she kept hidden." Angel said and I just cut my eyes over at him. Angel must of got the point because he put his hands up and took a step back. "My bad my nigga I didn't mean—" Angel said apologizing again but I wasn't trying to hear it.

"I want to—" Before I could finish speaking Angel cut me off.

"No wonder why your ass was relentless about finding a fucking nurse...Because you like Jada" Angel looked at me but he didn't smile.

"Chill out my nigga—" I said denying it and he just exhaled deeply.

"I don't think that's a good look for you." Angel said and I balled up my face.

"What do you mean by that Angel?" I asked in disappointment.

"I think that it's best if you just stay away from Jada. Don't pursue anything with her." Angel said shrugging his shoulders.

"But, why—" I asked because I genuinely wanted to know why he didn't think my liking for her was acceptable.

"CHINO! YOUR DAD IS OUTSIDE!" Nyla yelled out running through the double doors of the house. Nyla stuck her tongue out at Angel while running up the stairs. He looked a bit hurt when Nyla did that but, I always had a feeling it was something she knew about Angel. She didn't like him and that little girl wasn't afraid to express it.

"Thanks lil shawty." I said waving to her. Angel just watched Nyla run up the stairs until she disappeared. I clapped Angel up then I walked to the front door to leave out.

"Tell your pops...I said what's good." Angel said hesitant. I looked back at Angel and nodded my head up and down. I closed the doors behind me and walked up to my pop's car.

"Wassup pops?" I asked clapping him up as I got in the passenger seat. My pops turned to look at the front door and when I turned to see what his eyes were glued on I saw Angel standing at the door looking down on us.

"Every—Everything alright Chino?" My pops asked stuttering and I just nodded my head up and down. "How is Angel treating you?" My pops asked turning his attention from Angel over to me.

"Like the brother I never had." I said looking at Angel but, he was still standing at his door in the same position.

"For a reason..." My pops said putting the car in drive then he pulled off. He mumbled so it was kind of hard to hear what he just said.

"What did you say pops?" I asked confused and he just looked at me and smiled.

"I was just humming the words to a song I used to listen to back in the day." My pops said but I know he wasn't humming anything. Mumbled words came out his mouth that I just didn't understand. "Your mother can't wait to see you. She's in the kitchen preparing your favorite meal right now." My pops said changing the subject. I reached down in my right pocket and pulled out a stack of cash.

"Here you go pops." I said trying to hand it to him. My pops looked down at the money in my hand then he continued to drive on the road while shaking his head no.

"How many times do I have to tell you that I don't need your money Chino? Me and your mother are fine we don't want for anything son." My pops said declining my offer. I dropped the money down on my lap when I heard my phone vibrating. I pulled it out, tapping on the screen and held the phone up to my right ear.

"Yo, what's good" I said. My pops looked at me while I answered the phone then I turned to look out the passenger window.

"That nigga Mir will be out of the picture tonight. Make sure you're back home on time." Angel demanded. There it was again. That gut feeling that was causing me sufficient pain.

"No doubt." I said hanging up the phone on Angel. I sucked my teeth and dropped the phone on my lap.

"Who was that?" My nosey ass dad asked and I shrugged my shoulders.

"No one important...Where is the tape player? Dad I keep telling you every week let me upgrade your car but, you still want to be stuck in the 80's yo." I said laughing. I opened up the glove compartment and my pop's started laughing.

"What's wrong with my mustang boy? This car is still as good as new." My pop's said. I moved my parents into a new home and I paid everything off. I purchased my mother a new car but my pop's always rejected my offer whenever the subject surfaced.

"But, I have the money to get you any car you desire." I said and he got loud this time when he spoke.

"I told you Chino I don't want your damn money!—" My pop's yelled out. I shrugged my shoulders and continued digging around in the glove compartment so I could look for the TP. A second later curiosity killed the cat.

"Who is this?" I asked. I pulled a small photo out of the glove compartment and just stared at it.

"Just put that back into the—" My pop's kept his left hand on the wheel and tried to used his right hand to snatch the picture away from me but, I pulled back until I got answers.

"Nah, pops don't lie to me. I saw this woman's face before. Who the fuck is she?" I asked and my pop's banged his fist into his steering wheel while driving.

"Boy! You better watch how you speak to me I'm still your father!" My pop's yelled out but, none of that shit mattered right now. I nodded my head and went to the photo gallery on my phone.

"What are you doing Chino?" My pop's asked breaking out in a sweat. I knew I remembered her face from somewhere. Angel asked me to do some digging on Kia's aunt. I pulled up to her house and waited patiently. When she finally arrived home from work dressed in scrubs I took pictures so I could show him.

"This woman...This woman in this photo, her name is Tasha, right?" I asked looking at the picture in my phone then I looked at the picture my pop's had stashed in his glove compartment.

"Chino—" My pop's said exhaling deeply.

"Are you cheating on mom?" I asked. I was praying he said no because I didn't want to see my mother hurt.

"NO! IT'S NOT LIKE THAT CHINO...I WOULD NEVER CHEAT ON YOUR MOTHER!" My pop's said getting defensive.

"C'mon yo please respect me enough not to lie to me especially in my face." I said. I mean why else would a nigga have another bitch picture in his car. Keep in mind this photo was hidden in the glove compartment.

"Yes that lady name is Tasha." My pop's said confessing.

"Why is her photo in your car pops?" I asked confused.

"Why is her picture in your phone?" My pops asked trying to switch shit around but I wasn't in the wrong here...You see? I was never wrong.

"I asked you a question first pops be real with me." I said pleading at this point. My pops pulled over to the side of the road and took a deep breath.

"Because Chino. Tasha is your biological mother. You also have other siblings named Kia, Jada, Mir, and you're the youngest beloved." My pops confessed again and my eyes watered up. I can't fucking believe this shit. Damn, I'm supposed to be murdering my own blood brother tonight.

CHAPTER 31 CHINO

"Are you my father?" I asked tapping my right hand on my thigh. My pops kept both of his hands on the wheel while he was driving and kept quiet. A second later he looked over in my direction and shook his head no answering my question. "You played me for all these years yo!" I yelled out in anger. Who knows what the reason was behind the hidden secret but as a man...A grown ass man I just felt betrayed. Damn am I wrong for that?

"Now you know that's not true Chino...I would never hurt you son." My pops said making a right turn. I sat up in my seat and placed my phone down in my pants pocket.

"Hurt? How the fuck do you think I feel right now?" I asked and I heard him take a deep breath. A deep exhale that was necessary to calm him down.

"Chino—" My pops said in a low tone.

"Nah, since you know so much "pops." tell me how I fucking feel!" I yelled out. He made a left turn moving to the side so another car could pass by first.

"Whew, I understand that this bombshell angers you, but let me remind you that I'm still your father. Nothing can change that so watch how you talk to me son." My pops said warning me. He pulled in the driveway of his home while putting the car in park.

"My father? I mean honestly can I still call you that, sir?" I asked letting my emotions get the best of me right now. My pops turned the car off then took his seatbelt off while chuckling. I understood that the chuckle was a sense of comfort for him...He did that shit a lot when I was growing up.

"Now all of a sudden it's sir to you? The muthafucka that has been there since you were born. Running to the store at 3 and 4 in the morning to get you diapers. Teaching you how to fight, teaching you how to tie your sneakers and ride your bike. I was the nigga to remind you that it's not about how many times you get knocked down just make sure you get your ass back up and be better than yesterday. Putting your disobedient ass through school and loved your disrespectful ass enough to discipline you.

"Me and your mother working odd jobs just to have the money to sign you up for football. Just for your ass to quit a month later. You have been treated exceptional your entire life Chino and we have done right by you. After all I've done for you Chino you disrespect me and call me Sir instead of pops? You tried to make me feel exactly how you feel right now and let me tell you something, you succeeded but the thing is I've felt how you felt before. I stopped myself from feeling that hurt when I hit my 30's was it easy? Nah. But if I wanted to live my life I had to let go of that anger because I was directing it at the wrong people." My pops said to me.

I took off my seatbelt and shook my head. I was kind of confused what he meant by, *"letting go of that anger."* Unless he was hiding another secret in his life that he didn't tell me about. You see what I mean? Why the fuck can't muthafuckas just keep it real with me?! Just had me out here playing guessing games and shit.

"I'm not apologizing to you because I'm not the nigga that's wrong here." I said standing my ground.

"I didn't ask you to apologize Chino. You have every right to feel how you feel! You absolutely do and I'm not taking that from you but, don't turn around and treat me and your mother like shit just because we aren't your biological parents." My pops said and I started getting angry again. I just felt like he was trying to justify keeping this shit from me all these years.

"Why the fuck—" I said and my pops struck me in my chest with his right hand.

"Your mouth Chino." My pops said disciplining me again like I was a little boy.

"Make that your last time putting your hands on me pops I'm a grown man now and I don't live under your roof anymore." I said looking him in his eyes. I opened up the passenger door and I got out the car. My pops did the same thing holding his car keys in his right hand. The expression on his face, it was obvious he was biting his tongue. "Why is the truth just coming out now? Wait, what am I talking about truth? I still don't know the entire truth." I said gently tapping my hands on top of the roof. My dad looked at the front of his home and motioned for me to go inside.

"Go inside the house and ask your mother Chino. You'll get the answers you're looking for plus more." My pops said. I turned my head at him so fast you would think a truck was about to crash into us.

"Plus more? What the hell does that mean?" I asked. My pops stayed quiet and just shrugged his shoulders. I nodded my head up and down because now I was becoming fed up with this shit. I walked through the front door and my nose picked up on the smell of food so I knew where I could find my mother...It was time to confront her. I looked behind me and I noticed that my pops didn't follow me into the house yet.

"Mom I need to talk to you." I said walking into the kitchen. She turned around wearing her red chef apron and smiled at me.

"Chino...Papi I'm just waiting on the baked mac and cheese to finish up in the oven. I made a fresh pitcher of lemonade and I know you will love it baby, you always do." My mom said disregarding what I said. She opened the oven up to check on the food. I took a deep breath and walked up to the island table that was stationed in the middle of the kitchen.

"Cut the shit and tell me the truth." I said. My mother closed the oven and turned around. Her mouth dropped in shock. Them beautiful brown eyes filled with confusion and disappointment...Funny, huh? Now she feels exactly how I do.

"Wha—What—Excuse me?!" My mother yelled out. She reached for a kitchen towel and wiped her hands off while staring me down.

"You're not my biological mother...Tasha is, right? Why the fuck didn't you and pops sit me down and tell me this a long time ago?" I asked and My mother smiled and shook her head no.

"Honey, I don't know what you're talking about." My mother said shrugging her shoulders.

"YOU'RE STILL LYING TO ME!" I yelled out and I slapped my right hand on the island table. My mother jumped back and held both hands on her chest.

"Chino—" My mother said as her eyes watered up. I don't know if the tone of my voice scared her but she appeared to be threatened right now when all I wanted was the truth.

"Baby, just tell him." My pops said. I turned around and I see him walking up behind me entering the kitchen. Two tears dropped from my mothers eyes and she just pointed at my pops. A lot of rage was coming from this kitchen full of soul food right now.

"Why did you tell him James?! Why did you run your fucking mouth?! All I asked you to do was pick up Chino and bring him over here for dinner!" My mother yelled at my pops. She wiped her eyes and avoided eye contact with me. My pops remained calm as he started to shake his head.

"He found Tasha's picture in the car. I'm not sorry about it because he needs to know. I mean it was going to be a day he would find out eventually so why are you upset? Just tell him the truth...Finally." My pops pleaded with his wife. My mother picked up random silverware in her right hand and threw it in my pops direction. I moved out of the way so I wouldn't get hit with anything and she still wouldn't look me in my eyes.

"I'M NOT LOSING MY SON FOR THAT BITCH!" My mother yelled out referring to Tasha. I wasn't going to stop calling her my mother just because I found out that Tasha is my biological mother...Everything my pops said in the car was accurate the two of them always been there for me. They are my parents and that's what I know them as BUT, I still want to know the truth.

"Yes, you're my mother. You raised me but Tasha is my biological mother." I said and I could see the frustration and displeasure on her face when I said that. It was like a zombie targeting to attack a human. That's how my mother was standing in this kitchen right now. My pops saw the look in his wife eyes and he ran in front of me to protect me. My phone started ringing but I didn't bother to see who was calling.

"I'M YOUR FUCKING MOTHER NOT HER! YOUR CHOOSING THAT BITCH TASHA OVER ME?!" My mother yelled out with tears running down her eyes. The sweat beads were forming on her forehead. She was grabbing on my shirt making it bigger than what it was. I couldn't get her hands off me. She wouldn't let go.

"Calm down baby—" My pops said to his wife. He moved her back so she would get off of me but she started fighting with him now.

"GET THE FUCK OFF ME JAMES BECAUSE YOU STARTED THIS SHIT! YOU JUST COULDN'T KEEP YOUR FUCKING MOUTH CLOSED, COULD YOU?" My mother yelled out. My pops looked back at me and mouthed the words

"I'm sorry." in my direction. My mother walked back around the island table and slammed her hands on the navy blue tiles. She looked around at all the covered food and I knew that this soul food dinner was ruined.

"Are you going to tell me the truth?" I asked walking up to the table.

"Please just tell—" My pops said and I cut him off to speak.

"Just tell me pops...Please." I said looking at him. My pops looked at his wife and then he ran his right hand down his face. My phone started to ring again but I ignored it.

"I can't..." My pops said to me.

"What the fuck do you mean you can't?" I asked balling up my face.

"It's better if you hear it from your mother." My pops said pointing to his wife. My mother picked up a knife and she just looked at me pounding the knife on the tiles of the table. I pulled out my phone and I see I had two missed calls from Angel. I began to put two and two together and I knew I had to get to Mir before anyone else did.

"I need to see your car real quick pops." I said whispering to him.

"You're leaving?" My pops asked with a sadden face.

"I TOLD YOU! I TOLD YOU I WOULD LOSE MY SON!" My mother yelled out in tears as she continued to pound the knife faster. My pops walked over to his wife and gently took the knife out of her hands and he placed it into the sink.

"Chill out yo." He said trying to calm my mother down.

"Fuck you James! Every—Everything is your fucking fault." My mother said stuttering as she pushed my pops.

"I will be right back pops...I need to make a run. Just wrap my plate up and put it in the microwave. I gave you my word I promise." I said. My mother looked at me with more tears falling down her face than before. My phone started ringing again, I looked at the screen and saw that it was Angel again.

"Chino isn't coming back! He doesn't want anything to do with our family now!" My mother yelled out.

"Maybe, he just needs some air." My pops said assuming. He reached down in his pocket pulling his car keys out then he handed it to me. I looked at my mother but she didn't say a word to me. Not even an apology.

"I really need to go right now it's important." I said. My pops nodded his head up and down like he understood but my mother was standing there like her heart was broken. I left out of the kitchen leaving out of the front door and my phone started to ring once again. I hopped in the drivers seat starting up the car and I picked up the phone.

"Yo, what's good?" I said answering the phone. I looked behind me so I could pull out the drive way. I turned around and I saw my pops and my mother looking at me from inside of the house.

"Nigga I know you're spending time with your family but, when I call I need you to answer my nigga." Angel demanded. I disregarded my parents and gave my attention to this call I was currently on.

"A lot of shit just went down." I said referring to the overwhelming news I just encountered. "What you need?" I asked changing the subject.

"That muthafucka is about to get handled." Angel said in a serious tone on the phone.

"I thought you said later on tonight Angel...Damn, I didn't even get to eat with my family." I said.

"I can't wait any longer. I have to get revenge for Bella. I sent some niggas over there to his Aunt's crib to lure him in." Angel said and I pushed my feet down on the gas. Mir is family and for that reason alone I couldn't let this shit go down. I know harming Mir would make Angel feel better about Bella but I couldn't live with myself if I allowed it to happen.

"His Aunt's house?" I asked playing dumb even though I was headed there right now.

"Yeah my nigga. That bitch Tasha." Angel said and little did that nigga know he was calling my real mother a bitch.

"How long ago did you send them to her house?" I asked. I was curious to know if I had enough time to show my brotherhood to Mir.

"Why are you asking all these questions muthafucka?" Angel asked and my mind just went blank. Right now Angel thought I was still at my parent's house...He didn't even know I was on my way to protect Mir.

"Uh—" I said and Angel started laughing.

"Oh, I know what it is Chino—" Angel said and I began to get nervous because Angel was one smart muthafucka.

"What are you talking about Angel?" I asked making a left turn.

"You're hype about killing this muthafucka just like I am, huh?" Angel asked and I took a deep breath.

"I see you're not right about everything, huh?" I asked in a low tone hoping he didn't hear me.

"What you say my nigga?" Angel asked confused.

"Nothing...That was my pops talking in the background" I said lying. I pulled up to the house and all the lights were on which was a good sign that someone was home. "I will be there once I'm finished up with dinner." I said lying to Angel. I dropped my phone in the passenger seat and began to ruthlessly beep the horn.

"C'mon my nigga. I hope you hear me beeping the horn." I said praying that Mir would catch on. I looked around to make sure that I didn't see a truck pulling up. The front door opened up and Mir was dressed in all black. He was carrying a book bag walking in the direction of the car. I took a deep breath when I noticed he was going to be safe. "Yeah, that's right. Keep walking in my direction." I said watching Mir. I rolled the passenger window down and he got shook.

"FUCK!!" Mir yelled out when he saw my face. He turned around and started running. I jumped out the driver's seat and turned to yell at him.

"Ayo! Mir come here I put this on my life I'm not going to hurt you." I said telling the truth. Mir stopped running and he looked around checking his surroundings.

"That's your word?" Mir asked nervously.

"That's my word." I said and that shit was solid. Mir clenched on to his book bag and walked back over to the car. I moved the passenger seat down so he could get in the backseat.

"Angel sent you?" Mir asked wiping his forehead.

"I sent myself to save you. Thank God I got here in time before his army showed up." I said shaking my head. Mir placed his book bag on the side of him and he just looked around...I don't think he believed me when I said I wasn't going to hurt him.

"Kia..." Mir said rubbing his hands together.

"Huh?" I asked confused.

"Kia said she was going to do exactly what you just did. When I hear the horn outside just get in the car. My own sister was going to set me up?" Mir asked getting emotional. At that moment I knew he loved Kia to death. Just by his words he sounded betrayed and hurt. Trust me I felt the same shit today with my parents.

"I'm not too sure—" I said referring to Kia.

"Why are you even saving me right now yo? Who are you?" Mir asked uncomfortable sitting in the back seat.

"That's what family does." I said putting the car in drive.

"Family?" Mir asked dumbfounded and by the way he said that...He knew me and him wasn't brothers just yet.

"FUCK!" I yelled out when I see the all black Tahoe truck. Angel sent his niggas to come get Mir. "Duck down and don't move until I get back—" I said giving Mir specific orders as I put the car back in park. Mir did what I said but his ass was still asking questions.

"Why? Who am I hiding from?" Mir asked.

"Nigga just do it." I said hopping out the car and I jogged over to the driver's side of the Tahoe truck.

"Why the fuck are you here?" Benny asked. He was a little nigga that worked for Angel. He turned his truck off and hopped out the driver's seat.

"What you mean?" I asked trying to play dumb. I looked back at my car then I looked at Benny. "I'm trying to find that muthafucka Mir just like you." I said lying and Benny looked at me like he smelled bullshit.

"I mean Angel sent us here to pick this nigga Mir up...I know he didn't send your ass Chino." Benny said and he was right. "Let's just see what Angel has to say about you being here but, it looks obvious to me." Benny said smirking while pulling his phone out to contact Angel.

"What the fuck is that suppose to mean?" I asked getting offended.

"It means you're wearing a cape around your neck nigga. You're over here saving that nigga Mir behind Angel's back." Benny said with the phone up to his right ear.

CHAPTER 32 NYLA

"Where is your—" I heard someone creeping up on me from behind.

"Ahh!" I gasped. The apprehension presence startled me while my back was turned sitting on the bed. I closed my notebook repositioning myself...I see that it was Angel standing just feet away from me so I closed my notebook shut. I trembled with my number two pencil in my right hand and took a deep breath.

"I didn't mean to scare you baby girl I was just looking for your mother." Angel said staring dead at me while smirking. I continued to play with my pencil and I moved to the edge of the bed. I rubbed my left hand on my thigh and kicked the back of my feet against the bed. "Wait...Are you scared of me Nyla?" Angel asked. He spoke with such joy while that smirk was still on his fucking face. I looked up at Angel and returned the gesture...The smile I mean.

"I'm not scared of you or anyone else but I'm pretty sure you know that though." I said tapping the number two pencil against the bed. I didn't like this muthafucka and he knew it so for that reason I felt like he would pick on me...Not like a bully would though but pick my brain to see what I knew and little did he know my young ass knew a lot. I looked down at my book because I was sketching something that I had a vision about. Two people inside a mansion/home while an older male was sitting inside the closet texting someone. It doesn't make sense to me yet...A lot of my visions don't until I really take the time to understand. Angel was interrupting my process right now!

"I know one thing for sure—" Angel said. He looked back at the bedroom door then he rubbed both of his hands together.

"What's that?" I asked in a calm voice. Angel looked at my notebook and I grabbed it before he could. I placed the notebook behind my back and gave him my attention.

"I know that you wear your heart on your sleeve." Angel said to me and I started grinning.

"Define what you just said." I said talking to Angel like I was a teacher. He looked around the bedroom then rubbed his right hand through his scruffy hair.

"Uh, I mean—" Angel said stuttering and I just started laughing. Now at this point that smirk was off his face...Because he was getting intimated by me but, I was just getting started.

"You're stuttering so I will just help you out you won't have to owe me for the favor. Wearing my heart on my sleeve means exposing my true emotions. Making myself as a human vulnerable especially when I least expect it, right? Oh! Let's not forget this one...That I let all my feelings hang out there." I said jumping down off the bed dropping my pencil to the floor. Angel appeared nervous and I could tell that without looking at him. I assumed that emotion from his silence and when I did decide to look at him I was right. "Well since we're done talking about me, let's talk about you." I said pointing at him. Angel looked at himself up and down then balled up his face.

"What about me?" Angel asked confused. I walked over to the dresser and started tracing the outside with my middle finger...That was supposed to be a hint for his ass.

"The lack of secrecy when it comes to secrets." I said still focusing on painting a picture with my finger on the dresser.

"I don't have any secrets Nyla." Angel said in a low tone. He looked behind him to make sure no one was in the hallway.

"Can I ask you a question? Please be honest with me because I don't like when niggas—Excuse me, where are my manners? I don't like when people lie to me I get quite offended." I said turning to look at him. Angel looked like a frightened suspect getting questioned by cops. (I was the cop that he was afraid of.)

"I didn't lie to—" Angel said stuffing both hands down in his sweatpants pocket.

"Strike one...Three strikes and you're out. Fair warning..." I said pointing at him and I smiled.

"Nyla—" Angel said my name but I cut him off.

"Why did you allow all of us to live in this big ass house with you?" I asked. Angel looked down at the carpet floor while rubbing his lips together. "When someone is silent it's for two reasons...One they have something to hide OR two you're thinking of what to say next in your head to answer my question." I said and Angel started to shake his head.

"You know what...I think I'm just going to go find your mother—" Angel said turning around but when I spoke he stopped in his tracks.

"Your hands are sweating Angel." I said walking over to the window. I peeped through the blinds and I see Angel's security men dressed in all black guarding the gate.

"How do you—wait, my hands are in my pockets Nyla how would you know something like that?" Angel asked and I could hear it in his voice that he was petrified. I turned around from the window and motioned to his hands being in his pockets.

"Touch my hands." I said and Angel immediately shook his head no.

"Get the fuck out of here with that shit little girl." Angel said with more aggression than I saw before. I ran up to him and his eyes shot wide open. "WHAT ARE YOU DOING?!" Angel yelled out. He removed his hands from his pockets and held them out to stop me from attacking him...Which I wasn't. I just wanted to feel his hands and this dumb ass nigga fell for the trap. I squeezed on Angel's hands and three quick images flashed through my head. I don't know why my visions take so much energy from me but I fell back against the dresser and my mouth dropped.

"Oh my God—how many secrets do you have?" I asked as my eyes got watery. Angel wiped his hands off on his thighs and reached out to touch me but I pulled away. Something about the flashes reminded me of accuracy. "Wait, I've seen this before." I said wiping my eyes. I ran back over to the bed and I picked up my notebook.

"What are you talking about Nyla?" Angel asked fidgeting with his hands. I opened up the book to the page I left over sketching and there it was.

"It was you..." I said looking at the picture and a tear fell down my right eye.

"What—what was me? What are you looking at?" Angel asked nervously. He rushed over to me and I closed my book again. I wiped my eyes and took a deep breath.

"You're the reason why my mother was in prison for five years!" I yelled out. Angel wiped his forehead and he walked over to the bedroom door to close it.

"Aye, I didn't hire anyone to set Kia and Reem up." Angel said and that's when I gave him a puzzled expression because none of that came out of my mouth. "Why is that look on your face Nyla?" Angel asked walking over to me. I jumped on top of the bed while holding my book in my hand. Angel extended out his right arm so I would stop running from him.

"I never said you hired anyone Angel. You just mentioned it yourself. My mother also never told you her story about being in prison nor did she mention she got locked up with a male. That's funny...So how do you know any of this?" I asked and Angel just smirked at me. I knew at that fucking moment I needed to get away from him. I held on tightly to my book, jumping down off the bed and I opened up the bedroom door. Once I entered the hallway I looked around searching for my mom but, she was no where in sight.

"Nyla! Come here yo!" Angel yelled out with anger. That kind of anger that convinced me he had revenge up his sleeve.

"Don't you touch me!" I yelled out. I looked behind me and I see Angel running towards me.

"Mom! Mom where are you?!" I yelled out running down the stairs. I tried to keep up my pace and I could hear Angel. He was breathing heavy and not letting up. "Get away from me!" I yelled out again. I heard Aunt Jada coughing in her bedroom and I quickly decided to run to her for safety. I looked behind me and Angel suddenly disappeared.

"Little girl, have you lost your damn mind? Why are you running in my room like that? You're going to wake my daughter up." Aunt Jada said. She was looking at me like I was crazy. I closed her bedroom door shut and locked it. I placed my book on her dresser and bent over to catch my breath.

"Where is my mother Auntie Jada? It's important I need to talk to her!" I yelled out. Aunt Jada sat up on the bed dressed in a robe with a towel on her head. She used her left hand to pat her daughter on the back because she was sleep on her stomach.

"Girl...Why are you out of breath? It sounds like you need a damn nap...Come over here and lay next to your cousin." Aunt Jada said smirking but, she didn't understand how fucking important this was!

"I DON'T NEED A FUCKING NAP! I NEED TO FIND MY FUCKING MOTHER!" I yelled out and her daughter started crying.

"See what your little ass just did Nyla!?" Aunt Jada said annoyed. She started to hush her baby and pat her a little harder on the back so she would fall back asleep.

"You're not helping me I need to go look for my mom." I said fixing my posture. I caught my breath and started pacing her bedroom back and forth.

"Oh hell no you better get your little ass over here and put my daughter back to sleep since you woke her up. Damn, do you know how long it took me to lay her down peacefully Nyla?" Aunt Jada asked with an attitude. I continued to pace the room thinking about where my mother was. "You're so damn hyper all the time I think Kia needs to get you check for attention deficit hyperactivity disorder. You know get your little ass evaluated." Aunt Jada said smiling. Once she got her daughter settled down she repositioned herself to the edge of the bed. Since this bitch wanted to play with me I was going to play with her too.

"You mean to tell me after all them track marks down your arm and in between your toes that your brain cells are still working up there?" I asked smiling pointing to my temple and her smile erased off her face. "Did it hurt Auntie Jada when you said that long word? I mean you could of just abbreviated the word and called it ADHD." I said. Aunt Jada jumped up off the bed and rushed towards me.

"WHAT THE FUCK DID YOU JUST SAY TO ME YOU LITTLE BITCH?!" Aunt Jada yelled out grabbing on my shirt. "I'M NOT GOING TO TOLERATE ANY MORE DISRESPECT

FROM YOU!" Aunt Jada yelled twice as much. The alarming noise woke her daughter completely up this time.

"Get your hands off me you damn crackhead!" I yelled out pushing her ass but she wouldn't budge.

"I will fuck you up Nyla—" Aunt Jada tried to threaten me but, I pushed her again.

"I SAID GET YOUR HANDS OFF ME!" I yelled out. Aunt Jada grabbed my hands and three more flashes of her past went off in my head. "Oh my God..." I said. She let me go and I stumbled down to the floor.

"Every time you make that fucking face you creep me the hell out. What the fuck is wrong with you little girl?!" Aunt Jada asked anxiously as she backed up away from me. My eyes watered up and my heart started pounding.

"All of this is because of you Aunt Jada. .Angel inviting us to live with him wasn't a friendly offer. This shit makes sense now. It was a thought out and detailed plan because of YOU! My God...You took something precious from him years ago and his revenge has started. YOU DUMB ASS BITCH!" I yelled out. Aunt Jada knew exactly what I was referring to because she fell down to the floor in the fetal position.

CHAPTER 33 REEM

"Where you at yo?" I asked getting impatient. I was holding the payphone phone up to my right ear. I used my left index finger to block out the music in my left ear so I could focus on the conversation.

"I'm on my way Reem I told you already." Kia said annoyed but her background was beyond quiet compared to what I had going on over here. I looked around the bar and I see the bartender pouring double shots for niggas that couldn't handle their liquor. I looked behind me and this older lady was changing the music on the juke box.

"I don't give a fuck about what you told me Kia...I asked you a simple question and you still have yet to answer it." I said removing my left finger from my ear and I started to clench my fist together. "Now where is your ass at?" I asked again. Kia exhaled deeply into the phone and began chuckling.

"Inside a vehicle...About to pass a stop sign...Now I'm passing a gas station—" Kia answered my question but, her ass was being fucking funny.

"Oh! So you're trying to be a fucking comedian tonight, huh Kia?" I asked raising my voice. I noticed people staring at me so I toned it down a little. "Your ass was supposed to be here over an hour ago." I said and Kia made a noise on the other end of the phone.

"Listen, muthafucka I move when I want to fucking move NOT when you demand me being somewhere. I have a daughter and that is my first fucking priority—" Kia said and I quickly corrected her.

"That's our daughter and you act like she isn't a priority to me as well." I said and Kia stood quiet for a moment.

"All I'm saying is talk to me with some fucking respect Reem because you wouldn't like it if I spoke to you that way!" Kia yelled through the phone then she hung up on me. I took the payphone away from my right ear and placed it on the hook.

"Kia, Kia, Kia." I said under my breath while shaking my head. Ever since I got home from prison she has been acting different. Sounds like Kia is fucking with someone else but I don't want to be the one to assume anything...At least not yet.

"Everything good my nigga?" The bartender asked as I sat down at the bar. This nigga has known me since I was a young'n. I've been coming here since I was fifteen...I always looked older than what I was and during that time I would have muthafuckas in the bar hook me up with a drink. In return I would wash cars for free until I was old enough to buy my own damn drink.

"Yeah...Let me get another shot of vodka." I said pushing the stool chair closer to the bar. I dropped my head and rubbed my hands together because I couldn't get Kia off my mind. Anytime I felt this alone I would be in Tasha's bed fucking her from the back but I knew I had to have more self-control than that.

"You sure Reem? I mean you just got released from prison I don't think it's a good idea for you to go down this road...You already seem a little drunk—" The bartender said concerned. I elevated my head and balled up my face.

"Muthafucka what did I just say?! I didn't ask for a fucking sermon all I asked for is another drink." I said. The bartender placed a small white towel on his right shoulder and nodded his head up and down. I heard the entrance door to the bar open but I didn't look to see who it was.

"Here we are again...Do you remember me?" I heard a familiar voice asked walking up behind me. "Let me get the regular my nigga." He spoke again but this time to the bartender only. Then I see the stool chair moving on the left side of me. I turned my head and my expression was the same as it was before he entered this bar.

"The cab driver, right? Yeah...I remember you." I said. He extended his right hand out to shake mine without a smile.

"My name is Tywan." He spoke so calm and free.

"I don't think I could quite forget you after meeting you the other night." I said shaking his hand. The bartender came back over and passed two shot glasses in front of us.

"I see you still have that expression on your face...That expression that's full of questions." Tywan said looking at me then he repositioned his body to get comfortable in the stool chair.

"I'm just trying to handle whatever life throws at me my nigga." I said truthfully. I grabbed the shot glass, tilting my head back and threw the liquor into my mouth. "Why are you at the bar drinking? Aren't you on the clock?" I asked swallowing my shot. I looked down and saw that he had his work radio attached to his hip.

"I come here to drown out my problems...I always tell myself that a drink or two won't hurt me but the inner voice comes out and tells me to go ahead and take another shot. One or two drinks turn into fourteen or more if I don't black out. I'm here at this bar about six or seven days throughout the week." Tywan said then he started to down his shot. He motioned for the bartender to bring him another round.

"I keep telling your ass about this shit Tywan." The bartender said including himself into our conversation. I turned my head towards the music when I heard someone changing the genre to hard metal on the juke box.

"It's a bad habit that I'm trying to kick but it's hard." Tywan confessed.

"I'm assuming you drink the way you do because of Jada and the disappearance of your baby?" I asked for a better understanding. Tywan took another shot and pointed at the bartender for a third round.

"Jada leaving and my daughter missing plays a part in why I drink...Yes that's true, but it's much deeper than that." Tywan said running his right hand down his face thinking about his past. Why do niggas get so emotional when they ass start drinking?

"Nah I'm good my nigga." I said refusing another drink when the bartender came my way. One thing about me I knew my limits and I had enough liquor tonight. Tywan wiped his face again and started trembling with his hands.

"I use to run with this Spanish nigga back in the day and he had two brothers named Sanchez and JoJo or some shit like that...My memory isn't that sharp anymore. Me and the nigga used to move weight together ya know? From state to state faithfully a few times out the week. I enjoyed it because at that age I was living fast and made more money than I ever seen in my fucking life. One night before I went home I stopped by the Spanish nigga crib to drop off a bookbag to him.

"He left his front door unlocked and I was searching everywhere for him. I called out his name to tell him I arrived but I didn't get a response back. I thought something happened until I found him sitting in the hallway upstairs with tears falling down his eyes. I dropped the bookbag and I asked him what was wrong but, his eyes were glued on a family photo hanging up on the hallway wall. It was him, JoJo, Sanchez, and a young girl which he later confessed was his baby sister. He kept replaying the night in his head when a maid opened up the door and saw two detectives delivering bad news to his mother.

"He said it took him years to find out who murdered his sister I advised him to go to the police but, the nigga said he wanted revenge that was unforgettable...So unforgettable that he could taste it through his teeth. I told him I didn't want anything to do with his plan and since I refused, he said that I was dead to him. I was no longer a drug dealer because I didn't want to harm anybody so I got a job as a cab driver. All the money I had working with that muthafucka was gone! My mother's insurance got terminated, during that process of trying to get it back she was diagnosed with brain cancer.

"As her only child, I gave up all the money I had for the best doctors just so she could survive. Months later, all that money was used for treatments, medications and doctors. Overtime my mother got worse and she passed away shortly after. I was alone and broke...I wasn't making any real money as a fucking cab driver! So I started drinking...I drink because if I would of helped that nigga get revenge for his sister's murder then my mother would still be alive today. I haven't heard of any killings lately so you know what that means, right?" Tywan asked looking in my direction and I could feel my palms sweating.

"What—What does that mean?" I asked stuttering.

"He's executing his plan to perfection...Observing every detail so he can lay back and enjoy it. That nigga isn't ready for revenge at the moment he's having fun in the process that's why you haven't heard anything on the news just yet. I know how he thinks and I know how he moves." Tywan said pointing to his temple continually.

"The nigga...The nigga you're talking about is his name Angel?" I asked and I felt like my heart stopped when I asked that question.

"How did you know?" Tywan asked but, he had a smirk on his face while he spoke.

"WHAT THE FUCK!" I yelled out losing my balance. I didn't realize that I almost fell back out of the stool chair. The bartender and Tywan were looking at me like I was crazy but if they were in my shoes they would react the same. I was very timid right now, I heard the bar entrance door open up again. This time I turned my head and it was Kia walking through the doors. "Finally just the fucking person I wanted to see—" I said jogging in her direction. I looked back at the bartender to give him a heads up that I would be right back I didn't want him to think I was going to dip out without paying. I motioned for Kia to walk back outside because I didn't want to speak around anyone. I turned around and I saw Tywan smiling and winking at me as if he knew something that I didn't.

"What are you looking at Reem?" Kia asked me because I was just looking around like I was petrified... My emotions increased when I realized my daughter wasn't with Kia. This was the first time I actually saw Kia since we both been home from prison and I couldn't even focus on how beautiful she was right now because something was missing...Or someone at least.

"Where is Nyla? I asked you to bring my daughter with you." I said balling up my face.

"I'm the one taking care of her so I make the rules Reem." Kia said with an attitude but I didn't know where it was coming from. I reached out to grab her but she backed up away from me. "No uh don't touch me nigga." Kia said balling up her face.

"Come here yo...What the fuck is your problem Kia?" I asked and at this point it felt like I was chasing her ass because she continued to distance herself from me like I was contagious.

"I can smell the liquor coming out of your pores Reem...Get away from me." Kia said then she tightened up her jaw. I could tell that she was about to explode. "You fucked my mother that's my problem muthafucka and you got her pregnant behind my back!" Kia yelled out. A couple was getting out of their car to walk inside the bar and their mouth dropped when they heard Kia say that embarrassing shit.

"Your mother? Kia your mother passed away...She broke her neck falling down the stairs remember, baby?" I asked walking over to her and she slapped my hand out of the way.

"That's not my mother...Tasha is my mother." Kia said and my heart sunk to the bottom of my stomach. I felt like my forehead was sweating but, I knew the expression on my face exposed my guilt. I missed out on a lot of shit while being in prison because this was news to me. "What are you looking all nervous for honey? Because I know the truth now, huh?" Kia asked crossing her arms across her chest.

"Listen, Kia...I can explain—" I said taking a deep breath.

"No need Reem I didn't come here for an explanation nor an apology. Obviously that bitch had something that I didn't because you continued to go back to her." Kia said with tears in her eyes but she quickly wiped them before they fell from her loving face. I know I threatened Tasha telling her that if Kia ever found out about us that I would hurt her but it wasn't worth it. God showed Kia exactly what she needed to see so how the fuck could I be mad at that?

"Kia, all I want is you—" I said telling the truth and Kia looked at me like I disgusted her.

"I swear to God you will never have me ever again because I don't want you anymore Reem." Kia said wiping her face and she turned around to enter the parking lot. Seeing Kia walk away from me crushed my heart into a million pieces but, what did I expect? I was the one that done her wrong.

"DON'T HURT ME LIKE THIS KIA—" I said running up to her and I grabbed her right arm. Kia spun around and punched me in the chest.

"I asked you nicely not to fucking touch me Reem!" Kia yelled out and I backed away from her putting my hands up in the air...I didn't want to make her anymore more upset than she already was. "You also have another secret right?" Kia asked breathing a bit heavy and I shook my head no.

"I'm not too sure I know what you're referring to Kia." I said shrugging my shoulders.

"You have—I mean you had a brother named Jason didn't you?" Kia asked correcting herself because Jason was now dead.

"I never told you about Jason before." I said stepping back from her.

"That's the fucking problem you kept all of this from me!" Kia yelled out with more pain in her voice than closure. Jason was a deep secret that I kept hidden, how the fuck did she know about him?! I took a deep breath and smiled since she wanted to bring up my past...Now it was my turn.

"Kia...I'm not the only one with secrets here." I said and her voice began to crack.

"Excuse—Excuse me?" Kia asked and I could see her heart beating outside her chest.

"You murdered someone...Didn't you? Her name was Tatiana." I said and Kia just went off. She dropped her keys on the ground then she ran up to me punching me in my chest. Kia was beyond small so I was able to retrain her in my arms without any extra help.

"WHO TOLD YOU?! HOW DO YOU KNOW THIS REEM?!" Kia started crying as she tried to get out of my arms.

"Calm down baby." I said holding her tightly in my arms and she just exploded again.

"How many fucking times do I have to tell you?! I'm not your fucking baby!" Kia yelled out with more emotional tears than I have ever seen from her before. Kia shrugged her shoulders and started talking when she caught her breath. "So what...Yes I did it. I did what the fuck I had to do in order to save my sister Jada. I remember this night...As clear as day. I was laying in my bed watching the last episode of Baldwin Hills. Mir came in my room and handed me the phone saying it was urgent and Jada needed to speak to me. Jada was panicking on the phone telling me she did something terrible and if I didn't help her then she would go to jail for life. I told Jada to tell me where her location was and I would be right there. I stole the last twenty dollars out of my mother's purse for a cab just to make it to Jada.

I felt bad because that was money my mother was saving to get us dinner for the week and I stole it like a little thief. Why? Because when my sister called I came running without a question. I pulled up to this party Jada was at and the way she was panicking on the phone you couldn't tell because everyone else was just partying and minding their business. Jada didn't speak she just motioned for me to follow her. So we walked discreetly as possibly into the backyard of the party behind a shed that the family had on their land.

Jada pointed her index finger somewhere, I followed with my eyes and that's when I see the girl Tatiana laying there with cuts on her body. I leaned in further and noticed that she was stabbed to death. I looked at Jada hands and she had Tatiana's blood on her and scratches like the little girl was fighting for her life. I was so upset with Jada because my mother told us not to leave the house and her ass still went out like she was grown. Only difference is Jada had a body under her belt and she was just a teenager. I felt sick to my stomach I didn't want to know what went wrong here...I just wanted to hide this body and go home.

Me and Jada tuned the house party out while planning to get rid of Tatiana. I grabbed Tatiana's belongings before we decided on our next move. I knew we had to think quick though before someone saw us. We both dragged Tatiana as far as we could before we got winded. I was overwhelmed and my anxiety was getting the best of me. I bent over to catch my breath and I fell on Tatiana...I was completely covered in her blood. I heard police sirens and I told Jada to GET HER ASS HOME and get rid of the weapon that she killed Tatiana with. I kissed Jada and I told her I loved her...I always would.

We split up, Jada ran in the direction of home and I ran to the closest pizzeria shop to clean as much blood off me as possible. If I got caught that night or got hauled into the station for murdering Tatiana I would take the rap without a doubt even though I didn't do it. I love my sister that much to do anything for her" Kia confessed and my eyes shot open because danger was at her doorstep and she was too fucking naïve to see the shit.

"YOU NEED TO BRING ME MY DAUGHTER ASAP KIA
—" I yelled out and Kia wiped her face and looked at me like I
said something wrong.

"Why? What has gotten into you Reem?" Kia asked
dumbfounded.

"Muthafucka—Uh, Tatiana was Angel's sister and he's
coming after y'all...I think he knows what y'all did Kia." I tried to
speak to her with some respect but, I couldn't control my
emotions right now.

"Angel doesn't have any sisters dumb ass." Kia bent down to
pick up her keys and started laughing. "He only has two
brothers...What's really the problem Reem? Are you jealous?"
Kia asked sucking her teeth.

"Jealous? You think this shit is a game yo?!" I yelled out
pacing in front of the bar and Kia just stood there like she was
fucking cute.

"Yes nigga you heard me...You're intimidated that I found a
real man like Angel so now you're just saying anything to keep
me from him." Kia showed her true colors...She confessed what I
was hearing in the streets even the shit I heard when I was locked
up. IT WAS ACCURATE! Her attitude changed because of
another nigga...Another nigga that was plotting on harming her
ass.

"Bitch—You know what? So it is true Kia...you're fucking
with that nigga Angel, huh?" I asked and Kia shrugged her
shoulders confirming what I asked her. Shit, if Kia didn't want to
be with me anymore who am I to stand in the way of that? But,

one thing I know for sure is she better get my daughter away from that nigga before I end up hurting her ass and that was a promise.

"I have to get back to Nyla." Kia said trying to walk off but I knew in order to save her life I had to say something convincing from the night she murdered Tatiana.

"When you were cleaning your blood off in the pizzeria shop did anyone walk in the bathroom and see you?" I asked. Kia turned around and just looked at me like she was puzzled.

"What does that have to do with—" Kia was about to get smart but I cut her ass off to speak.

"DID ANYONE SEE YOU NIGGA?!" I yelled out and I could feel the veins popping on the side of my neck.

"Some older woman...Dressed in a maid uniform. Uh, nigga I don't know it happened a long time ago." Kia said shrugging her shoulders again then she looked down at the keys in her hands.

"That woman dressed in the maid uniform is my mother Kia. She saw you covered in Tatiana's blood." I said and Kia looked up at me and her eyes watered up again.

"I can't wait until Angel hears this shit." I heard someone speak coming from around the corner. I turned my head and it was Sanchez...Holding his phone out recording me and Kia's entire conversation with a smile on his face.

CHAPTER 34 NYLA

"You don't know what you're talking about little girl so just keep your mouth closed—" Aunt Jada said getting up off the floor as she wiped the tears away from her face. I was caressing Rose's back so she could fall back asleep.

"If I'm so dumbfounded, tell me why the fuck did you just get so emotional?" I asked concerned. I looked at Rose and when I saw that she dozed off again I covered her with the blanket. Aunt Jada charged at me and pointed her index finger at me.

"You little bitch—" Aunt Jada said with more anger in her bones than comfort. I jumped up off the bed so I could defend myself.

"Let me tell you something...If you ever put your hands on me again Aunt Jada I will tell my mother—Wait" I said rubbing the right side of my temple then I used my left hand to move her ass out of my way.

"There you go with that look in your eyes again." Aunt Jada said looking at me like she despised me. I turned around and my mouth dropped.

"The third flash—" I said staring at her and she just looked around the room like she was confused.

"What flash Nyla?" Aunt Jada asked then she sat down on the edge of the bed. "I don't see any cameras in this room what the fuck are you talking about the third flash?!" Aunt Jada asked getting frustrated because I just stood silent. She used her right hand and slammed it down on the bed. Then she turned around to make sure Rose was still sleeping.

"Of course you wouldn't understand...Aunt Jada you don't comprehend a damn thing I'll be surprised if you still knew your multiplication table." I said walking away from her but, when I heard her feet touch the floor I turned around to make sure she didn't harm me.

"DIDN'T I TELL YOUR ASS TO WATCH HOW YOU TALK TO ME—" Aunt Jada said getting loud and I started grinning.

"Nah, didn't I tell you if you touch me again then it was going to be a problem?" I asked and Aunt Jada just sucked her teeth.

"Nyla, I will—" Aunt Jada tapped her hands against her thighs to calm herself down. When I wiped the smirk off my face she returned to the edge of the bed and sat down.

"Tell me the truth Auntie Jada." I said moving over and I leaned back against the wall.

"The truth? About what?" Aunt Jada asked looking around the room like a lost child.

"Please don't insult my fucking intelligence...I'm smarter than you think." I said warning her.

"If you're so smart then you should know already." Aunt Jada said trembling with both hands on her lap.

"I get flashes in my head that only last about twenty seconds. I see shit but it's kind of hard to put the full story together. What you did was wrong Aunt Jada...I'm just trying to figure out why you did it." I said as I started to pace her bedroom floor.

"Nyla, Uh—" Aunt Jada said clearing her throat. I extended my arm out in her direction sticking my finger up so she would remain quiet.

"DON'T SPEAK YET." I said being cautious. I checked for anything out of the ordinary like holes in the room, loose vents or a mic hiding in the corner of her room including the bathroom. I didn't know what type of person Angel was and I was concerned that maybe he was hiding a recorder inside of her room to catch her slip up. Nothing caught my attention so I lowered my finger and proceeded to speak. "The girl you murdered...What was her name? I saw a gold chain and a composition book." I said with my eyes closed so I could remember the visions.

"Tatiana." Aunt Jada hesitated to speak but, when she said the victim's name her voice cracked like she was saying it with guilt and passion.

"Did my mother help you cover up the murder?" I asked and Aunt Jada started shaking her leg against the bed.

"Excuse me Nyla?" Aunt Jada asked playing stupid.

"C'mon yo don't lie to me...Why did my mother help you Aunt Jada?" I asked walking up to her and she took a deep breath before speaking. She stood up and walked over to her daughter and kissed her while she was sleeping peacefully.

"Kia helped me because she's loyal to me...Kia will always be loyal to you until she feels like you crossed the line. I just wanted to go out to the party that night just to see her face one last time." Aunt Jada said but when she said the pronoun "Her" I needed more clarity about who she was referring to.

"You're talking about Tatiana?" I asked for clarification.

"Yes...My mother told us not to leave the house that night due to all the shootings that went on in the summer time. I tried to fight temptation which didn't last more than five minutes because I disobeyed my mother. I told Mir and Kia I was going to bed early that night which was a lie. I went into my room and locked my door. Once I changed my clothes I snuck out my bedroom window and went down to the party to see Tatiana's beautiful face.
"I found her inside a party dancing on some nigga and I asked if I could talk to her privately outside. So me and her went into the backyard against the shed and I could feel that the vibe was off between me and her. I asked her who the nigga was and she laughed in my fucking face. Do you know what that bitch said to me?! Tatiana told me that she wasn't in love with me the way I was in love with her.

"That muthafucka played with my heart...She got my feelings so deep involved just to crush me and tell me she wanted to be with a nigga. At this point I was in tears but, my anger was growing and the more she spoke the more I was becoming numb towards her. I disrespected my own mother by leaving the house just to get broken up with at a fucking party...Do you know how fucking embarrassed and humiliated I felt Nyla?!"

"So you murdered Tatiana because she didn't want to be with you anymore?" I asked confused.

"I murdered that muthafucka because she confessed that she was just pursuing me because the cheerleaders in school placed a bet on my head. The cheerleaders told Tatiana if she could get me to fall in love with her then she could be on the team without even trying out. I was pleading to Tatiana in the backyard how much I loved her and how she was breaking my heart. I looked down in her hand and Tatiana was recording me so she could go back to school and show it to the cheerleaders.

"That's when I ran back into the party and I grabbed a knife out of the kitchen. I came back outside and I asked her nicely to give me the recording. Tatiana laughed and said no because I was going to mess her chances up with being on the cheerleading team. She walked away from me and I grabbed a fist full of her hair throwing her down to the ground. At this point she was kicking and screaming. I tongued Tatiana down one last time, kissing her on the forehead then I whispered that I was sorry for what I was about to do.

"I couldn't be humiliated like that yo because I was already getting bullied in school because of Mir. So I stabbed...I stabbed and stabbed until the recorder dropped out of her hand and she took her last breath. That's when I called the house and Mir picked up the phone. I told Kia if she didn't come right away then

I would be locked up for life...About seven minutes later Kia showed up at the party wearing a book bag and she helped me get rid of Tatiana's body." Aunt Jada was spaced out as she confessed about what she did to Tatiana. Multiple tears started running down her face as she surfaced her past again. I closed my eyes and took a deep breath.

"So you were into bitches in high school Aunt Jada?" I asked for a better understanding.

"Nah...I was just into her." Aunt Jada said and I closed my eyes.

"The third flash...It looked like my mother was inside the bathroom of a pizza shop. Did Tatiana have a gold chain on and did she have a book in her possession at the party?" I asked opening up my eyes. Aunt Jada looked at me like she was scared then she nodded her head up and down. "Where is it?" I asked and Aunt Jada shrugged her shoulders.

"You have to ask your mother...She got rid of everything." Aunt Jada said and I started to shake my head.

"Did you know that Tatiana is the little sister of Angel, JoJo and Sanchez?" I asked whispering and Aunt Jada jumped up with more tears in her eyes.

"WHAT THE FUCK DID I DO?!" Aunt Jada yelled out when she realized she fucked up. She looked over at Rose and the tears started falling from her face when she saw her daughter.

"Lower your tone Aunt Jada...If my mother is loyal to you, I guess I have to be too despite the wrong shit you did including dragging my mom into your mess." I said pointing to her.

"HOW DOES ANGEL KNOW—" Aunt Jada kept the same tone and I hushed her ass again. I just didn't want to bring any attention to her or me right now until I figure out what to do next.

"At this point it doesn't even matter...We need to get out of here. Do you have a phone or did you sell it Aunt Jada?" I asked looking around the room.

"You think just because I'm on drugs that I would sell my phone? I mean how else was I supposed to get in contact with my drug connect?" Aunt Jada wiped her tears then she started chuckling.

"I didn't think that was funny Aunt Jada." I said being truthful. She walked over to the dresser and grabbed her phone to hand it to me.

"I was just trying to lighten up the mood Nyla...I'm sorry." Aunt Jada said. I put in my mother's number into the phone but, the call wouldn't go through.

"Fuck I don't have any service in here...I have to step outside." I said. I looked back at my Aunt and she appeared to be so lost...I think she felt like that her entire life. "Lock your bedroom door I will be right back." I said walking out of the room. A few seconds later I heard the locks on Aunt Jada's door. I looked around to make sure I didn't see Angel then I walked outside still looking down at the phone in my hand.

"Damn! Where are you mom?" I asked out loud putting the phone up to my ear. I see a car come in through the gate but, as the car got closer I noticed it wasn't my mother. I exhaled deeply and called my mom again. "Mom—Mom...Pick up the phone." I said sitting down on the porch and the phone continued to ring. The driver's door of the car opened up, someone got out and then the door shut.

"You're the only one that showed up?" I heard someone say but, I didn't make out the face just yet.

"Showed up? What are you talking about?" I asked when I noticed that it was Teka. She was dressed in her nurse uniform and she just sat next to me on the porch. I ended the phone call and just held the phone in my hand...I didn't know if she was trying to be nosey but I didn't want to speak around her ass.

"It's the anniversary for Tatiana's murder. We usually do a candle lighting for her every year." Teka said and I scratched the back of my head.

"How did you know Tatiana?" I asked curious.

"I—Uh..." Teka started stuttering then she looked around to make sure no one was listening to her.

"I already know your secret...It's okay I didn't tell anyone besides my mother. So whatever you're about to say is safe with me." I said and Teka nodded her head up and down while clearing her throat.

"How did you know that dark secret about me Nyla? I'm not even going to lie sitting next to you feels a bit familiar" Teka said looking at me up and down. Then a second later she slid down away from me like I was deadly to be around.

"Tell me how you know Tatiana and I will tell you the things I know about you." I said moving closer to her and she didn't react. Teka shrugged her shoulders and started whispering.

"Uh—I was the quarter back for my football team in high school and I ended up fucking with Tatiana. The last time I saw her...Alive I mean she was dancing on me at this party then somebody came up to Tatiana and whispered in her ear. She told me she would be right back but later on that night I found out she was murdered." Teka said looking down at her nurse shoes.

"You didn't see who it was that pulled Tatiana away at the party?" I asked and when she turned her head to say no I started smiling when I realized my Aunt was in the clear.

"It was dark inside the party...I feel like I know but I don't want to assume." Teka said.

"It's probably your imagination Teka." I said waving her off then I looked down at the phone when I see my mother was returning my call.

"Nah...Honestly I think it was your Aunt Jada that murdered Tatiana." Teka said looking at me and that's when I realized that I spoke too soon.

—KASSANA WILSON

CHAPTER 35 SANCHEZ

"Sanchez, where are you baby?" Teka asked. I was holding the phone up to my right ear sitting behind the driver's seat of my wheel.

"I will be there soon. I just need a drink first." I said putting my car back in drive mode. I drove around the bar and the parking lot was completely full. There were two people standing in front of the bar having an argument. They looked familiar but I couldn't tell from afar. It was Friday night so I expected the bar to reach its capacity. I decided to park around the corner then walk to my destination.

"A drink? Nigga are you fucking kidding me?" Teka asked. She spoke with full disappointment in her voice.

"What's the problem yo?" I asked finding a parking spot. I parallel parked between two cars and turned my car off.

"The problem is you're supposed to be paying respect to your sister Tatiana tonight and you're not here at the gathering because ya ass decided to have a drink." Teka said exhaling deeply into the phone. I jumped out of the driver's seat and closed my door behind me. I still had the phone up to my right ear while carrying my car keys in my hand.

"Man, listen—" I couldn't finish because Teka cut me off to speak.

"I'm not a man Sanchez." Teka said getting defensive.

"I didn't say you was Teka it's just a figure of speech." I said with a straight face then I proceeded to walk towards the bar. "You should be used to the way I talk by now...Why the fuck are you being so sensitive?" I asked and Teka stayed quiet for a moment like she was thinking about something.

"Sanchez...Just get your ass over to the house now." Teka said in a low tone. I wasn't too excited about going to Angel's crib but I knew I had to put my feelings to the side to pay respect to Tatiana.

"Yeah I will...After I get my drink first." I said hanging up the phone and I put my car keys in my pocket. I continued to walk and I see this woman dressed in a suit with a messy bun in her hair. She was heading straight towards me. When I moved to the side she repeated to do the same.

"Who the fuck are you?" I asked as she stopped in front of me.

"I think the real question is who are you?" She asked stuffing her hands into her pockets with a smile on her face. I shrugged my shoulders and moved to the side...This bitch immediately did the same shit. I wanted my fucking drink and she was stopping me from getting that.

"BITCH IF YOU DON'T GET THE FUCK OUT OF MY FACE—" I said moving up closer to her. She used her right hand to move the bottom of her blazer to the side. I looked down and that's when I see her gold badge.

"Whew, I think you better back up before I hit your ass with an assault charge." She said smiling and she pointed for me to move back from her.

"I didn't put my hands on you." I said stepping back. The smile was even bigger on her face right now.

"Anything I say goes...Being a detective I turn nothing into something." She threatened me. "The name is Shay." She introduced herself. Shay extended her right hand out to shake mine but, I looked in the other direction and bit the bottom of my lip.

"Punk ass police." I said speaking under my breath.

"Excuse me nigga?" Shay asked walking up on me but, I just shook my head so I wouldn't have to repeat myself.

"What the fuck do you want? I don't know you—" I said and Shay clapped her hands together. She looked down at my hands and I just balled up my face.

"Your wedding band is impressive...I got checked into the hospital—" Shay said and I exhaled deeply and shrugged my shoulders. I didn't give a fuck about none of the shit she was saying right now I just wanted some liquor in my system right now.

"Listen...Weirdo...Detective, whoever you are. I'm craving a fucking drink and I have somewhere I need to be so if you don't mind—" I said trying to move around her but Shay grabbed my left arm aggressively causing me to stop in my tracks.

"Oh but, I do mind...You're not leaving until I finish telling my fucking story." Shay said and I pulled away from her with my face balled up again. She looked at me and smiled like she found this shit amusing. "Like I was saying, I got checked into the hospital the other day. The nurse that took care of me...Her wedding band match the one on your finger." Shay said and I nodded my head up and down because it was obvious who she was talking about.

"Nurse? You must be talking about my wife Teka." I said. Shay smiled and scratched her temple with her right hand.

"Teka?" Shay asked while laughing.

"What the fuck is so funny?" I asked getting aggravated.

"We both went to high school together...Shit, she is definitely a different person now." Shay said looking at the dirt under her nails.

"A different person? Her surgeries doesn't bother me...I actually support whatever she wants to do. I mean that's her body she can do whatever she pleases." I said in an encouraging tone.

"Are you drunk already or you're just naive? It's not the surgery that I'm talking about." Shay said erasing the smile off her face. "Did you know Pablo—I mean did you know Teka during high school?" Shay asked shaking her head. For a moment there I thought she said a nigga name but, I figured I was just tripping.

"Nah...I met her a few years ago. I would love to see what her sexy ass looked like during that time of her life but,—" I said. I stopped myself from talking because I was standing in front of a fucking stranger that so happened to be a cop...And I was venting to her. That was a big NO-NO!

"But what?" Shay asked looking me in my eyes.

"Teka tells me she used to get bullied in school and she wants to keep that part of her life buried forever so I don't bring it up." I said and Shay just started grinning.

"Teka wants to keep it buried for a reason...By the way that muthafucka wasn't bullied he—I mean she was very popular in high school." Shay said and there she go doing that slick shit again. Maybe she just had a lot of police cases on her mind and she was getting my wife mixed up with it so I didn't trip about the pronouns. Shay reached inside her right pocket and pulled out a picture that looked ancient. "I have to go...See if you can spot your wife." Shay said walking off. I looked at both sides of the picture and became confused.

"There's football players on one side and cheerleaders on the other side." I said looking back at Shay then I looked more into the photo and I see my little sister.

"Tatiana?" I asked confused. Shay turned back around and headed back towards me.

"That's your sister that got murdered, correct?" Shay asked standing in front of me.

"Yeah...But, she wasn't on the cheerleading team...Where is Teka?" I asked. Shit was becoming spooky at this point. Why was my sister in the photo when she wasn't an official cheerleader in high school and where the fuck was Teka in the photo?

"I never said Teka was in a cheerleading uniform in that picture." Shay said. I examined the picture intensely then when I looked up Shay was already down the street.

"Yo?! Where the fuck are you going?" I asked but she didn't respond back. She jumped into a vehicle and pulled off. "I need a fucking drink." I said. I heard commotion and I peeped around the corner...I see these two muthafuckas Reem and Kia. I went to the recording app on my phone and waited for one of these niggas to slip up.

"DID ANYONE SEE YOU NIGGA?!" Reem yelled at Kia.

"Some older woman...Dressed in a maid uniform. Uh, nigga I don't know it happened a long time ago." Kia spoke in a nonchalant tone.

"That woman dressed in the main uniform is my mother Kia...She saw you covered in Tatiana's blood." Reem said to Kia and she became silent.

"I can't wait until Angel hears this shit." I said holding my phone out as I looked at the two of them.

"SO YOU MURDERED MY SISTER BITCH?!" I yelled out feeling the same emotions I did when the detectives showed up on my mother's doorstep that night.

"Sanchez listen it's not even—" Kia put her hands up to speak but, I cut her off.

"Bitch shut up!" I yelled out and Reem rushed towards me.

"Ayo, my nigga watch your mouth when you talk to her!" Reem yelled out and Kia got in between us both.

"Where's my money pretty boy?" I asked smiling and Kia looked at Reem like she was confused.

"Nigga, I keep telling you I don't have any fucking money!" Reem yelled at me and I could see I was getting him frustrated...The same frustration that Shay had me a few minutes ago.

"What money is he talking about Reem?" Kia asked puzzled and Reem stepped back.

"This was my CO when I was in prison...He went through my files to see what I was locked up for and came across my dirt. I keep telling this muthafucka when we got locked up all that money disappeared." Reem said but I knew this bitch ass nigga still had money hiding somewhere.

"Sanchez, he's telling you the truth." Kia said trying to co-sign but, I pushed her back with my right hand.

"Bitch didn't I—" I said and Reem balled up his right fist.

"I'm not in prison anymore my nigga and I don't give a fuck about going back if you don't watch your mouth." Reem said. I looked down at my phone and started smiling.

"You know when Angel hears your confession, life will be over for you, Jada, and your daughter." I said and Reem started to breathe heavy...To the point Kia had to place her hand on his chest for him to calm down.

"MUTHAFUCKA! NOBODY BETTER NOT TOUCH MY DAUGHTER—" Reem said with tears in his eyes and I winked at him.

"Chill out Reem." Kia said patting his chest and Reem looked down at her.

"Chill out? How the fuck do you expect me to be calm when he just threatened our child Kia?" Reem asked and she just nodded her head up and down.

"Listen, my fucking heart is sitting at the bottom of my stomach right now too but I have to be calm in order to save Nyla and Jada." Kia said reassuring Reem.

"Save Jada?! Her ass is the reason why you're in this shit Kia." Reem said and now I was confused because I thought Kia took my sister's life.

"I'm not throwing my sister under the bus...I'm too loyal to her." Kia said shrugging her shoulders then she looked over at me. "Sanchez...If you delete the recording, I will tell Angel the truth without no hesitation." Kia said looking down at my phone.

"What are you going to give me?" I asked licking my lips and Reem charged at me.

"Nigga—" Reem said and Kia pushed her baby dad back while I still had a smile on my face.

"I have information about your wife that you don't know about...DELETE THE RECORDING." Kia said with tears in her eyes. I paused for a moment then I showed her that I deleted the recording. Kia wiped her eyes and took a deep breath. Reem moved to the side with his fist still clenched together.

"Tell me." I demanded putting my phone into my pocket but, I still had the photo in my hand that Shay gave me.

"Your wife...Was born a man and Teka didn't marry you because she loved you. Teka married you for another reason." Kia confessed and now. I was the muthafucka with tears in my eyes. No wonder why my wife...I mean my husband got fucking offended during our phone conversation.

"WHAT THE FUCK?! NAH YO AND WHAT DO YOU MEAN SHE MARRIED ME FOR ANOTHER REASON?" I asked letting all my anger and frustration build up. I looked at Reem and he was now smiling at me...Ain't it amazing how these fucking tables turn?! Kia came up to me and took the picture out of my hand. Her eyes were glued to it like she was searching for someone then she pointed down.

"She is the reason..." Kia confessed. I looked down to see Kia pointing to Tatiana...But, how the fuck was Teka connected to my baby sister? SOMEONE WAS GOING TO END UP MURDERED IF I DIDN'T GET ANSWERS.

—KASSANA WILSON

CHAPTER 36 ANGEL

"Yo—" I said answering the phone. I placed the phone on speaker to look under the mat to get my mother's house key. Every anniversary I would pick my mother up and bring her to my place in respect of Tatiana's candle lighting. At this moment my mom wasn't home so I decided to wait for her inside.

"Ayo, my nigga—" Benny said. I unlocked the front door and walked inside my mother's house. I placed her house key on top of a table that was next to the door.

"What is it Benny?! I'm kind of busy right now," I said locking the door behind me. I turned around and walked up the stairs.

"Uh...I have to talk to you—" Benny said stuttering and I balled up my face.

"Nigga, just spit it out! What the fuck are you stuttering for?!" I yelled through the phone.

I heard a beeping noise and I looked down at my screen. I had an incoming call, I took my phone off speaker phone and held it up to my right ear.

"Hold on Benny, someone is on my other line," I said as I proceeded to click over.

"Angel?" I heard a familiar voice say my name but, when I pulled the phone away from my ear to look at the caller ID the number came up blocked.

"Who the fuck is this?" I asked reaching the top of the stairs in my mother's house.

"Dr. Jacobs—" This nigga answered my question. I turned to my left and I smiled when I saw the bedrooms that belonged to me, JoJo and Sanchez growing up. I immediately turned to my right and I got the chills when I saw Tatiana's room door closed.

"What do you want?" I asked holding the phone up to my ear and I used my left hand to rub against the hallway wall...That feeling brung back a lot of unwanted memories so painful that I yanked my hand off the wall.

"When can I get the other portion of the money Angel? I'm going through a rough time right now and I'm backed up on my mortgage," Dr. Jacobs asked.

"You'll get the money when I'm ready to give it to you muthafucka." I said turning around and I exhaled deeply.

"Nah..." Dr. Jacobs said and I started to chuckle. I looked over at Tatiana's bedroom again and gained a knot in my stomach.

"Nah? Where did you pick up on the hood slang Dr.?" I asked but, he stayed quiet on the phone so I proceeded to speak. "Sounds like you been having a lot of niggas as your patients lately...What happened to the proper grammar? You know it goes a little something like this, *'Angel I disagree with your response,'* instead you just hit me with the word Nah." I said taking a step towards my sister's bedroom...Every time I got closer the knot in my stomach grew tighter.

"Listen, I did everything by the fucking book and I followed every small detailed direction. Even when I didn't want to do it...Now I need that money before I lose my home," Dr. Jacobs said.

"I said I will give it to your punk ass when I'm ready to give it to you." I said repeating myself and that was one thing that I despised was a broken fucking record.

"I will go to the cops and tell them everything—" Dr. Jacobs said threatening me.

"And tell them exactly what Dr. Jacobs?" I asked laughing. I was in front of Tatiana's bedroom and all of a sudden I felt like I was becoming suffocated. I reached down to touch the doorknob and I froze up like my entire body shut down.

"That mansion wasn't mine to begin with...I will tell them that you lured Kia and Reem into the house to rob it—" Dr. Jacobs said and I interrupted him.

"I didn't lure anyone Dr.," I said.

I took another deep breath and I opened up my sister's bedroom. The perfume scent that she use to wear in high school hit my lungs like she was still *living* on earth. Then I flicked the bedroom light on and her purple walls engaged with my eyes. Purple was Tatiana's favorite color...And everything in her room appeared to be exactly the same. Her bed was still messy from that night and she had clothes on her floor in the corner. She wore a size 10. My eyes watered up thinking about my sister.

"You still played a part in the crime muthafucka...You had one of your boys put a bug in Reem's ear about the mansion. Saying if him and his baby mom was to rob it then they wouldn't have to worry about money for a long time. I will also tell the police that you made me sit in the closet and alert them when they were doing the home invasion," Dr. Jacobs said.

I wiped my eyes when I realized I was still on the phone with this muthafucka. I sat down on the edge of Tatiana's bedroom and cleared my throat.

"You will get charged—" I said and he cut me off to speak.

"Nah muthafucka you were the mastermind behind all of this. Did you forget that I'm a doctor? The way I use my words are extraordinary and I will tell the detectives that you threatened my life," Dr. Jacobs said. "Let me ask you something...Why come up with a plan like this to get two people arrested?" Dr. Jacobs asked.

My past life flashed in my eyes again like it always did when I thought about this shit.

"I wouldn't expect someone like you to understand," I said shaking my head. "Let me tell you something if you ever threaten me again I will *gladly* remind you who the fuck I am. I will cut your dick off with my bare hands and stuff it in your mouth...You won't even have time to contact the police. Do you understand?" I said then I turned my head when I noticed the bottom of Tatiana's dresser cracked open. I got up to close it until something caught my attention.

"I understand Angel," Dr. Jacobs said and I nodded my head up and down.

"Good boy," I responded back to that nigga like he was my pet. I hung up my phone and placed it in my back pocket. Then I opened up Tatiana's dresser and inside was a torn up journal.

"Damn...I miss you sis," I said while picking up her property. I flipped to the end of the journal and I started to read when I see hearts all over the page.

"My last entry journal...

"I'm just speaking this into existence with it being my last entry for now, because I will start a new beginning on Monday. Tonight is the night that the most popular football player in my school invited me to a party. I've been a cheerleader for about a week now and my life has changed for the better. The only thing I feel guilty about is sneaking behind my brothers back with this secret because I know how they feel about me and cheerleading. Nevertheless, I get to break the news to Jada tonight at the party...That I can see her in my future forever and I have never felt this way about anyone else let alone a woman. I hear Angel and JoJo coming upstairs and I know they're coming to my room to bother me so let me put my journal away. I will pick it back up on Monday when I officially start my life as a cheerleader with Jada by my side.

Xoxo Tatiana"

"WHAT THE FUCK?!" I yelled out as I closed Tatiana's journal shut. I payed attention to my sister when I was younger how the fuck did I miss all of this yo?!

"What's wrong? What are you doing in here Angel?" My mother entered Tatiana's bedroom with her purse and car keys in her hand. I placed my sister's journal behind my back so my mother wouldn't catch me.

"I—Uh..." I said and my mother walked up to me like she found me suspicious of something.

"You know Tatiana's room has been the same since she left out that night...I haven't touch a thing AND YOU SHOULDN'T BE TOUCHING SHIT EITHER!" My mother yelled out and snatched the journal I had behind my back. I dropped my hands down to my side and my mother placed Tatiana's journal back into the bottom dresser.

"Ma...Tatiana wasn't on the cheerleading team in high school—" I said confused and my mother nodded her head up and down.

"Yes she was baby Tatiana made the team a week before she was found murdered," My mother confessed. She walked up to the desk in the bedroom and sat her purse and keys down. I balled up my face and just stared at her.

"Me and Sanchez told her how we felt about that shit. All them bitches—Excuse my language all them teens in school walking around in them short skirts. I didn't want that life for Tatiana...I didn't want her to grow up so fucking fast," I said.

My mother pointed at me with her right index finger. Truth was my mother would wear explicit clothing growing up to make money for us and I just didn't want to see my sister in anything provocative.

"Curse in front of me again Angel and I'm going to pop you in your mouth boy." My mother said and no matter how old I got she didn't give a fuck...Respect was respect in her eyes. "Did you hear what you just said?" My mother asked shaking her head while she spoke to me.

"What did I say wrong ma?" I asked with my hands up like I was in denial.

"You said, 'I...I this and I that,' when it wasn't about you Angel regardless of how you and your brothers felt about cheerleaders. I couldn't allow y'all to dictate your sister's life...She wanted to live her life and I encouraged her to follow her own path" My mother said but, I didn't agree with that shit.

"So you were alright with her being on the cheerleading squad?" I asked stuffing my hands down in my pockets.

"Alright? I was happy for Tatiana...Because she was happy for herself. She was finally doing something to be proud of without y'all negative asses trying to tear her down. Tatiana told me she made the squad and I told her to keep it a secret from y'all" My mom said smiling turning her head like she was reminiscing her deceased daughter.

"We never knew this—" I couldn't finish speaking because my mother walked up to me and tapped on my temple with her right and left index finger.

"Y'all went to a different school that's why." My mother said and I bit the inside of my mouth.

"I can't believe this shit...Why did you keep this from us? Does Sanchez know?" I asked and my mother balled her beautiful face up.

"Neither does JoJo—Wait," My mother said and she delivered the face expression of worry.

"What's wrong ma?" I asked staring at her.

"Where's JoJo?" My mother asked looking at me. I could feel my breathing picking up and my heart was starting to sink.

"I—um..." I said scratching my head because I couldn't find the right answer when the answer was I murdered my own blood brother because he was disloyal to me.

"I have been calling him and he doesn't return my phone calls...Tonight is Tatiana's candle lighting and I still haven't heard from my son," My mother said.

"Maybe JoJo is just doing overtime at work mom—" I said trying to make her feel at ease a little bit even though it wasn't the truth.

"Nah...I know he's not working," My mother said. She turned to grab her purse and keys off the desk then she looked at me.

"How do you know?" I asked breaking out in a sweat.

"He never works on this day...And a mother knows her child, something is wrong Angel," My mother said exiting out of Tatiana's bedroom. I went to follow after her because I wanted to calm her down.

"Where are you going Ma?" I asked then my phone started ringing. I looked at the incoming call and it was Benny, I answered the phone and placed it up to my ear. "Benny? I can't talk right now my nigga" I said leaving out of my sister's bedroom and I closed the door behind me.

"Angel...You're not going to be happy with what I have to say," Benny said. I looked around to see if I could spot my mother but she disappeared.

"Nigga spit it out!" I yelled getting annoyed because I was trying to deal with other shit right now.

"Chino got to the house before I did and I think he's protecting Mir from you." Benny said and my world became black and quiet when I heard that shit.

CHAPTER 37 CHINO

"So you didn't see Mir come out this crib yet Chino?" Benny asked sarcastically lowering the phone from his right ear.

"Nigga what the fuck did I just tell you?" I asked balling up my face. I looked back at the car to make sure Mir wasn't visible.

"I don't know muthafucka...Sometimes it's hard for me to comprehend when someone tells me bullshit—" Benny said smirking and I stepped to him.

"Nigga, what the fuck do you mean bullshit?" I asked looking Benny in his eyes. I heard a noise with three seconds in between, I looked down and I saw Benny tapping his phone against his right thigh.

"Why are you so defensive Chino? Unless you have something to hide." Benny said taking a step back towards me.

He looked in the direction of my car to see if I was hiding something but I jumped in front of him.

"I know you better take that fucking base out your voice when you're talking to me...I already told you. I was sitting in my car waiting for Mir to come out the house but, he never did. Next thing I know you pull up in your truck." I said and Benny turned around and started laughing. "What the fuck is so funny muthafucka?" I asked.

Benny leaned back against his Tahoe truck and moved his head to spit in the street.

"Angel wouldn't send two people for a job...He never does," Benny said and for a moment there my heart dropped but I know I had to think quick on my feet.

"Maybe Angel doesn't trust you to do this job alone. I have somewhere I need to be I hope you find Mir you know time is ticking." I said then jogged back to my car. I slipped in the driver's seat switching the gears so I could drive. "Stay low until I tell you to come up," I said whispering to Mir as I gave him simple directions.

"I'm so fucking nervous back here I can't even breathe," Mir said with a trembling voice. I looked out the passenger window as I drove passed Benny and I could see him holding his phone back up to his ear.

"I don't think I'm safe anymore...I know Benny is going to contact Angel to let him know I was here." I said under my breath and I quickly turned the corner. I banged my right fist against the steering wheel pouring out all of my frustrations. "I have to get you somewhere safe Mir," I said. First I made sure no one was following me then I motioned for Mir to come get in the front seat with me.

"You put your life in jeopardy to save me? I mean why did you do it?" Mir asked dumbfounded as he got in the passenger seat.

"Like I said before Mir...Family over everything," I said giving him a quick glance and his forehead was glistening from sweating profusely.

"Am I missing something?" Mir asked looking at me.

"I see I'm not the only one that didn't know the truth." I said shaking my head and I stopped at the red light ahead of me.

"The name is Chino...Grab a napkin out the glove compartment and wipe your forehead my dude," I said laughing.

Mir opened up the glove box and picked up a few napkins. He wiped his face and began to shake his legs from anxiety. The only reason I knew that is because my mother deals with that disorder. "I'm your younger brother...Tasha is our mother," I said pushing my foot down on the gas pedal to proceed driving.

"Tasha?" Mir asked laughing and all of a sudden the dancing in his legs stopped.

"What the fuck is so funny? What's going on with muthafuckas around me just laughing when I say some shit out of my mouth?" I asked balling up my face. Mir squeezed the napkins in his hands and shook his head.

"I don't mean any disrespect by it—Chino, is it?" Mir asked making sure he had my name correct before he continued to speak.

"Yeah that's my name my nigga" I said making a left turn.

"Tasha is my aunt...My mother was found dead at the bottom of the stairs with her neck broken," Mir said and I just felt so bad for this nigga.

"Sounds like you been lied to your entire life...Don't worry the two of us are in the same boat." I said then my phone started ringing. "FUCK!!" I yelled out when I see the name pop up on my screen.

"What's wrong Chino?" Mir asked nervously and I could see every ounce of worry on his face.

My phone continued to ring but I was looking around and driving like a paranoid suspect right now.

"Why the fuck are you looking around like that? Damn...Here I go getting nervous again I think I need another napkin." Mir voice started to crack like someone broke his heart. He wiped his forehead off and started dancing with his legs...His anxiety was making its presence known again.

"WHEN I PUT THIS PHONE UP TO MY EAR DON'T SAY SHIT MIR AND I MEAN IT," I said getting loud as I grabbed my phone. Mir didn't speak he just nodded his head up and down. I clicked the green icon on my phone and held it up to my ear. "Wassup my nigga?" I asked trying to control my breathing.

"Where you at Chino?" Angel asked in a calm voice.

"I—Uh...I..." I started stuttering. I had my left hand on the wheel while holding the phone up to my right ear.

"Damn nigga you can't even lie correctly," Mir said under his breath but it caught Angel's attention.

"What did you say Chino?" Angel asked into the phone.

"Uh—That was the radio Angel," I said lying to him. I switched the phone over to my left ear as I tilted my head. Then used my right hand to punch Mir in his arm as hard as I could.

The pain must have been intense because Mir dropped the napkins he had in his hands then rubbed on his arm to release some pressure.

"The radio? So you're in the car, huh? Are you coming back to the crib?" Angel asked and his questions were back to back like gunfire.

"Yeah...I—I had to run out to grab my mom some more biscuit dough for dinner tonight. Is something wrong?" I asked concerned and I knew the truth. Angel called me because Benny put a bug in his ear about me being somewhere I wasn't supposed to be at.

"Speaking of mothers...I just had a conversation with my mom about Tatiana and she kept a secret from me and my brothers growing up—" Angel said.

"What was the—" I tried to speak but Angel interrupted me.

"You wouldn't keep any secrets from me now would you Chino?" Angel asked and I felt like I had eyes all over me at this point. I didn't know how to answer the question but, I looked over at Mir and I see the look of hopelessness on his face. I couldn't let my brother go out like that...No matter how much time I had in with Angel.

"Nah...You know me better than that Angel." I said lying again and a second later Angel just hung up in my ear.

I stuffed my phone in my pocket and gave Mir my full attention.

"Muthafucka you could of got both of us killed...When I say shut the fuck up that's what I mean nigga! Do you understand?" I asked and Mir just dropped his hand from his arm and looked at me.

"You did mention that you were the younger brother, right Chino? I'm just trying to figure out why you're talking to me like..." Mir spoke with a smirk on his face. It was aggravating me because he wasn't taking this shit serious!

"DO YOU THINK THIS SHIT IS A GAME MY NIGGA? DO YOU KNOW WHAT I SACRIFICED BY DOING THIS?!" I yelled out and my eyes got watery because I was passionate about what I was saying. I made a right turn entering the neighborhood. I wiped my eyes and took a deep breath. "I watched this man murder *his own brother* in cold blood because he betrayed him...I don't want to end up like that. So when I tell you to do something that's what the fuck I need you to do." I said lowering my tone and Mir looked down at his lap as he began fumbling with his hands.

"His brother wouldn't happen to be JoJo, would it?" Mir asked in a broken tone like someone robbed him of something valuable.

"How—How did you know that?" I asked confused.

"JoJo was my best friend...He was murdered because of me." Mir said looking at me then he started going crazy in the fucking passenger seat. "FUCK!! WHEN ANGEL FINDS ME HE WILL DO ME JUST LIKE JOJO—" Mir yelled out with tears in his eyes. I made a left turn parking in the drive-way and I turned the car off.

"I'm not going to let that happen Mir, come on my nigga." I said placing my hand on Mir to calm him down. I got out the driver's seat carrying the car keys in my hand. Mir followed after me with his bookbag in his left hand.

"Mom? Dad? Where y'all at?" I asked walking in the front door. I entered the kitchen but neither one of them were in there so I walked inside the living room.

"I thought you said—" Mir said with a confused face and I cut him off to speak.

"It's a long story...These are the parents that raised me," I said giving him clarification. Mir looked around at the pictures of us hanging on the living room wall.

"What's wrong son?" My dad asked walking into the living room. I placed the car keys on the table and took a deep breath. Before I could speak my mom came up behind my dad with tears in her eyes.

"No—No, No, No, No, No." My mother said staring at Mir and the tears dropped from her face down to the floor.

"What's wrong baby?" My dad asked my mother but, her eyes were glued to Mir and she didn't budge. "Chino...Who is this?" My dad asked giving his full attention to me.

"That's Mir." My mother said wiping her eyes and I just gave her ass a puzzled look. "Chino he cannot be in this house," My mother said. I looked over at Mir and he was just as confused as I was.

"WHAT MOM? WHY NOT?" I yelled out and my dad slammed his right hand against the table.

"Can someone tell me what the fuck is going on please?!" My dad yelled out.

"His presence...Every time he is around something bad happens" My mother took a few steps towards Mir but, my dad held her back.

"Excuse me yo? Mir have you met my mother before?" I asked looking at him.

"No—No I never saw her before EVER." Mir said putting his hands up in the air to persuade me that he was telling the truth.

"How the fuck did y'all find one another?!" My mother yelled out in disappointment. "I took you in Chino to keep you away from evil like this." My mother said and my dad continued to hold her back.

"EVIL?! WHAT DID I EVER DO TO YOU LADY?" Mir yelled out to my mom and I motioned for him to move back.

"Chill out Mir...Mom what is wrong with you?" I asked wanting answers. "Dad are you going to stand here and not say shit yo?!" I asked and he shrugged his shoulders.

"You know how long it took me to calm your mother down after you left the first time? I'm not arguing with her ass again." My dad said and I sucked my teeth because this shit was ridiculous.

"CHINO GET HIS ASS OUT OF MY HOUSE BEFORE IT'S TOO LATE SON!" My mother yelled out pointing to the door with tears falling from her eyes again.

"What type of shit is this mom? I come to you for help and you throw us out like that?!" I yelled out. My dad let my mom go and she turned to look at Mir.

"I'm not throwing you out baby I'm throwing his ass out of my house!" My mother yelled out. I looked at Mir and he started clenching his jaw together while holding on to his bookbag.

"Well we come as a package! That's my fucking brother!" I yelled out.

"TIME IS TICKING CHINO HE HAS TO GO! NOW!!" My mother yelled overtop of me. She turned her head to look at the clock hanging on the living room wall.

"Come on Mir...I don't know what's going on around here." I said tapping his right arm so he could follow after me. I opened the front door up and I noticed that Mir wasn't behind me...But, my mother was.

"Chino?" My mother said my name.

"WHAT MOM," I said disregarding her because my eyes were looking for Mir.

"It's too late son" My mother said as she stared at the front door. I followed her eyes to see what she was looking at and my heart started to sink.

"Going somewhere my nigga?" Angel asked standing outside my mother's door.

CHAPTER 38 CHINO

"Where the fuck are you going Chino—" Angel asked smirking at me. I looked back at my mother who had an expression of concerns on her face.

"I—I was just—" I said turning to face Angel then I glanced behind me to see if I spotted Mir. From the moment Angel showed up I broke out in a sweat but, this moisture was different. It was like every time this nigga spoke I perspired more. Maybe fluids increased because I knew there was about to be some consequences for my actions.

"Stop turning around when I'm talking to you my nigga...Are you looking for someone Chino?" Angel asked stepping to me.

"I wasn't—" I said then I stopped speaking when I caught myself fumbling over my words.

"Come on baby boy I know you better than that remember I took you under my wing when you were a young'n. I know you're hiding something because you can't stop stuttering...And the sweat coming from your forehead looks like you ran multiple laps around the basketball court." Angel said putting me on the spot. I used the back of my hand to wipe my face then I turned to look at my mom...I felt like my back was against the wall and I needed a little help.

"Mom?!" I yelled out. My mother looked at me and took a deep breath.

"Nah yo...Don't bring your mother into this shit. You know what? Take your ass back in the crib let's talk" Angel said pointing at me. I turned around to go back in the living room and my mother was just giving me the death stare but, not saying shit. "I heard you made dinner?" Angel asked my mother.

"Yes I did Angel." My mother said answering his question and she forced a smile. My dad entered the living room and observed everything that was going on.

"Well, can you make a nigga a dinner plate or should I make it myself?" Angel asked my mother then he rubbed on his belly. It appeared that he was flirting with my mother but, it was hard to tell. Why? Because Angel was a sarcastic muthafucka...He smiled at everything no matter how dark he was feeling.

"I can make—" My mother couldn't finish speaking because my dad interrupted her.

"No, honey I will do it," My father said offering. Angel circled around the living room then he flopped onto the sofa.

"Well I see who wears the pants in this relationship," Angel said winking at my dad.

"Muthafucka you watch your mouth in my house—" My dad was about to charge at Angel but my mom jumped in front of him with her hands on his chest. I stood in place but, I was staring around to see if I spotted Mir.

"Your house?" Angel asked laughing as he got more comfortable on the sofa. "Why are you getting so defensive pops? Damn all I want is some food" Angel said to my dad. I looked over and I could see the anger and frustration pouring from my pops face. My mom lowered her hands from touching my pops and he clenched his fist together.

"What did I tell you?! Didn't I tell your ass that one day this was going to get out of control—" My dad said to my mother then Angel started laughing.

"Man...Take your ass to the kitchen and make my plate nigga" Angel said and at this point I had enough of this shit.

"WATCH HOW YOU TALK TO MY POPS ANGEL," I said stepping to him and Angel stood up from the couch.

"Damn nigga and I thought it wasn't a tough bone in your body...I know you better back the fuck up before I break both of your fucking legs Chino." Angel said and the smile disappeared from his face. My mother came up to me and my dad then she took a deep breath.

"Baby just go make the plate." My mother said to my dad. He just stared at Angel like he despised him then he proceeded to walk to the kitchen. When my dad disappeared she turned her attention towards me. "Chino...Just sit down baby I don't want anything to happen to you," My mother said and I gave her a baffled look.

"Just sit down?" I asked then I noticed something that I was concerned about. "How the fuck did you know Angel was going to be here mom?!" I asked stepping back. Angel looked at me and pointed to the chair in the corner...He motioned for me to sit down.

"Watch how you speak to me boy—" My mother said to me.

"It's something going on that you're not telling me about." I said and she avoided eye contact with me when I mentioned that. Angel walked around the living room and he touched the wall with his index finger.

"I haven't been in this house in a few years...Still looks the same but, the feeling is dissimilar. A lot of betrayal, lies and unforgiving memories when you step foot in this home." Angel said with his back towards me. My heart was racing for Mir damn, I just wanted to know if he was safe at least. "I'm not looking at you Chino but it seems like something or someone has your attention...Speak your mind my nigga. Damn that food smells amazing...I know you put your foot in that mac and cheese, didn't you?" Angel asked turning around then he looked at my mom.

"Angel listen—" I said and Angel shook his head while sitting back down on the sofa.

"Nah uh...Every time a muthafucka tells me to listen they just end up lying to me. You know I received a phone call from Benny earlier and he told me you were parked outside of Mir's house before he showed up, is that true?" Angel asked rubbing his hands together.

"Angel—" I tried to explain myself but his voice grew louder.

"Muthafucka is it true or not?!" Angel yelled out.

"I told you Chino...I told you every time Mir is present that some shit goes down." My mother said and I just bit the inside of my mouth.

"How would you know that mom?" I asked confused.

"I'm the one asking questions right now nigga...You saved Mir didn't you Chino?" Angel asked and my mother just started shaking her head like she was disappointed in me.

"I did what I felt was right." I said telling the truth then my pops entered the living room and he walked up to Angel.

"Don't get none of this damn food on my carpet," My dad said handing Angel a plate of food.

"Get the fuck out of my face you see grown folks talking," Angel said to my dad. My mom motioned for my pops to get out the living room before he got hurt. Angel stuffed a fork full of mac and cheese into his mouth. He started smiling then sat the plate of food on the living room table.

"Let me show you something Chino...Get your ass up yo," Angel said swallowing his food. He grabbed me by the back of my shirt and pushed me into the hallway. I heard my mom make a sound and I gave her a look that I was alright. "You see that shit right there? What the fuck do you see?" Angel asked and I see the back door opening and closing like someone ran out before he showed up.

"The back door is wide open" I said and Angel pushed me back into the living room. This time he was a bit more aggressive and I fell down on the carpet floor.

"I'm fine mom...I'm a grown ass man I can handle my shit," I said watching my mom run to my aid. I exhaled deeply and got up off the floor.

"Stupid ass nigga...You did what you felt was right and this nigga went ghost on your ass. You tried to show loyalty to the wrong muthafucka and he LEFT YOU BEHIND!" Angel yelled out. Whether Mir disappeared or not I was glad that he got away...Even if it cost me my life.

"My God...My God!" My mother yelled out.

"You should've stuck with me Chino I would of kept you safe now let's go for a ride." Angel said grabbing a piece of chicken off his plate. He took a bite, wiped his hands off and pointed to the door.

"Are you going to do me like you did JoJo?" I asked swallowing the spit down my throat.

"Angel, please don't hurt my son." My mother pleaded and I looked at her.

"Mom tell me the truth...At this point that's the least you can do for me," I said. My mother walked over to my baby picture that was on the wall and she rubbed it with her hand as if she was reminiscing.

"Tasha...I used to work wit Tasha down at Atlantic Care. Me and her both worked as nurses on the 2nd floor of the hospital. Tasha would come into work and express the emotions she was feeling...She was pregnant with you at the time Chino so I thought that's where her mood swings were coming from. Tasha said all three of her kids were driving her crazy and were out of control...Kia was being grown at a young age, She had suspicions of Jada liking other females and last but, not least Mir.

"Tasha said she caught weird objects under Mir's bed like duct tape, blades and scalpels. She mentioned she walked into his room a few times and it smelled deadly like he been dismembering animals but, she didn't have any proof. Tasha was overwhelmed and I told her to go home for the night that I would cover the rest of her shift. It never came out of her mouth but, the way she was stressing it just seemed as if she couldn't handle another child. I have been trying to get pregnant for years but that muthafucka soldiers don't march." My mother said referring to my pops.

"So after my shift I went to see how Tasha was doing at home and when I walked in the apartment building...A body came falling down the stairs and a moment later I heard this woman's neck snap in two. I looked up and I saw Tasha looking down at me smiling and all she said was, *'She deserved it.'* I stared at Tasha's belly and I came up with a plan immediately...I told Tasha if she gives me that baby in her belly then I wouldn't tell the cops what really happened. We even came up with a written contract agreement that when she gives birth you belong to me," My mother said and she smiled at me.

"You black mailed her yo...You also took me for pity? Is that what you're telling me? Because you couldn't have a child of your own?!" I yelled out and Angel started laughing like something was funny.

"Watch yourself Chino! I loved you...I did right by your ass I did everything a loving mother was supposed to do. You were better off with me and I proved it! You see how Tasha's other kids turned out compared to you...You are NOTHING LIKE THEM BASTARDS. You actually had a father in your household raising you." My mother said stepping towards me then she cleared her throat. "I also told Tasha I didn't want you to know the truth and to keep her evil ass kids away from you." My mom confessed again.

"Evil kids mom? Jada, Kia and Mir are a part of me!" I yelled out with tears in my eyes. "How could you say some fucked up shit like that?" I asked and she punched me in my chest. Angel found that shit amusing.

"NO THEY AREN'T! I RAISED YOU...YOU ARE MY FLESH AND BLOOD!" My mother screamed and I stumbled back holding my chest because she punched me like she was a nigga. "Why did you have to do it Chino? Why did you have to go back and save Mir?" My mother asked looking at me shaking her head.

"Family looks after family...You taught me that!" I yelled out.

"We need to go now Chino—" Angel said pointing to the front door.

"Promise me you won't hurt my son Angel," My mom pleaded.

"You know I can't keep promises beloved," Angel said with a straight face. I knew since I betrayed him that my life was over with but, thank God I found some closure before I leave this earth.

"PROMISE ME OR I WILL CALL THE COPS!" My mother yelled out running up to Angel.

"When are you going to fucking learn that I'm untouchable?" Angel asked moving my mother out the way.

"Tell Chino the truth Angel!" My mother yelled out and now I was more confused than ever. What the fuck did Angel have to hide?

"What the fuck are you talking about?" Angel asked looking at my mother.

"Angel knew this entire time that Tasha was your biological mother...Angel was tasting your loyalty Chino and you failed baby." My mother confessed and my heart broke in two.

CHAPTER 39 MIR

"Mir? Hello...Is this you on the phone? Speak to me!" Kia yelled into the phone. I didn't have anywhere else to go and I know backtracking probably wasn't safe...But, I ended up right back where I started. At Tasha's house...Hiding out.

I felt my chest was becoming too heavy to carry, my breathing was so loud I could sell it for half the price if a rapper wanted to purchase the noise. The sweat was dripping off my body like a two for one special at the gym...Yet my mind was still cloudy as ever.

"Yeah...It's me big sis I haven't been defeated yet." I said speaking into the phone. I was standing in the middle of the living room with the front and back door locked. I didn't feel safe I guess that's the reason why I'm constantly looking over my shoulder even though I was alone.

"What the fuck is that supposed to mean?" Kia asked playing stupid but, my beloved sister was far from that.

I didn't answer her question I walked up to the window and began peeking out of the blinds. "Where are you Mir? I was worried sick about you" Kia said softly like she was concerned but, she wasn't fooling me.

"No you wasn't worried about me Kia...I'm all alone out here. Well I was before JoJo got snatched away from me," I said. I heard the screeching sounds of tires coming down the street and my heart dropped. For a moment there I thought Angel caught up to me until I noticed it was one of the neighbors across the street...Driving like he didn't have any sense.

"How do you know about JoJo? Who told you about that—" Kia tried to finish speaking but I cleared my throat.

"Well, I can't give JoJo all the credit because I met someone tonight that's family. Out of all my years living on this earth who would've guessed that loyalty would come from a muthafucka that was my best friend and a muthafucka that didn't even know me; for more than an hour?" I said talking about Chino. My paranoid ass walked up to the front door just to make sure it was locked...I didn't want to be caught slipping up.

"I'm sorry I don't know what you're talking about Mir—" Kia said lying to me again.

"I know I haven't been the best brother growing up for you and Jada. I had trauma and unresolved issues in my childhood...My memory is so fucked up and I don't remember much but, you knew this first and Kia you still tried to throw me out into the fire to burn alive. I thought you loved me yo...I thought you had my back." I said getting emotional and I heard Kia sniffing through the phone.

"I do love you Mir—" Kia said and I punched my right fist on the black sofa.

"YOU'RE FUCKING LYING TO ME! YOU DON'T LOVE ME...YOU AND ANGEL SET ME UP!" I yelled out then it was suddenly quiet on the phone.

"I—I...Uh..." Kia said stuttering and I started shaking my head.

"See how quick your speech turns into stuttering...You can't even convince me at this point. Why did you do it? Why did you deceive me Kia? It was supposed to be family first or did you forget that shit?!" I yelled out. I looked back at the front door then I proceeded to walk into the kitchen.

"I COULDN'T DO IT ANYMORE MIR! I COULDN'T FUCKING COVER FOR YOU AND THE SHIT YOU WERE DOING! IT WAS COSTING ME A PRICE TO LIE AND YOU NEEDED TO BE DEALT WITH! YOU PUT OUR OWN SISTER ON HEROIN! YOU'RE A FUCKING MENTAL CASE!" Kia yelled out finally showing me, how the fuck she truly felt. Kia exhaled and took a deep breath.

"Ever since you were younger...The animals you received as birthday gifts would end up decapitated or a creature being cut in half just for the fun of it. Then you would bury them in the backyard and make me and Jada attend like it was an actual fucking funeral. At that time you were still a child ya know? So full of potential but, you couldn't get out of that dark place; that was holding you back. As you got older I would notice cuts on Jada and you would injure her because you felt like it.

"I was the one that came to YOUR rescue so you wouldn't get in trouble EVERY FUCKING TIME! It went from you murdering animals, harming your sister to growing up being a real life murderer beloved. We aren't kids anymore my nigga and I will not cover for you...So I felt like setting you up for Angel was the right thing to do. I mean you did murder his wife Mir," Kia proceeded to add in.

I used my left foot to kick the kitchen table...I have to stop allowing people to provoke me because it's like pouring gasoline into the fire and once I explode I'm suddenly the bad guy.

"It was a fucking accident! It was just an accident Kia!" I yelled into the phone.

"You have too many killings on your hands Mir...Every death was not an accident my brother," Kia spoke like she was schooling me. "It's time for you to live in your truth—" Kia said.
I started chuckling then wiped off the sweat from my forehead and rubbed my nose.

"When are you going to start living in yours?" I asked and the silence was covered by Kia thinking.

"What the fuck are you talking about?" Kia asked.

"Chino told me about Tasha...He said that she is our biological mother Kia and he is our fourth sibling. You wasn't going to tell me, right?" I asked.

"Mir just turn yourself in before Angel finds you," Kia said disregarding my question.

"Don't change the fucking subject! I didn't ask to be this way—" I said and Kia started to yell again.

"YOU CAN'T KEEP BLAMING YOUR CHILDHOOD! YOU HAD A CHOICE TO BE A SURVIVOR OR A FUCKING VICTIM! YOU CHOSE TO BE A VICTIM AND TO STAY IN THAT DARK PLACE!" Kia yelled out. "You can't keep using what you been through as a child to justify your behavior...You need help muthafucka," Kia said.

"You will be needing more help than me beloved." I said pulling out a chair and I sat down at the table.

"Excuse me?" Kia asked confused but I could hear her voice trembling when she spoke.

"Ask your daughter...Ask Nyla about the Lopez club. Then let me judge you on how fucked up your life will be when you find out the truth...Victim or Survivor, right?" I asked cracking a smile. "We all have a choice, don't we sis?" I asked and I took the phone away from my ear.

"MIR! MIR! DON'T HANG UP THIS FUCKING PHONE! WHAT ARE YOU—" I could hear the pain in my sister's voice when she screamed through the phone. I saw the back door knob twisting and turning. I jumped up out of my chair and ended the call I was on.

"FUCK!! YOU SCARED ME LITTLE BOY—" Tasha said entering the house holding her keys in her hands. She closed the back door behind her and locked it. Then she walked over to the counter and sat her belongings down. Something caught my attention when she walked passed me so I stretched my hands out and walked up to her. "What the fuck are you doing?" Tasha asked getting offended.

"Why do you smell like that?" I asked backing up from her.

"Smell like what nigga?" Tasha asked.

"Reem's scent is all over your work clothes...How could you do that to Kia?" I asked reaching for the counter and I leaned back against it.

"I could ask why do you ensure the things you do but, me and you both know you won't tell me the truth," Tasha said shrugging her shoulders. She took her badge off her nurses uniform and stared at me. "You're not really blind Mir, are you?" Tasha asked placing her work badge down on the table.

"How did you know?" I asked finally giving her eye contact.

"Because a mother—Never mind, I knew this entire time Mir." Tasha confessed but, it sounded like she was going to say something else before that.

"Why did you keep up with my lie so much?" I asked curious.

"I'm not sure if you were running away from what happened to you in your childhood because I didn't question it. I just figured maybe you just wanted to be invisible and block out the world but, when JoJo told me the truth about what you did to Bella. I knew I played a part in it...So I went along with the lies of you being blind," Tasha said.

"Why didn't you turn me in when you knew the truth? It seems like everyone is against me at this point," I confessed.

Tasha nodded her head up and down then she walked up to the table, pulling out a chair and she sat down.

"I failed you once when you were a child so I felt like this was my favor back to you. So if cops asked about what happened to Bella I could cover for you because in my mind you were blind." Tasha said and my eyes blew up because how the fuck did she know my secret?!

Tasha stretched her feet out then she stared at me like she was reminiscing.

"I was a young mother getting pregnant back to back and every nigga I came across didn't want to stick around. I always thought them muthafuckas were the problem until I realized how weak minded I was. I'd been working in the hospital before I got pregnant with Kia. However I was overwhelmed; to the point where I would make myself sick and fragile. Kia came into this world and things went good until I gave birth to Jada and you." Tasha said and I balled up my face.

"So you covered for me out of guilt?" I asked feeling sick to my stomach.

"No! Let me finish...My sister came along and told me she wanted to take care of y'all. I felt like I needed the help so why not? Plus I was getting more sleep than I ever did before. Then one day my sister told me she was going to give herself the, *'Mother,'* title even though y'all muthafuckas belonged to me! I was furious but, I knew she could do a better job raising y'all than

I could. I mean growing up she basically raised me herself...So even though I was y'all biological mother that was something y'all didn't know because we kept it a secret.

"Months passed by and I thought at that stage in my life that I was honestly ready to be a mother. I had a savings account, food in the house and cable. I asked my sister if y'all could stay at my house for the weekend just so I could get used to motherhood for a bit. One thing I wasn't honest about was telling my sister that I met this random man while she was raising y'all and I allowed him to move in my house. My sister asked me specifically if I had to work that night because if I did then y'all could come over another time. I lied I told her I didn't have to work but, damn I just wanted my fucking kids! My children that I gave birth to...

"I wanted y'all under my roof even if it was just for the weekend. I know I was supposed to be home bonding with y'all but, I was trying to work every double that was offered to me in the hospital. I felt like what's the harm in leaving y'all home with my man for a few hours? I wasn't too concerned about leaving y'all at home because he was helping me...Lord knows I had a lot to be cautious about. One night I came home and you were in the bathroom naked in a fetal position. I dropped my purse and car keys to the floor to see what was wrong...I didn't know my stomach was going to turn until I looked behind you. Mir you was bleeding profusely...My child you was in so much pain. I tried to lift you up and your rectum fell out of you.

"I checked on Kia and Jada and they were sound asleep. I yelled for the man that was watching y'all to give me answers but he disappeared. He took all his clothes from the closet and went ghost. I didn't know he was going to rape you Mir and that's why I feel like I failed you. I didn't want to call the police because I was the one at fault when I didn't know that man no more than two weeks but, he was living in my house. I also didn't want to get in trouble because that night I also found out that I was pregnant with that man's child. I was a nurse so I tried my best to put you back together...Little did I know I just broke you more. I took y'all back to my sisters house and she called me two days later.

"She said something was off with you Mir and asked did something happen at my house? I denied every accusation that she threw in my direction. She threatened me that she was going to call the police and I told her to WAIT! I was coming over to tell her the truth but that was also a lie. I went to her apartment building and because I wanted to save my own ass I had to get rid of my sister...It didn't matter if she was family or not. So I broke her neck and threw her down the stairs. My sister's death was ruled as accidental and I couldn't be more happy.

"I took y'all back in my house and kept my last pregnancy hidden from y'all all these years. I later found out that the man that raped you was a registered sex offender. He got released two days before I allowed him to stay in my fucking house. Now you see Mir? Everything you did or was doing came from that trauma in your childhood. I wasn't there to save you so I disregarded the animals you slaughtered and I kept a blind eye to you cutting your sister with blades around the house. If I would've been there for each one of y'all; from day one, maybe y'all would of turned out better. *But, I loved myself more*...I had to choose myself over y'all." Tasha confessed with a broken spirit.

I knew something happened to me but, maybe I was blocking out the truth because it was too painful to relive. Could I honestly call Tasha my mother now?! Nah, because a mother wouldn't do the shit she did to me no matter how bad life got. I looked over at the knife sitting in the sink...Before I could react her phone started ringing.

"Hello—I just got home please don't ask me to cover anyone's shift because I'm tired—" Tasha said as she wiped her eyes then her mouth dropped. "WHAT?!" Tasha jumped up from her seat and the tears flowed more heavily this time.

"What happened?" I asked concerned and Tasha took the phone away from her ear and held on to her chest.

"My worst fear came true," Tasha said crying.

"WHAT THE FUCK HAPPENED?!" I yelled out wanting to know the truth.

"I used to work with this nurse down at the hospital her name is Humia...She said Jada just overdosed." Tasha said and she fell down to the kitchen floor.

CHAPTER 40 ANGEL

"Is it true Angel?" Chino asked while sitting in the passenger seat of my car. He tapped his right hand against the car window anticipating on a response back from me. I looked at him from the corner of my eye and sucked my teeth.

"Nigga, you're not in the position to ask me any muthafuckin' questions." I said with a little more aggression in my voice. "Do you think that nigga would risk his life for you Chino? Be careful how you answer the question." I said making a right turn while keeping both hands on the wheel. Chino's pride was holding him back from understanding how much this nigga hurt me doing shit behind my back.

"To be honest Angel...I wouldn't give two fucks if Mir would of done it for me. I didn't stick my neck out there looking for *any* loyalty back. I did it because I been in his situation before.

I know how it feels to lose oxygen because you feel alone. We try to do the right thing in life and no matter how much we stay on the path to recovery, the devil attacks us. Niggas like us are bound to fail...I didn't want that for Mir, I wanted to be his way out," Chino admitted. He accepted every consequence that was about to come his way.

"THAT MUTHAFUCKA MURDERED MY WIFE CHINO!" I yelled out and I slammed my right fist on the wheel. Chino took a deep breath and stared out the passenger window.

"You have took the lives of more people than I can count on my hands and feet. Shit, you murdered your own brother Angel. Mir isn't a saint in this lifetime and neither are you. I backed you up on the shit you did even when I didn't agree with it Angel." Chino said and I kept a straight face while making a left turn.

"Your loyalty should have been with me my nigga," I spoke in disappointment.

"But, Mir is my brother," Chino said.

I shrugged my fucking shoulders.

"THAT NIGGA DOESN'T GIVE A FUCK ABOUT YOU!" I yelled out and my breathing started to pick up. I had entirely too much shit on my mind to the point I was blocking out my phone going off.

"Your phone is ringing," Chino said to me.

I rolled down the driver's side window to get some air. I felt like I couldn't breathe. I pulled my phone out and placed it to my right ear.

"Hello," I said answering the phone without looking at the caller ID.

"Why are you breathing so heavy Angel? Did something happen son?" My dad started to panic through the phone.

"Dad I'm busy right now." I said trying to control my breathing.

"I'm going to send you my location...You need to get your ass down here now," My dad said in a whisper.

"For what—" Before I could finish speaking my dad started yelling through the phone. It caught Chino's attention because he looked at me and dropped his head.

"JUST GET YOUR ASS DOWN HERE ANGEL!" My dad yelled a bit louder this time. I took the phone away from my ear and my dad hung up on me. A second later his location came through my phone.

"How did you know Tasha was my real mother?" Chino asked lifting up his head. I glanced over at him before I answered his question...It was about time he knew the truth.

"Do you remember that severe infection you had in your body when you were about thirteen years old?" I asked and Chino delivered a puzzled look.

"How would you know something like that Angel...I didn't know you when I was that age" Chino said and I started smirking.

"Yeah...But I knew you Chino. I was in high school at the time and it was career day. My father wanted us to spend the day with him. Isn't it funny that JoJo had the choice of skipping school that day but, he still showed up to first period before the bell rang. JoJo said he didn't want to be seen hanging around a cop all day. But, years later the nigga ended up being a cop in his life. Sanchez was messing around with bitches at the time and he figured being under my father's wing for the day would make him look less attractive.

"I was the only one left and since my brothers already told my dad that they didn't want to participate in career day I just decided to tag along. That was the first time I ever got inside a police car and damn, it was uncomfortable...I felt forced because I didn't want to let him down. I felt like it was my duty as the older brother to make my father proud. I thought we were going to arrest muthafuckas all day but, we got down to the police station and he was doing paper work for a few hours. My dad saw the look of displeasure on my face then he asked me if I wanted to see something cool. He showed me the evidence room, I saw the amount of drugs packaged up and my ass fell in lust. It wasn't until he told me how much drug dealers make in a day that's when I fell in love. Another cop came into the evidence room and said that there was a situation down at the hospital.

"My dad said that's the only action we were going to get all day so we decided to show up. My dad spoke with the nurse and he told me to sit in the waiting room. Tasha showed up at the hospital crying saying that her son needed her. That's when I found out that you had a severe infection and needed a blood transfusion. Tasha pleaded to the nurses how she was the biological mother and she could do the procedure so you could live," I confessed. I looked over at Chino and he had tears in his eyes.

"You knew this shit since I was thirteen and you never bothered to tell me the fucking truth Angel?" Chino asked heartbroken and wiping his face.

I started smiling and I nodded my head up and down.

"Now you understand how the fuck I feel when you keep secrets nigga." I said then looked down and Chino balled up his fist. This nigga can try to get buck with me if he want to...I won't hesitate to put a bullet in his head.

"Why did you wait until I got older to come into my life?" Chino asked. I looked down and he released his fist but, his hands started shaking. I turned the corner while slowing down. I quickly looked down at my phone and saw that I was a few feet away from my dad's location. When I put my attention back on the road I noticed multiple cop cars parked down the street with their lights flashing.

"You were only thirteen...You wasn't ready for the street life Chino. I gave you a few years to get healthy before I made my move. Now I see you were never built for this shit." I said pulling over to the side. I parked the car and opened up the driver's side door. "Stay the fuck in the car," I demanded. I spotted my dad standing behind his car talking to another detective. He saw me approaching him and came walking towards me.

"Man, why the fuck would you tell me to come here with all these cops dad?" I asked lowering my tone around his fellow officers. My dad turned around, flashing a smile to a someone walking by then he turned his attention back at me.

"Muthafucka I'm a cop! What are you trying to say?" My dad asked balling up his face.

"Why did you ask me to come down here...I'm busy." I said looking back at my car to make sure Chino didn't go anywhere.

"I have to show you something." My dad said walking around to the front of his car. He looked at me and motioned for me to get in the car. I see two people handcuffed in the back of his vehicle.

"Who the fuck is this?" I asked looking at my dad.

"Angel get your hardheaded ass in the car and just shut your mouth for a minute." My dad said shaking his head. I got in the passenger seat of his car, a second later my dad joined us. I looked back and I see Tasha and Mir.

"You got off easy nigga...You're lucky I didn't catch you," I said smiling at Mir. He broke out in a sweat and looked at my dad for comfort.

"Angel be cautious about the shit you say...Everything is recorded in my car." My dad said gesturing me to watch myself.

"I'm sorry about what happened to Bella. I didn't mean for tha—" Mir tried to apologize and I cut him off.

"Bella was fucking around with you behind my back so you must have been doing something better than me. That girl even went to the extreme of taking a baby that didn't belong to her—" I said and Mir's mouth dropped to the floor.

"Wait, Bella didn't give birth to Charlie?" Mir asked with tears in his eyes...Shit he seemed more disappointed than I was and I was married to her deceiving ass!

"Bella couldn't have kids nigga...That baby existed but, she didn't belong to Bella. Jada gave birth to that baby girl," I said.

A tear dropped from Mir's right eye and he tried to wipe his face off using his shoulder since his hands were cuffed.

"What the fuck—" Mir said in a panic.

"NO! THAT CAN'T BE TRUE MY DAUGHTER DIDN'T HAVE A CHILD—" Tasha said raising her voice. My dad just made a noise sitting in the driver's seat.

"Jada is your daughter now Tasha? Damn, you actually claim your kids?!" I yelled out smirking. Mir looked over at Tasha and she balled up her face.

"FUCK YOU!!" Tasha yelled out. I looked down at her hands behind her back then rubbed my lips together.

"You helped Mir cover up Bella's murder, huh? Is that why you're in handcuffs with your mental son?" I asked laughing.

"No...That's not why. Tell him the truth Tasha." My dad said and the smile quickly erased off my face.

"Tell me what?" I said raising my eyebrows looking at my dad.

"TELL HIM!" My dad yelled out pointing to Tasha.

"I was fucking around with your father Angel," Tasha admitted staring at my father.

I looked at him and shrugged my shoulders. That muthafucka couldn't stay faithful to my mother so him cheating didn't surprise me not one bit.

"So the fuck what? That has nothing to do with me—" I said and Tasha started to chuckle like something was funny.

"Yeah it does sweetheart because shit gets deeper. I was having an affair with your father for three months...I felt like we were seeing enough of each other so I wanted your father to come home with me. This muthafucka told me he couldn't and when I asked him why do you know what he said to me?! This selfish son of a bitch told me he had a wife, three teenage boys and a daughter at home. He said he wasn't leaving his family for a whore like me. So my tongue became sharp as a knife, the skin under my nails grew fire so aggressive that it would burn a muthafucka if I even flinched.

"He broke my heart in pieces that couldn't be recovered and I needed your father to pay for what he did to me. I went over to my sister's house to breathe because I was suffocating in my own house. I came across Jada's diary and my stomach turned. Jada confessed how she was in love with this bitch name Tatiana who I later found out was the daughter of your dad. I told Jada if she didn't murder Tatiana then I would separate her from Kia and Mir.

"You see...I knew Jada couldn't survive without her siblings because both of them were her soft spot. Kia and Mir completed Jada so I knew she wouldn't tell me no. Jada cried that she didn't want to do it...

"That Tatiana just became a cheerleader and she was finally happy in life but I didn't give a fuck. Y'all father broke my fucking heart and he needed to feel the same way I did! I got called into work and Jada called me panicking saying Tatiana wasn't moving...I told Jada that she did an excellent job and to call Kia. I knew Kia would back up her sister because they were raised like that. Your father called me heartbroken on the phone that night...He asked if he could come over so he could be in my arms. I didn't refuse because me and him were two broken people sharing a bed together." Tasha said looking my father in the eyes.

"Y—You...You got Jada to murder my baby sister because my father rejected you?!" I began stuttering and now I was the one with tears in my eyes. Mir looked at me and started smiling.

"No...Not because he rejected me Angel but, because your father rejected us." Tasha said in a low tone.

"Us? What the fuck are you talking about Tasha?!" I screamed out.

"Tell him detective." Tasha said winking at my dad then he looked at me.

My dad took a deep breath before speaking to me.

"Tasha told me she was pregnant with my child and I told her to get the abortion...I couldn't bring a black baby home to my family. I just didn't want to lose what I had at home because I couldn't keep my dick in my pants." My dad said reaching to comfort me but I moved his hands out the way.

"WHAT YO?!" I yelled out. "OH MY GOD!" I screamed with tears coming down my face and I swung the driver's side door open.

"You lied to me!" Mir yelled at Tasha but, she didn't seem to budge. It was like whatever she lied to Mir about didn't bother her. "You told me the man who raped me was the man who got you pregnant." Mir said breathing deeply and my eyes shot open.

"I had to make my story sound good son," Tasha said smirking at Mir.

My dad grabbed my arm and I looked at him like I despised him because I DID!

"NO! DON'T YOU FUCKING TOUCH ME!" I yelled at my dad. I wiped my face and headed back towards my car.

"Where are you going Angel?!" My dad asked.

I stopped in my tracks and turned around to face him.

"So career day… When the cop told you to go down to the hospital! He didn't say that shit because it was a coincidence. YOU had to go to the hospital because that was your son!" I yelled out and I looked back at Chino sitting in the passenger seat.

"Me and Tasha did the procedure to give Chino blood for his severe infection...That's why I left you in the waiting room of the hospital for more than an hour. Mir told me what Chino did to save him...And you're not going to hurt my son Angel." My dad confessed…

Now his bitch ass was claiming Chino as his son.

CHAPTER 41 ANGEL

"I know that look in your eyes son...Don't do it." My father tried to whisper in a low tone so I wouldn't cause a scene...But, y'all know I wasn't a dumb ass nigga. I was smarter than that! My driver's side door was open and this nigga was standing a few feet away from me. He trying to comfort me, little did he know it was too late for saving. I looked over at Chino sitting in the passenger seat and that muthafucka's legs were shaking like he was on a rollercoaster.

"FUCK YOU NIGGA! AND DON'T CALL ME YOUR SON!" I yelled out at him.

"Angel...I know you're hurting beloved." My dad spoke in arrogance like he wasn't in the fucking wrong! My sister lost her life because of his actions.

"YOU DON'T KNOW A MUTHAFUCKIN' THING!" I yelled out. I banged my right fist into my steering wheel. My dad looked over at Chino to gesture him that everything was going to be alright.

"Let Chino go Angel just walk away from this." My dad said and I shook my head no.

"Chino has to pay for what he has done to me." I said getting emotional with tears in my eyes.

"Angel—" My dad said clearing his throat and I placed my right hand under my seat to pull out my burner. I didn't give a fuck about the cops standing at the end of the corner.

"Since your punk ass want to defend Chino...Why don't you take the bullet for him pops? I mean why not, right? Since we all family here." I said shrugging my shoulders then I wiped my eyes with my left hand. The anticipation was still wrapped around my burner under my seat. Chino sat still then readjusted his body in the seat.

"Angel, I'm telling you right now if you pull a weapon out on me you better be prepared for what's going to happen next." My dad said looking at every move I was making.

"The fuck is that supposed to mean nigga?" I asked getting offended.

"I'm a cop Angel...My men will shoot you down until you take your last breath." My dad looked over at his officers still standing down the street then he turned his attention back at me. My breathing started to pick up like a bad habit I couldn't get rid of.

"You betrayed us nigga...Your careless affairs caused your own blood daughter to get murdered. You knew Tasha was behind Tatiana's murder this entire time didn't you?" I asked and he pointed his index finger at me.

"No! That's not true! When I entered Tasha's home to arrest Mir for the murder of Bella. I saw Tasha trying to hide a journal. I asked her what was in the journal and she just told me to call you down here so you could hear what she had to say. I didn't know Tasha was going—" My dad tried to confide in me but, I wasn't trying to hear shit right now.

"Nah, you didn't know you were going to get caught. I can't believe you did this to my mother all these years! Playing fucking games behind her back yo. She sacrificed every muthafuckin' thing for you...She even slept with men to feed us when you wasn't around and you do this shit?!" I yelled out then I leaned up in the driver's seat. My dad stepped back to put some distance in between us so he could protect himself. AS ALWAYS! That muthafucka only cared about himself. "Answer my question...You weren't around a lot when we were kids because you were fucking other women, right?" I asked and my dad turn his head to spit in the middle of the street.

"Your mother wasn't enough for me Angel...She was so fucking weak." My dad said balling up his fist.

"MY MOTHER WAS EVERYTHING SHE NEEDED TO BE, FOR YOU MUTHAFUCKA!" I yelled out. Thinking back and hearing my mother cry herself to sleep at night got me in my feelings all over again. Before I could point my burner at my own father...A bitch ass cop walked up behind him.

"Hey!! Is everything alright over here?" A cop in uniform asked my father. I let go of the gun under my seat and wiped my emotions off my face. My dad looked at the officer but, didn't answer his question.

"Angel let my son go." My dad said whispering so the cop didn't think it was a hostage situation.

I looked at Chino but, that nigga couldn't look me back in my eyes. That's when I realized I was mad at the wrong fucking person...Chino was right he was doing what he needed to do for family. I looked at the door and motioned for Chino to get the fuck out my vehicle.

"Come on son." My dad said waving for Chino to come over to him. Chino closed the passenger door shut and stood behind my dad...I mean our dad.

"You won't be sticking around for Chino much longer." I said slamming my driver's side door. I started up my vehicle and rolled down window.

"Excuse me?!" My dad yelled out in disbelief. "What the fuck is that supposed to mean Angel?" My dad asked me and Chino knew exactly what I was talking about. I looked at my dad and smirked before driving off on his ass. I grabbed my phone out of my pocket and tapped on my recent contacts. I clicked on the second name and placed my phone on speaker.

"What's good my nigga?" Benny asked in a calm voice.

"Do you still have that recording?" I asked. Benny didn't answer my question with actual words he just made a noise on the phone agreeing with me. "Take it down to the station and ask to speak to the Captain. Give the recorder to him and tell the Captain he has a closed case with the last name 'Graves'. Her death wasn't an accident...It was a homicide involving someone on his very own police force," I said. I made a right turn heading towards my house.

"Say no more my nigga." Benny said and I heard my phone beeping. I looked down and it was my mother calling me. I ended the call with Benny and clicked over to the other line.

"Hola madre," I said in Spanish.

"Que esta mal?" My mother asked in her accent.

"Ma I need to speak to you about something," I said. My mother stayed quiet on the other end of the phone. "Did you know dad had another—" Before I could fully ask the question my mother interrupted me to speak.

"Another child? Yes I knew papi" My mother confessed and my eyes shot open from disbelief.

"Why didn't you tell me this shit before?" I asked and my mother took a deep breath. I slowed down at the stop sign before I continued driving down the street.

"Watch your mouth Angel! I'm still your mother!" She yelled through the phone. "I had a feeling when y'all were kids...But, I wasn't too sure I didn't have any proof. Until he came home smelling like another woman that's when my gut was telling me I was right. It wasn't until Tatiana passed away that I began having dreams. My mother always said when one life ends another one begins. Your father didn't treat y'all any different but, it was the look in his eyes that something or someone else was missing. When Tatiana passed I needed comfort but, your father ran off…

"So I followed behind him to see who had his attention more than I did. A woman…A black fucking woman greeted his muthafuckin' ass outside and he cried to her while rubbing on her belly. Tatiana was OUR CHILD! His ass was supposed to be at home consoling me but, instead he went to another fucking race. I was sick to my stomach. I made it my duty to see what this woman's child looked like…And he reminded me so much of Tatiana. The only difference was he was mixed with black. That night I came over to your house and you had that woman and little girl in your kitchen.

"My rage and bitterness came out all over again…Just like it did when I found out your father had a child behind my back. I was angry because that black child looked just like your guest standing in that kitchen. It was more of them monkeys like each one of them were spreading…I was so broken by what your father did that I felt like it happened all over again when I saw their faces." My mother spoke like she was traumatized yet unapologetic.

"I'm sorry that you had to go through that ma—Wait, Chino was security in my house all these years why didn't you say anything before?" I asked deeply concerned making a left turn.

"Because I didn't want you, JoJo or Sanchez to look at your father any differently. Plus, even though you and Chino never knew y'all were brothers all these years y'all certainly did act like it." My mother said and she paused before she spoke again. "Now…I was honest with you Angel…I need you to be honest with me son." My mother said in a low tone.

"Wha—What?" I asked stuttering.

"Is JoJo alive baby?" My mother asked me. My mind went blank, my hands started to tremble on the steering wheel and my heart was beating through my shirt. How the fuck was I supposed to tell my mother that I murdered my own brother because he was disloyal?! Nah...That shit wasn't right yo.

"Why are you asking me this ma?" I asked in denial.

"I lost one child already...Please tell me if my son is alive Angel." My mother said and a second later she began weeping on the phone. Damn, the sound of her cries always brung back memories.

"Please forgive me ma." I said feeling like shit.

"AN—AN-ANGEL! NO, NO, NO—NOT ANOTHER CHILD!" My mother screamed out again. I arrived at my house with more shame than I came out with.

"I didn't mean to hurt you ma." I said sounding like a frighten little boy. My security opened the gate for me but something caught my fucking attention.

"ANGEL MY HEART IS BROKEN ALL OVER AGAIN!" My mother poured every emotion she was feeling into the phone.

"Mom—I'm so sorry but, I have to go." I said balling up my face and I hung up the phone on her. I noticed Sanchez dancing around his car with a double stacked styrofoam cup. I pulled up behind him, turning my car off and I jumped out of my vehicle.

"What the fuck is this? Sanchez is this *blood* my nigga?!" I asked raising my voice a bit when I caught myself about to bust my ass in front of my house. I moved to the side and saw that it was blood leaking from his trunk down to the ground.

"I needed to handle something don't worry." Sanchez said playfully tapping my right shoulder. He looked down at the blood leaking then he started laughing like shit was funny.

"What do you mean, *'don't worry,'* muthafucka? There's fucking blood right here in the front of my house and you don't expect me to panic?! You're going to make it hot for me nigga." I said to Sanchez. He looked inside his cup with one eye like it was a magnifying glass. When he noticed nothing else was inside he threw it down to the floor. "If the cops come around here; me and you will end up in prison." I said picking up the trash he just purposely dropped.

"Nah...Chill out Angel." Sanchez said smiling then he started stumbling. I grabbed his arm so he wouldn't fall and hurt himself.

"Muthafucka are you drunk right now?" I asked and Sanchez just shrugged his shoulders.

"I mean I can still keep my balance so I wouldn't say I'm that intoxicated," Sanchez said. He tapped me again then he chuckled. I leaned Sanchez on the side of his car then I walked over to the step to sit the cup down until I got inside my house to throw it in the trash. "Look at this my nigga." Sanchez said. I turned around and this muthafucka moved from the spot I placed him at. He opened up his trunk and winked at me. I walked behind the vehicle to see what he was trying to show me.

"Is that Teka? Nigga that's your wife!" I yelled out and I looked at Sanchez. He didn't seem bothered at all. "Why would you do that to her Sanchez?!" I yelled out moving to the side.

"Her?" Sanchez asked then he raised his eyebrows.

"What's funny you fucking idiot!" I yelled out getting frustrated because all this nigga did was laugh in my face. My security heard the sound of my voice and came outside the house to see what was wrong.

"Let's just say she wasn't the person we thought she was," Sanchez said.

"Ayo! Come here!" I yelled out waving for my security to come to my aid. "Get rid of this vehicle and clean this shit up before someone shows up. Sanchez go in the guest room and sleep that shit off. You stink my nigga." I said smelling the liquor coming from his pores. I moved over and Sanchez just followed me.

"I thought we—We...Were supposed to celebrate the life of our baby sister tonight?" Sanchez asked in a drunk tone...At this point the nigga couldn't even keep his eyes open.

"Nigga you speak French now? What the fuck are you stuttering for?" I asked pushing him out of my way. I heard the front gates to my house open up but, I didn't turn around to see who was arriving. "Take your ass in the house and lay the fuck down...Damn, fucking with you is making me sweaty. Who the fuck is this?!" I yelled out.

One of my security men grabbed Sanchez and took him in the house. The other two came over and started to get rid of evidence. A car pulled up and I didn't notice who it was until I saw the make and model of the car. I waved to my security for them to hurry and clean this shit up. I walked up a bit so Kia wouldn't come any closer...I didn't want her to see what Sanchez did. Kia parked the car and got out...Someone else got out of the car with her.

"Angel...There's something I need to talk to you about." Kia said closing the driver's side door and I just stared at her for a second.

"You covered up the murder to protect Jada, right?" I asked and her mouth dropped.

"Listen Angel I didn't know Tatiana was your sister—" Kia tried to say her plea but, I shook my head.

"Is that shit supposed to make me feel better yo?!" I asked stepping towards her. I looked over and the nigga Kia showed up with tried to defend her.

"Ayo, watch how you speak to her my nigga," He said balling up his face and I started laughing.

"Reem? That's your name, right?" I asked with a smile on my face. He looked over at Kia for answers.

"You told this nigga about me?" Reem asked Kia and she immediately shook her head no.

"No! I never mentioned your name around Angel before...How do you know that?" Kia asked me and I shrugged my shoulders.

"I guess me and you are even beloved." I said smiling and she just gave me a puzzled look.

"Even? What the fuck is that supposed to mean?" Kia asked in a low tone. Reem looked over at Kia then he stared at me from a distance.

"I knew you were involved with the murder of my sister a month after the detectives came to my mother's door and announced that she was dead. I planned, I planned and I planned how I was going to make you feel the greatest pain that y'all muthafuckas caused me and my family. I knew about you and your siblings since y'all were teenagers. I was playing along this entire time...I knew Bella was fucking around with your brother Mir the moment they became intimate.

"You know I have eyes everywhere Kia. A bug was put in my ear that Jada was struggling at her job and couldn't pay rent. I gave JoJo laced heroin to give Mir but, your brother didn't know the drugs were tampered with. Somehow Mir convinced Jada to try it and her ass got hooked on it...Just like I planned.

"Then I murdered JoJo because I told him to cut Mir off but, they continued to have a friendship behind my back. So for that reason my own brother had to be dealt with. If I would have known your MOTHER Tasha was involved just as much as y'all was I promise I would've made her life a living hell but, I just found out," I confessed.

"How did you—" Kia stopped speaking because she lost her breath. She leaned against the car to keep her balance.

"Don't worry...Teka couldn't hold water. I knew the moment she got the DNA results. Now let's get to you and Reem" I said pointing to the two of them.

"What the fuck do I have to do with this shit? I didn't know your sister Angel." Reem said holding his right hand up to his chest.

"Y'all were a team...Which meant y'all niggas came as a whole! You involved yourself muthafucka," I said. Then I walked over to the back of my vehicle and leaned against it.

I reached down in my right pocket pulling out a piece of gum and I tossed it into my mouth.

"Why do you think you were in prison for five years just like Kia, nigga?" I asked with a smirk on my face.
"YOU DID THAT TO US MUTHAFUCKA?! YOU SET US UP?!" Reem yelled out. He tried to charge at me but, Kia pulled him back.

"No...Is this true Angel?" Kia asked me.

"Oh my God." I leaned up off my car and started laughing. "This one is going to put the icing on the cake beloved," I said licking my lips.

"What are you talking about Angel?" Kia asked and her hands started shaking.

"MOMMY!" Nyla yelled out and I popped a bubble in my mouth from the chewing gum. She came running down the stairs in her pajamas.

"Step back baby...Go with your daddy." Kia pointed to Reem but Nyla walked over to me.

"Nyla, I said go with your daddy." Kia said stepping towards Nyla then she looked at Reem.

"Mom...Angel is my father." Nyla said standing right by my side. Reem looked at me like his little heart was broken. He held his hands together and turned to walk away.

"I waited until it was the *right* time Kia! Remember April 2008 you went out with your friends to the Lopez club. You had too much to drink so you went back to your room and passed out ALONE. Well at least that's what you thought.

"Your body was more attractive when you were laying unconsciously on the red silk sheets in the hotel room. Before I raped you I whispered in your ear that you were going to pay for your actions. Since my sister's life was taken for no fucking reason I was going to make sure y'all world came crashing down...Just like mine did when I found out Tatiana was gone for good." I said winking at Kia.

"No—No, No that can't be. Reem come back!" Kia yelled out as she fell down to the ground with tears running down her face. "How do you know Nyla is your daughter Angel?" Kia asked panicking and breathing heavy.

"Nyla has the same gift that Tatiana had before she was murdered." I confessed and the tears continued to pour from Kia's beautiful face.

"I remember you said Nyla, *'NEEDED US'* but, I never questioned what you meant by that." Kia said with her lips shivering. "That's why you weren't surprised when Nyla was having visions...You've seen all of this before." Kia said and her mouth dropped.

www.ingramcontent.com/pod-product-compliance
Lightning Source LLC
Chambersburg PA
CBHW050119030726
47505CB00007B/1949